Published by Avenstar Productions.
Paperback ISBN: 978-1-7350108-8-5

Visit Mark Wayne McGinnis at
http://www.markwaynemcginnis.com

To join Mark's mailing list, visit
http://eepurl.com/bs7M9r

D1489850

OTHER BOOKS BY Mark Wayne McGinnis

SCRAPYARD SHIP SERIES
Scrapyard Ship (Book 1)
HAB 12 (Book 2)
Space Vengeance (Book 3)
Realms of Time (Book 4)
Craing Dominion (Book 5)
The Great Space (Book 6)
Call To Battle (Book 7)

TAPPED IN SERIES
Mad Powers (Book 1)
Deadly Powers (Book 2)

LONE STAR RENEGADES SERIES
Lone Star Renegades (also called 'Jacked') (Book 1)

STAR WATCH SERIES
Star Watch (Book 1)
Ricket (Book 2)
Boomer (Book 3)
Glory for Space Sea and Space (Book 4)
Space Chase (Book 5)
Scrapyard LEGACY (Book 6)

THE SIMPLETON SERIES
The Simpleton (Book 1)
The Simpleton Quest (Book 2)

CHAPTER 1

September 2049
P1AL *Facilities, Palo Alto, California*
Jack

Jack let out a long, measured breath and wondered if he should pray or something. *A little late for that,* he thought. He took a deep breath and then grimaced, feeling the pain in his rib cage. Just a little reminder that came with the latest loan that these were the sort of guys you paid back. On time. Every time. With interest. A spindly looking pink and yellow cleaning bot was outside the window—seemingly, it was deciding what to do with a sports drink carton in the gutter. Abruptly, the bot snatched it up with its articulating claw and tossed it into a nearby trash bin.

Jack glanced over to Bartholomew "Bart" Pulldraw, who gave him his third enthusiastic thumbs-up for the morning. Bart returned his attention to his Strontium 5 Power Core, the $40,000 laptop computer he'd required Jack to purchase for him at the commencement of this project. Sure, Jack thought, *Go ahead. Pile on the credit card debt, kid.*

Bart was a living, breathing cliché of the disheveled, irreverent software engineer. To say he was large was an understatement. But Jack wouldn't call him obese either. He was somewhere in between the two. His manner of dress was off-putting to those who first met him. He's unique in that he watches decades old TV reruns—shows nobody else remembers and tries to dress to emulate them. And Bart liked hats. Seemingly, the same hat could never be worn twice. Jack imagined Bart's apartment stacked with an assortment of fedoras, Stetsons, bowlers, chapeaus, stovepipes, and maybe even sombreros—although he'd yet to wear a sombrero into the office.

Glancing Bart's way, Jack considered that he'd never seen the top of the man's head, his hair, or much of his forehead, for that matter. This was not the time to develop a new concern for Bart's hairline, however.

The big digital clock on the wall showed the time, 7:00 a.m., Pacific time. That meant it was 3:00 p.m. in Geneva—where the CERN Hadron Collider was located and being readied for today's test.

Jannith Burroughs, Jack's twenty-three-year-old admin assistant, set down a cup of coffee on his desk. "I know you like to get your own coffee, boss…but I can't stay still. Can't sit. Can't do anything." She forced in a deep breath. Her eyes drifted over to the clock. "It won't be long now. It all comes down to this?"

Jack shrugged. "It'll be okay. Either way, it'll be fine," he said, putting on a confident smile and offering her a fatherly "I know what I'm doing" nod. But he wasn't feeling anywhere close to confident. This technological roll of the dice had involved two years of exhausting, mind-numbing work. None of Jack's thirty-three Particle One Accelerator Laboratory (P1AL) employees had been granted a vacation for a year. The hours had been long. It wasn't uncommon for employees to work through the night and be found the next morning sleeping at their desks. With that said, special monetary incentives had been promised for all. This was a team effort, and they were all poised to become millionaires—for

Jack, a multimillionaire. From the elderly janitor, Bill Myers, on up to top scientists, such as Gordon Tooley and Rosa Hernandez, stock options were guaranteed to all. Everything hinged on the next few hours.

"Here they come..." Jannith said, looking nervously out through the office window. "We have science and technology reporters from National Geographic, the SmithsonianWORLD, Popular Science, Discover, and Quantum Science News. Oh no...I see logos from CNN, BRAVE-TV News, and Time-NBC too...Oh God...I think I'm going to be sick," she said.

Jack stood up and glanced around the office space. They'd already done a major cleaning over the last few days. Jack said, "Bart...that Doritos bag and those cans of Red Bull *RAD!*... all that goes into the trash. Trish, feet off the desk. Come on, people, let's all at least try to look professional. And nobody talks to the press! Anybody speaks to you, send them to me."

"Got it, boss."

"Copy that, Jack."

"Do I have anything in my teeth?" Lara from accounting said, widening her mouth to a coworker.

They'd set up a partition of sorts for the media people to stay behind. Basically, a few tables set up with stacks of disposable tablets with all the technical briefs stacked within. At the top of the room, where the team huddled, stood an old-school podium.

Jannith's voice bellowed behind Jack, welcoming and ushering in the media teams—basically reporters and their camera operators. Several teams brought along a dedicated audio person as well. Within five minutes, there were over forty of them clamoring around within the confined space for the most optimal positions for watching the test.

"And this is our illustrious leader, theoretical physicist Dr. Jack Harding. He'll be able to answer any of your questions...set the stage for what will be occurring in just under an hour from now," Jannith said and smiled, taking a step back, looking relieved to once again be out of the spotlight.

Jack stepped up to the opposite side of the tables, behind the podium, and tried to look relaxed. As if this was just like any other day at P1AL. His eyes were drawn to a small video monitor that had been placed on the table. The angle of the screen was such that he could see himself standing there. *What a fucking disaster.* His suit looked cheap, which it was. His hair needed combing, and the three-day cool stubble look he was going for just made him look pathetic.

"Welcome, everyone. And thank you for coming," he said, now looking into a half-dozen camera lenses.

A pretty female reporter with sandy-blonde hair, wearing a red dress with a white-knit cardigan covering her shoulders, said. "Hi, I'm Trinity Watson…Time-NBC News. Um, Dr. Harding… can you give us a quick overview of what we'll be witnessing here today? Why it's important?"

Damn, she looked familiar. Why was he suddenly thinking of lilacs? "Be happy to."

"And in simple English…" another, this one a young African American male reporter, added.

Jack offered a reassuring nod, simultaneously feeling an overwhelming need to scratch his groin. *Damn cheap detergent.* "This test, this real-time example, will show the world just how accessible particle science is about to become in the year 2049. There is an excess of thirty-thousand particle accelerator/collider facilities located all around the world. Most are too small to make the kind of scientific breakthroughs we see from multimillion-dollar facilities such as FLIN in Madrid, CORSH outside of Chicago, and, of course, CERN, who've just added another thirty miles of track outside Geneva. Limited by funding, small accelerators can't hope to achieve the magnetic field strength needed to replicate experiments. The Large Hadron Collider at CERN has the advantage of miles of superconducting magnets and the funds to keep them cooled to operational temperatures. Without a strong magnetic field to steer and speed up charged particles, small facilities can't hope to reach the speeds needed for groundbreaking research into the fundamental properties of the universe."

"And you have some kind of software?" Trinity Watson asked.

It hit Jack. *Four months ago. The Rust Bucket. We had drinks. Too many. Shit. What did I do?* He carried on, fighting the urge to put his hand down his pants and scratch his balls. "Yes. It's called ROAR. ROAR, short for Replication Of Accelerator Runs, is a quantum particle imaging application that will revolutionize particle accelerator experiments and the entire field of particle physics."

Looking to his right, Jack realized Bart was now standing next to him. He had changed hats and was now wearing an honest-to-God black pirate hat. A skull and crossbones emblem hung off-kilter at its brim. Jack wanted to slap the hat from Bart's big head but acted as if it was no big deal instead. "This is Bartholomew Pulldraw, the lead design engineer of the software." Deciding to break his own rule, Jack added, "Why don't I let him explain a little more about ROAR?"

Bart sniffed and swallowed as he seemed to be formulating his thoughts. He said, "Working with experimental observations and mathematical calculations using quantum computing, ROAR takes the data from previously run short- and long-beam accelerator experiments and processes them through all possible scenarios and outcomes. ROAR then utilizes a high-throughput neural network that learns through cause and effect patterns how to predict experimental outcomes based on their design. After this initial learning phase, you can input experimental parameters into the ROAR application, such as type of particle accelerator, length of accelerator track, particle speed and energy, strength of magnetic field, and which particle activity the experiment is focused on. ROAR uses quantum computation to run the experiments and utilizes priming from the neural network to give a predicted outcome. This can be done for both electrostatic and electrodynamic accelerator experiments."

I just had to do it...had to let him open his big stupid mouth...

The room went quiet. The reporters gaped at Bart. Trinity Watson pursed her lips. The young black reporter bent his microphone toward Jack, limp and defeated.

Bart moved back to his laptop and tapped at a few keys. Happy to take cover, Jack moved back to the antiquated podium, shuffling a stack of papers. He remembered lilac lingering on his sheets the next morning, so many months ago. Even Alice mentioned it. *I'm such a moron.*

Suddenly, a three-dimensional construct took shape high overhead at the center of the room. Bart smiled. "Not only that, but ROAR also works as a holographic 3D imager that can simulate imaging of the particle collision experiments in real time, scaled up to be seen by the human eye."

The hovering, rotating image was breathtakingly beautiful and seemed to alleviate some of the media's irritation at the technical gobbledygook Bart had been spewing over the last few minutes.

"This imaging software allows you to zoom, pause, hover, rewind, and slow down the moment of collision so it can be observed with a resolution that was previously unachievable. Rather than analyzing data that is a product of the collision, we can now see the individual particle interactions with the naked eye."

Bart made a move toward the podium as if to say, "See? I know what I'm doing." Jack placed a hand on Bart's back, not giving up his spot. "Yes, I know that all sounds incredibly complicated. Even my head is spinning listening to that. Basically, what we're about at **P1AL** is allowing for amazing new scientific breakthroughs not just from the big multibillion-dollar facilities but from the little guys like us. ROAR allows for that, and today, we're going to prove it."

"How so?" an ancient, pot-bellied reporter with cigarette-stained teeth asked.

"By conducting the exact same experiment CERN is preparing to run within the hour. Their almost one hundred miles of accelerator track up against our measly mile. We'll let the scientific community determine for themselves the results in real time."

"So, you're saying that with this ROAR product, particle experiments that were previously impossible for smaller accelerators... the same kind of engineering becomes possible?" Trinity Watson asked.

The woman had some smarts in addition to being a knockout, Jack thought. No wonder he slept with her. Why didn't he call her? Then he realized how sexist he was being when he noticed that she was looking at him sideways—as if reading his mind.

"Yes, with high-quality and high-accuracy modeling and imaging," Jack added.

Another science reporter asked, "Talk to us about the other test. The one CERN is conducting...that you're trying to emulate."

"Sure," he said, acknowledging the older man, who looked intrigued by what they were doing—*a good sign*. "Well, CERN is prepping to do experiments on the gravitational properties of antimatter in their ALPHA-g containment tube. They've spent months producing the antiprotons and honing the beam of particles into their vertical drop tube. The idea is that they are going to let antiprotons free fall within the ALPHA-g and measure just when the antimatter explodes, allowing them to calculate the gravitational properties of antimatter and antiatoms."

"Okay…so you will be doing the same experiment…here and at the same time?" "Yes, but for a fraction of the cost and with even faster test results and analyses."

Jack knew ROAR was already preprogrammed to simulate the gravity drop of an antihydrogen atom. They were ready to show the world and, more importantly, deep-pocketed investors, their technological achievements.

Bart was still at his terminal when he piped up again. All eyes went to the oversized pirate. "Our modeling system will come to the same results as CERN. You can take that to the bank, people. We've already tested, well…simulated, an antimatter drop in preparation for today with containment tube parameters…the same as what is expected with their ALPHA-g test. We just need their exact, final test parameter numbers. They'll be releasing those in…" Bart looked over to the wall clock, "three minutes."

Bart was right. They'd left little to chance. All they now needed were those exact parameters so that the simulated test they were running was indeed exactly the same as CERN's.

The room had gone quiet, which only increased Jack's sense of looming dread. *Next time I won't wear underwear. The suit is dry-cleaned. It's the damn briefs.* Bradley washed everything, including Jack's underwear, with dollar store detergent.

Jack tried to look self-assured, giving Trinity a confident nod of his head. Did she remember him? What did they talk about? He was sure he drank too much. He had a tendency to talk too much when he drank like that.

Thirty seconds to go, and they'd have CERN's specific test parameters. Then Bart would input them, and they'd be off and running. Jack thought about the three and a half million dollars of debt accumulated over the last few years in preparation for this. For right now. This was their moment. In ten seconds, they'd have the parameters. Fifteen minutes after that, both CERN and P1AL would commence their respective tests simultaneously. Jack looked out into the tension-filled room and at his thirty-three dedicated employees. He wondered, *Am I looking at a roomful of soon-to-be millionaires or the soon-to-be-unemployed?*

"Parameters coming in now!" Bart yelled, raising two chubby fists high in the air while staring intently at the display before him. Then he looked up–their eyes met. It was then that Jack knew they were in trouble. That they were truly fucked.

CHAPTER 2

TitusBane, Space Technologies Facility, Houston, Texas
Locke

Travis Locke took in the TitusBane facility's industrial, high-tech surroundings with its preponderance of glass and stainless steel while he was encircled by a procession of eight of the world's most highly acclaimed engineers and rocket scientists. At forty-one, tanned and handsome, Locke wore his longish dark hair strategically neat but mussed up just to avoid conveying too stodgy an appearance. It was important that there be an impression of wildness about him, an unpredictability.

Just under six feet tall, Locke stood out from the others adorned in their long white lab coats. He dressed to impress—always. Today, he wore a charcoal gray Dormeuil Vanquish IX, an impeccably tailored suit. One of three identical suits he'd purchased two months earlier while on a business jaunt to Paris. The suit, estimated to have cost twenty-four thousand euros, also happened to be the same suit worn by actor Ross Price in this year's 2049 James Bond thriller. To complete his ensemble, Locke wore an Hermès Etriviere belt and a pair of seventeen hundred euro Italian Salvatore Ferragamo calfskin Oxfords.

En masse, the contingent approached a pristine, twenty-foot-high by fifteen-foot-wide sliding glass door. Within, Locke could just make out a control room off to the left and to the right, the gargantuan *pièce de résistance*–another compartment, housing a rocket's prime propulsion system, the TitusBane CRX2221. An engine three times more powerful than even a SpaceX Quant L35 Powerplant, with a vacuum thrust of 6,130 kN.

That's one fucking beast of a rocket engine–Locke thought, feeling his heart rate elevate. *God, I love my job,* he mused. He rose on his tiptoes to see above the others. Laid out horizontally, the thing was immense. This latest version's test platform, Locke knew, burned liquid oxygen (LOX) and rocket-grade kerosene (RP-1) propellant. In today's competitive world of rocket science, this was the no-frills, old-school, tried and true, brute-force approach.

"I'm sorry, but before we enter…please…this compartment adheres to ISO Level 5 clean-room standards," a short, balding engineer said, holding out a stack of white clothing. "For contamination reasons—"

"Yeah, got it, Chicken Little, we don't want the sky falling," Locke said, cutting him off and accepting the clean-room apparel. Before touching the rest of the apparel, to minimize contamination, he dragged the white latex-free gloves over his hands. Then came the crinkly white bodysuit, a hood buttoned up around his head, and a thin cloth mouth cover. He finished by slipping on the DuPont Tyvek booties and the shower cap–like bouffant. "With what I'm investing here, I'm in agreement we don't need any proverbial flies in the ointment."

They continued, slowing as they funneled into TitusBane's Number 3 Control Station, positioned off to the left. It wasn't large, but it sure was impressive. Like something one would expect to see on a spaceship's bridge. There was a cohesiveness of heavy glass panels and polished chrome all about. Even the ceiling was artful and futuristic, having a reflective equiangular spiral that seemed to move on its own, like an anaconda slithering into a comfortable position overhead. The myriad inset blinking lights on the control panel were dazzling—all set into a fifteen-foot-long, gently curved console with a distorted Jockimo cast glass facing.

A hand came to rest upon Locke's shoulder. Locke, a germaphobe, did not appreciate being touched, even through his multiple layers. It was Dr. Engleton, TitusBane's head of operations. Tall and gray-haired, there were whiskers from his bushy, unmaintained mustache trying to escape the sides of his mask. Best to ignore the man's intrusion into his personal space, Locke offered the eager rocket scientist his most genuine, affable smile from behind the mask—a smile Locke had rehearsed in front of bathroom mirrors most of his adult life.

"Stumbles should be expected. The complexity of what we are attempting to do here at TitusBane is...well, it's beyond what you may be able to technically comprehend," Dr. Engleton said, unclipping his card key badge and holding it up to the reader adjacent to the door. "I'm sorry if that comes across as a little condescending or insolent."

For the span of a nanosecond, Locke's smile indeed faltered. *Just keep it up, you pompous shit. Go ahead; patronize me a little more...* Locke thought, but nodded his head in feigned appreciation, his smile back to its practiced perfection.

"Hey, we're still in the game...we're still in the running, Mr. Locke," Engleton added with a toothy grin. "And after today's prime ignition test, who knows...maybe we've even pulled ahead a little bit."

Engleton was referring to the most competitive, nasty space race of all time. TitusBane was just one of five—or maybe it was six, now—multibillion-dollar space technology firms vying for a prize like none other. Ever. And that was just here in the US.

Other countries were in the race as well. Twenty years prior, in 2029, a NASA subterranean Mars project, coined the Inaugural Basin Expedition, had shot drilling probes below the surface of Mars in a number of different regions.

After examination of the transmitted raw data, the determination was made that Mars held an immense treasure trove of precious and rare metals such as silver, gold, and platinum, as well as elements such as osmium, iridium, and palladium. That was all that was needed to divert commercial resources already being focused on the moon over to the distant red planet. Thus far there had been a number of separate manned geological expeditions by the US, Russia, and China, and thousands of geological samples had been taken. Then, by accident, living alien life had officially been discovered, a scientific revelation that rocked the world.

One particular organic sample was brought back from the third US space expedition. Discovered within the deepest of Mar's underground lakes was the microscopic creature UM55562145, subsequently renamed the Mars egret, because when magnified adequately, it looked like a heron-type bird taking flight. Exciting as it was, the determination that mankind was not alone in the universe was nothing compared to what was later discovered about the tiny organism. The Mars egret was determined to have a life span of no less than five centuries, if not longer. Like all life on Earth, DNA evidently was the basic blueprint for life on Mars, containing the chromosomal instructions for this organism to grow, develop, and survive within its dark, oh-so-cold habitat.

There was something about Mars egrets' telomeres, those little shoelace-tip ends of the chromosomes, that differed significantly from anything found on Earth...those throwaway DNA sequences on Earth were the secret to eternal life on

Mars. Early experiments conducted by labs in both North Korea and Iran (not sanctioned, of course, by any international health regulatory organizations) showed that the organisms, once injected directly into mice and later into chimps, cured most forms of cancer within days, capping chromosomes to slow cell splitting.

The research suggested that the injection could prolong all life, not just the lives of the ill. None of the animals injected had died thus far. Unfortunately, all attempts to breed the same organisms on Earth had failed. It wasn't long, though, before the media got wind of the Mars egrets' extended life span and the ongoing experiments. The potential to cure devastating diseases—the implications of human life being extended...perhaps without end...created a craze.

Within the relative blink of an eye, the Mars egrets had become an all-encompassing obsession, not only within the scientific community but with the worldwide public at large.

As fruitful as the exploration missions had been, it was now time to fully exploit Mars for all of its natural resources. The lands of Mars weren't owned by anyone—laws simply didn't exist there yet. Greed and power had become the guiding forces, a dangerous combination, be it government bodies, mega-corporations, or the wealthiest of individuals.

It wasn't long before land rights disputes started to arise. Not only what country would achieve the rights to certain geographical regions, but more importantly, in this global corporate environment, what industrial complex would achieve certain regional rights? As posturing quickly elevated into threats of war, actually putting military boots on the ground to fight tooth and nail for certain territories, finally the United Nations stepped in, coming up with a far more amiable and civilized prospect: have a mad-dash Mars land-grab event, such as that of the Oklahoma Land Rush of 1889. Soon, spread across the entire Martian landscape, equal two hundred by two hundred-mile land parcels had been designated, each identified by a constantly broadcasting communications beacon.

There would be an actual starting line for the land rush. And there would be rules, a whole lot of rules, designed to keep things fair. For one thing, teams had to get to Mars, land, and check in several days prior to the event. Martian off-road buggies had to meet certain engineering requirements, which would keep the playing field even, so to speak. The first team that reached a beacon simply had to enter the team's code to take ownership.

So there they were. New revolutionary methods of space travel were being developed to overcome the seven-month journey. New technologies for robust base stations and the construction of aquatic mining operations capable of withstanding the harshest of conditions were just a few of the requirements for human life on Mars. The good news? There was no shortage of new financial investment. Trillions of dollars had already poured in, and multiple competitive teams around the world were building their own rockets and designing all sorts of new Martian base stations. Most would not get to Mars in time for the race.

Engleton again spoke, bringing Locke back to the here and now.

"I get it. Conventional space rocketry of old will not cut it. We know that…we're not here to waste your time, sir. Yes, yes, time is indeed of the essence…getting there, and, more importantly, getting back to Earth as fast as humanly possible."

The scientist is correct, Locke thought. Above and beyond the pure economics of getting those egrets back to Earth in a timely manner, it seemed that many, if not most, were going into shock along the way. Prolonged space flights were simply a no-go at this point…the typical fourteen-month round trip, using conventional rocket technology, was out of the question. So multiple rocket technologies were being studied and prototypes constructed, ranging from ingenious to utterly ridiculous.

One thing was for sure: Travis Locke's investment technologies (and there were several) would put him first on Mars, where he could set up a viable base station and soon bring home the proverbial bacon. Those little bastards, those Mars egrets, would make him a god among corporate chieftains.

"I am sorry that we are…um…somewhat behind schedule. A mere two months, considering all that we have accomplished, is a small price to pay for such amazing results, no?"

Locke didn't answer but knew a period of two months could easily be the difference between success and failure.

"Just be patient…let us do what we do best," the scientist said, handing Locke a clipboard. "We'll need four signatures, one at the bottom of each page, indicated by those little yellow sticky signature tabs."

I know what fucking signature tabs are…Locke wanted to snap back. However, his voice was silky smooth as he accepted the clipboard. "Talk to me about today's test. What specific results can we expect?" Locke asked, speed-reading the first of the sheets—an overview of today's test and the expected result parameters that needed to be met—a kind of milestone check-off document.

The scientist droned on and on about the test. The man was slow. A slow talker, a slow mover, and worst of all, slow to develop a next-generation rocket. It wasn't difficult to determine where the bottleneck in TitusBane was. He was staring at it.

Locke elegantly dug through layers to remove his David Oscarson Jacques De Molay fountain pen from his suit jacket's inside pocket. Tapping the four-thousand-dollar writing instrument against his mask-covered lower lip, he perused each of the three succeeding pages. "Everything seems to be in order." He signed at the bottom of each page with his normal trademark flourish then replaced the cap on his pen. He didn't return the clipboard to Engleton. "Shall we go inside? I'm excited to get up close and personal with the CRX2221 rocket engine...since I've paid for its development."

The group of scientists shuffled in closer behind them. Locke, turning to the others, offered up a masked million-dollar smile and said, "I'm sorry...would it be possible to proceed on by ourselves first? I have some, well...tough questions to ask the good doctor here, and it would be best if we have some privacy."

Locke ignored the indignation on their faces. "Dr. Engleton, tell me...are you familiar enough with the various specifics of this test today to conduct things yourself? Or, do you require one or more of these more directly involved scientists to assist you?"

Engleton's bushy brows came together. "I am quite capable of running any test within this facility alone...I can assure you of that."

Locke raised both palms and turned to the others. "Thank you, everyone...thank you very much. No need to waste any more gowns and gloves right this minute. Enjoy the rest of your day." He watched as they filed out from the control room. Several glanced back, clearly unhappy at being excluded from such an important occasion. A few cast doubtful glances at their boss before they left them to it.

"Shall we?" Locke asked, gesturing toward another set of double glass doors. Dr. Engleton used his card key to gain access to the test facility. It was truly awe-inspiring. Locke doubted NASA had any facility that could compare. It had been quite some time since the budget-constrained government agency could compete with what commercial enterprises could now accomplish. Only time would tell if NASA would even be around in the next decade.

The test compartment was the size of an indoor football field. Its surrounding walls towered over one hundred and fifty feet high–the white ceiling a mass of painted, crisscrossing ventilation ducts and pipes. But it was what sat in the middle of the room that captured Travis Locke's full attention. A rocket engine–foreboding in its physical size, not to mention its capacity to produce so much raw, explosive power.

Together, the pair circumnavigated the looming CRX2221 rocket engine while Dr. Engleton blabbered on and on about fuel efficiency, weight distribution, and other tech-speak. Locke wanted to turn the volume off, to stop the droning, but no such knob existed. Some of the technical regurgitations Engleton spewed, Locke already knew. Much he didn't. And didn't care to know, for that matter.

Having completed their up-close-and-personal tour, Dr. Engleton ushered Locke out of the test facility back into the control room.

"Most impressive, Dr. Engleton. I must say, I am beyond inspired by what you and your team have achieved here," Locke mocked.

The rocket scientist took the praise with arrogant pomposity–like, *what else did you expect?* With his reading glasses perched upon the tip of his nose, Engleton busied himself at the console. "Fortunately, everything is completely automated. All systems and subsystems are automatically monitored; readings are digitally captured." Without raising his head, his eyes glanced up–a rueful smile tugging at the corners of his mouth. "One slap at our thunder button here and...off we'd go!"

Locke settled his eyes on the big red button situated at the center of the console. Then he glanced up to the ceiling. *Not all systems are being monitored,* he thought. For instance, unbeknownst to any of the employees here, video monitoring systems were currently off-line.

"Ready for blastoff?" Dr. Engleton playfully asked, his palm poised directly above the button.

Locke glanced out through the large observation windows. Bright, circulating red warning lights indicated a dangerous test was imminent. A repetitive alarm sounded. Locke was well aware that there were countless procedures in place to ensure that no one would be inside the restricted test area at this juncture. One such procedure was having a team of scientists sitting within the control room. Another was motion-detection indicators—which, like the video monitoring system, had been hacked and disabled.

Suddenly looking at Engleton, Locke's eyes went wide. "Oh no...the clipboard! I...I left it on the table inside." He craned his neck as he spoke and pointed to a small metal table at the far end of the engine-thrust cone.

Dr. Engleton waved away the problem. "I'll just print off another set after—"

"And my pen, too, unfortunately." Locke grimaced and pointed back to the clipboard and the pen lying upon it. "Sorry to be such a bother...but I venture to say that David Oscarson Jacques De Molay fountain pen probably cost as much as your car."

Engleton's eyes narrowed at that added bit of detail.

Locke was fully cognizant that the thin cloth mask he still wore covered his practiced smile, but he employed it anyhow. One could never be too charming, after all.

The scientist hesitated. He would be considering important safety protocols right now, Locke speculated. Weighing them against the next infusion of his desperately needed investment dollars. Locke cleared his throat gently.

"Hold tight...be right back," then Engleton stopped in his tracks. "Please don't move from right where you are. Don't touch anything. I'm breaking about thirty safety regulations right now." Out came his card key and with a quick tap against the reader, the rocket scientist was back inside the test facility, lumbering past the window. Reaching the small metal table, he snatched up the clipboard and the expensive pen.

With a shake of his head, Engleton looked back toward Locke, only to be confused. Locke wasn't standing where he'd expected him to be. Only when he turned his head several degrees to the right did he see Locke, now standing at the center of the console. With his mask tugged down around his chin, Locke offered the man a sad, even sympathetic smile as he slapped the big red thunder button.

The CRX2221rocket engine ignited in an instant.

As if all the fires of hell had been summoned forth, the engine rumbled to life, followed by an ear-shattering explosion of erupting rocket fuel. One moment Dr. Engleton was standing there–the next, he was a silhouetted skeleton, momentarily gyrating, writhing, caught in a six-thousand-degree furnace blast. Locke thought he heard the man's screams, but perhaps he only imagined that.

Fortunately, the test seemed to be a resounding success. Unfortunately, no trace would be left behind of the obliterated scientist. There would be no record of how such a terrible accident could have occurred. But it had to be done, Locke knew. There would have been little time for more corporate politics–a slow-moving human resources department changing over the leadership for such an important project. Perhaps moving forward, there would be more progress and far fewer delays.

Locke watched as the rocket engine, its propellant fuel supply exhausted, went silent. As his eyes scanned back toward the rear of the engine, he did feel some remorse. His favorite pen had been a personal gift from the crown prince of Saudi Arabia, Mohammed bin Salman bin Abdulaziz Al Saud.

CHAPTER 3

Three months later
P1AL *Facilities, Palo Alto, California,*
Jack

The winding metal staircase was like an enormous corkscrew driving deep into the earth. With each step, Jack's footfalls echoed off the cleaved subterranean walls. Normally, he would have taken the lift down, but the power had already been cut.

Just like how his life was trending these days.

Piece by piece, things were being taken away from him. He almost laughed.

Woe is me.

It wasn't like him to be such a defeatist.

Things will turn around…won't they?

Now, catching his breath after descending hundreds of feet, he felt the familiar chill in the air. Oddly, he felt more at home within these rock walls than anywhere else—here where his particle collider was situated. A collider he would now shut off permanently, at least as far as he was concerned.

When he'd purchased the property, the offices aboveground, along with this vast complex of caverns and tunnels underground, Jack thought he'd made the deal of a lifetime.

The tunnels were the main reason he'd bought the abandoned military facility in the first place. Actually, he'd purchased only a portion of the subterranean property. Major Earl Cotton bought the other, even larger portion. The major's purchase included an underground cavern large enough to hold a downtown skyscraper.

Jack had run into the major a few times over the years. For decades, the moon had been a gold mine of opportunity, since the Chinese discovered its hidden quarries of rare earth elements. The elements—all kinds of oxides, lanthanides like yttrium and scandium, and twenty or so other indistinguishable silvery-white soft heavy metals—exhibited unique chemical properties as well as different electronic and magnetic properties. All elements a world hooked on high-tech couldn't live without.

Suffice it to say, twenty-plus years earlier, in the mid-2020s, the mad rush to exploit the moon was on. Big time! The California Gold Rush of 1848, when gold was first found by James W. Marshall at Sutter's Mill, was nothing compared to China's Captain Chin Lee's National Space Administration, CNSA. Lee was the first to bring back lunar geological samples from deep beneath the cratered surface. The mad dash for moon resources created a market for lunar transportation. As a result, myriad space vessels were constructed, particularly vessels for exploration, excavation, and mining, and the space transport business boomed. However, the demanding use placed on such vehicles gave rise to another business—repair and refurbishment.

Major Earl Cotton's underground company, BrutForce Labs, had filled that void as a repair contractor, servicing such firms as Mira Flight Industries, Rockwell, Boeing, Corbin Space Engineering, SpaceX, even NASA. He'd apparently made a pretty penny at it, too, if Jack were to believe even half of what the major had shared in some of the casual conversations they'd struck up in the tunnels. Jack's gut twinged with modest jealousy. A little bit of that kind of success. That was all he'd been trying to do at the **P1AL** labs with the ROAR program. Instead?

Crash and burn, baby.

A remorseful grin gnarled the corner of his mouth.

Too bad the major can't repair and refurbish my entire existence.

Jack took in the clean, sleek collider complex spreading out before him. Failures aside, he was proud of what he'd built here. Proud, and now saddened that he'd bungled his once-in-a-lifetime opportunity. He set off, skirting the main control structure. He headed down the northernmost tunnel and track, the suspended large tube which peeled off into the distance, following its circuitous route.

The **P1AL** collider consisted of an approximately mile-long ring of superconducting magnets. When operational, inside the track, two high-energy particle beams traveled at close to the speed of light before they would, ultimately, collide. That was when the real work started—the analysis of a whole other world inside humanity's own reality—a subatomic world with its own unique laws and remarkable events.

A world, Jack realized, he missed dearly.

He made a sharp left into a somewhat narrower branch of the shaft. Ten feet above him, secured to the rocky ceiling, was a cluster of heavy conduit lines that powered the facility. Turning left and then left again, he continued to follow the conduits. Five minutes later, he'd reached the bank of six dark gray, floor-to-ceiling metal cabinets. Some had been originally installed by the military years prior. Some were installed about several years ago, just prior to building the **P1AL** collider facility.

A dull humming sound emanated from each of the cabinets. Jack opened the door of the far cabinet and stared blankly at the large main power breaker to the underground **P1AL** facility. He began to reach for it, then thought better of the action. It was going to get really dark down here after he shut off the power. He felt for the flashlight protruding from his front left pocket.

Clang!

The abrupt metallic sound echoed off the surrounding rock walls. Startled, Jack's gaze darted around. The sound had come from further down the shaft. Twenty feet away stood the BrutForce Lab's breaker cabinets. Jack looked back to the open breaker door beside him. He had expected to be alone down here. Did he really want to kill the power?

Later.

He shut the cabinet door and strode on toward BrutForce Labs and the loud noise he'd heard just moments before. He had the same sort of bread-crumb kind of trail to follow via the overhead conduit lines. Several rights and lefts later, Jack entered the main cavern of Major Cotton's lab space. He stopped and gaped at the sheer immensity of the former underground water aquifer. A chill rippled down Jack's spine. There was something eerie about this place—a contradiction in imagery that jarred the senses. The cold gray walls gave way to warm sunlight streaming in from somewhere up high above. A million dust particles danced within golden rays of light, life in a dead space.

Jack surveyed the multiple raised metal platforms and support structures—like a giant's abandoned erector set—and what must have been the various spacecraft testing stations or docking depots. High above, overlooking it all, was a horizontally constructed structure built into the rock itself. The facility's main offices, where Major Cotton overlooked his toiling troops, Jack supposed.

Once a military man, always a military man.

As Jack tentatively progressed farther into BrutForce, it became evident the place was no longer in business. Some scattered equipment remained strewn about. Even several spacecraft in various states of disassembly stood in a few of the docking bays–huge metallic specters in the dim light–but there was no human in apparent attendance.

"Can I help you?" came a booming baritone voice from Jack's left. Jack whirled.

The man was wearing an orange hard hat and grimy overalls. Jack recognized him straight away. "Major Cotton? Earl? It's me, Jack Harding, um, from next door…so to speak."

The major stood near Jack's height at six feet, but age feathered through his close-cropped hair and neatly trimmed beard. The major's startlingly blue eyes could pierce a man's soul. When he looked at you, Jack thought, you knew he could tell the measure of you with a single glance.

He probably thinks I'm as FUBAR as they get.

If he did, the major gave no indication. "Oh yeah…Jack. You just wandering around these tunnels, or did you get lost?"

He'd said it with a smile, but Jack suspected the major was truly curious.

Jack jabbed a thumb behind him. "I was over at the breakers…heard a noise. Thought I'd check it out. Ended up here. Can I ask…are you shutting down the place?" Jack gestured with a hand to the seemingly abandoned facility. "No more money in fixing moon craft?"

The major's brow wrinkled, then he nodded. "Oh yeah…no. Actually, ship engine repair is still good business. But I'm moving operations."

The man looked about the cavern and sighed. "I am going to miss this place though. Still own it, but would be happy to sell for the right offer."

He eyed Jack, a twinkle in his blue eyes. "You know, if you wanted to expand P1AL, I could make you a great deal."

Jack grimaced. "Ah no...that's...just no."

A pang of longing twisted Jack's gut. He would have loved to take the major up on the offer, but he didn't think the man would accept an IOU as legal tender.

Jack now saw what had made the loud clang. A pulley system dangling from steel cables swung back and forth from a suspended overhead crane arm. Every so often, it swung into a metal girder.

"Where are you moving?" Jack asked. "Seems this is the perfect locale to do the type of work you do. Out of the way of California's restrictive noise ordinances and everything."

"Oh, it is! There's no mistake about that. Only problem is, it's not on Mars."

"Mars?"

"Come on, man. Don't you read the papers? Yeah, Mars. The great Martian land grab? Like the one here on Earth back in the late 1800s. In Oklahoma? You know—the big Oklahoma Land Rush. Settlers back then could stake unassigned acres of land for something like a buck and a quarter. Same kind of thing's happening now. Only it's not the Sooner State. Now world governments are offering big corporations and anyone with the chutzpah and a ship a similar kind of deal. Mars is being apportioned—parceled off—for near chicken feed. And let me tell you, Jack...what geological and mineral resources we found on the moon? Ha! They'll be bupkis compared to what's up there on that little red planet!"

Jack had heard about the great Martian land grab. Hard to miss, really. It had been big news months earlier. Every Tom, Dick, and Harry had thrown their hat, not to mention their millions, into the ring. The problem that had stymied each and every one of them, though, was the fourteen-plus months or more it took to get to Mars and back. The magnitude of propellant it took to power a trip like that was sorely problematic. Jack scoffed.

I've got plenty of my own problems.

He nodded and turned to leave, giving the major a half wave as he departed.

"Let me know if you change your mind and want to buy this place. Offer still stands."

Jack smiled. "Good luck, Major. Send me a postcard once you're situated on Mars."

"Roger Wilco. Hey, you never know. Maybe you'll join us one day. Build a particle collider on Mars!"

"Why not?" Jack laughed as he walked back toward the breakers. He thought of a million reasons why not.

And most of them I owe people on THIS planet.

CHAPTER 4

P1AL *Facilities, Palo Alto, California,*
Jack

"Don't do that, Alice…" Jack scolded, hefting another cardboard box onto a collapsible table. He closed the lid and used a tape gun dispenser to seal it shut.

"How much longer we gonna be here, Jack?" his eleven-year-old charge asked, continuing to spin in circles in his office chair.

"Yeah. How much longer are we gonna be here, Jack?" The second plaintive whine came from Bart. He sat slouched, in a thirty year-old Mandalorian visor no less, opposite Alice and matched her rotation for rotation. The executive office chair creaked and groaned under the pressure.

"It would go a little faster if I had some help," Jack hinted not so subtly.

"Yeah. You should have hired one of those moving companies like, uh, Two Men and a Robot," he suggested.

Subtlety had never been Bart's forte. His cheeks had to be red from the blunt force of his mental face-palm.

"Now, why didn't I think of that?" Jack sneered. "Oh, that's right. Because moving companies cost money. Something I am deplorably short of at present. So, instead I'm stuck with one guy, the child, and a roller skate."

Jack grimaced and tossed a quick glance in Alice's direction. "I wasn't talking about you."

She shrugged. "I know."

The incessant squeaking halted as Bart sat tall. "Hey, hold on now. Do not trash talk Leia. She is a brilliant piece of automobile engineering. She gets two thousand miles per charge! I'd like to see NASA get that kind of mileage." He scoffed. "Maybe we'd be to Mars by now."

He pushed off with one foot, arms outstretched like an airplane, and made whooshing sounds as the creaking resumed.

"Just stop it!" Jack begged.

"Why?" Bart retorted.

"Because it's extremely annoying."

Alice snapped her bubblegum. "But it's not like it's even yours anymore. Whoever owns the chair now can tell him to stop," she reasoned.

Jack glanced her way. His initial irritation quickly turned to something else—*admiration*. At eleven, the kid was beyond her years in smarts. Her IQ was far higher than his own...and just about anyone else's. "He's going to hurl, kiddo. And I'm not going to be the one to clean it up."

"No...of course not. Why should you?" she responded matter-of-factly. "Like the chair, it's not your building anymore. Let the new owners clean it up."

Jack flashed back to that day it all went wrong. Three months, one week, and three days ago. He looked over the empty room. How different the place looked now, just a hollow space full of memories and the ghosts of dreams.

Alice slowed her own rapid revolution down by dragging her feet on the polished concrete floor. Jack noticed that her once-gleaming white tennis shoes were nearly the same color as the gray concrete. Their decorative crimson hearts were now just a faded pink. A baby toe could be seen peeking out of her left shoe. As if he couldn't feel any worse...his adopted children's shoes were in no better shape than those of a homeless person.

A thin crease formed between Alice's blonde brows as she caught him looking at her shoes. "It's the style now...retro-shabby."

He hefted up another box. This one, like the eight before it, was full of books on particle physics and quantum theory. Alice jumped up and began rifling through the titles. Jack shooed her away.

"That's not an actual thing...retro-shabby...you made that up," Jack said, as the tape dispenser made its *sssffftttt* sound.

Alice shrugged. "Oh...by the way, Bradley wants to talk to you, Jack."

"Isn't that your nanny?" Bart asked.

Jack let out a frustrated breath and nodded. Bradley Gibbs. Nanny extraordinaire and most likely to ram a spoonful of sugar down your throat if you disagreed with him. "He's got my cell number...he can call me any time."

"No, he wants to have a sit-down family meeting tonight." *Supercalifragilisticexpialidocious.*

"It's not his job to call for family meetings," Jack said. He placed several binders, labeled with the **P1AL** logo, into a plastic black and yellow storage container. The binders contained human resources regulations for Particle One Accelerator Laboratories— the company he no longer owned. Correction. He *owned* the company, but not the laboratory and all the buildings necessary for the company to run.

"Why don't you just let me deal with Bradley, okay? I can handle it." He stood up, straightening out his aching back. Truth be told, the disgruntled nanny was the least of his worries. For nearly a week, he'd been hard at it here, closing shop in his shuttered Palo Alto, California, particle accelerator facility. *I gambled, and I lost.*

Jack sent a wary glance toward the large floor-to-ceiling windows and the view to the parking lot outside. They had already sent someone to collect what he owed them, twice now. The guy had been big, a modern-day Shylock sent to knock Jack around. Next time, the guy had promised…*It'll be broken elbows and kneecaps.*

"This you?" Bart said, holding up a framed photograph in both hands, his nose mere inches from the glass. He glanced over at Jack, then back to the photo. "Good God! What happened to you?"

Jack bit back a scathing retort. At least Bart was up out of that damned chair, helping…sort of.

Jack knew what photo he was staring at. Alice scurried over, peeking over his arm.

"Come on…I look the same…well, nearly." He snatched the picture from Bart's clutches and looked for himself. Jack stared at the eight-by-ten framed photograph. Yeah, it was him, all right. Taken about twelve years ago, on a lake back in Stockholm, Sweden, where he'd gone to university. He looked at the person sitting next to him those years earlier. Jack and his best friend—both shirtless—were seated within a borrowed, meticulously restored 1938 17' Gar Wood Split Cockpit Chris Craft motorboat. They looked happy, not a care in the world.

"What about the person sitting next to me?" Jack asked, angling the framed photograph toward Alice.

Alice took another hard look, squinting as she inspected every detail of the man sitting to his right. "My…father?" Her Swiss-German accent was abnormally strong in her distraction. "He looks a lot different than I remember him." She tugged at the frame, bringing it closer to scrutinize. "Are you certain this is my father?"

"Yeah, that's your father…and my best friend. That's Oliver."

"His nose is ginormous," Bart commented over his shoulder.

"Well, Alice got her mother's nose, thank goodness."

"Where was she?" The way that Alice's 'w' took on a 'v' sound was a dead giveaway that Alice was half listening, half remembering her childhood. Most of the time her accent was barely noticeable anymore.

"Elsa…I think she was the one taking the picture. She must have been."

Alice pursed her lips, still absorbed in the photo image. Jack knew that her incredible mind was working something out. Attempting to make the puzzle pieces fit together just right. But this would be one puzzle that would never be reconciled.

Oliver and Jack first met when they were both in their early twenties, in pursuit of their bachelor's degrees at the prestigious KTH Institute of Technology in Stockholm. Enthusiastic and geeky, they were paired as lab partners in an elementary quantum theory class. They grew close, studying mathematical formulas and drinking *brännvin*, a Swiss vodka. They shared their dreams and hopes for the future together, working within the highly competitive and exciting field of particle science. Jack had been more seriously inclined toward studying than Oliver, who was both a jokester and a romantic. He also was naturally brilliant, a gift which excused him from having to study as much as Jack did.

Jack glanced over at Alice. *Like father like daughter.* When Oliver first met Elsa, Jack worried he'd lost his best friend to her. But nothing could have been farther from the truth. The three of them became the Three Musketeers—inseparable—the very best of friends. For Jack, a foster kid brought up in the system, bounced around like a ping-pong ball, they were the closest thing to family he had ever experienced. As for Oliver and Elsa, both were only children, and their parents had long since passed away. So, Jack became their de facto adopted brother, giving all of them some semblance of an extended family.

Eventually, Jack returned home to the US, having graduated with a bachelor's degree. Accepted into Stanford, he went on to earn a doctorate in physics.

Although he hadn't seen them very much over the years, they did keep in touch. The whole family had come over a few years back, kids and all. They had done Disneyland and all the other major California theme park attractions, made a whole trip of it even though the twins were barely toddlers. Truthfully, Jack had mostly stayed in contact with Oliver. They'd made time for Skype calls and emails as much as their busy schedules permitted. Which wasn't as often as it could have been. Not in hindsight.

Then again, it often seemed like no time had passed between chats. Oliver was the consummate prankster. Their last call had been about a gag gift Oliver had sent him. Damn. What had it been? *Oh yeah–that ridiculous stuffed ferret.* He had been adamant that Jack keep the mangy thing. Swore it was an important part of particle science history. At one time in the distant past, the beady-eyed rodent had been used to ensure that hundreds of feet of vacuum piping were cleared of any debris.

Overselling the bit, if you asked Jack. It seemed absurd, especially since he was talking about the infamous CERN Hadron Collider facility in Geneva, Switzerland, where he'd worked.

Jack had googled the wacky-sounding story to see if Oliver was pulling his leg. He wouldn't have put it past him. Turned out the story was true. Energetic little ferrets were known to have an affinity for burrowing and clambering through tight spaces, making them the perfect species for such a job. Many decades earlier, when CERN had just opened, its smallest and furriest employee, a ferret, had been tasked with ensuring that hundreds of feet of vacuum piping were cleared, often in between tests, by pulling a rag saturated with a cleaning solution through the long maze of piping…that was until Jack's particular taxidermied animal was mistakenly zapped–someone had forgotten about the poor rodent–flipping the ON switch for the collider and sending eighteen thousand volts into its little body.

"Jack? Earth to Jack…"

He peered up and saw Alice looking at him. "Sorry…spaced out there." He raised his brows. "What?"

"I asked you if you miss them."

He nodded. "More than you know, kid."

It had been two years ago that he got the long-distance call. A social worker with a heavy French accent had yammered on the line. She had been frantically trying to reach him.

"Monsieur…is this Monsieur Jack Harding? You live…are you in Palo Alto, California?"

"Ah yeah…I'm Jack."

"And you are, how do I say *ami*…um, friend, to Oliver Johansson?"

"Yes, Oliver and I are friends…what's this about?" he asked, growing concerned.

"Pardon…so sorry to say, but Oliver, your friend, has died. A terrible accident. A plane crash."

"No. No, no, no! You must be mistaken…I just spoke to him last week. He was in Geneva. So, you're mistaken, miss."

"They were on holiday. En route to Paris," the woman affirmed.

Jack swayed, his knees buckling, as he reached for something to grasp onto. "Not the whole family? Please tell me, not the whole family." Jack swallowed, trying to find his voice. "All of them? They're all…dead? All seven of them?"

"No, monsieur. Just Elsa and Oliver have been identified. Yes, they are dead."

Jack let that sink in. He was devastated. The loss of his two dearest friends—how was he going to cope without them? He wiped a combination of salty tears and running snot from his nose. The woman continued.

"The children. They are headed to you now."

"Wait...what?"

"The twin boys, Lucas and Oscar, who are three; Charlie, five; Alice, nine; and Julia, who is eleven years of age. They will arrive at San Francisco International Airport in seven hours. They are accompanied by Mademoiselle Renee Dubois..."

Jack couldn't speak. Could barely organize his thoughts. Sure, this impossible contingency had, in fact, been agreed to. Years ago. It was a subsection of both his and Oliver's last will and testaments.

Jack barely remembered any of the details. But that was how he'd been informed, two years prior, that his two dearest friends had died when their Boeing 737 jetliner crashed into a potato field in rural France, and he had abruptly become the custodian of five devastated little kids. With no living family, Jack became their family.

A large shadow drifted across the concrete flooring. The silhouette of a hulking shape moved past one window, then another. Strange. It was Saturday morning. No one should be around here.

Elbows and kneecaps.

"Bart, take Alice. I want you to go into my office and close the door. Lock the door."

"Why?"

"Just do it...GO!"

CHAPTER 5

Jack closed his eyes and tried to steady his breathing. *Kneecaps and elbows.* That's what the threat had been the last time they'd sent someone to collect on his monumental debt. Selling the laboratory had fulfilled a promise to meet the worst of the debt. But even that wouldn't cover everything. It was barely enough to save his kneecaps...once the sale went safely through all the bank channels. Too bad the bulk of his debt was channeled through less scrupulous lenders. *Deep breaths. Think of something to say.*

He only hoped Bart would follow directions and keep Alice in his office. He'd have to try to keep his screams in check. Panic welled in an acidic burst in the back of his throat. Jack glanced around for something to defend himself with. He saw a long-handled broom propped against a wall, a stapler lying in a nearby shipping carton. Bart's helmet. *Crap!*

What a fool he'd been. So sure that their technological breakthrough would revolutionize an entire industry. But it turned out CERN had gotten wind of their plans three months prior to the fateful day and had altered the rules of the game. And why wouldn't they have? P1AL was on the precipice of making

CERN's business model obsolete. So on **P1AL**'s big day, when the test parameters showed up on Bart's display, they were all wrong. They were for a different test model. Yes, they would be letting antiprotons free fall within the ALPHA-g and measure when that antimatter exploded in free fall, but CERN had changed over to a different damn collider track. Every one of **P1AL**'s calculations had been set to Track 31A, not Track 31B.

In the end, doing their best to keep their quickly sinking ship afloat, **P1AL** had displayed other preconfigured animations. Sure, the holographic 3D graphics were impressive, and Jack had managed to look cool, calm, and collected on the outside...all the while dying on the inside. The media personnel had played along, keeping their cameras running. But it was evident. They knew this was a bust—just another crazy, albeit well-intentioned scientist falling flat on his face. The nail in the proverbial coffin had been the way Trinity Watson had looked at Jack. Like the pathetic turd he was.

The door to the street shook with a heavy knock. Jack didn't want to open it, but he knew making them force their way in would be much worse for him in the long run. Possibly bad for Alice, too, which he simply couldn't have. Bart, though? He momentarily toyed with the concept of hanging Bart's ass out to dry—but he knew he wouldn't do it. Even after his spectacular failure, the brilliant nitwit had stuck with him. Jack had to give him points for loyalty. Of course, it wasn't as though he had to beat feet to find other employment. Pretty sure Bart's mother didn't charge him rent.

Jack swallowed hard, grabbed the Swingline stapler, squared his shoulders, and flung open the door.

"We all out of corned beef...so, pastrami...we use pastrami." The middle-aged Latino man held up a large white bag in surrender on the other side of **P1AL**'s entrance. Grease stains spotted the paper. Jack stared at the man wearing the red polo shirt with a monogrammed DroneDash emblem across his chest. Only now did he remember he'd ordered Reuben sandwiches from Stan's Deli down the street. It appeared no one was coming to break his legs–not today at least.

"I'll take that," Alice said, hurrying by him. *Great job keeping her in the office, Bart.* She grabbed the bag from the delivery guy.

"Thanks…I hate pastrami though…just saying." She reclaimed her seat in his desk chair, opened the bag, and inspected the contents.

Jack let out a long breath and waved goodbye to the driver. On the bright side? Guess he still had at least $32.75 worth of credit. The card on file had still worked.

Alice said, "You worry too much, Jack." She smiled. "So, can we eat?"

"Oh yeah…starving!" Bart huffed as he came jogging into the room, red-cheeked and sweating. Jack shot him a reproachful look.

He shrugged. "What? She's quick."

Jack shook his head as Bart pulled up his old chair next to hers. The relief he felt must have been evident on his face as he pulled up one of the storage bins for his own makeshift seat. Alice distributed the sandwiches and fries and little packs of mustard…and ketchup. *I hate mustard,* Jack thought.

"Hey, boss, we have drinks?" Bart asked.

"Didn't order any. And I'm not your boss anymore, Bart. I'm not the boss of anyone anymore."

"Can I get that in writing?" Alice quipped.

"Funny girl. I think we have a few Mountain Dews and Cokes left in the fridge."

Alice scampered off toward the break room. He heard the refrigerator door open and then close again. "Cups? You know I hate drinking from cans…"

Jack chuckled. Each of the adopted kids was quirky in his or her own way. Alice didn't like drinking directly from cans, even if cleaned with soap and water. It grossed her out. "In the cabinet near the sink!" he yelled.

He took a bite of his Reuben and listened to the metal cabinet doors being opened.

"Aaaahhhh!"

The bloodcurdling scream was ear-piercing. Bart and Jack jumped up at the same time. Jack was the first to sprint toward the break room, wondering if Alice had cut herself on something sharp. Maybe slammed her finger in the door? He turned the corner just in time to see Alice standing stock-still in front of the tall, open metal cabinet–looking up. All body parts intact.

"What's wrong? What happened?" he said, hurrying to her side.

Bart turned the corner. "She okay?"

Eyes as wide as dinner plates, Alice finally turned her gaze toward Jack. "You don't see it? It scared the living crap out of me. How's it…doing that?"

Jack turned his gaze to the inside of the cabinet. He'd forgotten it had already been cleaned out, with its contents of cups, plates, packages of plastic forks and spoons, and small boxes of wax birthday candles all packed away. Even the metal shelves had been dismantled for shipment.

That's when he saw it. Two beady eyes stared back at him.

"What the hell?" Bart exclaimed.

Jack bent at the waist, holding his gut, and laughed out loud. Bart's brow furrowed, wrinkling at the concept that maybe, just maybe, Jack had finally gone round the bend. Bart took a wary step backward.

Jack's guffaws subsided. He placed a consoling hand around

Alice's tiny shoulders. "Relax, guys. That's just Thom-Thom. It's a ferret. One that spent some time at a taxidermist."

She stared at it there, way up at the top of the cabinet, upside down, and slowly nodded.

"Your father sent that to me a few years back. A kind of joke. Funny, I've been looking for ol' stuffed Thom-Thom for years... gave up looking a few months back—"

"I know it's a ferret, Jack. *Mustela putorius furo.*"

Bart giggled. "Stinky weasel thief."

Alice and Jack both turned with a baleful stare.

Bart shrugged. "I watch Animal Galaxy."

Alice shook her head and gave a little stamp of her faded tennis shoes. "That's not what scared me!"

"Well what, then? That thing can't hurt you. It's not like it's alive."

She took in a patient breath, held out her arm, and pointed. "It's...it's...just floating there."

Jack gave it a good look. She wasn't wrong. It appeared to be, well...hovering, near the top of the cabinet. He tilted his head this way and that, trying to figure out just how it was being suspended up there like it was. He crouched down lower to better see beneath it.

"Must have its tail caught in a crevice or something." Jack reached in and grabbed for the ferret's long tail. A tail, he discovered, that was not caught in the least. He nudged the critter with his arm and sent it tumbling out into the break room.

Alice jumped backward, bringing both hands up to cover her mouth. A scream punctuated the air. Jack looked at her. Eyes wide, she shook her head and pointed to Bart, who promptly ran from the room. Alice and Jack watched, paralyzed, as the furry rodent gently rose and bounced off the ceiling tiles, descended a foot or so, and then rose and settled on the ceiling. The motion made Jack nauseous. Once again, its two beady upside-down eyes stared down at them.

Alice tugged on his shirtsleeve. Jack looked down at her.

"Besides the fact we don't have any cups, I think your ferret broke gravity."

CHAPTER 6

Bart was hesitant to give a helping hand with capturing the elusive Thom-Thom from the ten-foot-tall ceilings. Using the broom, Jack mostly managed to just bat the stuffed rodent around from one location to another. He'd knock the thing right side up, and it would start sinking, like a slowly deflating helium balloon. He had to assume Oliver had somehow rigged the thing with something like that, just to freak him out.

Jack stretched up too-short fingers to snag it, but the damned thing just rolled over, belly-up, and bobbled back toward the ceiling. Eventually, he stacked several storage bins on a table, climbed on top of the makeshift mountain, and grabbed the ferret.

"Hand it to me before you drop it," Alice said with outstretched hands.

"Drop it?" Jack repeated, hesitating on his topsy-turvy perch.

"Come on. You know what I mean. Hand it down to me."

He did as told, his mind churning over the possibilities.

"What do you suppose is making it do that?" Bart asked weakly. He took a nervous step backward.

Jack said, "There's got to be a simple explanation. Maybe the ferret's bloated with some lighter-than-air element, likely helium or hydrogen. Maybe some kind of sealed internal bladder that magically keeps the little hairball suspended in the air. Granted, I probably should have noticed that ages ago."

He jumped down and disassembled his Rubbermaid Jenga. Alice looked at the ferret. More like examined it. Closely. A miniature scientist in the making. Jack handed one of the bins to Bart and reached for another.

As if to reassure himself, Jack reiterated, "It's from Oliver, Alice's father. My best friend. Has to be one of his pranks. Probably just a helium balloon inside it with some sort of delayed activation. I just regret I won't be able to return the favor."

"Sounds like this buddy of yours had a seriously weird sense of humor."

He scoffed. *Says the Mad Hatter.* Jack stacked the bins on a trolley to haul them to the front door and nodded.

"Only two things Oliver was ever serious about–science…" He cast a forlorn look at Alice, who continued studying the ferret, "and family." He walked over to her. "How about I zap your sandwich in the microwave? Heat it up a tad?"

"Uh-huh."

"That is a brilliant idea!" Bart chimed and sauntered off to retrieve his own sandwich.

"You should wash your hands, kiddo…who knows what microbes are crawling around on that thing."

"Jack…"

"Yeah?" he said, about to leave the room.

"Look at this." Alice cradled the body of the ferret like a baby but let the tail fall free. It floated up like a wayward kite on a string. "There's nothing inside the tail. I felt around on it. No balloon in there, no nothing." She stared back at him with a quizzical expression. She looked at Thom-Thom, held the ferret out in front of her, and let go. It fell upward.

CHAPTER 7

En-Route to the StarCall Facility, Northern California Carolina Locke

The driver spoke over his shoulder, "We're ten minutes out, sir. Arrival time to the StarCall Facility will be close to one thirty…and yes, we'll be precisely on time this afternoon."

Locke didn't comment. Instead, he continued to stare out the side window of his rented Maybach Landaulet EV Deluxe. The mostly hand-crafted automobile was big–really big–more akin to a street yacht. Far preferable to more pedestrian limos or oversized SUVs. With a five-million-dollar sticker price, the luxury motor carriage turned heads as it quietly cruised the streets. Locke spotted several young boys on bicycles racing along on the sidewalk outside. They tried to keep pace with the Landaulet, their feet pedaling faster and faster. His mind flashed back to a fond memory of his own youth.

To date, Travis Locke had purposely killed twelve separate individuals over the span of his life, the first being Donny Newton, who had been seven years old, just as Travis had been at the time. As far as the rest of the world knew, the two boys had headed out one morning on their mountain bikes to explore the wooded and well-worn trails surrounding their Northern

California mountain neighborhood. En route, an argument had erupted between the two young boys. All these years later, Travis could not remember what it was they were quibbling about. What he did remember, though, was how satisfying it had been to hear the other boy's skull hit the bottom of the ravine.

The boys on bikes faded in their pursuit, not unlike how Donny, with his asthma and his annoying wheeze, had fallen behind when Travis sped away from the argument. The opportunity had been far too tempting to ignore when he came upon the lookout site. He dismounted and headed over to the cliffside, waiting as Donny's telltale gasping approached. He stood there on the precarious ridge overlooking the wilderness hundreds of feet below and looked back over his shoulder, acting as if the argument had been long forgotten, before pointing downward. "There's an old ramshackle cabin down in those trees. Like a secret fort."

Donny dismounted and threw down his bike, apparently still miffed about being left behind. He peered down while shielding his eyes from the bright glare of the morning sun, shaking his inhaler in his free hand. "I don't remember seeing any kind of cabin down there," he huffed, gasping in albuterol. When Travis remained still, gaze trained down the cliff, the other boy exhaled in a great burst, "You're full of shit."

"Nah," Travis kept his voice happy, excited even. "You can see part of it. At least one small corner." He held out an extended finger and pointed down at the distant tree line. "See that super tall tree there? The one that's like twice as tall as the others around it?"

"Yeah, I see it."

"Now look right below it...in that open patch at its base."
Donny leaned forward and squinted. "I don't–"
Travis had taken a large step backward. His two-handed

47

shove was enough to send poor Donny Newton stumbling over the edge, his protest cut short. Strangely, the boy didn't scream or cry out. Perhaps it had been the shock of the situation...suddenly falling fast, knowing he was about to die...absolutely nothing he could do about it.

Travis waited, watching as Donny hit the bottom of the ravine below before hefting his friend's bike up and tossing it over the edge. He marveled at how both the bike and the boy landed with parts at impossible angles. How fascinating it had been, the similarities between the two after the fall. Bones and metal, metal and bones.

The simple fact was Travis had been aware he possessed abnormal tendencies even before the youthful cliffside incident. That he was a diagnosed psychopath hadn't been revealed to him until he was in his late teens, but a part of him had always known. Such labels meant little to him then, and even less now that he was forty-one. In truth, everything in life was a means to an end. Wasn't that the underlying rule of survival in the wild...the world? Did a lion giving chase stop to consider the morality of killing its prey out on the Serengeti? No, of course not.

"Sir."

Locke looked up, seeing his driver standing beside the now-open car door. The man held out a hand.

Locke slapped it away. "What...you think I can't lift myself out of a damn seat? Leave me be." He spat the words before climbing out and taking in the expansive aeronautical facility with its multiple sleek-looking outbuildings and glimmering lift pads off in the distance.

"Ms. Copeland called," the driver said, "She is en route... perhaps ten minutes out."

Locke nodded, not surprised his executive VP of legal affairs was going to be late again. Sarah typically arrived late. If she hadn't been so competent a lawyer, not to mention easy on the eyes, he would have fired her long before now. An attractive woman in a position of power at his side was a look he wore well, and Locke was keenly aware of that fact. Besides, he had to give her props—Sarah was as ruthless a businessperson as anyone he had ever met. She'd been relentless in her pursuit of a position in his company and seemed just as invested as Locke was at being the first to bring back a spaceship full of still-living Mars egrets.

If only that investment in the project translated into being more punctual. Locke tugged the cuffs of his Armani grisaille and satin blend suit in place. The lighter fabric was much more ideal for the humid North Carolina morning when compared to some of the more expensive suits in his closet. It wouldn't do to walk into the StarCall facility looking unkempt. He turned his wrist to watch the second hand tick on his Girard-Perregaux Quasar Tourbillion, the fifteen-thousand-dollar watch moving with silent precision.

"Send her in once she arrives." Locke stalked past the driver, not waiting to hear his confirmation of the instructions.

"Mr. Locke, what a pleasure to see you this morning. Would you care for a cup of coffee?" The red-haired receptionist hustled around the side of her desk the moment Locke stepped through the door.

"Thank you, but no." He flashed his careful smile, pleased at the flush the expression elicited on the woman's face. "Are the engineers prepared for our meeting?"

She nodded vigorously, her kitten heels dancing on the tile floor. "Oh yes! Absolutely. We have the best, er, the nicest conference room set up for you and..." She trailed off, her blue eyes finally moving from Locke's face to the door, just now noticing that he wasn't accompanied as she'd expected him to be.

"Ms. Copeland. She took a last-minute call from an investor

in Tokyo." He shook his head, allowing his full lips to turn down just so at the corners. "You know how hard the time differences can be to manage for some."

The fiery bun at the top of the receptionist's head bounced as she nodded vigorously in opposition to the crystal-clear fact she had no concept at all. "Oh, it's so nice of her to take calls at any time! Your company is most impressive."

Locke cleared his throat pointedly. *Come on, you bumbling fool, let's get on with it.* He had such a distaste for small talk. It curdled in his mouth.

The young woman flushed even deeper, making Locke wonder if perhaps her head would burst right open from the extra blood flow to those plump cheeks. She followed his gaze over her shoulder toward the hall and skittered to turn a hundred and eighty degrees. "Right this way, sir, uh, yes, right this way."

Locke followed behind her clicking heels, the smooth soles of his Italian leather Testonis silent on the shining tile. He entered the room. All four heads swiveled. Dr. Binderkampf shoved thick frames further up his twitching nose, a nervous gesture that Locke had despised since the first time he'd met the physicist. One seat over, Theodore Steinbluum tapped his pen on the thick folder in front of him, pointedly checking his watch. Emry Vashtin, the boy wonder of the group at only thirty-five, with six different degrees all earned from either Brown, Princeton, or Yale, barely looked up from the notepad he was scribbling on illegibly. Last but not least, Peter Valeni's balding head reflected the cool blue light from the bulbs set deep in the ceiling.

Not just the engineers.

Unperturbed, Locke smoothly circled behind the men, rounding the table to pull out a chair on the opposite side. He folded his hands atop the polished wood between them and dispensed with any notion that greetings were necessary. "Shall we begin?"

Peter snorted, his roots in the "construction" business never quite polished away, despite the fortune his Mafia-made family had accumulated. "You walk in, what, five minutes late, no apologies, no 'how are yas,' and you're ready to get right to business? Ha! That ain't how we do business in my town."

Gazing coolly at the middle son of the Valeni family, Locke arched one brow. *I could buy and sell your older brother twice over...don't even get me started on you, you little prick.* "My apologies. I assumed we were all here under the same purpose." He turned his attention to Dr. Binderkampf. "It's my understanding that today's report leaves a lot to be desired in terms of progress."

The physicist's bulbous nose twitched again, sending his glasses on a downward trajectory, disrupted at the last moment by that annoying push on the black plastic in the middle.

Locke sighed audibly. *Get a fucking fitted pair of spectacles, you imbecile.* "Doctor, I've told you before, I'm perfectly capable of understanding your reports. I'm keenly aware that the past two tests did not go as planned, and I'd truly like to be given a reason to keep...supporting...your research."

"You ain't the only one 'supporting' here, buddy. I'm not sure I like your tone," the ham-fisted thug opposite him sneered.

"Gentlemen, gentlemen. I recommend that we wait for Ms. Copeland to join us." Steinbluum stopped tapping his pen, substituting his left heel instead.

"Ms. Copeland is here." Sarah Copeland's voice carried from just outside the door; the velvety-smooth tones slid smoothly, like the honed blade of a jeweled dagger being sheathed.

Locke felt the same possessive jolt he felt each time he saw the sleek blonde lawyer. Her honey-gold strands were pulled into a smooth bun; her makeup was classy; and her suit was cut just so, making it obvious that she had curves in all the places men liked them. "Glad you could join us. One never knows how long those international business calls will last." He stood, presenting her chair for her.

"Thank you for waiting." Her eyes didn't leave Locke's as she sat—the closest, Locke knew, that she'd come to apologizing for her tardiness. "Now," she turned to the men opposite them, the feral smile that had first interested Locke in the young lawyer three years ago now greeting Valeni. "If I recall, your support is approximately one-third that of my client, so perhaps you could do us the favor of speaking one-third as often. Vashtin, Emry, I believe? I would so prefer if you could give us your full attention."

The prodigy's pen slowed as he glanced up, his gaze clearly worlds away.

"Honestly, I don't know why anyone bothers to parade him out for these sorts of meetings. Dr. Binderkampf, I suppose it will be you to give the update." Sarah's pen poised to take notes, completely unruffled by the chest-heaving anger simmering at her from Peter Valeni.

Balls of steel, Locke thought, fighting the smug smirk that wanted to show itself. *And the gaze to match.* He admired the strength and poise reflected in her gray eyes as she stared Valeni down. Still, it wouldn't do to burn any bridges until he was certain that the results of the third test at this facility were as dismal as he was anticipating.

"I, uh, the last test was not optimal. It was, well, it did okay...initially. The numbers looked to be just below target until the atmosphere was breached. The ion thruster was unable to maintain mass propellant at the proposed rate once out of line with the gravitational pull due to energy conservation needs for the life-support systems on board." The scientist looked nervously over at the mobster to his left. "So, um, we were thinking that perhaps one of your other research centers has found a more compact generator option? Collaboration has often yielded great results in the scientific fields."

Locke lofted his eyebrows in response. Sarah replied for him. "Mr. Locke is not at liberty to discuss his other ventures at this time. Should he deem it necessary, there will be appropriate paperwork drawn up well beforehand. By me."

"Uh, yes, well…the problem areas continue to be power and weight. Unless you plan to send an entirely unmanned vessel to Mars, it appears unlikely that it can be done in the sub-two-week time frame you are demanding. The LOX and RP-1 can't create adequate propulsion across the atmosphere to continue the forward motion needed at the appropriate rate to…well.

"The problem at this point isn't so much the liftoff. It's everything that happens after. The generator on board is too small; the ion thruster supplement is only able to work optimally within a gravitational pull, which could be solved by less of everything. Less space. Less equipment. Less life support. More power. More fuel for combined fusion and chemical propellants."

"If I wanted an unmanned space shuttle, I'd work with one of the leading drone companies. I'm not. I'm working with StarCall." Locke steepled his fingers, waiting for the scientist to continue.

"Right. Uh, yes, of course. Well, have any of your other investments, perhaps, sorted a way to build a lighter craft?"

Peter leaned forward, his interest rendered across his face like a bad oil portrait. *Amateur,* Locke sneered inwardly. It was suddenly clear that this meeting was as much about the stumbling blocks of the research as it was an attempt to gain knowledge. Knowledge that *his* money had paid for.

"Dr. Vashtin, would you care to contribute to this dilemma?" Locke eyed the boy wonder. It was a pity, so much education, so much money, and still…failure.

"It's a true preponderance, the quandary of adequate energy. A perplexity that has impacted humanity since the first fire was built, epochs ago."

"An eloquent 'no' would suffice." Locke shrugged nonchalantly. "Gentlemen, I believe the time has come to sever our working relationship. Thrice now, I have been generous. Thrice now, you have disappointed me."

"I do believe you'll find in the contract you signed a clause of three full years financial backing." Theodore Steinbluum's toothy grin grated on Locke's nerves.

"Interesting." Locke leaned across the table as he stood. "I believe you'll find that my lawyer is much better than yours when it comes to drawing up contracts."

"I *am* our lawyer."

"Indeed." Locke sniffed lightly, already cruising past the men at the table on his way to the door. He had no doubt that Sarah had written in loopholes Steinbluum had overlooked. She always hid them so well. "Valeni, I'll remind you that I am awaiting Ms. Copeland in my car. See that she returns to me shortly."

Not that Locke had any concern for his lawyer's safety. Still, sometimes it could be so satisfying to watch cheap men squirm when they were outmaneuvered.

CHAPTER 8

P1AL Facilities, Palo Alto, California
Jack

They had all agreed to ignore the ferret until their work was done. Easier said than done, but the bank had only given them until Monday to be out of the building. Secretly, Jack harbored the fear his kneecaps-and-elbows friends would soon be paying a visit, so he wanted to get a move on.

By late afternoon, Alice and Jack had the P1AL office pretty much packed up. Bart spent most of the time executing complex mathematical computations to determine if their trailer payload would exceed his Ford EV GoJo! Smart Car's tow capacity. Between his seven-year-old Volvo-Fiat EV200 and Bart's precious pride and joy, Jack figured they could just about fit the pittance that remained of his once-ambitious company.

The underground accelerator track and control room portion of the facility, along with all its associated engineering systems, was still intact. He'd assumed the next owner would want to keep that aspect operational—why else purchase a fully functional, albeit relatively small particle accelerator/collider facility in the first place? The tunnels were the main reason he'd bought the abandoned military facility in the first place. Scores of the hollowed-out corridors warrened beneath the operations buildings. They had made a perfect place to construct the accelerator—no expensive excavation needed.

After the second Cold War of 2028, when budgets fell under the ax, the military had undergone some serious streamlining and had to sell off a lot of underutilized properties for a song.

Lucky for me, Jack sighed. *Or maybe not so lucky.* If things didn't turn around soon, he was going to be looking for things to sell off himself.

On the drive home, Alice gave him a gentle reminder. "Better go faster, Jack...we have less than a half hour." She gestured to the digital clock on the Volvo's dash.

"Half hour?" he said, trying to remember what appointment he'd forgotten about tonight. It was the weekend, and he couldn't imagine making any plans.

"The meeting...Bradley's meeting?" Alice said.

Jack stifled the urge to roll his eyes. "Oh yeah. And what is it exactly he wants to meet about?"

She raised her palms up in mock surrender. "Beats me...but I'm not getting in the middle of things between you two. And Julia's already said she's not even going to listen."

Jack sighed. To say things could get contentious between Bradley and Jack would be an understatement. The man often crossed the line from competent employee to pushy nanny who forgot he was not the actual parent. It wasn't totally Bradley's fault. The problem was, Jack relied on him far too much. With everything going on of late, Bradley had become the de facto parent—shuttling kids back and forth to school, ensuring doctors' and dentists' appointments were kept and after-school sports practices were synchronized, even assisting with homework. All this in addition to the normal nanny duties of doing laundry and preparing meals for the seven. And above all the rest, there was

Charlie, the middle child, who had come to Jack as a perfectly healthy kid and now struggled with special needs—a kid destined to spend the rest of his life restricted to his electric wheelchair.

Each kid was two years older than when he or she had arrived. The twins, Lucas and Oscar, were now a rambunctious five. Charlie, at seven, possessed a sweet demeanor and, despite his condition, still shouldered the role of caretaker, mediating arguments among the brood, helping Bradley with the laundry, and keeping a brotherly eye on his younger brothers. Then there were Jack's girls. Alice was eleven going on thirty, and Julia, at thirteen, wore snark like a fashion accessory.

They drove in silence for the next few miles. Jack noticed Thom-Thom was on Alice's lap, partially covered by her pink hoodie and held down in place with one hand. Although he'd told her they'd think about the floating stuffed rodent later, in reality, he'd thought of little else since its discovery in the cabinet. The scientist in him kept trying to sort through the facts. Without meaning to, Jack had begun to develop and dismiss multiple hypotheses, ideas based on what they had seen. In his mind, Jack ran through possible experiments to help them turn conjecture into theory and then into fact. His mind already churned through the possibilities while discounting low-probability tenets.

They slowed and pulled into the driveway. The long, steep drive serpentined between four massive and majestic Monterey cypress trees. Up ahead loomed his nineteenth-century brick Victorian. Horas B. Harding, Jack's great-great-grandfather, had built it. Good old Horas had moved west from New York and had taken full advantage of the California Gold Rush of the 1850s. Although the four-story mansion hadn't always stayed in the family over the past one hundred and eighty years, Jack's grandfather, Collin Harding, had repurchased the rambling old structure from a foreclosure sale back in the late 1950s.

The home was worth millions in today's market. Jack certainly wouldn't have been able to afford such a thing—especially with his current money problems. He'd inherited the twenty-six-room monstrosity and its iron-clad clause that no mortgage or lien could be attached to the house or the five acres of land surrounding it. So, on paper, he supposed, he was a millionaire. Didn't prevent him from having to scrounge for nickels, dimes, and quarters in between couch cushions for the kids' lunch money on more than one occasion. The house, in all its glory, would do nothing to help him keep his elbows and kneecaps intact.

"See, we're not so late," he said, pointing through the windshield.

Up ahead, Bradley was at the side of the old Ford Electroline, lowering the powered handicap ramp. Charlie sat in his wheelchair on the platform. He twisted around in his seat to see who was coming down the drive. With a wide grin, he waved an enthusiastic hand. Although Jack couldn't hear him, he could read the boy's lips—*Look, Jack's home!*

Bradley offered his own half wave and tepid smile. The remaining kids piled out the other side of the van and stampeded for the house. Jack pulled in behind the Electroline, shut off the engine, and Alice and Jack stepped out.

Bradley barked, "Hey! No one goes into that house without carrying a grocery bag!"

Ignoring him, the twins ran to Alice instead, each latching onto a leg with enough force to nearly topple her over. Both five-year-olds looked up at her.

Lucas said, "I saw Oscar pick his nose and eat a booger."

"Did not!" Oscar said, scowling at his brother.

Alice mock-frowned. "Hey…what did I say about snacking before dinner?"

Both boys laughed overdramatically while Bradley gave a disapproving glance. Jack watched them trail Alice into the house. Two years and he still felt like he was on the outside looking in— except with Charlie.

"Jack!" he called.

Closing the Volvo door, he moved toward Charlie with a tired smile. Charlie had taken control of his Karman XO-202 Full Power electric wheelchair and drove it in his direction. The mechanical wonder was top-of-the-line. At $10,000, it had better be. Jack would be paying for it for the next fifteen years. He tousled the boy's hair and put his briefcase in his lap. "Can you take that in for me, Charlie?"

"Sure thing!" He zipped away–always happy to help.

"Oof!" Jack grunted. Bradley offloaded three paper grocery bags on him.

"Careful!" he warned. "That one has a full chicken in it… hold the bottom of the bag, for goodness' sakes."

"Yeah, Jack," Julia mocked, carrying her own bag. He noticed she had added several new colors to her long wavy locks. Apathy was Julia's factory setting, or so she would have everyone believe. If you looked past the rainbow hair, the kid cared too much. Jack remembered her tear-streaked face and puffy eyes when he picked them up at the airport two years ago. As the oldest of the Johansson kids, she had felt the greatest impact at the loss of their parents. Eleven years made for a lot of memories. Now, at thirteen, she lived behind a wall, one no one appeared to have much success getting through. Especially Jack.

But emotions got through. They showed up in the most awkward ways, like when she'd hacked the school's grading system and took vengeance on some mean girls last year for poking fun at Alice.

Like a line of pack animals, they all trudged up the cement

switchback ramp toward the home's double front doors. Two years had changed a lot of things for these kids. And for Jack.

*****

Later, after dinner, dishes were washed, dried, and stowed away. They adjourned to the music room. One of many rooms in the old house Jack saw no need for. But Bradley had chosen this room for their family meeting, and Jack didn't care enough to protest.

They all found a seat, and Bradley, standing in the middle of the room, waited for them to quiet down.

"Thank you for allowing me these few minutes."

Jack shrugged. "Of course...what's on your mind, Bradley?"

Bradley was close to thirty-five, medium in height and weight, with thinning curly blond hair. He wore stone-washed blue jeans–high, belted right above the waist. Sharp sleeve creases sliced down the sleeves of his blue-striped button-down shirt. The tails of the shirt tucked neatly into his high-riding pants. The fact that Bradley was gay was a nonissue in their household– who someone loved or a person's sexual orientation made no difference to Jack. However, with that said, Bradley was always ready for confrontation concerning the way he looked, talked, or walked, or anything pertaining to his overall demeanor. He was a contentious little man, and Jack, for one, did his best to give him a wide berth.

"I just wanted to say...and it pains me more than you know...I am hereby giving you all notice."

"What does that even mean? You don't look like you're in any pain, so why fake it?" Julia sneered.

"Giving notice of what?" Charlie asked, a deep line creasing his forehead.

"He's telling us he's leaving," Alice said, narrowing her eyes toward Bradley.

Both twins began to cry.

Alice waved them both to come over and sit upon a knee.

Jack sighed heavily. This was not the first time Bradley had given notice. In fact, it was the second time this year. It was all part of the song and dance he brought out when he wanted a raise. All that was missing was the jazz hands. Jack had half a mind to tell him it was curtains. There was nothing to give... unless he took IOUs.

Bradley had never done his routine in front of the kids before, though. A niggle of worry tugged at his gut. With two bawling five-year-olds to contend with now, Jack wished the nanny had stuck with his regular timing of threatening to quit once the kids were all in their rooms for the night.

"Thank you, Bradley. I know it must have been a difficult decision. You'll surely be missed." Jack's blunt statement shocked even the twins into silence.

If looks could kill, he'd be lying dead on the one-hundred-and-twelve-year-old hardwood floor. He almost withered under Bradley's baleful stare. The nanny stationed both manicured hands on his narrow hips. Bradley wanted an argument...a plea from Jack to stay. Besides the money. He certainly deserved both. What he accomplished on a daily basis was amazing. But the well was dry. There was no more money to offer him.

"Where are you going, Bradley? Do you have another job... with another family?" said Charlie, his young face filled with honest concern.

"Not with another family. I'm branching into the corporate sector...but, yes, I have secured other employment. Something a little more—stable."

"How much notice are you giving us? I'll need no less than

two weeks. Three would be better. I will need to run an ad," Jack continued.

Bradley cleared his throat and pulled at his buttoned-up collar. "Ahem…yes. Well, you see, I'm afraid that won't be possible. It was a requirement of the new job offer. I have to start first thing Monday."

"That's in less than forty-eight hours," Jack rasped, dry-mouthed.

"I know, and I feel absolutely terrible about it, but my hands are tied. I have obligations of my own, and I'm afraid, well… again, this was a difficult decision, but tomorrow—Sunday—will be my last day. I will miss all of you children…miss you terribly." Bradley blinked away the accumulating moisture in his eyes.

Uh-oh. It struck Jack then—their indispensable nanny just might not be bluffing.

CHAPTER 9

Harden Estate, Palo Alto, CA
Julia

The storm had blown up suddenly. After Bradley had dropped his bombshell news, Jack had urged everyone into early baths and bedtimes. Julia suspected that was just so he could nurse his woes with an early scotch. The evening sky had been clear as Bradley wrestled the twins into a bubble bath. Charlie had been carried to bed and his wheelchair put on charge. Julia and Alice had gone to their respective rooms.

At least Julia had at first. When she had slipped into her sister's room to stash her tablet–Bradley had officially put her on notice for spending way too much screen time on Tik Tok–Alice was nowhere to be found. When Julia's younger sibling burst in moments later, chest heaving and out of breath, Alice just said, "Oh, hey. I was just in the bathroom."

At that moment, one of the twins, head piled with bubbles and ass naked as a jaybird, streaked down the hallway and past the open door, Bradley screaming behind him.

"Lucas! Lucas, you get back here this instant, young man!" Hot on his heels was an equally naked and bubbled Oscar, laughing his head off.

Julia narrowed a doubtful look at her sister. "Bathroom, huh? With Double Bubble and Toil and Trouble? Yeah. I don't think so. You're up to something."

Alice gave a defiant pout and crossed her arms. "Am not!"

Julia sauntered toward her younger sibling and waggled an accusatory finger under her nose. "I call baloney. You're absolutely the worst liar in this whole family. You give it away every time."

"Oh yeah?" Alice defended. "How's that?"

"Let's just say Mom and Dad should have named you Thumper instead of Alice." Julia pointed to Alice's worn-out shoes, thumping a staccato rhythm on the floorboards. "Your toe is a tattletale."

Alice looked down and groaned. She threw her hands in the air in surrender then slapped the outside of her thighs. "Man! No wonder Bradley seemed suspicious when I said I didn't take the milk!"

Julia nodded as she slid her tablet into Alice's pillowcase. "Also, just a helpful hint–if you're trying to successfully convince someone that you did *not* take the vinegar either, try not to spill it on yourself. You smelled like the salad bar at Golden Corral."

Alice shrugged. "The twins were doing an art project, and they were out of paste. I used the milk and vinegar to make homemade glue. It's a really cool chemical reaction when you think about it. When you add the vinegar to the milk, it separates the milk protein, casein, from the liquid. Neutralize the acetic acid of the vinegar with a little baking soda and–ta-da–moo glue!"

"Yeah? Well, guess what, Bill Nye. I'm not covering for you if Bradley comes looking. What are you up to this time, anyway?"

Alice set her jaw. "Nothing."

The repetitive tapping filled the silence of the room. Julia grinned. Alice looked down at her foot and groaned.

Julia stepped in closer. "Fess up, midget, or I'll snitch on you just to get Bradley off my back for a while."

Alice let loose a gush of expelled air. "Okay, fine! I can't believe you're resorting to blackmail–my own sister–but I guess I don't really have a choice. Wait here."

Alice turned on her heel and scurried to the door. She gripped the doorjamb with both hands and cautiously poked her head into the hallway. A disintegrating trail of white bubbles stretched the length of the hallway runner, little popping mountains of long-chain alky groups on the fading Persian, but no twins, and more importantly, no Bradley. She took a hesitant step into the hallway as Julia watched, then broke into a sprint down the narrow passageway.

A few fleeting moments later, she popped back into the room, holding a lumpy, red bundle of fabric. Julia could make out some of the white lettering–S-T-A-N.

"Jack's old uni sweatshirt? You're doing laundry? Big whoop," Julia scoffed.

Alice shook her head vigorously. "No, no, no. Wait till you get a load of this!" she jabbered and walked toward her desk. With her back to Julia, she set her precious cargo down on the desk surface and, with great aplomb, whipped the sweatshirt away to reveal the ferret.

"Ta-da!" she exclaimed. Julia stood motionless.

"Right?" Excitement twinkled in Alice's eyes. "Isn't it the most awesome thing you've ever seen?"

Julia blinked her own brown eyes. "A stuffed rat?"

Alice's eyes narrowed. "It's not a rat. It's a ferret."

"Ferret…rat…just don't let Bradley catch you with that mangy old thing. God, it's disgusting!" Julia's face puckered.

"Disgusting? Try amazing! Have you ever seen anything like it?"

"Yeah," Julia replied. "On the glue traps the janitor lays out at school."

Alice gestured emphatically. "Come on, Julia! Look at it. It's floating!"

One eyebrow arched high over Julia's eye as she tilted her head. Alice slowly turned to face Thom-Thom, who sat, frozen in a forever snarl, completely stationary and quite rooted to Alice's desk. Alice leaped forward.

"Wait a second. That's not supposed to happen. Come on!" She grabbed the immobile rodent and shook its wiry little body. "It's supposed to float!"

"Float?" Julia laughed. "Whatever, Einstein. You'd better toss that thing in the trash before you get rabies or something."

Alice scowled. "I'm not going to catch rabies, stupid. And I'm not throwing it away. It's important." Anguish cracked her reedy voice. "It was Dad's."

Her accent dramatically altered the pronunciation of "was." "Don't you ever miss them, JuJu Bee?"

Julia scowled and stomped toward the motionless ferret. She picked it up and prodded it. "Yeah. Guess so."

Alice whirled on her. "Guess so? Doesn't anything affect you anymore?"

"What's the big deal?"

"Jules, our parents…our parents are gone. I sometimes have trouble even remembering what they looked like anymore. Jack and I found a picture at the lab when we were packing up. I didn't even recognize Dad. I don't know how much Charlie remembers. And I don't even think the twins remember them at all."

"So what? They're gone. They're not coming back, and we're stuck here," Julia gestured to the peeling wallpaper, "in this crusty old dump with Jack the Genius. Some genius. More like Jack the Loser. Lost his business. Lost our nanny. How's he going to take care of us, Alice? Face it. We're probably going to get split up and put in foster care."

"Don't say that! You can't say stuff like that! But don't you see? That's why I need to find out why this ferret floats! Maybe Dad came up with something really awesome. Something that Jack could use somehow to get back on his feet. Something to help keep us all together."

"Great, Alice, except for one thing...the stupid ferret doesn't float!"

Julia threw the white rodent to the ground...only that wasn't where it landed. In fact, it didn't land at all. The creature spiraled toward the floor, ass over nose until its pinkish underbelly faced the ceiling. Just before it hit the floorboards, it seemed to gently bounce off an invisible hill and began a slow ascent.

"What the heck?" Julia muttered.

Both girls stood riveted as the ferret sailed on, bouncing off the trim on the door frame and back into the room, dancing along the ceiling there.

"See?" Alice cried. "See? I told you it floats! Like a furry white bubble."

Julia watched, slack-jawed, as her sister clambered atop her desk chair, trying to retrieve the floating ferret. From another part of the house, she heard Bradley bellow.

"You two get back here this instant!"

The teen looked back at the floating animal and mumbled under her breath. "Double bubble, toil and trouble."

*****

Lightning shocked the room into a moment of brilliant daylight. Julia bolted upright in her twin bed, clutching the comforter, knuckles blanching. She stole a furtive glance at the

digital alarm clock on the bedside table. 3:00 a.m. Sleep just
wasn't going to be an option tonight, she thought. As if Alice's
little discovery wasn't enough to keep the wheels in her brain
turning, thunder rolled ominously beyond the window glass.
Julia's heart hammered against her rib cage as she tried to catch
her breath. She forced a swallow, but fear lumped in her throat.

"Rain, rain, go away," she mumbled the old nursery rhyme her
mother had taught her.

Mother Nature, on the other hand, had a different idea
altogether. In defiant response, she ripped open the sky once
more, illuminating Jordan Flint, the hot pop star of the moment,
whose poster was thumbtacked to the wall; the lop-eared stuffed
rabbit missing an eye; the scattered collection of cosmetics on
the dresser; and the other random bits of flotsam that totaled the
teen's existence.

Julia dove back under the covers until the last *basso profundo*
rumble died away. She peeked over the top edge of the blanket.
More lightning flashed. Julia began to count.

"One thousand...two one thousand...three one thousand...
four one thousand..." Every second meant five miles. She stared
up at the ceiling, at least where she assumed the ceiling would
be. Without the illumination of the lightning, the space above
her had been plunged into an abysmal blackness. "Five one
thousand..."

Craaaack!

Okay, now she had to pee. Despite the urgency, she remained
rooted to the mattress, the gravity of fear competing with the
pressure on her bladder. A crease furrowed between her eyebrows
as the corners of her mouth tugged decidedly downward.

"Grow up, stupid," she admonished herself. "It's just a
freakin' storm."

The reprimand held little comfort when she considered that

was probably just what her parents had thought the night their plane went down over Paris.

Julia ripped away the covers and swung her feet over the edge of the bed. Her painted toes disappeared into the pile of the fur rug. Faux, of course. At least no animal Julia knew of sported a bright purple coat. Not that she would have tolerated real fur anyway. Even at thirteen, she was an avid believer in animal rights, not to mention a staunch vegetarian. Her particular eating habits often drove Bradley to distraction over the dinner table. Like they had tonight when she started describing the offensive practices at many chicken farms in lurid detail. She couldn't help but smile when the nanny and Jack had slowly pushed away the cordon bleu on their plates as Julia munched quite contentedly on her carrots.

Things weren't quite so funny right now though. Ever since the turbulent night of her parents' death, Julia positively hated storms. And violent electrical ones were the worst. Authorities claimed it had not been lightning that had brought her parents' plane down. The fuselages of most modern aircraft were specifically designed like Faraday cages to keep electrical current away from the contents inside. Yet, despite what the official report detailed, the fact remained that the plane had exploded after flying through a particularly violent summer storm, and then Julia and her siblings had wound up here.

Julia padded silently but quickly across the floor and into the hall. A framed photo, the last one taken of the Johanssons as a whole family, hung on the wall. She considered what she had said to Alice—about the possibility of them getting split up. It had been mean. She knew it. It had been automatic though. A knee-jerk response to the pain she felt inside. In reality, she couldn't bear the idea of losing any more members of her family. Maybe Alice was right. Maybe if they solved the puzzle of the floating ferret, the solution could be used to help them all stay together.

The glass of the photo caught the jagged reflection of another lightning strike from her bedroom window. Julia jumped. She shuffled forward, head down, staring at her toes.

"One thousand...two one thousand..."

Right now, though, she just wanted to get to the bathroom, flip the light switch, do her thing, wash her hands, and rush back to bed, pulling every piece of herself back under the blanket, where she could lie to herself and say everything was okay and nothing could hurt her–and she might just believe it.

"Three one thousand..."

A thunderous crack rent the sleepy silence of the house. Julia sprinted the last few feet into the bathroom and slammed the door behind her.

She collapsed against the closed door, slid weakly down to the floor, and hugged her knees into her chest.

"Mom...Dad...I miss you." She murmured it like a quiet prayer as the silent tears streamed down her cheeks.

CHAPTER 10

Locke's Estate, Monterey, CA
Locke

A white-hot bolt sliced through the anonymous blackness of the night sky. Its light flashed through the walls of glass overlooking a broad swath of the Pacific Ocean. The sudden harsh glare accentuated the shadows under Locke's sharp cheekbones–cheekbones that could cut. They paired ironically well with his murderous side, a physical manifestation of the killer instinct inside.

As he stood brooding inside the towering five-story structure of his cliffside Monterey home, the fact that his soul, if indeed he had one, was black as the outside night didn't bother Locke in the least. His ambition burned far bright enough to light his way.

But Locke's flat dead eyes, eyes like the great whites that flocked to Monterey each October, looked out over the dark water. He considered the sharks that lurked below the churning waves. Such efficient killing machines. A great white could smell a single drop of blood in the water from nearly two thousand feet away. A furrow rent Locke's nearly flawless forehead in two. Just like *Carcharodon carcharias,* he smelled blood in the water–only this time the floundering prey was his own damned company!

He growled and drove a balled fist into the glass. The double-paned balcony door spider-webbed into a dozen wild, haphazard cracks. Droplets of blood welled over the surface of his knuckles as he drew back his hand, but he made no move to tend them.

A groan came from the California king bed behind him. Sarah Copeland slept, spent from a vigorous lovemaking session. Locke drew in a deep breath, centering himself. Focusing.

A metallic chink echoed across the white marble floors as Locke flicked open the eighteen-carat white gold Ligne 2 Champagne lighter. A manicured thumb coaxed a brilliant orange flame into existence. He delighted in his own power for an instant, a crooked smile tugging discreetly at the corner of his mouth, watching the dancing sparkle of the four-hundred-plus diamonds. The amusement was fleeting, however. He pulled the flame to the end of the Sobranie Black Russian gripped firmly between his thin, set lips. Granted, Sobranies weren't the most expensive cigarette in the world, but Locke had developed a taste for them while on a business trip in Moscow years prior. He took a long drag, encouraging the tip to glow.

He'd developed a taste for something else on that trip too.

His upper lip curled over his perfect veneers in a near-feral snarl. He dragged on his silk robe and cinched it roughly at the waist before storming down the sinuous ribbon of the helical staircase to the lower levels. A jagged crystal chandelier—angled panes of staggered, sharp glass—suspended precariously in the open eye, hanging like the sword of Damocles. Its delicate tinkling as Locke stamped down the steps belied the mortal injury it could render should any piece of it shake loose from its shackle. Locke pressed forward, unfazed.

"Open!" he ordered. The voice-activated glass-paned door slid open, suction popping as the airtight room's vacuum seal broke. Locke smiled coolly. Air wasn't what he had intended to prevent escaping when he had first considered the design of this room.

"Nooo," an anguished voice cracked as the door resealed behind Locke. "No more."

It was the screams.

Dr. Arnold Binderkampf hung, weak and bleeding, at the center of the room. One eye, purpled and lacerated, had so swollen that the lid burgeoned out beyond his cheekbone. His arms and legs splayed awkwardly behind him like a bird in flight, bound with zip ties that cut harshly past the curly red hairs on his arms and into his pasty skin. His head slumped forward as he sobbed.

An ironic chuckle emanated from the shadows.

Locke slipped casually in and out of the columns of light and dark created by the harsh lighting of the room.

"No more?" Locke shook his head gently, his voice a low gravel, the smile dissolving from his lips. "Why, Dr. Binderkampf, 'no more' would imply that you have already given something."

He stopped just in front of the agonized physicist. Binderkampf choked back running snot and squeezed his purpling, distended eye shut. Locke bent to catch Binderkampf's gaze. Binderkampf was too weak to look away.

"And you, Doctor, have given me exactly…nothing!" Locke drew back his fist. Binderkampf winced, but the blow never came. Locke melted back into the shadows.

On the ride home from StarCall, Locke had brooded. Yes, the lab had fallen dismally short of expectations, a fact Locke simply could not abide. He could also not abide, however, the possibility of starting over from scratch with yet another company—of some other Musk-wannabe beating him to the punch and robbing him of the Mars pennant. He had dug his nails into the armrest of the Maybach, scarring the leather as the idea threatened to make him lose control.

Loss of control.

When he considered it, it hadn't been Valeni's condescending sneers or Vashti's vacuous ramblings that fomented the boiling ire in his blood. It wasn't even the annoying female reporter who shoved her microphone in his face, asking questions as he left the lab, although he had fleetingly regretted dismissing her as harshly as he did. She had been quite beautiful.

No, it was the emasculating impotence in failure to control the outcome of StarCall's efforts. The solution had crystallized in Locke's mind. He didn't need to cut ties with StarCall.

He needed to assert control.

He'd ordered his driver to return to the lab and retrieve Binderkampf. Locke would motivate the lead physicist to produce viable results. Locke would just have to put up with those fucking glasses.

A properly motivated team would work better, more efficiently—more output for less input—and Locke could stop throwing good money after bad. He would control the bleeding. A sardonic grin twisted his mouth.

At least where the lab was concerned.

Locke studied Binderkampf's mangled face.

"Please," the man whispered. "Do what you want to me, just please...don't hurt my family."

Locke raised a curious eyebrow. He tapped a long finger against his leg, lost in thought. He cocked his head.

"Hm," Locke finally responded. "An engaging concept. Perhaps I *have* been using the wrong incentive."

He strolled slowly nearer the bound scientist. "And where would your family be right about now, I wonder? Tucked quite safely in their beds in suburbia, I imagine. Dreaming sugarplum fantasies."

Locke drew close enough to gently pull a matted red lock from Binderkampf's damp forehead, twisting the wet curl around his index finger. "It would be such a shame if something, or someone, turned those dreams into a nightmare."

Locke yanked the scientist's head back at an unnatural angle. Binderkampf screamed.

"What do you want? Just tell me what you want," the man sobbed.

Locke growled through gritted teeth. "I want results."

He let the man's head drop and melted back into the shadows.

"Have you ever heard of the *lastochka*, Dr. Binderkampf?" Locke's voice drifted from the darkness. A pained look of puzzlement crept over Binderkampf's swollen features before Locke continued. "No. No, I don't suppose you have. It's a different language, certainly. Russian, to be precise. Much like your $E=mc^2$ and $F=ma$. Foreign. Unintelligible. Yes, a different language altogether. I didn't have much of a grasp of Russian when I first visited Moscow, but the gentlemen I did business with there, many of them former Soviet soldiers, gave me a very informative education."

Binderkampf jerked as Locke appeared unexpectedly at his side and whispered in his ear.

"Ohhhh, and I was a very eager student, Dr. Binderkampf. That's how I learned about the *lastochka*. The swallow." Locke pointed. "That's the Russian name for the rather awkward position you find yourself in at the moment. Apparently, it was used quite frequently by the Russian military and, would you believe, the police. Yes, the swallow and the elephant—don't ask me what the Russian obsession is with animal names for torture—were used to elicit desired information from prisoners and suspects and enemies of the state. The Russians taught me so many new and wonderful ways to get what I want. And, in case you hadn't noticed, Doctor…" Locke opened the jaws of a metal alligator clip and attached it to the lobe of Binderkampf's right ear. "I always get what I want."

Locke disappeared back into the dark, leaving Binderkampf shivering and immobile.

"This one doesn't have an animal name," Locke's disembodied voice called from the dark. "They say this one is 'A Call from Putin.'" A distinct buzz hummed throughout the room. The strident column of light surrounding Binderkampf dimmed as his jaw clenched involuntarily. His entire body arced with the force of the electric current before the light steadied once more, and his body fell slack.

Locke strode back into the light. He circled Binderkampf, a sleek lion round his prey. "The Russians had a name for these men who showed me these new and wonderful things. The *avtoritet*–the authority. I admired them, the way they controlled Russian society. Drove business. Created…change. That's what I'm after here, Doctor. Change. A change in the way we accomplish space travel. It's time for a new authority. Make no mistake, Dr. Binderkampf, I will be the authority on the Mars egrets. I will win the Mars race. With…" Locke reached for the breaker switch once more. Binderkampf groaned weakly. "Or without you."

*****

Sarah shifted in the bed as Locke slowly ascended the staircase, casually wiping a smear of red from his angled cheek. Her golden hair spilled across the black silk sheets, moonlit waves that hid her beautiful face. Locke stood at the top of the stairs, looking at her lithe body twisted in the bedclothes. She'd slept through his…discussion…with Dr. Binderkampf as he'd expected her to. He was glad the soundproof room had performed to expectations. It would have been a shame to have to dispose of something so beautiful. He'd just as soon burn a Picasso. A tragic waste. He walked over and sat on the edge of the bed. He drew his Sobranies and lighter from the pocket of his robe.

Of course, if it stood between him and what he wanted, he would burn the grand master himself.

Locke lit a cigarette.

He'd burn him right to the ground.

The wavering flame danced in Locke's dark eyes. A rustle of silk sheets whispered behind him.

"Where have you been?" Sarah Copeland's sultry bedroom voice murmured as he dragged on the cigarette.

Locke snapped the lighter closed.

"A meeting."

Sarah squinted sleepily at the bedside clock. "At 3:00 a.m.?"

"I wasn't satisfied with today's meeting at StarCall. I decided to talk some sense into those stupid fucking scientists," Locke growled through gritted teeth. "A million goddamned degrees and not one fucking brain between them. But I think we've finally come to…an understanding."

The sheets swished as Sarah sat up and pressed her bare breasts against his back. She snaked her arms around his waist.

"Personally, physics has never really been my forte." She turned him around forcefully. "I've always been much more interested in…biology."

She moved to plant a passionate kiss on his mouth and was rewarded instead with a violent slap. Her pale ivory cheek pinked almost immediately under the protective hand she drew instinctively to her face.

"What the hell, Travis?" she balked, unintimidated by her

nakedness. She swung a retaliatory hand toward him. He caught her wrist deftly in mid-swing. Almost clinically, he observed the storm raging in her gray eyes, a storm that rivaled the one raging outside. Despite his anger, Locke grinned. Sarah kept it tempered most of the time, but he knew the violent passion roiling inside the blonde-haired lawyer. It was one of the things that had attracted him to her in the first place—someone who wasn't afraid to challenge him.

Didn't mean he would ever allow her to win.

He arched a single brow. "If biology is truly where your interests lie, perhaps you should consider pursuing a different career? I hear the corner of Marathon and Western in downtown LA has a brilliant view of the Hollywood sign. You could do some sightseeing in between jobs."

Sarah scowled. He got her, and she knew it.

At least until the next skirmish.

Without taking her eyes off him, she reached down and retrieved the sheet. Wrapping it around her, she slid off the bed.

"I see. So, you're not severing ties with StarCall, then?"

"No."

"As your lead counsel, my opinion…"

"Has a zero net worth to me at this juncture. Thank you, Ms. Copeland."

Sarah blinked, her jaw slightly agape. Finally, she snapped it closed and moved to retrieve her clothing as Locke strolled to the tall windows and stared dispassionately out into the night.

"Will that be all…Mr. Locke?"

"Maybe just one more thing," Locke suggested. A hint of a smile crept into the corners of Sarah's generous mouth.

Locke turned to face her. "Do you know what I would absolutely love?"

A tinge of playfulness entered Sarah's voice. "What's that?"

"Someone with a brain."

Sarah's shoulders fell.

Locke elaborated. "Someone with a brain enough to work the actual science and get me to goddamned Mars."

CHAPTER 11

Hidden Tap and Barrel Bar
Jack

"It's a whole other planet," Bart bemoaned over the colorful paper umbrella poking out of his drink. Jack took one look at the wiggling silver deely boppers on Bart's head and sighed.

"What is?"

"Wherever it is that women are from, man."

Jack pushed his empty scotch, his third, to the edge of the bar. He gave a silent chin wag to the bartender, then buried his head in his arms and sighed—loudly.

After Bradley had dropped his bomb earlier in the evening, Jack had called Bart to meet him at the bar. It had been his full intent to drown his misery in Glenfiddich 18 Year. He couldn't seem to do anything else right lately, but at least he could still pick a proper scotch. His choice of friends, however, was questionable. The alien antennae atop Bart's head wobbled. Ah well. Bart was a good guy, if deplorably lacking in social graces. Not to mention, he was buying.

"I can't even talk to them," Bart blathered. "Sometimes I think we don't even speak the same language.

Jack lifted his heavy head. "Well, you know what they say. Men are from Mars. Women are from Venus."

"Maybe. But that was written, what…fifty years ago?" Bart said, making a face. "Anyway, my mom's a woman, and I talk to her all the time. Of course, when you've always lived in the same house as someone, I suppose it's different. By the way, she says you and the kids are invited over for brisket Sunday, which," Bart looked at his smartwatch, "yikes, is today. Crap! My mom's gonna be *meshuggener*!"

Jack squinted at his own watch. The numbers blurred. When they finally came into focus, his eyes widened. It was late.

It may have been late, but the Hidden Tap and Barrel was still hopping. Traditionally, the bar only ever closed for two hours every day between 9:00 a.m. and 11:00 a.m., just long enough to slough out the day's detritus, spritz up the joint, and gear up for another round of craft beers and cocktails from the inventive mixologists behind the bar. Jack surveyed the motley assortment of trendy Silicon Valley techies trying to interface their hardware and software. On a better day, he'd probably be one of them. These days, however, life just kept throwing out a 503-error code—out of resources.

His gaze wandered up to the flat-screen television up behind the bar. KTVU was rerunning the 11:00 p.m. news. Jack started when he spotted the familiar curve of Trinity Watson's figure against the impressive backdrop of StarCall Labs. Goddamn, but that woman was beautiful.

He thought of the inebriated evening at the Rust Bucket and groaned.

Yet another example of something I've screwed up.

The bar chatter drowned out the sound of Trinity's voice, but Jack followed the closed captioning running along the bottom of the screen. Apparently, the science correspondent was reporting on the Mars race. Jack smiled wryly. At least he wasn't tangled up in that business, he thought. He was perfectly satisfied keeping his failures on a less universal scale. Literally. He watched as Trinity tipped her microphone in Travis Locke's direction as the stony-faced billionaire came barreling out of the labs. Jack scowled as he watched Locke practically shove the microphone back in her face. Trinity stumbled, nearly falling.

Bart remained oblivious to the television. He was busy working on his watermelon-kiwi margarita. Or, at least, he was trying to. Instead, all he was really doing was chasing the straw around with his mouth. Every time he pursed his lips forward, the paper cylinder rotated in the pink slush, staying just out of reach. It was like watching a pouty bulldog chase its tail. The irony wasn't lost on Jack. The visual analogy conveniently summed up his life.

Just throw me a Milk-Bone and call me Rover.

He huffed and grabbed the full glass of amber-colored liquid the bartender slid in front of him. He took a healthy swallow.

"Where did we go wrong, Bart? ROAR was perfect," Jack groaned.

Bart looked up from his futile pursuit, the springing silver spheres on his head belying the sudden seriousness on his round face. "What are you talking about? It *is* perfect. ROAR does exactly what it's programmed to do. It's a freakin' reverse-engineering miracle! It takes the data for any given scenario, works quantum computations that would turn the human brain into gazpacho, and runs hypothetical experiments ad nauseam. Then, because I'm rather brilliant…" his gaze wandered over a passing brunette in a tight skirt, "if underappreciated, it utilizes priming from the neural network to spit out what's gonna happen. No muss. No fuss. No guesswork."

He looked on despondently as the brunette settled into a cozy booth with a guy with a movie-star smile and too much product in his hair, and giggled coyly. "If only I could program it with the data that would show me how to get a date."

Bart took a noisy slurp of his drink through a straw. He ignored Jack's eye roll.

"What wasn't perfect was the human element," Bart continued. "When you start throwing in vectors like greed and jealousy, the whole equation goes out of whack. Those boneheads at CERN couldn't stand the thought that our little program was going to make them obsolete." He took a long pull from his straw until the sound of suction rattled in the bottom of the empty glass.

"So," he continued, "they jacked up the numbers. Made sure we'd fail."

Before Jack could agree, Bart grabbed his head, knocking the alien headgear askew. "Gah! Brain freeze! Brain freeze!"

He smacked the bar surface several times in rapid succession. The software engineer's right eye twitched as his shoulders tensed up around his ears. Jack looked around hopelessly, uncertain of how to help.

"Try rubbing the tongue up against the soft palate," a feminine voice suggested from behind Jack's left shoulder.

Jack swung his attention away from Bart and his temperature tribulations and swiveled on his barstool. Trinity stood right behind him. In the flesh. The incredibly beautiful flesh. She'd changed since the news, her outfit appreciably less professional—a merlot-colored off-the-shoulder fitted modal blouse that exposed the subtle curve of her creamy neck with hip-hugging black leggings. Her long legs started out at her full hips and lingered all the way to next Friday. And the heels she wore hovered just between sensible and sex kitten, not to mention the marvelous things they did for her glutes.

"Huh?" It was the only word Jack could muster—half because he hadn't expected to see her here, half because of the scotch, and half because the blood was rushing somewhere other than his brain.

She gestured. "His tongue. Not yours, of course."

Her face beamed with a genuine smile. Jack considered getting lost in that smile. Instead, he shook himself from his reverie and chuckled dryly.

No way was he going to have a repeat performance of the Rust Bucket.

"Anyway," Trinity continued as Bart's face contorted into several odd expressions. "The cold from the margarita's constricted the blood vessels back there, and the brain interprets it as pain. The quicker you warm them up again, the faster the pain sensation fades. The scientific name is called sphenopalatine ganglioneuralgia."

Bart's eyes rolled in his head as he suddenly slouched into a more serene and relaxed position. "You can call it Emperor Palpatine for all I care, miss."

Jack shot him a disapproving stare.

Bart shrugged. "All I know is it worked. Thank you so much."

He cocked his head and narrowed his eyes at Trinity. "Hey. Don't we know you? Don't we know her, Jack? Wasn't she one of the reporters at the ROAR launch debacle—oof!"

Even if Trinity's little palate thing hadn't done the trick, the pain receptors in Bart's brain would have abandoned his headache and rushed to his shin, precisely because that was where Jack had just kicked him. Bart scowled at his former boss and vigorously rubbed at his leg.

Trinity looked puzzled, having missed Jack's subtle assault on the software engineer. She nodded. "You're right, Mr. Pulldraw. We met at P1AL Labs. Trinity Watson. Science and technology correspondent for KVTU out of Oakland. Um, are you okay?"

Jack inserted himself between Bart and the reporter. "Don't worry about him. He's absolutely fine. He was just about to go make a call. His mother worries, you know."

He eyeballed Bart, who gave a pronounced pout but obligingly slid off his stool and skulked toward the opposite end of the bar.

"Yeah," Bart mumbled as he moved away. "She likes to know I'm not out doing anything, you know, stupid."

He drizzled a little more emphasis on the word stupid, staring balefully at Jack before limping off. Jack stood staring at Trinity for a moment before shaking it off and pulling out Bart's abandoned stool for her to sit.

"Thanks," she murmured.

"Can I get you a drink?" Jack burst out, a little too eagerly.

Trinity shook her head. "No, I'm fine. Thank you, though."

Jack cleared his throat, then grabbed a bowl from the bar and shoved it under her nose. "Beer nuts?"

"Really, Dr. Harding, I'm fine."

Jack withered at the use of his professional name.

"Guess after that night at the Rust Bucket, just 'Jack' isn't an option," he mumbled. "Look, I'm truly sorry. I guess I drank too much—it's just we were out celebrating the successful test run of ROAR¬—and I never drink that much."

He caught her sidelong glance at the four empty whiskey glasses.

"Hardly ever drink that much," he amended.

"What are you talking about?" Trinity asked.

Jack looked puzzled. "I, uh, just didn't want you to think I was a one-night stand kind of guy, is all."

Trinity shook her head. "Wait. You think we *slept* together?"

"Didn't we?" The pitch of Jack's voice ratcheted a little higher.

Trinity shook her head and laughed. Jack scowled. "Well, I don't think the concept is *that* humorous."

"No wonder you didn't talk to me after the ROAR demonstration. I just thought you didn't want to talk to me because I was a reporter. You know. Because the test failed?"

"Yeah, thanks for pointing that out."

"I really just wanted to tell you what a cheap shot it was for the guys at CERN to pull that switch on you. I truly believe it would have worked."

Jack looked up, hopeful.

"And as far as sleeping together that night at the Rust Bucket? You were a perfect gentleman. Despite my best efforts."

"Oh?"

Trinity nodded. "And a little bit of a geek. Kept me up all night talking."

Jack's brows knitted together. "About what?"

"Hm, let's see. *Pilot Wave Theory as a Deterministic Approach to Applied EmDrive Quantum Mechanics,* I think it was."

"My doctoral dissertation from Stanford?"

"Mmhmm. It was quite riveting…right up until the part where you snored."

"I snored?"

"Sure did. That's not what I usually inspire in most guys."

A fleeting thought twisted Jack's mouth into a frown. "What about Travis Locke? I saw tonight's news broadcast. You okay?"

Trinity's face soured. "Travis Locke is an ass in Armani. Do you know he actually hit on me once at a charity function? Cornered me in the coatroom. Said I should be honored. Got pretty aggressive when I turned him down. You know, maybe 'aggressive' isn't exactly the right word. More like 'assault.' He's damn lucky I didn't bring him up on charges."

"Why didn't you?"

"For one, Locke has more money than God. And I'd be willing to bet he has more judges in his pocket than a billiard table's got balls, anyway. It would have been a case of he said, she said. Nobody at the event witnessed the altercation."

Trinity shrugged. "That's the thing about Locke. On the surface, he's Teflon. Nothing sticks. At least it hasn't...yet." A small smile played on her lips.

"You think you have something on him?" Jack queried.

Trinity played with the bowl of beer nuts. "Maybe. That's why I went to interview him at StarCall Labs tonight. Locke's company, Locke Industries, has a horse in the Mars race. He's been hiring out big tech firms like TitusBane in Texas and StarCall here in California, monopolizing facilities and personnel to develop a viable propulsion system. Locke's PR people would have us believe they're on the cusp of a major breakthrough."

"And?" Jack asked.

"You see, that's just it. I think it's all smoke and mirrors. Or at least smoke, anyway. There was a horrible accident at the TitusBane facility in Houston. One of the scientists on Locke's team accidentally got trapped in the firing bay when a rocket was being tested. Burned to a crisp."

"Gnarly," Bart interjected, holding out a Cosmo for Trinity.

Jack grimaced and grabbed the drink from him. "Gnarly? Okay, Point Break."

Bart assumed an unsteady hang-ten pose. "What? I surf."

"Internet doesn't count, genius," Jack admonished. He turned back to Trinity. "You think Locke had something to do with it?"

"I'm not sure. One thing I do know...I want to see somebody beat Locke's ass."

"Physically or metaphorically?" Jack asked with a crooked grin.

"Yes," she replied. Trinity reached for the Cosmo and took

a swallow. "After I saw you at **P1AL**, Jack, I remembered that night at the Rust Bucket. You talked so passionately about life, the universe…and everything. You talked about floating up there among the stars. Forget about ROAR. Why aren't you involved in the race to Mars?"

Jack scoffed. "If I had Locke's kind of money, I'd already be there."

Bart nodded vigorously. "He would, too. Jack's concept for a quantum vacuum thruster is spectacular…"

"And completely theoretical. There's still so much we don't know," Jack stated zealously.

Like how I'm going to take care of those kids. How I'm going to pay Charlie's medical bills.

He took the last swallow of scotch lingering in the bottom of his glass. He wasn't certain if it was the whiskey or the fact that he had hit such rock bottom that he had no fear of falling further.

Hell. Here goes nothing.

He turned to face Trinity. "What I *do* know is I owe you a proper date. Would you do me the honor, Ms. Watson, of accompanying me to dinner…say, the day after tomorrow?"

Jack tried to ignore Bart's elbow in his ribs and concentrated instead on Trinity's smile.

"That sounds nice…Jack," Trinity replied.

He stared at her blankly for a moment, in disbelief she had accepted. Finally, something had gone his way. He shook himself alert. "Yes. Okay, yes. That's wonderful. So, I'll pick you up at, say, seven?"

He was rewarded with yet another jab from Bart. Jack held up an index finger. "Would you excuse me, Trinity, for just one moment?"

He wheeled and hissed in a menacing *sotto voce*, "What, Bart!"

"Are you forgetting? You won't be able to leave the house in the evenings. Bradley quit. There's no one to watch the kids."

Jack slapped his forehead. "Dammit! I didn't think it through. You can watch them for me, can't you? The twins love their uncle Bart."

Bart shook his head. "No can do, brother. That's Mom's canasta night. If I don't drive her to and from the hall, she'll be kvetching from now until Rosh Hashanah."

"Crap! Okay, okay. I can do this. I am not going to screw this up!" He turned to Trinity. "How do you feel about a nice, home-cooked meal?"

"At your place?" Trinity asked.

"Yeah. Sure."

"I had no idea you cooked."

"Neither did he," Bart chuckled under his breath. This time the software engineer received the elbow jab.

"Yeah, it'll be great. I'll see you around seven."

"Around seven. Great. Well, I'd better head home. It's pretty late."

"Me too," Jack replied. "See you the day after tomorrow."

He watched Trinity's hips sashay as she walked out of the bar. She turned and gave a small wave just before she stepped through the door and into the wee hours.

As soon as she was out the door, Jack collapsed on the bar, head down, groaning. Bart patted him on the back. "No worries. I'll have Mom cook an extra brisket."

CHAPTER 12

Harding Estate
Jack

The explosion would detonate at any minute now.

Jack braced his head in his hands, anticipating the spontaneous separation of his cranium from his shoulders. The incessant pounding of his pulse coursed through his basilar artery, playing like an old Irish jig in his cranium and making him queasy as hell. Jack groaned audibly.

Lord of the Dance, my ass.

Right now, he'd like to take the little leaping leprechaun and his Irish buddy Jameson and give 'em both the old what-for. Or maybe he'd just sic the twins after them, he mused. He watched Oscar and Lucas stomp through the living room and into the kitchen, roaring like three-foot-six dinosaurs.

Oscar tore open the refrigerator door and snagged a head of green leaf lettuce in a chubby little hand.

"I'm an herbivore!" he declared before chomping down and tearing a hunk of the vegetable loose with his teeth.

"Hey! That's for the salad, young man!" Bradley reprimanded. Before he could rescue the greenery from the first twin, the second twin barreled past with two Slim Jims hanging from beneath his upper lip like long, meaty fangs.

"But I don't eat plants! I'm a carnivore! I'm a T-Rex! Rowr!" Lucas growled.

"Yeah?" Julia warned as she ghosted into the kitchen. "Your arms are sure short enough, pipsqueak. But you'd better watch it. You keep eating those gross Slim Jims in front of me, and you'll be just as extinct."

"I traded," Lucas declared.

"Traded?" Julia asked as she ducked into the pantry for a bag of potato chips.

"Traded fair and square."

"What did you supposedly trade off?" Jack mumbled from his spot on the sofa.

"JuJu Bee took my Hot Wheel. I took her snacks."

Jack shrugged. "Fair is fair, JuJu Bee."

Julia huffed indignantly. "I did no such thing. Why would I want one of his stupid cars? And *don't* call me JuJu Bee."

She tore open her bag of chips and stomped toward the living room.

Bradley called after her. "Do not fill up on junk food, miss. You are all going over to Mrs. Pulldraw's for brisket later. Oh, but I still have to make the salad...and schedule the Uber...and pack! Oh good gracious, I'll never get it all done before I have to leave. Now, where's my packing tape? I swear it was just here."

"Whatever," Julia muttered as she plopped into the overstuffed armchair.

Jack watched as the room spun like a merry-go-round, a matter compounded by the frenetic activity of his soon-to-be ex-nanny. Bradley zipped back and forth through the house, rattling off information, packing suitcases, and labeling boxes. As Jack watched the boxes stack, he realized he hadn't truly been aware of just how long Bradley had been a part of their lives. Long enough, apparently, to accumulate two large Samsonite bags, seven assorted U-Haul boxes, and a potted Ficus.

What on earth was he going to do without him?

No, really, Jack thought. How in God's name was he supposed to manage this household without Bradley's experienced organizational skills? It occurred to Jack he might want to pay attention to what Bradley was saying as he whizzed past for the seventh time in as many minutes. He braced against the pain and put all his effort into focusing on the nanny's words.

"And don't forget, on Tuesdays, you need to make two trips to the school for pickups. Once at the regular time, and once after five because Alice has Mathletes and has to stay late. Usually that's when I squeeze in a trip to the grocery. Just be sure to make a list and stick to it. If you don't, these animals," he gestured to the Jurassic twins, "will whine and cry and goad you into buying three different kinds of chocolate cereal and make you forget all about the toilet paper."

"Is that why we had to use tissue for a week that one time?" Charlie mentioned as he wheeled into the room.

"You found tissue?" Julia mumbled through a mouthful of potato chips. She slumped onto the sofa next to Jack and kicked her feet up on the coffee table. "I had to use an issue of Jack's *Popular Mechanics.*"

Jack threw her a confused, if pained, look. "Was it the Elon Musk Draco thruster issue?"

Julia nodded.

"I looked for that for days, you know."

"Don't bother looking for last month's *Scientific American,* then." She jammed her hand back into the chip bag but grabbed empty air as Bradley reached over the sofa and swiped it from her grasp. She scowled.

"I just vacuumed, ma'am. I will not have you making more

crumbs. I fully intend on leaving this house cleaner than I found it," Bradley said. He turned on his penny loafer and headed back toward the kitchen. Julia shrugged and pulled another bag from behind a throw pillow.

Jack suppressed a smirk. "You're looking rather dapper, sir." He gestured to the bright bowtie the middle Johansson child wore.

Charlie straightened the polka-dotted accessory. "Mrs. Pulldraw likes it when I dress up. She says it makes me look extinguished."

Julia laughed. "I think you mean *dis*-tinguished. Next time you go see Doc Harris, have him check and make sure your brain is still in there."

"Oh my gracious!" Bradley blurted as he burst back into the room. "I nearly forgot! Charlie has a 10:00 a.m. doctor's appointment on Wednesday. He cannot be late. It took me three weeks to get the appointment in the first place, and if you're late, they make you reschedule."

"And this one's really important, Jack," Charlie urged. "Dr. Harris is going to let me know if I'm a good candidate for a bone marrow transplant."

His eyes glittered with the prospect of hope. For most people with Charlie's condition, the outlook was pretty bleak. Leukodystrophy came in a variety of forms, each with its own specific challenges, but they all shared a comparable end...an end none of them wanted to think about. With a bone marrow transplant, they could put off the inevitable—at least for a while longer. Jack fervently hoped the doctor would sign off on the procedure. He'd figure out how to pay for it later. These kids had already experienced enough loss in their young lives...enough pain.

Jack squinted. Right now, he'd be happy to just eradicate the throbbing pain in his own head.

"I need some aspirin," he moaned. He hefted himself from the sofa and headed for the bathroom medicine cabinet. He flipped the light switch and leaned over the vanity to study his face in the mirror. Yikes. He looked like hell. He thought back to all those nights and weekends at university when he'd tied one on with Oliver and Elsa and cheerily got up the next morning to attend classes.

Yeah. Those days? Gone.

The memory of his old friends tugged at his gut. Not just because he missed them, but because he felt like he was failing them. Oliver and Elsa had trusted him to take care of their children, and here he was–failing miserably. Like his effort with ROAR. He'd fallen flat on his face. Smacked right into the ground. Gravity was not on his Christmas card list.

He huffed. Maybe Trinity was right. Maybe he should have put his efforts into the Mars race instead. Bigger men than him had failed. The thought momentarily distracted him from his hangover woes. At least he'd be in good company.

Except for Locke, he surmised. His lip curled. He'd love to beat that jerk at his own game.

The problem, he mused, was gravity. Newton's law of universal gravitation clearly outlined that the force of gravity is proportional to the product of the masses of two objects and inversely proportional to the square of the distance between their centers of mass. In layman's terms, for a rocket launch to make the difference between flight and just taking up real estate on a launchpad, the engine has to produce a thrust that is greater than the total mass of the vehicle–to break the pull of gravity. And the bigger the rocket and the further you intend it to go–like, say, Mars–the more propellant that's required, increasing the total mass and jacking up the whole equation. Too much excess mass and the endeavor would blow up in your face. Jack grinned wryly. *Just like too much excess Jameson's could make your head explode.*

He abandoned his ruminations on space travel and pulled the medicine cabinet open. He grabbed the aspirin bottle and struggled to work the cap loose, gritting his teeth. The vein in his neck bulged with the effort.

"You know it's a childproof safety cap."

Jack let out a startled scream. The now-open bottle of pills sailed into the air. A shower of generic white tablets showered down on him, skittering off the surface of the countertop and scattering every which way. Some slid into the basin of the sink. Some bounced on the floor. Jack wheeled around to see Julia chuckling in the doorway.

"What?" Jack snapped.

"Bradley says we'd better get a move on if we don't want to be late to Mrs. Pulldraw's."

"Fine." Jack looked around at the mess he'd made. "But I need to clean this mess up first. Where's the broom?"

Julia shrugged. "Last time I saw it, one of the twins was riding it through the house, chasing Alice. Maybe she knows."

"I never should have let them have that *Harry Potter* movie marathon over Halloween." Jack groaned. "Where is Alice?"

"I dunno where she is now, but I saw her snooping around your stereo system earlier."

Jack's brows knit together in a sharp peak. "What was she doing around the stereo system?"

"How am I supposed to know? You know, Jack, if you want me to babysit all the time, you're going to have to start paying me." With that, Julia wheeled around and headed back down the hallway. Exasperated, Jack blew the hair off his forehead and shook his head. He stepped over the mess and headed for Alice's room.

"Hey, Alice!" he called. "I was wondering if you'd seen…"

Jack never finished his sentence. As he opened the door to Alice's room, his jaw dropped in stunned disbelief. There, floating in the middle of Alice's room, was a Corvette. A 1978 candy-apple-red Corvette Stingray.

CHAPTER 13

Harding Estate
Alice

"What in the hell is that!"

It was more of an exclamation than a question, Alice mused as Jack suddenly burst into the room and observed the car floating, rather magically, in midair. After he'd let the epithet fly, his jaw remained slack as he stood there in stunned disbelief. Pride tugged a smug little smirk around the corners of Alice's mouth. It was pretty amazing if she did say so herself.

"Um, it's a car? A Hot Wheel if we're going to be specific," Alice shook her head. She had rather expected him to grasp the obvious.

"I can *see* it's a Hot Wheel. I can also see the guts of my $3000 vintage Hartley Holton tower speakers spewed all over the floor."

Alice's eyes widened at the pricey dollar figure Jack assigned to the stereo equipment. Her gaze cast askance at the cannibalized speaker, woofer, and tweeter hanging limply from red and yellow wires. It was so much electronic spaghetti. She gulped. She'd had no idea the equipment was so valuable.

"I can put it all back together, Jack. I swear," she assured, scrambling toward the technological detritus. She picked up a page of loose-leaf paper festooned with a diagram sketched in crayon. "I made notes. Lots and lots of notes. A connects to B, then B fits into C—"

Jack slowly shook his head, his elevating blood pressure flushing crimson over his neck and cheeks. He grabbed both sides of his head, gripping tufts of hair in balling fists. "What have you done?"

"I just needed the neodymium magnet from inside the speaker. To test my theory," she quickly replied, showing him the makeshift levitron she had built. "You know, about what was making Thom-Thom float? I thought…maybe, somehow, something was causing a magnetic field around Thom-Thom, and the force was possibly canceling the force of gravity? You know?"

Jack took one measured step toward her and the levitating, rotating Corvette. He looked down at the heavy, circular ringed magnet that had formerly been housed inside the speaker. The metal car spun slowly and steadily, hovering several inches above its surface, marking three hundred and sixty degrees every five seconds.

He growled through gritted teeth. "What I know is I've had those speakers since I was fifteen. Paid for them with my own money. Must have mowed a hundred lawns, dripping in sweat."

Jack laughed, a tinge of insanity licking around the edges. "You should have seen my foster mom's face when I showed up on the doorstep with those monsters balanced in an old rusted-out Radio Flyer. She must have yelled at me for hours. How did I expect to fit something that big in a plastic garbage bag? Guess she'd already made up her mind then about keeping me."

He slumped onto the corner of Alice's bed and buried his head in his hands. Alice took a cautious step toward him. She laid a tentative hand on his shoulder. She jumped back when he abruptly raised his head and stood.

"But you know what? I dragged those monsters with me from home to home. The one thing I could actually call *mine*. And I kept them. Kept them in mint condition."

The room fell quiet.

"I'm really sorry, Jack," Alice offered to fill the void of silence.

"Sorry?" Jack snapped. "Is that what I'm going to tell Valeni's goombahs when they show up to break my legs?"

Alice's pixie face pinched in confusion. She shook her head in consternation.

"Wait. What? Who?"

She jumped to her feet, her leg brushing against the rotating car. It slid slightly off its axis of rotation and began a list to one side. Alice was oblivious.

"Why is somebody showing up to break your legs, Jack? Is somebody coming here to hurt you? You should call the police!"

"The police?!" Jack stopped talking. His face puckered like he'd just vomited something foul. The muscle in his jaw tweaked with tension. He exploded into abrupt, jerky motions as if he'd suddenly come into contact with a live wire pumping seventy-two hundred volts. He rapidly waved his hands in the air.

"Forget about it. Doesn't matter. What's done is done." He started pacing, weaving his way through the detritus of the discombobulated sound system. "Dammit! If only ROAR had worked!"

Alice, though her mind was mired in a confusing jumble of thoughts, stepped forward. She tried to be supportive.

"But ROAR *would* have worked, Jack. You said so. They changed the numbers on you. It wasn't your fault."

"Yeah," he scoffed. "And it wasn't my fault your parents went and died either, but it seems I'm paying the price for that too."

Alice let the hand clutching her colorful diagram fall to her side. Her shoulders slumped.

"Christ!" Jack stared despondently at the pile of pieces. "I thought maybe I could sell the damned things and at least scrape together some money to throw at Valeni. But now that idea's—well—worthless."

"Worthless." He snorted, slapping his hands against his thighs. "Pretty much like everything else in my life."

Jack waved a dismissive hand toward the scattered bits and bobs. "At least clean this stuff up, will ya? And hurry up. We're already late for dinner at Mrs. Pulldraw's."

Jack slammed the door. The already wobbly Hot Wheel spun in a gradually wider ellipse.

"Don't worry about it," Alice murmured. "I don't think I'm hungry anymore."

The Corvette finally fell out of orbit, clattering off the magnet into a tiny, upended cast-iron wreck onto the floor.

*****

"This is the song that never ends. It just goes on and on, my friend! Some people started singing it, not knowing what it was, and they continued singing it forever just because this is the song that never ends…"

"Shut your pieholes, will ya! And stop singing that *stupid* song!" Julia snapped at the twins, who rewarded her with a duo of perfectly-timed Bronx cheers. Apparently, they didn't appreciate the scathing review of their boisterous balladeering.

The pair of them had been singing the same monotonous tune at the top of their five-year-old lungs since they had left the house and piled into the Ford Electroline van to start the drive to the Pulldraws. Alice didn't acknowledge them. It was as if she didn't even hear their caterwauling. She stared out the window, past the blur of smearing raindrops at the streaking red brake lights of passing cars.

Meanwhile, the boys eyeballed each other and exchanged wicked little smiles. The pert cupid's bows of their mouths opened wide, and they offered up a stridently off-key rendition of "John Jacob Jingleheimer Schmidt."

A worn high-top sailed past Oscar's ear from the back of the van and clipped Jack in the elbow where he sat in the driver's seat.

"Hey!" Jack whirled around as best he could without losing control of the vehicle. "Cut it out. Do not make me pull this van over!"

"But we're hungry!" Lucas complained.

"Yeah! Are we there yet?" Oscar chimed.

"And you two," Jack addressed the twins. "Domingo and Pavarotti. Ixnay on the ingingsay, all right? My head's splitting."

The boys seemed to have other ideas.

"I don't speak Spanish, Jack. And I'm not Pava...Pava... rotten," Oscar grumbled. "I'm Oscar! And he's Lucas! My brother!"

"Nuh-uh," Lucas grinned. He hooked a chunky little thumb into his own chest. "He called me Domino! That means I'm a pizza! And I'm gonna eat myself up! And none for you!"

The twins' interest became absorbed in their own little mock battle. Alice, on the other hand, battled hot tears streaming down her cheeks.

"You okay, Alice?" Charlie asked as his sister twisted her body away from his penetrating gaze.

"No, she's not okay, genius. Jack went nuclear on her back at the house," Julia whispered tersely under her breath.

Charlie's eyes widened. "Why?"

Julia kicked her feet up, one shoeless, and crossed them at the ankles on the bench seat in front of her. She ignored Oscar pinching his nose and shrugged diffidently. She slouched down and powered up her tablet. The glow of the screen dissolved her features into an amorphous blue haze. "What? Am I the club secretary now? Was I supposed to take notes?"

"That's not very nice, JuJu," Charlie admonished his big sister. He adjusted his bowtie, which had tilted off-kilter.

She snorted. "Neither was destroying his prized stereo system."

"Alice!" Charlie's head swiveled toward Alice. The abrupt movement immediately knocked his tie crooked again. He sighed in frustration and straightened it again. "You didn't! After all Jack does for us?"

"Does for us?!" Alice whipped to face her wheelchair-bound brother. Anger and frustration flashed in her eyes. She whispered harshly, "When are you going to realize, Charlie? Jack doesn't care about us at all."

She folded her arms stiffly across her chest. "He just got stuck with us."

A pained look passed across Charlie's delicate features. He slowly shook his head. "No," he finally managed. "No, that's not right. Jack loves us. That's why he was working so hard at the lab. To try and make a better life for all of us."

Alice caught Jack's probing gaze in the reflection of the rear-view mirror. She leaned forward and cupped her hand around her mouth so only her siblings could hear. "Wrong. The only reason he was working so hard is 'cause he got himself in some kind of trouble."

Charlie scooted to the edge of his wheelchair seat. "Trouble? What kind of trouble?"

Alice stole a glance to make sure Jack wasn't listening. "I think he borrowed money."

Charlie sat up. "People borrow money. What's so weird about that? Mom and Dad used to get money from people to help with their work all the time."

"Mom and Dad got grants. That's different from borrowing. I think Jack borrowed money from the wrong people. Jack said somebody named Valeni was coming to," her voice dropped to a nearly inaudible whisper, "break his legs."

Julia leaned back against her seat. "Well, that's just great! Sounds like the guy Mom and Dad trusted to take care of us can't even take care of himself!"

Alice waved her hands, trying to shush Julia. "Keep it down, will ya?"

Julia shrugged her off. "No. I will not keep it down. It was bad enough when Bradley announced he was quitting. Do you realize what will happen if something happens to Jack?"

The sudden stark reality hit Alice like a two-ton lead weight. "Garbage bags."

Julia nodded.

Charlie's seven-year-old brows knit together in confusion. "Garbage bags? I don't get it."

"Jack said when you go into foster care, you carry most of your stuff around in black, plastic garbage bags," Alice said. She let that sink in.

A half-hearted smile broke across Charlie's face. "That's okay. Who needs a fancy old suitcase anyway? I mean, we'll still have each other. Right?"

Alice couldn't look her brother in the eye. Julia just slowly shook her head. Oblivious, the twins carried on their antics in the seat in front of them.

"I don't think we're gonna be able to stay together," Julia suggested. She gestured. "There are five of us, little man. The twins? They're a handful just by themselves. And you? You come with your own user's manual and can of WD-40. What family's gonna have enough space for all of us?"

Tears began to glisten in Charlie's eyes. Alice looked out the van window. The rain had stopped, clearing the view to the open expanse of stars in the night sky.

"If only there was a way we could get up there," she said, tracing the pattern of the Big Dipper against the glass with her index finger. "Up there, there'd be space for all of us."

CHAPTER 14

Pulldraw Home
Jack

"Is it a girl thing?"

A cloud of garlic-scented air wafted under Jack's nostrils as Bart whispered in his ear. Jack wrinkled his nose and pulled away.

Bart grinned crookedly as he adjusted the stovepipe silk top hat on his head. "Ooh, yeah. Sorry about that. Mom went a little heavy-handed with the garlic on the brisket, but look at it this way—you'll be safe on Ventura Boulevard."

Jack cocked his head and squinted at his former programmer.

Bart tapped the top of his hat. "You know. Tom Petty? 'Free Fallin'? 'All the vampires move west down Ventura Boulevard'? Ah, never mind. Forget it. Anyway, I know the garlic's a bit much, but they haven't touched a thing on their plates."

He gestured toward the opposite end of the oak table and the oldest three Johansson children, who sat slumped in front of full plates. Charlie pushed limply at his slab of brisket with his fork. Alice balanced her delicate chin in her hand as her elbow rested next to her plate. Julia stared blankly at the wooden cuckoo clock hanging on the antique rose wallpaper. She jumped when the little yellow bird popped out and announced the eighth hour.

"I'll tell you what it is," Myrna Pulldraw posited. "He probably let them fill up on junk food before they came over. Chips and candy. Stuff that'll rot their little teeth, no doubt. No elbows on the table, miss."

She eyeballed Alice, who immediately sat ramrod straight.

"Ma!" Bart interceded.

She wagged a silver serving spoon in his face. "Don't you 'Ma' me, young man. You're just as bad. Don't think I didn't find the empty box of Bagel Bites in the trash. And no hats at the table. If I've told you once, I've told you a thousand times."

Bart grimaced and sank into his own seat, defeated.

"At least I can always count on my little *bubelahs* here to have an appetite!" Myrna turned toward the twins, who eagerly held up their empty plates to be refilled.

She heaped a steaming mountain of fluffy white potatoes onto Lucas' plate. Oscar's pouting lip belied his irritation at being second in line. A wide smile broke out across his face, however, when he realized his pile was bigger than his brother's. He stuck out his tongue.

"I promise, I didn't let them eat anything, Mrs. Pulldraw," Jack insisted. "No way was I going to ruin their appetites for your delicious brisket."

Myrna looked down at Jack's own full plate and balanced a polished hand on an ample hip.

Jack managed a weak smile.

"Well, don't think you're getting any rugelach as long as there's still food on your plate, sir."

"Roo-guh-luck? Yesh!" Lucas squished through a mouthful of potatoes and jammed a triumphant fork in the air.

"Don't talk with your mouth full, sweetheart." Myrna tousled his hair and moved to clear some of the dirty dishes to the kitchen. She gestured toward the girls and Charlie. "You three.

If you're not going to eat, you can clean. Come with me to the kitchen. Charlie, you can dry. Let's go, you sad sacks."

She scuttled them off to the kitchen, leaving Jack and Bart alone with the twins. Bart turned toward his old boss. "So, what's really going on? Why is everybody so down in the dumps?"

"Ru-ge-lach. Ru-ge-lach!" the boys chanted, drumming in time on the tabletop.

"Okay. Maybe not everybody."

Jack sighed long and hard. "I don't know. I may have sort of gone a little Oppenheimer on Alice before we came over."

"What? Alice? The kid's a saint! What on earth could she have done that would have made you blow up?"

Jack leveled a look at Bart. "She dissected my Hartleys."

Bart sucked in a breath. His hand clapped over his mouth. "No! Not the Holton towers!"

Jack nodded.

"But those were so cherry! If you ever wanted to unload those, you could have gotten two thousand for them easy."

Jack slowly shook his head and held up three fingers.

This time, Bart expelled the air. "Three grand?"

Jack sat forward. "Yep. Had a guy on the line ready to pay cash. I was hoping I could use the money to hold off Valeni's thugs for a little while. At least until I can figure out a way to get back on my feet."

Bart dropped his voice to a near whisper. "Just how long do you think you can dodge him, Jack? There's only so far a man can run, you know. I mean, unless you're planning on pitching a tent on Mars or something."

Jack gave a half-hearted chuckle. "That's not a half-bad idea. Anyway, the buyer was even going to handle pickup...until Alice made it fifty-two pickups. At least, that's how many parts it looked like she had spread on the floor."

"What was she trying to do?" Bart asked.

"I don't know. I think she was trying to figure out what was making the damned ferret float."

Bart grinned like a proud uncle.

"Our own little Maria Goeppert-Mayer!" He referenced the German-born American theoretical physicist. "Do you know she came up with the nuclear shell model of the atomic nucleus?"

"I know Goeppert-Mayer, Bart," Jack interrupted, but it fell on deaf ears.

"It was her mathematical model that explained why certain numbers of protons and neutrons in a nucleus result in stable atomic configurations," Bart rambled on. His brow suddenly furrowed. "So, what was Alice's working theory?"

Jack frowned. "Magnetism. She levitated a 1978 Corvette Stingray."

Bart's jaw dropped. "A Corvette?"

"It was a Hot Wheel." Bart's mouth formed a silent "O." Jack continued explaining. "She built a levitron."

Bart nodded like the answer should have been blatantly obvious. "With the neodymium magnet from inside the speaker."

"Exactly. The kid built a levitron out of my $3,000 vintage stereo system when I could have just ordered one for $39.99 off the internet."

Bart shook his head. "No, you couldn't have."

"What are you talking about?"

"You couldn't 'cause you, my brother, are flat-ass broke."

"I heard that, Bartholomew David Pulldraw!" Myrna shouted from the kitchen. "I will not have you using that kind of language! As long as you live under my roof, you will live under my rules, young man!"

Bart withered and dragged Jack to the family room where they could speak uncensored. They sat on the sofa. It crinkled as the protective plastic gave under their weight. Jack looked vaguely uncomfortable. Bart remained cheerfully oblivious.

"What did she do? Spin the Hot Wheel like a top?"

Jack nodded. "So it would orient around the local magnetic field and precess around it. As long as you create a gyroscopic effect that would allow the car to reorient itself. Otherwise, even the slightest nudge and the acting forces would just push it back down the gravity well."

"Hold on!" Bart scowled. "Magnetism depends on specific properties of objects. Magnetism can either pull the two objects together or push them apart, depending on which way the magnets point. And a classic Hot Wheel is made out of metal. That's not going to react the same way carbon-based matter like a ferret will."

He sighed and leaned back on the sofa, locking his hands behind his head. "Guess we'll have to wait on that Nobel Prize."

"Maybe," Jack suggested after a protracted silence.

"Wait. What?" Bart asked.

Jack sat forward on the edge of the cushion. "I said 'maybe.' Granted, organic matter doesn't usually react to a magnetic field like, say, a metal would. It's going to depend on what is going on with the electrons in the material. I mean, think about it. Every electron is like a tiny magnet itself. Most materials, like fabric, wood–fur–only feel a small magnetic force because they've basically got a million little magnets–electrons–pointing helter-skelter, with equal numbers pulling and pushing, give or take."

Bart stared blankly. "So?"

Jack stared at him. "What if they weren't?"

"You lost me."

"Okay, listen. Remember how I was talking about the car and the gravity well?"

"Yes."

"Well, subquantum kinetics suggests that, kind of like a magnet, gravity should have two polarities. A matter-attracting gravity potential well—"

"Like the force that pulls the Hot Wheel down."

"Exactly. And it can also have a matter-repelling gravity-potential hill. Furthermore, the theory is that the polarities are going to coincide with the polarity of an electric charge. Theoretically, protons will create gravity wells—"

"—and electrons will create matter-repelling gravity hills!" Bart sat up, his head bobbing in excited comprehension.

"Now, when Oliver sent me that furry little rat—"

"Ferret," Bart corrected.

Jack sighed. "Fine. Ferret. When he sent me the ferret, he told me some story about it getting zapped inside the Hadron Collider. What if that massive charge altered Thom-Thom at the atomic level?"

"What do you mean? Like mixed up his protons and neutrons?"

"And his electrons. What if, basically, Thom-Thom's mass excess is now jacked up, and his molecular makeup is negatively charged, creating a gravity hill that effectively repels the forces of gravity?"

"You'd need a mass spectrometer to determine the atomic condition."

Jack nodded slowly. "I think there's still one floating around the lab. If the creditors haven't snaked it yet."

The magnitude of the concept demanded a heavy silence.

"Is that kind of thing even possible?" Bart whispered, finally breaking the stillness. "And, hell, even if it was, how in the hell could you hope to replicate it?"

A slow smile began to spread across Jack's face. "Wouldn't it be great if we had some sort of program that would let us run theoretical simulations? Oh, wait. We do."

Bart jammed a fat fist into the air and yelled at the top of his lungs. "ROAR!"

A loud clatter echoed from the kitchen.

"My rugelach! Bartholomew!"

CHAPTER 15

P1AL *Labs*
Jack

"Do you *know* what happens to soft guys like me in jail, Jack?" Bart bemoaned for the millionth time since they arrived on the **P1AL** campus. The sliver of moon that had been shining in the sky since the rain had stopped had ducked behind a dark cloud, plunging the night into an inky black once more.

Jack was glad for the darkness. He stole a glance at the display on his watch. As of twenty-eight minutes ago, the **P1AL** labs were technically no longer his property, and he had no legal right to be poking around. But he and Bart were on to something. He was sure of it. They just needed to get inside and use the mass spectrometer. The spectrometer and some of the other equipment had been lumped in along with the property itself when the bank foreclosed. He didn't *want* to break in, but where else was he going to find a mass spectrometer at 12:28 on a Monday morning?

It wasn't like they had one on the counter next to the burrito microwave at the 7-Eleven on Waverley.

Jack lifted his forehead from his cupped hands against the darkened window and looked at Bart standing next to him, quaking in his silver headgear. Jack pointed. "Dude, I'd be more worried about what happens to guys who wear colanders on their heads."

"Hey!" Bart straightened his shoulders bravely for about half a second until the pop of a twig cracking sounded in the dark. Then his voice dropped back down to a whisper. "I'll have you know, this is the official religious headgear of the Church of the Flying Spaghetti Monster and, as such, is worn by thousands of devoted Pastafarians all over the world. I just thought, since we were venturing out tonight on a potentially dangerous mission, that maybe we could use help from as many different deities as possible."

Jack shook his head. "Don't let your mom hear you. I'd be more afraid of her than the guys in jail."

Bart shivered. "Yeah."

The two men continued around the perimeter of the building. "By the way, that was really sweet of her to agree to watch the kids."

Bart shrugged. "They're like the grandkids she's never had. 'And never *will* have if you don't get up off your *tuchus*, you schlep, and marry some nice Jewish girl,' she's constantly moaning. I keep telling her, it's not me!"

Jack swiveled his head and tossed his friend a dubious glance.

Bart motioned to himself, head to toe. "Hey, I am putting this prime, Grade-A meat out on the market. Not my fault no one's buying."

Jack waved at him to be quiet. The pair pressed up against the building as the crunch of radials on loose gravel echoed through the parking lot. The rotating yellow beam of the bubblegum light atop the private security truck swept just beyond their toes. They collectively held their breath as the vehicle meandered past without incident. Relieved breaths escaped both their lips.

"Whew!" Bart gasped. "That was close. This sure would have been easier if we could have just gone in the front door."

"Did you not see the convincing lockbox?"

"Oh yeah. Man, that thing was massive. Guess they were serious about the whole eviction thing."

"You think?" Jack rolled his eyes. "Too bad for them they didn't think to secure the secret entrance."

Bart pulled up short and smacked a beefy arm across Jack's chest. "Shut...the...front...door."

Jack winced and rubbed his pecs. "What'd you do that for?"

"The whole time I worked for you and we had a *secret* door?"

"I mean, yeah. Sort of."

"And you didn't *tell* me about it?"

"Well, technically, it's kinda right there. In the name."

Bart threw his hands in the air and frowned. "Nope! That's okay. I see how it is. Exploit my genius, sure, but deign to induct me into the secret club? No, that's too much to expect, I suppose."

He started to walk away toward the sloping hills of scrubby desert behind the building.

"It's not that–" Jack began.

Bart cut him off. "No, no, no. Really. Don't trouble yourself."

Jack stumbled after him, tripping over a rock in the dark. "You're not listening, Bart. I couldn't–"

"Couldn't share with your best friend? The guy that's stuck it out with you even when you've fallen flat on your face? Really. What does that say about you, Jack? I mean, as a person?" Bart brushed past a stand of *Artemisia californica*, California sagebrush. Its spicy, slightly bitter scent wafted through the air.

"Would you shut up, dummy? I couldn't tell you about the door–"

"No. I'm not upset. I've come to terms with this. Been

happening to me all my life." Bart turned, colander and all, to face Jack. "I've just gotten used to people letting me D…OWN!"

Bart disappeared into a sudden cloud of dirt and dust. Jack stopped, looking at the empty expanse of space his eccentric friend had occupied only moments before. He shook his head from side to side before taking several strides to stand at the edge of a hole in the sandy earth. Jack looked down into the void, hands stationed firmly on his hips. The bit of moon peeked from behind the clouds, casting a wary silver light over the landscape.

Bart lay at the bottom of the hole, arms and legs akimbo, looking like a husky Pinocchio.

"I couldn't tell you about the secret door because it wasn't a door, you dumbass. It was a tunnel."

CHAPTER 16

P1AL *Labs*
Bart

Bart's head swiveled a hundred and eighty degrees around the crumbling brick walls. Insistent roots pushed through the disintegrating clay and mortar, nature reclaiming what man had abandoned long ago.

"I don't get it," Bart stated. "I've been down in our accelerator tunnels. They look nothing like this–gah!" He frantically swiped at a hanging spiderweb that had caught in the curled foot of his upended colander. The colander clattered to the ground, the metallic sound echoing hollowly through the deserted corridor.

Hopefully deserted.

The nervous thought niggled at the back of Bart's brain as Jack played the beam of his Maglite through the darkness. The interminable black swallowed the column of light after only a few feet. It swallowed every last hint of Bart's *chutzpah* too. He resisted the urge to grip the back of Jack's shirt and hold on for dear life.

"Yeah, the labs only use a portion of the tunnel system that was located under the building," his friend continued. "I explored a lot of it when I first bought the facility, but it just goes on for miles. There's tons of old storage space down here—big empty rooms that branch off the main corridors. God knows what kind of stuff Uncle Sam stored in them. The military had a ton of places like this—all across California. Bases with standard military installations aboveground and entire networks of subterranean tunnels below."

"Like an iceberg," Bart murmured.

"Exactly," Jack agreed.

"Let's hope we don't wind up like the *Titanic*," Bart chuckled weakly.

"If we do," Jack warned, "I am not playing the part of Rose. Just saying. I am not kissing you."

"Fine by me!" Bart agreed wholeheartedly but secretly thought how much he would prefer slipping off the edge of a floating door into the icy depths to being in this tunnel.

"Anyway," Jack continued, "once the military moved out, a lot of the tunnel systems just fell into disrepair. This section we're in now branches off from the section we used for our collider. I probably should have had the more dangerous arteries sealed off, but that would have required money."

Jack pulled up short. Bart's bulk skidded to a stop as Jack held up a warning hand.

"Wait. I think this is it," Jack said. He waved the flashlight beam over a nearby section of wall to expose a dark, narrow gap. "I think this is the entrance to the collider maintenance tunnels."

He squeezed his head and shoulder first into the opening, taking his flashlight with him as the rest of his body followed. Bart was plunged into darkness. Something skittered nearby.

"Um, Jack? Buddy?" Bart's voice sounded thin and reedy. He leaned forward, reaching blindly for the obscured entrance.

"Yipe!" Bart squealed like a Girl Scout as Jack popped back

through the opening and grabbed Bart by the fleshy part of his upper arm.

"Quit messing around, will ya? Come on."

He pulled Bart toward the opening and slipped through once more. Bart thrust his left leg through the opening and let momentum carry the rest of his frame through the narrow crevice.

"Jack?" Bart called, though his voice was choked, his lungs constricted by the unforgiving rock pinning him from both sides.

"Jack!" he wheezed. "Pretty sure Einstein disproved this theory."

"What theory is that?" Jack asked.

"Two objects cannot occupy the same space at the same time. Get me the hell outta here!"

Jack gave a hearty tug—okay, maybe a few—and the two men tumbled in a tangled heap on the other side of the gap. The Maglite spun across the floor, its three-hundred-and-sixty-degree spins casting wild shadows on the wall. It eventually slowed, the cast of its beam illuminating the impressive beam pipes and accelerating structures of the collider. Even though it was only a fraction of the size of CERN's collider, the architecture of it was magnificent.

Bart's jaw dropped in awe. "Wow."

"More like ow. You can get off me now," Jack mumbled from beneath Bart's bulk.

"Whoa, yeah. Sorry about that, man. Let me help you up."

He helped Jack to his feet. Jack picked up the flashlight and trained it on the collider. The pair stood there for a moment, simply admiring.

"I know, right?" Jack agreed. "Even though I've seen it a hundred times, it's still pretty incredible. Really sucks that it's not mine anymore. We could have made history."

Bart thumped him on the back. "We still can. Let's go find that mass spectrometer!"

*****

Bart might not have been so confident if he had seen the crisscrossed scars spiderwebbing across the face of the thug sitting in the idling SUV just outside the **P1AL** building. His face looked more like a AAA road map than it resembled any human visage. A livid white twist of tissue transected his left eyelid, the socket sunken for lack of a spherical occupant. The gelled black hair atop his head brushed the headliner of the Yukon's roof as his brawny torso spanned the breadth of the tan leather driver's seat that was pulled back as far as the car's specs would allow.

A tendril of smoke wisped under his nose from the direction of the passenger seat. He made no move to wave it away. He just sat.

Staring.

Stoic.

Serious.

Like the 9mm Glock lying patiently on the black denim of his thick thigh, the blood on the textured grip was nearly invisible in the darkness, but he knew it was there. The concussed security guard knew it was there too. At least, he probably would once he actually woke up. The yellow light on his truck was dark. The vehicle was parked next to the SUV.

"Did youse see where they went?" The accented voice of Peter Valeni finally prompted the leviathan to move.

The black leather of the big man's jacket creaked as he turned. "No, boss. They were there one second. The next? I dunno."

"Well, keep lookin'. That mook owes me big, and I intend to

119

collect. Even if it's outta his hide." Valeni scoffed. "He thinks he can dodge me by sneakin' around in the middle of the night, he's got another think coming. I don't like when people try to cheat me outta what's rightfully mine, Sal. Like Locke."

Valeni took a long, deep drag on his cigarette. After a few seconds, he let loose a stream of blue-white smoke. "I know Locke is trying to edge me out of the Mars deal, but I say nothin' doin'. I may have got this far in life tradin' on the family name, but this is one Valeni who's gonna be respected for something besides fear. You hear what I'm sayin'?"

"Loud and clear, boss."

Valeni took another drag. He pointed vigorously at the building, ash from his cigarette threatening to drop on the floorboards. "They're in there. I know they are. We'll wait here until they show their ugly faces. And, if we have to," he took another deep inhale on the Marlboro, "we'll smoke 'em out."

He laughed as he blew another streamlined cloud of steely blue smoke out before him, and his foot kicked several glass bottles at his feet. The liquid inside sloshed. Only the dirty rags stoppering the necks kept it from spilling onto the floor mats.

CHAPTER 17

P1AL *Labs*
Jack

CRASH!

"I'm okay! I'm okay!" Bart whispered tersely, the anxious tension in his voice practically guaranteeing him a spot in the Vienna Boys' Choir. His warbling soprano echoed in the near-empty offices of what had once been a bustling collective of like minds bent on breaking new ground in the world of particle physics.

Now, Jack thought, it was just an empty honeycomb of abandoned cubicles and deserted workstations.

"Watch what you're doing!" Jack warned. "You know we're not supposed to be here, and we need to find that mass spectrometer before that security guard gets suspicious and starts poking his nose around here."

Bart righted himself, dusted off the dingy film of dust that had settled on his Cal Tech sweatshirt, and steered a wide circle around the empty wire trash can that had tripped him up. He jogged to Jack's side. "So, you really think the mass spec can give us the readout we're looking for?"

The two men headed through a glass door simply marked

"Lab." Jack nodded.

"Well, basically, mass spectrometry can accurately measure the mass of various molecules within any given sample. We'll take a sample of Thom-Thom's tissue, vaporize it in the mass spectrometer, and it'll pass into the ionization chamber. Once it's ionized, the mass analyzer will sort and separate as each ion of increasing mass crosses the finish line at the detector, and the computer will do its magic and spit out a spectrum. Thank God the guys at MIT finally downsized those bad boys and made them affordable. Did you know that some mass specs like the NICOLET 6700 can cost fifty grand or more?"

Bart looked like he'd just sucked a lemon with hot sauce. He grumbled under his breath. "Woo hoo. MIT. Blowhards."

Jack chuckled. The rivalry between Bart's alma mater, Cal Tech, and the East Coast school was well established.

"And they have the dumbest mascot ever."

"Beavers?"

"Yeah. Dumb, right?"

Jack paused and looked at Bart. "And remind me what the Cal Tech mascot is again."

Bart stuck out his lower lip so far it would have put Angelina Jolie to shame.

"So, where's this stupid mass spectrometer supposed to be anyway?" he responded, drastically changing the course of the conversation. Jack bit his lip, swallowing an amused chuckle.

"Right here," Jack pointed. It was actually an innocuous-looking little device—maybe two-foot square. Jack swiped the black backpack off Bart's shoulder and unzipped it, drawing the toothsome Thom-Thom from his hiding place. Jack looked over at Bart.

"You have the analysis software downloaded on your laptop, right?"

Bart nodded, grabbing the bag from Jack. "Yup. Just hand me that cord there, and we'll get hooked up to the spectrometer. Geesh! That thing really is scary looking."

"Have you looked in the mirror lately?"

"Oh, ha-ha."

Using a pair of finely pointed dissecting scissors, Jack took a sample of Thom-Thom's tissue and loaded it into the mass spectrometer.

"Here goes nothing," he said, throwing a glance toward Bart and pushing the button to initiate the process. The initial hum and whir of the machine startled the two men at first, as they both jumped back a fraction.

"Is that all it does?" Bart finally ventured.

"What were you expecting, Igor? Lightning bolts?"

Bart shrugged. "I dunno. Something."

The two men stood in protracted silence as the mass spectrometer did its thing. Suddenly, the laptop screen glowed to life as data started feeding into the graph, sharp, stark spikes and deep plunging valleys appearing along the x-axis.

Jack started shaking his head vehemently. "No, no, no. Wait, wait, wait. This can't be right. Look at the relative abundance levels here and here. Are you seeing what I'm seeing?"

"Honestly, man, I speak Python, Kotlin, JavaScript, Ruby, and even a little Klingon, but this shit? It's all Greek to me. What am I looking at?"

"This is impossible. This is wrong," Jack pulled out a pencil and pad of paper from his bag. He hopped onto a nearby stool and started jotting down computations, speaking commands into the calculator app on his wrist-comm.

Bart looked on in confusion. "When you say, 'wrong,' what's that mean? He's just got a few extra neutrons or something? Is he like the Switzerland of particle physics now?"

Jack suddenly stopped. He dropped his hands into his lap and stared at Bart, though his gaze was actually a million light-years away. "Everything we know to exist is comprised of atoms, right?"

Bart nodded.

"And inside those atoms, there're protons, neutrons, and electrons. In any given atom, we might see a slight variance in the number of, say, neutrons to protons. But there's one established relation that never varies—there is always going to be an identical number of protons and electrons."

Bart pointed to the computer screen. "So, is that what that says? Was our theory wrong?"

Jack jumped from his stool. The pad fluttered to the ground with his pencil as he grabbed Bart's hands. He slowly shook his head from side to side. "No. Our theory was spot on. Thom-Thom's atomic structure has somehow been altered. Like, radically altered. His proton-electron ratio is totally out of whack. His electron count is through the roof!"

Jack burst into crazed laughter and twirled Bart around in an impromptu ring-around-the-rosy.

Bart laughed along with him, albeit a little on the nervous side.

"So, it's positive?" he asked as Jack spun him around. Jack suddenly stopped, leaving Bart a bit wobbly.

"No!" he answered heartily. "It's completely negative! And it's perfect!"

*****

"Oh, I get it. 'Cause electrons are negatively charged particles." Bart rolled his eyes. "Stick to science, bro. Comedy is not your forte," Bart suggested. "So, what do we do now?"

Jack cupped Bart's fleshy jowls in both hands. He looked into Bart's blue eyes. "Now, my genius pal, you work your magic."

"I al-waysh did like Gan-dawf," Bart mumbled through squished cheeks.

Jack released him and grabbed his abandoned legal pad from the floor. He reviewed his notes and scribbles. He paced the length of the lab, his pencil thrumming a rapid rhythm on the pad.

"Now that we know the *what*, we've got to figure out the *how*," Jack muttered.

"Right!" Bart agreed. "That's where ROAR comes in."

Jack wheeled to face him, the exuberance on his face starting to fade. "Of course, it's not going to do us any good unless we can get the exact data of the original incident when Thom-Thom was zapped—what testing protocols were being used in order to run the data through ROAR and prove veracity."

Now, it was Bart's turn to get excited. He scuttled over to his laptop. "We don't need the data."

Surprise flooded Jack's features and morphed into consternation. The crease between his brows deepened with frustration. "Yes, we do. If we just start putting in random parameters, we're no better off than we were the day of the initial ROAR test. There's got to be over a billion different combinations. It's impossible!"

"Nah!" Bart waved him off as his fat fingers flew over the keyboard at the speed of light. "You've just gotta come at it from a different direction."

"What are you talking about, Bart?"

"Reverse engineering! I think I can write a subroutine for the ROAR program that can extrapolate the exact parameters that were in place when our little furry friend went over the rainbow bridge. Then we can use that data in conjunction with information on the existing atomic substructure of some other physical matter, like, I don't know, your hair gel," Bart pointed to Jack's styled locks, "and run it through a battery of ROAR simulations to replicate the effect."

Jack stared at him blankly for a moment, then suddenly rushed forward. "Good God, why hasn't some woman scooped you up, you brilliant, brilliant man?" He planted a fat, wet kiss on Bart's cheek.

"I don't know, man. I've been asking myself that same question for years." Bart promptly gave his cheek a swipe with his shoulder. "I'm beginning to think it's because I've been hanging out with you too long."

A clatter sounded somewhere beyond the light of the lab—somewhere in the darkness. Jack leaped for the light switch and plunged the room into near blackness. The only light was from the glowing blue of Bart's laptop screen. Jack peered out the lab windows and rapidly motioned to Bart.

"Shut it all down!" he hissed. "Shut it all down!"

"I can't just shut it down!" Bart typed frantically. "I gotta save the data first!"

"Dammit!" Jack cursed. Bart was right. He tossed nervous glances back at his friend, holding his breath and peering through the darkness to determine if their presence had been discovered.

"Got it!" Bart whispered. Finally, Jack let loose a long, relieved expulsion of air as Bart slammed the laptop shut, shoved it into the backpack, and hurried to Jack's side. "What is it?"

"I don't know. I don't see anything. Maybe we'd better get out of here. I guess we can try to sneak back later to run tests."

"Roger that," Bart agreed. He chuckled nervously. "Can't run tests from a jail cell."

Bart slunk off into the darkness, making his way back toward the crumbling tunnel. Jack sucked in a deep breath and followed behind.

"Come on. Galileo did some of his best work under house arrest."

*****

The pair beat feet back through the collider access tunnels and toward the narrow gap that led back to the surface. Faint echoes chased behind them, causing more than one wary, nervous glance back over a shoulder, but no faces materialized out of the darkness.

Bart's backpack kept slipping off his rounded shoulder, the weight of his laptop and the jerky movement of his frantic, uneven jog disputing Bart's desire to keep it stationary. He gave yet another frustrated tug on the strap as he tried to keep up with Jack, who loped several strides ahead. Bart had quickly lost his lead to the fitter man. Marathon gaming was not a big calorie-burner.

"Wait up, will ya?"

Jack looked back at him and waved him on. "No. Come on, man! Put some hustle in it. I don't know what'll be worse if we get caught–getting slapped with a charge of criminal trespass or getting slapped by your mother when she has to drag all the kids down to the station to bail us out."

The mental debate seemed to prompt renewed momentum in Bart's pace as they reached the gap. They squeezed, one by one, through the narrow passage, Bart forcing his bulk through once more. The uncertain beam of Jack's Maglite flickered as he clicked it on, training it on the uneven ground. It couldn't keep pace, however, dancing wildly in Jack's grip as the men stumbled headlong over crumbling brick and loose rock.

"Come on," Jack urged. "It's this way."

He swung the beam right, then left. A worried twist warped his mouth. "I think."

Bart stumbled along in his wake, concern worrying at the corners of his eyes. The bunching clutch of wrinkles belied his distress at Jack's sudden, uncertain navigation. Bart's tennis shoe skidded on a loose rock. He reached out through the darkness to the dilapidated wall for balance. He quickly withdrew his hand when it landed in a small cleft in the brick and crunched on some unknown thing. He shook his fingers violently and rubbed the contaminated hand vigorously on his pant leg.

"Bleh! Has anyone ever gotten lost in this tunnel system?" he asked Jack, a slight quaver in his voice.

"I don't know," Jack answered brusquely as he hesitated at a fork in their path. "I mean, I don't think so."

The light traveled down the abysmal dark of one tunnel. Its beam, though strong, couldn't penetrate further than a few feet, exposing a relatively intact section of whitewashed brick and finished concrete floors. Jack didn't remember this artery from their path into the accelerator maintenance tunnel. It almost looked like the entrance to another lab—similar in architecture and construction to the network of tunnels and lab spaces P1AL used—though he couldn't fathom why it would be so far removed from the main network. He looked down at the backlit display of his sports watch and noted the step count. They'd clocked nearly half a mile from the collider tunnel. You didn't usually isolate a lab—

—unless you wanted to keep what was inside it a secret.

Bart's labored breaths brought Jack's attention back to their current quandary. Jack swung the beam toward the only alternative route. Narrower, congested with sage roots and piles of disintegrating brick from walls that had lost the battle against nature, it looked far less inviting. Jack bobbed his head and took a wary but determined step.

"This is the way."

Bart peeked over his shoulder. "Are you sure about that?" He wheezed and heaved, bent over, palms bracing on the tops of his knees. "I mean, I know you said no one ever got lost in these things, but what about *buried*?"

As if to prove his point, brick and rock shifted ahead of them, sending up little flurries of dirt and dust to dance in the shaft of light.

"I'm just saying that way looks a lot more stable." Bart pointed toward the solid brick tunnel.

Jack shook his head, though the thought did worm at his resolve. "Nope. This is definitely the way. Let's go!"

He took off. Bart took a deep, disappointed breath and dashed after him.

They dashed helter-skelter down the narrow corridor, dirt and stone showering down on their heads as the vibrations from their running feet worked less stable particles loose. But Jack pressed forward. He was almost certain this was the way they had come in. He kept throwing his arm across his face, trying desperately to block the grit from getting into his eyes and maintain his grip on the flashlight.

He failed. On both counts.

"Dammit!" he cursed as he instinctively crushed his eyes shut against the foreign matter. The Maglite hit the ground with a solid thud. He stopped short. In the uncertain light, Bart barreled into his back and knocked him flat. Jack ate a mouthful of dirt.

"Oof!" he mumbled through the mixed taste of metallic conglomerate and bland grit of sandy loam. He tried to foist Bart off him. "Be careful, will ya? This—"

He didn't get the chance to complete the thought. The overburden above their heads came crashing down, burying them under soil and rock.

CHAPTER 18

P1AL *Labs*
Jack

They always said there was a light.

Jack, however, reflected that someone upstairs must have made a major clerical error. With his stellar track record, he didn't stand a snowball's chance in hell of getting past God's bouncer at the Pearly Gates. He considered how he had bungled through life—the fuck-ups, the failures...

The snowball stood a better shot.

He scowled as he studied the brutal, intense face of the angel floating above him. One black eye returned a piercingly studious gaze right back at him. The other eye, or at least where there should have been an eye, was divided by a winding rope of pale white cicatricial tissue.

Funny. That's not how I pictured St. Peter looking at all.

The "angel" wrapped a monstrous, beefy hand around Jack's forearm and hoisted him free of the collapsed tunnel. Dirt showered from Jack's body, pebbles skittering, as the big man tossed him unceremoniously to a patch of unforgiving ground nearby. Bart was already waiting there, coughing vigorously. Dusty smears covered the software engineer from head to toe. The only thing that wasn't covered in filth was Bart's pearly whites as he flashed Jack a weak grin.

A trickle of blood oozed from a laceration on Jack's forehead. Something had smacked him with a decent wallop. His vision swam as he squinted his eyes for focus. Jack's muddled brain tried to piece together what had happened.

Did the damn tunnel collapse in on us?

"Well, well, well. Jack Harding." The oily charm of Peter Valeni's voice slithered.

Yep. And I've gone straight to hell.

Jack made a feeble attempt to dust himself off and stand. He wobbled, held his arms out till the world stopped, then slowly straightened. He was still about a foot and a half shy of the one-eyed behemoth's height, but he took a small modicum of pride from standing head and shoulders over Valeni's balding pate.

"Valeni! Hey! Fancy meeting you here. You like tacos too? I heard they had awesome food trucks out here," Jack rambled.

"Knock it off, Harding," Valeni snapped. "You know exactly why I'm here. We followed you and your little girlfriend here so we could collect my money."

"Really?"

Valeni bobbled his head on a thick neck. He sneered. "Really."

"Wow. That's too bad then." Jack made a pantomime of patting down his pockets. "I seem to have left it in my other pants."

"You'll be wetting your pants once I let Sal have a go at you."

Jack took a haughty glance at the big man who stood near Valeni's left shoulder, leaning casually on the pommel of a Louisville Slugger. "Not my type."

"What is your type then, huh, smart guy? Type A? Type B? How's about we spill some of your blood all over the ground here and find out exactly what your *type* is?" Valeni bristled at

Jack's defiance. The definitive slide and click of Valeni's gun eroded some of the bravado.

Some.

Jack threw his hands in the air in a gesture of mock surrender. "What are you going to do? Shoot me? Dead men don't pay debts, and you know it."

Jack's head exploded in its own version of the big bang theory.

Damn. I think that's the Little Dipper.

Before he could confirm any constellation in the galaxy of stars swirling in his brain, Jack took a little dip of his own as he stumbled under the blow of Valeni's pistol butt to his temple. Now blood trickled down both sides of his dirt-streaked face.

Hey. A matching set.

Jack felt a tug at his pant leg. Bart quivered on the ground. He looked up at him with imploring eyes. "Come on, Jack. Cut it out."

Valeni scoffed. He waved the gun at Bart. "I'm guessing Round Boy there's the brains of your particular operation, huh, Harding?"

Jack looked down at Bart.

"Please," he begged.

Jack swung his gaze back to Valeni and his goon.

"Maybe dead men don't pay debts," Valeni agreed reluctantly, holstering his weapon. "But properly incentivized men tend to make good on what they owe. What do you think, Sal? One bone for every grand he still owes me?"

Jack's eyes flew wide. That was a lot of bones.

Shit.

This time, Jack waved his hands at Valeni in earnest. "Now, hold on a minute, Valeni."

"Man, oh man," Bart moaned.

The crack of wood against bone echoed through the desert night. A white-hot pain seared through Jack's shoulder. He dropped to his knees.

Valeni squatted next to him. The loan shark leaned in. "I lent you a large sum of money. Normally, I don't extend that kind of credit to just any *goombah* off the street, but for you, I was willing to take a risk because of what you promised. You promised you had tech—tech like nobody's ever seen before. Stuff that'd blow people's minds. Something that could finally help people look at me like a legitimate businessman and not just another knuckle-crackin' *ginzo*. Turns out, Jackie, you *lied* to me."

Jack laughed weakly but derisively. "Welcome to the party, pal."

Valeni laughed back with equal sarcasm. He lightly slapped Jack's face twice. "Now, I came here tonight incensed. Wasn't I incensed, Sal?"

The big man nodded silently.

"In fact, I was so incensed, I was considering setting your little Love Bug on fire."

Bart gasped. "Leia!"

Valeni held up a finger. "The peanut gallery is officially closed for comment. As I was saying, I considered using a special cocktail to properly toast that Volkswagen, hoping you would grasp the gravity of your situation."

"Leia is a SmartCar, *not* a Volkswagen!"

Valeni shrugged. "Whatever. They're both German, right? Anyway, things were about to get lit when I start wondering why you two *pompinaras* are futzin' around out here. You don't even own the joint anymore, am I right?"

He slapped Jack upside the head. Jack winced.

"I said, am I right?" Valeni repeated.

Jack nodded slowly.

"So, I start thinking maybe we should watch just a little bit longer. See what youse are up to. So, we watch. And BAM! You're gone. I mean, one minute you're here and the next, poof! Like a coupla fuckin' fairies. Ain't nothin' else around here 'cept the goddamned building. We check the front door, but it's locked up tighter than Fort Knox. I figure you got some other way of getting in. Turns out you did. Who knew about these freaky tunnels, eh? But why would you want to get into a place you don't own no more and risk getting buried like King Tut unless it was to snag something of serious value that you left behind? Something you could use, say, to square your debt with me?"

Jack's gaze involuntarily drifted to Bart's backpack before he could stop himself. Valeni followed his gaze. Bart wrapped his arms around the bag protectively.

Valeni nodded to Sal. "Get the bag."

Bart scrambled backward. "No, wait! Hold on just a second. I don't owe you a thing, and this bag is mine."

Sal plucked the backpack from Bart's scrabbling grip like plucking a ripe piece of fruit from a tree. He tossed it to Valeni, who caught it in his outstretched hands. Both Bart and Jack lunged.

"No!" they cried simultaneously. Sal grabbed Jack from behind. Jack's face pinched in anguish as his injured shoulder twisted in the big man's grip.

Valeni raised a thick, curious brow. "Wow. Whatever's in here must be worth a mint. Let's see, shall we?"

Gritting his teeth against the pain, Jack tugged against Sal's brawny hands. Even if Valeni was able to boot up Bart's laptop–a likelihood Jack sincerely doubted–it was farfetched that the loan shark would be able to interpret the information they had gathered from the mass spectrometer. Jack felt confident he could readily explain it away as useless data.

What he *didn't* think he would be able to explain away as easily was the presence of a floating ferret. If Valeni saw Thom-Thom float, Jack was as good as sunk.

At best, the rodent would scare the crap out of the gangster. He'd likely lose control of it, and it would float away into the atmosphere, making the data in Bart's computer the only existing link to an antigravity solution. And if Valeni kept the computer?

They were fucked.

At worst, Valeni would realize exactly what he held in his hands and its implications for mankind—and the Mars race. Then?

Then they were royally fucked.

Each click of the zipper teeth sent a lightning bolt coursing through Jack's battered body. It was all going to be over in a few seconds. This was going to go down as the biggest screwup in his rich history of screwups. Part of him wished fervently Valeni had just left him to suffocate in that pile of dirt and brick. It would have been an easier fate to deal with than facing the kids—than facing Charlie—and letting them know, once again, that he had failed them.

A bitter grin contorted his lips.

Would be easier than facing myself.

Valeni worked the zipper all the way open. He slid his hand into the recesses of the backpack and slid out Bart's Strontium 5 Power Core. He whistled long and low.

"Sweet piece of merch you got here. What'd this set you back? Or should I say, what'd this set *me* back? I'm assuming you didn't use my hard-earned funds to buy company letterhead."

Jack looked away, refusing to make eye contact with Valeni. Valeni's eyes narrowed. He nodded at Sal, who jerked Jack in Valeni's direction.

"Mr. Valeni asked you a question," Sal grunted. Jack scowled, still refusing to answer.

"Forty thousand dollars!" Bart piped.

"Forty Gs!" Valeni exclaimed, his jaw dropping.

Jack's gaze snapped toward Bart, ire burning hotly.

"They were going to hurt you, Jack. More than they already have. Come on. It's not worth it," Bart pleaded. A beat passed. "Think about the kids."

"I *was* thinking about the kids, you idiot," Jack hissed.

Valeni clucked his tongue. "Oh, come on now, Harding. He's not an idiot. I'll grant you he ain't much to look at, but, like I said before, out of the two of you, he's definitely the higher IQ."

Valeni tossed the computer through the open window of the SUV. "Okay. Forty grand down. Only two hundred and sixty thousand to go. Let's see what else you've got in here, huh?"

He jammed his hand back into the bag and hissed as he rapidly drew it out again. He took a closer look inside. "What the hell do we have here?"

Slowly, he drew Thom-Thom from the bag, gripping the creature by the scruff of the neck. He turned its pointy face with its shifty, beady little eyes toward his own. If he hadn't been so tense about the potential outcome of the scenario, Jack might have laughed at the resemblance between the two. As it was, he hadn't taken a breath for the last sixty seconds.

"What's this, Harding?" Valeni turned Thom-Thom's weaselly little face toward Jack. "Your emotional support animal?"

Jack stole a glance at Bart, hoping beyond hope the Cal Tech grad knew of some obscure algorithm that would determine a positive outcome for their current predicament. Bart only offered a weak shrug.

"No?" Valeni queried. "So, what then? Some freaky little lab experiment? Like glow-in-the-dark mice or something?"

He chortled at his own creativity. Even Sal let loose a reserved chuckle. Valeni stared Thom-Thom in the face once more. "Pah!

Ain't nothing more than a piece of junk. Just like *you*."

Valeni moved to chuck the ferret down into the open backpack...only down was not the direction Thom-Thom went.

A gasp escaped Bart.

"What the fuck?" Valeni exclaimed.

Sal loosened his grip on Jack. Jack took advantage of the momentary lapse and dove forward, the tips of his fingers just grabbing Thom-Thom's tail before he floated out of reach.

The sudden, insistent peal of a car bleep pierced the night as the unconscious security guard in his nearby truck slumped forward, his head hitting the steering wheel. None of the three men standing moved even a fraction to look. They all just stared at the furry white rodent grinning toothily in Jack's hands.

"I bet people ain't never seen *that* before, huh, boss," Sal murmured.

When Valeni finally found his voice, it came out as a low whisper. "No, Sal. No, they haven't."

A slow, measured smile broke out across Valeni's face.

CHAPTER 19

Harding Estate
Jack

"You look like hell." Julia uttered the words matter-of-factly as she reached past Jack to the kitchen cupboard for a mug.

"Good morning to you, too, and watch your mouth," Jack groaned.

She surveyed all the questionable injuries—scratches, scrapes, and other assorted bruises—scattered up and down his shirtless torso and snorted.

"Why? What are you gonna do about it...Jack?" She dropped the intentional double entendre.

The pastel rainbow of her ponytail swayed as she gave a haughty little flip of her head. She grabbed the handle of the coffeepot and filled her mug nearly to the brim with the steaming black brew and strode back toward her room. He heard the definitive slam of a door.

Jack sighed. She was right. He sat slumped on a stool at the breakfast bar, a pack of frozen peas Ace bandaged around his shoulder, skin a palette of harsh colors—intense pink, darkening to red in spots from the cold of the frozen vegetables, and deep indigo purpling to black where blood vessels had erupted beneath the surface of the skin. Valeni had let him and Bart go last night.

You'd think that would be a good thing, right?

Jack groaned audibly instead. He would have almost rathered Valeni let Sal beat him to a pulp and just owe the loan shark for the rest of his life than for Valeni to have let him off the hook as he did.

Well, not entirely off the hook.

Valeni had confiscated Bart's computer and Thom-Thom.

Jack had protested–heartily. He winced as he brought his coffee cup to his lips.

And he had the split lip to prove it. Right where Sal had planted a solid left-cross that had brought Jack to his knees. Valeni had agreed to leave Jack alone–for the time being.

"But keep your wrist-comm on, huh?" the gangster had warned. "Consider yourself on the payroll. And the money I gave you? We'll call it an advance. For services to be rendered."

Valeni had left Bart to scrape Jack up off the desert floor and hightail it out of there before the security guard came all the way around. The pudgy little software developer had helped him pile the sleepy kids into the van back at the Pulldraw house, begging him to go to the hospital to get his shoulder looked at.

"Yeah, yeah," Jack had grimaced as he secured Charlie's wheelchair in the van. "I'll go."

"When?" Bart had asked.

"When it's free," Jack had snapped before pulling out of the drive and heading home.

Now, as the throbbing intensified, he almost wished he had taken the advice. Although, with the way he felt, he probably would have just saved everybody the trouble and bypassed the ER and gone straight to the morgue. He squinted at the blinking digital clock on the microwave. The blurry blue numbers read 7:00 a.m. Jack moaned. Four more hours before he could pop a few more acetaminophens.

Damn.

If only he had something stronger.

Is it too early for scotch?

He slowly brought his fingers to his temples, careful not to touch the lacerations there, and rubbed, hoping to whatever God was listening that his life would somehow come back into focus. And it had better do it soon, he thought, because he was starting to see things. His blurred gaze settled on the small naked child in front of him. Jack blinked until his vision cleared. The cherub was still there.

"Oscar?" he ventured. "Why are you naked?"

The twin stood before him with a scowl, tiny potbelly poking out before him, lower lip pursed. "I can't find my Captain America underwear."

"Okay," Jack reasoned, not quite understanding the dilemma. "So, wear your Batman ones."

Oscar stamped his bare foot. "No! No Batman. It's the first day, and Captain America was the first Avenger. I have to wear Captain America."

Jack shook his head and immediately regretted the maneuver. "Wait. I don't understand. First day of what?"

"First day of the school week?" Oscar held up his hands and shrugged. He blew an impatient raspberry when he realized Jack wasn't getting it. He ticked off on his pudgy little fingers. "Every week is just the same. Monday is Cap. And Tuesday is Iron Man. Black Widow is on Wednesday. Then there's Thor's Day. Hee hee. Friday is Hulk, and Saturday's Hawkeye."

Jack's forehead creased. "What about Sunday?"

Oscar folded his arms. "Sunday, I don't wear no drawers. Charlie says they call that commando."

Jack dropped his head into his arms.

"Oh dear God, Bradley. Please come back. How am I going to manage without you?" he muttered under his breath.

"Well, you'd better figure it out, Einstein, cause the first bell rings in twenty-five minutes," Julia interjected as she walked past him once more, this time to toss her mug into the sink. She reached down to grab her schoolbag from the front hall and slung it over her shoulder just as Lucas blew past her and threw open the pantry door. He hefted a five-pound bag of rice off the bottom shelf and, with wild abandon, ripped it open, spilling its contents all over the tile of the kitchen floor.

Momentarily forgetting about his injured shoulder, Jack leaped from his perch on the stool and threw his hands into the air. "Lucas! What in the hell do you think you are doing?"

His shoulder immediately reminded him of recent events. He cringed.

"It's a hundred days of school," Lucas explained. "Teacher says we gotta bring in one hundred of the same things. I'm bringing rice! One, two, three…"

From the substantial mound on the floor, the five-year-old began plucking individual grains, counting each one as he thrust it into a plastic sandwich bag.

"I'm bringing buttons!" Oscar told his brother proudly.

"You'd better bring some clothes while you're at it," Alice mentioned as she stalked through the room and stormed out the front door. Jack watched her stomp by, a genuine look of confusion on his face.

"What's her problem?" he asked Julia as Lucas continued counting grains of rice.

"I'm looking at it," Julia quipped. She turned on her heel and began to follow her sister out of the front door. "I'll be waiting in the van."

"Good morning, Jack!" Charlie called cheerfully as he

wheeled into the room from the first-floor hallway. "Did you make the lunches yet? Oh, and I hope you cut the crust off the twins' peanut butter and jelly. They won't eat, otherwise. Last time they got in trouble because they threw their sandwiches across the cafeteria and accidentally started a food fight."

Jack seemed to remember receiving a call a while back, but he had been busy trying to get ROAR off the ground.

"Lunches?" Jack mumbled.

Charlie smiled. "Don't worry about it. I can do it. I used to help Bradley all the time."

He piloted his chair into the kitchen and grabbed the bread from the counter. As Jack watched the young boy deftly maneuver a rounded dollop of creamy golden peanut butter onto a slice of Wonder Bread, he had the sudden and harsh realization that the seven-year-old was more adept at adulting than he was.

Jack looked back at Oscar, who was ass up, digging in a basket of folded laundry. "Wait! Where'd you find buttons?"

"Off your shirts, silly!" Oscar mumbled through the clothes. Suddenly, he popped up, holding his underwear high. "I founded him! Captain America!"

He sprinted through the kitchen, knocking the plastic bag out of his brother's hand. The upended bag emptied, grains of rice skittering across the ceramic tiles.

"My rices!" Lucas cried. "Oscar!"

Jack watched helplessly as Lucas took off running after his twin. "My shirts?"

CHAPTER 20

StarCall Labs
Locke

Locke's lazy gaze took a detour along the generous curve of Sarah Copeland's hip, traveled down the slim line of her thigh, and paused at the sudden tension tugging at his inseam. He discreetly adjusted his pants and silently admonished himself for allowing himself to be distracted from the task at hand. As pleasantly distracting as it was for him to survey Sarah's physical qualities as she leaned over his desk to point out the salient points of the revised contract with StarCall Labs, he needed to retain control or his efforts to win the Mars race would become a futile pursuit.

"As legal representative for StarCall Labs, I have Dr. Binderkampf's signature here and here," Sarah's mellifluous voice dripped like sweet honey. "Although, truth be told, I cannot fathom why he would accept these terms."

He had a little…incentive.

"The contract's brilliant, don't get me wrong," Sarah continued, turning to face Locke. She leaned casually against the edge of the extra-wide executive desk.

God, what I wouldn't give to take her on this right fucking now.

"I mean, after all, I drafted it. But it wholly turns over all proprietary rights to Locke Industries. They will still have 100 percent access to the laboratories and equipment, but you retain all rights and ownership of the physical property and any developments, including intellectual property. Basically, they're doing all the work, and you're reaping the benefits."

Locke tented his fingers together and brought them to his thin lips. He looked out the top of hooded eyes at her. "And the problem with that is?"

She shook her head. "Oh, it's no problem. Unless you're an employee of StarCall Labs. It's just, this is a groundbreaking theory they're going after. If they succeed—"

Locke shook his own head.

"When," he corrected.

"Fine. *When* they succeed, they've basically conquered space for peanuts."

Locke stretched his lanky legs out in front of him and stood. "Which is no more than monkeys should expect."

He strode toward the large window overlooking the test floor. His cold eyes observed the hurried scampering of white-coated scientists bustling along below him. He tapped the glass with a manicured finger and smiled coolly. It was rather like watching animals at the zoo.

He reveled in the success of his little tête-à-tête with Dr. Binderkampf. The stagnation that had mired the Mars efforts just twenty-four hours before seemed to have evaporated. The good doctor had reported to work that morning fueled with the new theory he brought to Dr. Vashtin and the other members of the team. When they had questioned him regarding the rainbow assortment of lacerations and bruises on his person, he waved them off, albeit gingerly, claiming he'd gotten in a car wreck. Everyone had recommended he go home immediately to tend to his wounds, but the suggestion drove the bespectacled physicist into a paroxysm of violent behavior.

"No time! No time! We have work to do!" he exploded, his face flushing beet red as spittle flecked his split lip.

Locke grinned. "We have work to do indeed, Doctor."

Locke pushed away from the glass and walked toward the elevator in long, loping strides. He tilted his head toward Sarah and held out a hand. "Let's go see what our little monkeys are up to, shall we?"

*****

"We need more power," Binderkampf mumbled, his speech impeded by his swollen lip.

Preaching to the choir.

The thought rambled through Locke's brain as he watched the rotund scientist reach an index finger toward his glasses to foist them back up the bridge of his bulbous nose. Locke glared. Binderkampf froze. He lowered his hand, leaving the spectacles to lie exactly where they were. Instead, he gestured toward the brown-skinned scientist beside him. He winced with the effort.

"As Dr. Vashtin here has mentioned previously, the quandary which most deep space missions have come up against time and time again is how to provide adequate power to propel a manned spacecraft enormous distances through the recesses of space without burdening the payload with heavy propellants and the hardware necessary to transport them," Binderkampf explained. "The limits of conventional propulsion technology are, well, frustratingly limiting, to say the least."

Locke rolled his eyes and sighed. "Uh-huh...yes, yes. We've already established that, Dr. Binderkampf. And, if I'm not mistaken, it is the exact reason I have employed you and your little three-ring circus act. But as amusing as the circus may be, tragedy can strike…at any moment."

He glared at Binderkampf to drive his point home. "For instance, do I need to remind you what happens if the lion tamer's lion gets hungry?"

Binderkampf swallowed with some degree of difficulty. "Yes, yes. I mean, no. Of course not. I realize that, of course." He hobbled toward the nearby whiteboard and picked up a dry-erase marker. He flinched as he twisted off the cap. It let out a screeching squeak. "What if, then, we took traditional propellant out of the equation altogether?"

"Really?" Locke arched one perfectly shaped, dark eyebrow. "How?"

Binderkampf nodded eagerly. "Electrogravitics."

"Excuse me?" Locke said.

"Electrogravitics? It's the physics that studies the interrelation between electricity or electromagnetism and gravity."

Locke's brows knit with interest. He snapped his fingers at Sarah and motioned toward an abandoned chair in the corner of the room. She quickly grabbed it and rolled it closer to Locke, who lowered into it. He crossed one ankle over the opposite knee. He gestured to Binderkampf.

"Go on."

"You've heard of Nikola Tesla, of course."

Locke nodded. "Of course. Who hasn't?"

"Well, the study of electrogravitics can be traced back to Tesla's experimentations with high-voltage shock discharges. But there was another pioneer in the field, Thomas Townsend-Brown, who did extensive work to establish the correlation between electrostatic and gravitational fields. Allow me to explain," Binderkampf suggested when he noted the slightly blank look on Locke's face.

147

"By all means," Locke replied.

The marker squeaked along the whiteboard as Binderkampf scrawled out an equation in blood-red ink.

$$m_g \propto q$$

"A charged body, in theory, generates a gravitational mass." He pointed to the lowercase "m" with the subscripted "g." "Now, that mass is directly proportional to the size of its electrical charge. The larger the charge, the greater the gravitational mass."

Doubt began to seep into the downturned edges of Locke's mouth. "So, instead of two hundred tons of propellant, you're saying all I need is a really long extension cord?"

Binderkampf started to waffle. "No, no, no! That's not what I'm saying at all, Mr. Locke! Please, hear me out."

"I'm listening, though not for very much longer."

"I'm not speaking of electricity in the traditional sense as much as I'm discussing electrical charge—positive or negative. Brown created a device he called a gravitator. Effectively, this device altered the ambient gravitational field, relying on the inherent charge of the gravitational mass. A positive charge would create a matter-attracting force, much like the gravity we experience here on Earth, while a negative charge would, in fact, repel matter, thus creating, well," he put his one good hand on his hip, "gravitational thrust."

For the first time since Locke had entered the room, he thought he could see Binderkampf's eyes—well, eye—glittering. Even the apathetic Vashtin seemed to spark with some semblance of excitement at his colleague's revelation. At least, it was the first time with any degree of confidence Locke could determine the kid had a pulse. His eyes swiveled back to Binderkampf, who had stepped forward. His voice, sandpapered with strain, dropped to an excited whisper.

"Imagine, if you would, a spacecraft which could alter its polarity at will, creating a gravity-potential well before the ship. A matter-attracting gravity-potential well. The ship would be continuously drawn forward, pulled by the artificially induced attractive force. Theoretically, it would be as if you parked a planet the size of Jupiter right in front of it, and the gravity would yank it along without so much as a fart from the ship. This pull-and-tug effect could be maintained throughout the entire course of a long-range space mission."

Binderkampf let the enormity of his words sink in.

Finally, Locke spoke. "Why have I not heard of this before?"

Before Binderkampf could answer, Vashtin interceded. "Well, even though Townsend-Brown held several patents for his work, mainstream academia has mostly sidelined the phenomenon demonstrated by Dr. Townsend's work because it directly violates Einstein's theory of general relativity. Dr. Einstein himself once tried to incorporate gravitational concepts and electromagnetism into his theory but failed. Relativity simply could not predict the correlation between the polarities of charge and gravitational field."

Locke slowly drew his long fingers down the length of his jaw. He could feel the raw tension of held breath quivering in Vashtin's slight frame—in Binderkampf's broken body. He considered the physicist's proposed new direction. It was wholly theoretical, of course, and, as it currently stood, got him no closer to Mars than he had been with that charcoal briquette at TitusBane. But unlike the massive rocket system whose payload nullified any realistic intention of a successful Mars mission, this?

This held promise.

He ruminated on his would-be competitors, other billionaires who, at some point and level, had picked up the baton in the space race: Galvin Finn with the JumpSpace program; Richard Drake, with his less-than-stellar Plato 5 Industries; Amazon's latest chief, Brenda Fisk, and her always-conservative Blue Origin endeavors. These were but a few of the lofty visionaries who sought to take yet another "giant step for mankind" in the twenty-first century.

Who gives a crap about mankind?

A dark smile twisted at the corner of Locke's mouth. He was in it for no one but himself.

And now, he had an edge on those altruistic dipshits.

Binderkampf's theory was based on something vetted academia likely considered pseudoscience at best. Therefore, it was highly unlikely any of their reputable scientific teams would deign to pursue it. Locke looked down at the conference table, where the newspaper had fallen open to the real estate section.

It wasn't even that the theory was flawed, Locke thought.

It just couldn't be predicted.

The gravel of Locke's voice shattered the silence. His intense gaze bore down on Vashtin. "You said Einstein's relativity couldn't predict the correlation between the polarities of charge and gravitational field."

Vashtin swallowed long and hard. He nodded slowly. "That is correct. To properly apply what Dr. Binderkampf is suggesting, we would need some method to ascertain the quantum aspects of gravity and determine the specific effects alterations at the subatomic level would have."

"And do we have such a method?" Locke asked, the acerbic bite of impatience beginning to gnaw at his gut.

Vashtin exchanged nervous glances with Binderkampf. Finally, Binderkampf took a hesitant step forward.

"At this time, Mr. Locke, I'm afraid no one has developed the requisite tech to make those calculations."

Silence hung like a funeral pall over the room as Locke remained quiet. Motionless. Suddenly, he slammed a fist onto the table. Binderkampf cringed and cried out. Vashtin cowered, quivering behind the whiteboard. Even Sarah, normally so aloof, grasped her ample bosom as her heart leaped unexpectedly in her chest.

Locke's violent, abrupt move had caused his perfectly coiffed hair to fall across his dark eyes. It veiled his stormy gaze as he glowered at the two scientists. "Why can't you animals just give... me...what...I...WANT?"

He lunged on that last word, upper lip peeling back over his teeth in a feral snarl.

Just then, Peter Valeni burst in through the conference room doors, Sal following dutifully behind.

"Maybe because you been working with the wrong animals," he uttered, a smug smile across his narrow features as he held the snarling ferret out in front of him.

CHAPTER 21

Pacific Grove Science & Technical Academy
Alice

It all had to be a bad dream.

That was the thought rattling around in Alice's mind. The careening disaster that seemed to be her life could not actually be real.

She probably shouldn't have allowed herself to get so distracted. She probably should have been paying attention to Mr. Osterberg prattle on about when Thomas Edison invented the first electric light bulb.

January 1879?

Alice laughed internally. Any real student of science knew that Sir Humphry Davy, a British inventor, had succeeded in that pursuit nearly seventy years prior to Mr. Edison's great Menlo Park discovery. Davy had affixed two wires to a battery, then run them to a charcoal strip, which glowed with the subsequent charge. Humphry's endeavors, not Edison's, produced the first arc lamp.

Duh.

Normally, Alice rather enjoyed science class. She loved school as a general concept, in fact. Pacific Grove Science and Technical

Academy just made it even cooler. The tuition-free charter school offered students a unique learning environment where faculty encouraged them to set goals, formulate ideas, and research and discover answers—in the lab and in the impressive school library, which, through a cooperative program with Cal Tech, afforded students access to many published scientific journals and papers. Many students, in fact, went on to design real solutions for real-world problems. Alice, for one, loved exploring new ideas and concepts and figuring out what made the world tick.

"Curiosity! The age-old question of 'why,'" she remembered her father saying. "That's where all the truly brilliant ideas come from."

Moisture began to well in the corners of her eyes as she recalled how he used to tweak her nose when he said it. She closed her eyes against the threatening tears and inhaled. If she concentrated, she could almost feel the rough scratch of the wool in his cardigan against her cheek as he held her. Smell the sweet smell of his cherry pipe tobacco. She remembered how he would purse his full lips, blowing little smoke rings, challenging Alice to poke her tiny fingers through before they dissipated. His rich, warm chuckle at the pouty pucker of her tiny mouth when each ring mysteriously vanished into thin air.

"Where did it go? How did it disappear, Vati?" she would prod him, calling him by the Swiss-German term for *father*. "Is it magic?"

"It's not magic, my *schätzl*, my little treasure. It's science!" He blew another circular puff of smoke and pointed at it. "You see, smoke is a combination of unburned fuel, like the tobacco in my pipe, and tiny little drops of water."

"Tiny. Like me!" Alice exclaimed.

"Yes, *schätzl*. Tiny like you." He would blow another puff of smoke until it swirled around his head, looking like an ephemeral crown. Appropriate, Alice thought as she remembered. For her, he had always been her king.

"The ash? The unburned fuel? It eventually spreads out so widely it becomes part of the dust floating in the atmosphere. The water, on the other hand, well, it never really goes away. It only changes, evaporating into vapor. We cannot see it, but it is always there."

"You'll always be there, Vati, won't you?" she had asked.

He had kissed the top of her head. "Of course, schätzl. Of course."

Except he wasn't.

She hadn't wanted them to go. She had begged them to take her with them. But her father and her mother had gotten on that plane to go to Paris, and they never came back. On vacation, they had claimed—only Alice couldn't remember any luggage. Just her father's briefcase. She only remembered because she had devised some great scheme to hide in her mother's carry-on bag. She recalled the last thing her father said to her.

"Don't ever be afraid to ask questions, my sweet Alice. Only if you ask the questions will you ever find the answers."

That's all she had been doing when she had dissembled Jack's speakers—asking questions and looking for answers. It seemed the only thing she managed to find was trouble though.

And now, she was caught in this awful nightmare. Her parents were gone. She was stuck with a guardian who obviously didn't want her or her siblings, and her little brother—her sweet, loving, happy-go-lucky brother—was not only stuck in a wheelchair because of some rare, debilitating disease but was living on borrowed time.

Life wasn't fair.

"Ms. Johansson?" Mr. Osterberg's nasal address shook Alice from her reverie.

She hurriedly dragged her sleeve across her face to wipe away the angry tears that had started to fall. "Yes, Mr. Osterberg?"

The science teacher's bushy mustache twitched under his pointed nose. His eyes narrowed with concern. "Are you okay?"

Osterberg blinked in confusion, looking so much like one of the classroom lab mice searching blindly for the cheese at the end of the maze.

No, Alice considered. *I am so not okay.*

She sniffed. "Um, no, Mr. Osterberg. Can I go to the bathroom?"

Osterberg tugged at his bowtie. "Certainly. Go right ahead. Take the hall pass."

He gestured toward the plastic tag, hooked by a key ring that hung by the door.

Alice pushed away from her desk, grabbing her satchel on the way out, snatched the pass off the hook, and barreled through the door into the empty hallway.

*****

She didn't go to the bathroom. Instead, Alice headed straight for the library. Alice had always found comfort in libraries. Some had totally succumbed to the digital modern world with their integrated workstations and disposable tablets. But not this one. Well, not completely, anyway. The pervading scents of woody paper, slightly sweet, and the damp, musty undertones of decay reminded her of the forest near their Switzerland home–a place where pine needles and leaves crunched underfoot as the family went for long strolls along the trail to the nearby lake. The rich, earthy leather of old book bindings stirred up scents of juniper and birch tar, an almost smoky smell that evoked memories of her father's study.

But perhaps the thing she loved most about libraries was answers. Libraries were like walking into a neatly ordered brain. All the facts you could ever hope to glean, catalogued and organized in nice, neat rows. You just went to the proper section and plucked the knowledge you sought right off the shelf or workstation.

Alice sought answers. Answers that offered some explanation as to why Thom-Thom seemingly defied the laws of gravity and could mysteriously float. Answers to why her father had sent the ferret halfway across the world to Jack. Surely such an accomplished scientist as her father would have wanted to explore the implications of the ferret's altered state on his own. Given her own inquisitive nature, she could not fathom that her father's curiosity had not prompted him to investigate.

Then again, maybe he did.

The librarian, a tall, skinny woman with a long beaky nose and hair pulled back in a painfully severe bun, looked up over her wire-rimmed spectacle at the sudden commotion as Alice burst into the room. The heavy wooden doors swung in gradually diminishing arcs over the worn green carpet, fat brass hinges squeaking loudly until they finally came to a rest, and silence settled over the room once more.

Alice stood frozen, knees slightly pulled together as she gripped her book-sack strap tightly in both hands. A few clusters of students, open research materials spread out on the wooden tables before them, stared at her sudden intrusion on their intellectual pursuits. Alice shifted the weight of her backpack to the opposite shoulder.

"Sorry." Her voice, though barely above a whisper, echoed in the quiet library.

The librarian scowled, annoyed wrinkles deepening in the wide expanse of her bare forehead. She brought a bony finger to her dry, lined lips. "Shhhh."

Alice bowed her head in shame.

"Do you have a hall pass?" the librarian whispered harshly as if speaking at full vocal volume was a felony.

Alice nodded and produced the labeled pass. The librarian sneered down the length of her long nose and gave a dismissive "humph." She directed Alice toward one of the tables. Alice gave a polite nod and slinked to her seat.

Once seated, Alice slipped her laptop from her backpack and set it on the table. She powered it up and logged on to the internet. She typed in her father's name.

"Oliver Johansson," she murmured out loud as she typed and quickly looked up to see if the librarian had heard her. The librarian busied herself checking in returned books, scanning each one's barcode into the system.

The search engine rapidly generated a list of scholarly journal articles her father had published.

Functional Integration in Quantum Physics.

Unified Mathematical Treatment to Address Statistical Anomalies in Quantum Measurements.

Heady material beyond even Alice's remarkable IQ.

The search also threw up a newspaper article from *Tages-Anzeiger*, one of Switzerland's largest print news outlets.

"CERN SCIENTISTS AMONG VICTIMS OF FREAK AIRLINE CRASH."

Alice's heart skipped a beat. She maneuvered her finger on the touchpad of her laptop, positioning her finger over the link to the article. Her finger hovered. She took a deep breath, bit her lower lip, and clicked.

GENEVA, Switzerland – An Styrfjäder Air jet carrying 152 people, including two prominent scientists from the CERN Hadron Collider staff, lost contact with air traffic control just a few short minutes after departure from Geneva on an international flight to Paris on Friday when it was purportedly struck by lightning and standard communications were disrupted. After undisclosed malfunctions prompted the crew to send a distress call prior to landing at Charles de Gaulle Airport, the pilot was forced to attempt an emergency landing in a potato field outside the city. Automatic systems failures resulted in the plane coming down hard, forcing debris into the engine. According to official reports, the engine then caught fire and caused the plane to explode, killing all 152 passengers and crew on board. Drs. Oliver and Elsa Johansson, noted quantum physicists at the nearby CERN facility, were among the deceased. Sources at the CERN facility indicated the Johanssons' travels had nothing to do with CERN operations but were for "personal reasons" requested just days before the flight by Dr. Oliver Johansson and, curiously, just days before another scheduled ALPHA-g test to study antigravity at the collider facility. The couple leaves behind five children. An evaluation of the plane's recorded flight data and cockpit conversations by investigators has not been able to determine what bearing, if any, the lightning strike had on the incident.

Alice felt a harsh tug at her gut as she read the events leading up to her parents' deaths. She could almost imagine the heat of the flames singeing their skin and clothing as the plane exploded around them. But what disturbed Alice more than the horrible vision of her parents' plane bursting into flames was why they were even on it in the first place.

Alice had never known there was a scheduled antigravity test at CERN around the time her parents died. It was not something her father would miss—not unless he had good reason.

Like knowing that he possessed something that would render the current CERN testing obsolete.

Alice looked up.

Thom-Thom.

What, or who was in Paris? Alice no longer harbored any belief her parents had just been "going on vacation."

"Don't ever be afraid to ask questions, my sweet Alice. Only if you ask the questions will you ever find the answers." She heard her father's voice echo in her memory. She definitely had questions. She looked back at the grim news article on her screen and shivered.

Yeah, Vati, but curiosity sure didn't work too well for the cat, did it?

CHAPTER 22

StarCall Labs
Locke

"Is that a cat?" Locke's features pulled back in disgust. "What? Is that your way of calling me a pussy, Valeni?"

A puzzled look flitted across Valeni's face as he first looked at Locke and then at the slightly feline features of the animal frozen in his beefy grip. He chuckled broadly. "I ain't insinuating nothing, but you go ahead and infer all you want, Locke."

"Careful, Valeni. It's ill-advised to exhaust one's entire vocabulary in a single sentence."

The derisive comment halted Valeni's laugh track in an instant. "That ain't funny, Locke."

Locke drummed the table. "Oh, I don't know. I found it rather amusing if I do say so myself."

Valeni took a heated step forward. "Yeah? Well, we'll see who's got the last laugh when you see what I brought to the table."

Locke's eyebrows lifted in unison. "Roadkill?"

A ripple of laughter undulated through the room. Even Sarah tittered for a second before she brought a manicured hand over her red mouth. The red deepening in Valeni's cheeks almost matched the shade.

"No, smartass." He waggled his free hand at Binderkampf and Vashtin. "I brought you an answer that all your little Einsteins couldn't figure out."

The tension in the room hovered, waiting for Valeni's big reveal. Locke grew impatient. "Look, *Peter*, if you hadn't noticed, the grown-ups in the room were in the middle of a big meeting discussing *important* things. So, if you'll take your little pet and let us get back to business, we need to..."

His voice drifted as everyone in the room watched the creature leave Valeni's hand when he loosened his grip, and it floated, bouncing off the ballasts of the fluorescent lights, bobbling uncertainly, then lofting up toward the acoustical ceiling tiles above their heads.

Valeni crossed his arms across his broad chest and grinned.

"To figure out how to make your shit float?"

Most of the jaws in the room fell slack, watching the ferret drift along the ceiling of its own accord. Locke just studied it with keen interest, the dint of a sparkle in his black eyes. Binderkampf took a cautious step forward, placing himself directly under the little furry beast.

"Is it a balloon of some sort?" he asked.

"No, it ain't a balloon. It's a floatin' ferret, genius. Christ! How many box tops did you have to save for that fancy-schmancy degree, huh, Doc?"

Vashtin circled under it, his eyes white and wide against his dark skin. "It's almost as if it's being buoyed atop a gravity hill."

He grabbed a long pointer off the ledge of the whiteboard and poked the animal. As the ferret rolled onto its belly, it started a rapid slide toward the floor.

"It's falling!" Vashtin cried.

"As if into a gravity well," Binderkampf murmured almost

reverently.

The pointer clattered to the floor as Vashtin fumbled to catch the ferret, flipped it back on its back, and watched as it began another steady rise back toward the ceiling, clawed feet first.

Binderkampf turned to Locke, who had not so much as moved a muscle during the entire sequence of events. Emboldened by what they had just witnessed, the battered scientist took a brave step toward the stoic man.

"Mr. Locke, I don't know where this animal comes from, but it seems to prove the theory that Dr. Vashtin and I are suggesting. Somehow, this ferret is generating its own gravity hills and wells, allowing it to manipulate gravitational forces. If we can study it, determine exactly what is generating those gravity-potential fields, we could perhaps replicate it and apply it in our propulsion tech."

He waited for a reaction from Locke. Finally, Locke stood. He strode silently toward the floating animal and stared at it for a moment or two. Without looking away, he addressed Valeni.

"Where did you acquire this item of keen interest, Mr. Valeni?"

Glad to finally be taken seriously, Valeni tugged the lapels of his leather jacket straight. "Let's just say the aforementioned item belonged to an *employee* of mine."

Locke looked dubiously at the stalwart Sal standing rigidly behind Valeni. Valeni followed Locke's gaze and shook his head. "Nah. Not him. Another guy. Name of Harding. Jack Harding. Gave it up to pay for his...company health care."

"And what does this Harding do for you, Mr. Valeni? Works for your 'construction business,' does he?"

"No," Valeni answered. "I told you before. I'm...diversifying. It's like how I got into business with you, Locke."

Locke took a deep, measured breath. He was starting to lose patience with the Italian. "So, this Harding is a businessman, then?"

"Nah. He's some kinda scientist." He pointed to Binderkampf and Vashtin. "Like youse two, but better lookin'. At least until Sal took a crack at him, huh?"

Valeni let out a braying laugh and slapped Sal on the back.

"A scientist, hm?" Locke mused. "Any particular field?"

"I dunno. Some sort of physicist. Used to own that lab out in Palo Alto. You know. The one with the racetrack for molecules?"

"The collider?" Binderkampf ventured.

Valeni nodded. "Yeah. That's the one. Till he jacked things up five ways from Sunday and went nose up. In fact, that's where we had our little, uh, company meeting, and I divested him of this particular...asset. He don't own the lab no more, but him and his marshmallow pal were sure as hell acting like they still owned stock. Caught 'em sneaking around in some secret tunnel system that runs under the joint."

"Was the ferret the only 'stock' you divested them of?" Locke asked.

"No," Valeni answered. He motioned to Sal, who brought over the backpack and drew out Bart's laptop. "They had this too."

Valeni set the laptop on the conference table. "That's a Strontium 5 Power Core."

"Translate," Locke demanded.

Vashtin stepped forward. "It's an incredibly powerful computer, Mr. Locke. You only have a system like this if you're running really brutish software with enhanced visual applications. Granted, it's not going to achieve the 148.6 petaflops of the DOE's Summit system—that's got 2.41 million cores, of course—but this was probably being used to make massive calculations in fractions of seconds."

"Like, say, calculations to ascertain the quantum aspects of gravity and determine the effects of subatomic alterations?" Locke suggested.

Vashtin stared at him and nodded very, very slowly. "If someone had written a program that could make those calculations, yes. This machine would likely be able to run it."

A beat passed. Locke gestured to the closed computer. "Well?"

Vashtin leaped forward and quickly opened it. He booted the machine up. His face fell when he was confronted with Bart's security screen.

Vashtin straightened, tension creeping back into his features as he looked into Locke's stormy eyes. "It's password protected. But even if we bypassed the security, I'm not exactly certain what I'm looking for."

He cringed, almost waiting for Locke to deal a crushing blow. Instead, Locke turned calmly to Valeni.

"Mr. Valeni. You say this Harding is an employee of yours."

Valeni shrugged. "Yeah. Kind of."

"Then I do think you should prepare your company for a hostile takeover."

"Wait. What?" Valeni shook his head.

Locke turned to Sarah. "I think it's high time to retain this Dr. Harding's services, Ms. Copeland, don't you?"

Sarah blinked coquettishly from beneath long lashes. "And what if the usual incentives don't work?"

Locke smiled. "Don't sell yourself short, my dear. You can be extraordinarily convincing when you want to be."

His eyes traveled up and down her lithe body. "Some parts of you more than others."

She smiled coyly. "So, you want me to offer the *full* benefits package then?"

"What I *want* is Jack Harding's tech."

CHAPTER 23

Pulldraw Home
Jack

"I have nothing against you, Jack, hand to God," Myrna Pulldraw kvetched. "But if Bart doesn't start getting out more and stop running the streets with you till all hours of the night, doing heaven knows what, he's never going to find a girl."

She led a sheepish Jack through the house. "Do you even *know* how much Borax I had to throw in the wash to get rid of all that grime he brought home on his clothes last night?"

She threw her hands in the air. They slapped the apron stretched across her wide midsection as they fell. "Last night? What am I talking about? More like this *morning!* Where on God's green earth did you two disappear to in the middle of the night like that?"

She didn't give Jack a chance to even try and respond. "Not that I minded watching the kids. Unlike you two, the five of them are little angels. The twins ate seven *sufganiyot* each and passed right out."

Jack's eyes widened.

Seven?

Usually if he ate even one of the sugary, deep-fried jelly

doughnuts, he'd be in a sugar coma for a week!

"I'm only mentioning it because I'd hate to die without ever becoming a *bubbe*. He's down there."

They reached the basement door.

"I'm really sorry to have kept him out so late, Myrna. It won't happen again."

"And if your word was a bridge, I'd be afraid to cross it. Humph." She folded her arms and waddled off toward the kitchen, where Jack could smell something else baking.

It's a wonder how Bart keeps his svelte form.

The sarcastic thought jogged through Jack's thoughts as he jogged down the steep basement steps. As he came to the foot of the steps, Jack felt he had walked into Supanova Comic Con. A three-foot model of a vintage USS *Enterprise*, comprised entirely of Legos, sat in a strategically lit glass case. He watched, mesmerized, as the beam of light morphed from red to yellow to blue, then dissolved to an eerie green before repeating the sequence. A life-sized cutout of Leonard Nimoy stood next to the case, cardboard hand raised in a Vulcan greeting. The cartoon bubble emanating from his mouth contained Spock's most famous quote: "Live long and prosper."

A low hum caught Jack's attention. His gaze swung to the crossed lightsabers on the wall—one red, one blue—locked, it would seem, in an eternal battle. A series of framed comic books, an *Avengers #4, a Batman #182*, and an *Amazing Spiderman #9*, hung along the pine-paneled walls. That was just the framed stuff. It occurred to him he was staring at a fortune in print.

The room was warrened with stacks of comic books and graphic novels. He picked the top one of the stacks.

Plasma Girl and Her Death Rays of Doom?

The cover art was a sort of Manga-style depicting a very curvy, green Lycra-clad femme fatale in a spread-eagled action pose. What really caught Jack's eye, however, were the two deadly-looking lasers apparently shooting from her rather buxom chest.

Yeah, Myrna. And I'm the reason Bart hasn't found a girl yet.

Jack continued surveying the collectibles when his foot crunched on something. He looked down to see an empty Doritos bag under his foot. He bent to retrieve it.

Well, where there's Doritos, Bart can't be far away.

"Bart?" he called out as he wound his way through the stacks. "Yeah!" Bart called. "Back here!"

"Where?" Jack rounded the corner and stopped.

"Mission control, my friend," Bart declared proudly, hands positioned confidently on his hips and sweat pouring in rivulets down his face. Jack's friend was surrounded by an odd amalgamation of whirring central processing units; a web of colorful, bound wiring stretching crisscross overhead and underfoot; graphics processing units; and a host of various other and sundry equipment Jack couldn't put an identification to.

It's like the Geek Squad puked in here.

He gestured to the vast array of equipment. "Have you been up all night?"

"Who? Me?" Bart stepped forward, knocking into a pyramid of empty energy drink cans. "Okay, yeah. Maybe. Might want to watch your step. Girls' day off and all. Sorry about the temperature. All this equipment generates a ton of heat."

"What is all this?" Jack asked.

"I felt really bad about what happened last night. How's your shoulder, by the way? Anyway, like I said, I felt bad about Valeni taking the furry, you know–" Bart made a funny fang face in a comical imitation of Thom-Thom's countenance. "And while I couldn't really do anything about that, I figured I could at least try to do something about the computer he took. So, I cannibalized my gaming system, took the GPU from it, and I had all these old

CPUs lying around I bought off eBay. By themselves, they're not much to sneeze at, but I figured if I stacked the—"

Jack held up his hands and motioned for Bart to stop. "As much as I appreciate whatever it is you're trying to explain to me, buddy, I had a helluva morning and would appreciate the condensed version."

"Yeah, of course. Sure thing." Bart looked around and surveyed his handiwork. "I am Bart. Hear me ROAR."

Jack shook his head. "Wait. You're telling me that you jerry-rigged a computer system that can run ROAR out of a couple of old office computers and a PlayStation?"

Bart cleared his throat. "An Xbox and some old office computer, thank you very much. I did have to borrow a Lambda deep-learning workstation from my old roommate at Cal Tech. It has four graphic processing units and a generative adversarial network that can handle the 3D holographic output ROAR generates."

Bart scratched the back of his head. "And if he finds out what I did to it, he's gonna want my *Batman #121*."

"That the first issue with Mr. Freeze?"

Bart nodded.

Jack's gaze wandered over the massive thing Bart had built. He ran his hands gently along the sheaths of wires. "Bart, this is incredible. Really, it is. But we don't have the data to input into the program and run simulations. Valeni took it with him when he took the computer. Last night was our last chance, and it was a long shot at best. That's it. We blew it."

The harsh revelation did nothing to wipe the goofy grin off Bart's cherubic face as he slowly shook his head from side to side.

"What?" Jack prodded.

"Remember just before we ran back into the collapsing tunnel? How we thought we heard somebody?"

Jack nodded. "Yeah, probably Valeni and his goon trying the front door."

"And remember how you kept telling me to hurry up and I told you I couldn't rush it because I was saving the data?"

"Yes, Bart. I expect there's a point soon."

"Well, where do you think I was saving it, genius? It was taking so long because I was uploading it to the cloud."

The ramifications of Bart's admission started to hit Jack. "So, you can access it from anywhere. Like your mother's basement."

"Like my mother's basement."

Silence hung between the two men for several moments. Bart placed a hand on Jack's shoulder. "We can use the new subroutine I've written and reverse engineer Thom-Thom's data, then run as many simulations as we want. We can duplicate his antigravity properties with...anything. We would just need—"

Bart's face suddenly fell.

"What?" Jack interjected. "Don't stop! You were on a roll! We would just need access to a collider to replicate the original circumstances...Like at P1AL," Jack groaned.

"Like at P1AL," Bart agreed solemnly.

"I don't need a collider," Jack continued. "What I need is a freaking miracle."

"What you need is a watch!" Myrna called down from the landing. "It's past three thirty! And Bart, don't forget you're driving me to canasta."

"Oh crap!" Jack exclaimed, scrambling up the stairs.

"Don't forget your brisket!" Myrna yelled after him. "I got it wrapped up on the server for you. Pop it in the oven for fifteen minutes at 325."

"Why? What happens at three thirty?" Bart called after him.

"Carpool!"

CHAPTER 24

Pacific Grove Science & Technical Academy
Jack

The rain came down in sheets. The dry landscape of California, so recently susceptible to rampant wildfires, gratefully drank in the torrential downpour. The five dripping children standing on the curb under the teacher's umbrella–not so much.

Jack hadn't felt his wrist-comm vibrate. He had left it in the van while he was down in Bart's basement celebrating their small win and pondering their next hurdle. Truthfully, he was dodging Valeni, should the gangster decide to call. It never even occurred to him that the children might need to reach him.

It should have.

To use one of Mrs. Pulldraw's favorite words, he felt like a total schmuck.

He jumped from the driver's seat into the pouring rain to help the teacher load the kids, including Charlie's wheelchair, into the Electroline. The teacher held the umbrella as Jack operated the chairlift. The water ran in rivulets off the sloping canopy and dripped right into Jack's face. The young teacher was so caught up in her own conversation, she didn't realize she was inadvertently soaking him.

"I'm so sorry we couldn't wait inside, Mr. Harding. The school's having a bit of a pest problem, so we are having it fumigated. Everyone had to be out of the building by three forty-five, or we would have had to reschedule the appointment with the exterminators," she prattled. "We sent it home several times in the parent newsletter."

"He's not our parent," Julia quipped from the back seat, where she tried to towel off with a sweatshirt someone had left in the van.

"Oh!" the teacher exclaimed. "I just assumed—"

"I'm their legal guardian," Jack snapped as he secured the restraining straps for Charlie's wheelchair.

"My goodness! Must be quite a handful for you and your wife."

"I'm not married. Boys! Get in the van. Now!"

The twins, who had been delightedly splashing in puddles on the sidewalk, burst into synchronized pouts and slowly climbed into the van and their respective car seats.

"It's okay, Jack," Charlie offered in his usual cheerful manner. "It's just water. And the human body is made up of almost 60 percent water anyway. Achoo!"

Charlie let loose a powerful sneeze that would have saturated Jack if he wasn't already soaked to the bone. He blinked slowly and mentally counted to ten.

The young woman made another attempt at being friendly. "You know, there are some wonderful parent support groups here at the school—"

Jack cut her off in mid-sentence. "Thank you for waiting with them. We really need to get going."

"Oh. My gracious, yes. I suppose there's homework and baths and dinner—"

Jack's eyes flew wide. Images of full-breasted curves and hip-hugging leggings flashed through his mind.

Dinner!

*****

After the ninety-minute drive home, made oh-so-much worse by the torrential weather, Jack wrangled the kids inside and started to get ready for his date with Tiffany. Jack tossed the twins into the bathtub, tossed the wet clothes into the washer, and tossed the brisket into the oven.

"Fifty minutes and 325 degrees," he mumbled frantically as he set the dial on the oven. "Right!"

He clapped his hands together and ran into the master bedroom to jump in the shower himself. Ten minutes later, he was digging through his closet looking for a shirt. Oscar had been thorough. Every single Oxford Jack pulled from the rack hung thready and bare, devoid of even a single button.

"Son of a bitch!" Jack cursed under his breath. His hand fell across his suit–the one suit he owned–and, coincidentally, the one he had worn to the ROAR demonstration months before. There was a white button-down shirt tucked inside the jacket. Oscar had missed it!

Yes!

Jack rallied and picked out a tie that wasn't too garish. He settled on a subtle blue paisley.

Distinguished, but not stuffy.

"Looks like dancing sperm." The fashion assessment came from Julia, who leaned against the doorjamb. Her hair was still wet, and it stuck to her "Save the Whales" T-shirt.

Jack looked down at his tie. "You think so?"

Julia gave him a baleful stare. "So, is that what this thing is tonight? Some kind of hookup?"

"No," Jack replied indignantly. "It's just dinner."

"Yeah. About that. I think eating meat in general should be punishable by law, but what you've done to that brisket is absolutely criminal."

"Wait. What?" He sniffed the air. There was the distinct scent of burning food. "The brisket!"

Jack flew to the kitchen, where Lucas wore a costume fireman's hat and held the spray nozzle from the sink toward the open oven, which billowed black plumes of smoke.

Jack held out his hands. "Lucas, wait! No!"

He jumped in between Lucas and the oven and was rewarded with a solid blast of cold water as Oscar teetered on a barstool behind his twin and wrenched the faucet on full blast. Alice stood next to the oven, waving a dishrag to fan the smoke.

"I think you were only supposed to have this on for fifteen minutes, Jack," she coughed. "You had it on fifty."

He dove toward the sink and turned off the faucet. Then he turned, dripping, to look at the charcoal briquette sitting on the rack.

"Aw, come on," he groaned.

"Jack," Charlie called. "Do we have an extra blanket? I don't feel so good."

Jack grabbed some potholders and pulled the brisket out of the oven. "I think there's one in the hall closet."

"I'll get it for you, Charlie," Julia muttered and followed her brother from the kitchen. "Jack's busy having a midlife crisis. Come on, Tweedledee and Tweedledum."

She pushed the twins out in front of her and steered them toward their bedroom.

"Great! What am I supposed to serve now?" Jack groaned, surveying the wrecked dinner.

"Maybe you should try seafood," Alice suggested, snickering.

"You could tell her you caught it yourself. It would explain why you look half drowned, at least."

Jack looked down at what he was wearing. The suit and his one good shirt were drenched. He looked at the clock. Six forty-five.

Trinity would be here in fifteen minutes.

Jack leaned down and grabbed Alice gently by the wrists. "Look, Alice. I know you're mad at me right now and, honestly, you probably have every right to be. It's just, well, try to understand. I'm a theoretical physicist. Everything I know has a formula. Parenting? Parenting doesn't. It has a million different variables, and it doesn't follow any set of ordered rules. And that just confuses the hell out of me. I promise, I'll try harder to be better, but tonight I *really* need your help."

Alice looked him straight in the eye. "You don't deserve it."

"I know. I know. I don't. But the woman coming to the house tonight? She's a reporter. Now, I'm not 100 percent certain, but I think I—well, Uncle Bart and I—I think we figured out what's making Thom-Thom float."

Alice's eyes widened to saucers. "Wait! You found out?"

Jack nodded. "What's more, I think we may have found a way to make the same phenomenon occur in other objects."

Alice jumped excitedly. "That's—that's amazing!"

"It is amazing, but it's also dangerous."

Alice's sudden exuberance clouded. "Dangerous? How?"

"A lot of people would love to get their hands on this kind of scientific breakthrough. People who probably aren't afraid of doing terrible things." Jack's shoulder twinged, and he thought about Valeni and his goon.

Alice bit her lower lip. Her gaze fell down and to the right as if she were considering something. She looked back at Jack.

"So, what does this reporter have to do with it?" she asked.

"Honestly, I like her."

"Is she pretty?"

"Well, yes, but that's not the only reason. I think she might be able to help me keep things safe."

Alice cocked her head. "Like an insurance policy?"

"In a way. I'm thinking of telling her a little about what we've discovered. She knows people. I'm hoping maybe she can put me in touch with someone who might be able to help me get the lab back so we can make sure our theory holds water. And, if something happens to me–"

"What? What's going to happen to you? Does this have something to do with all the cuts and bruises you have? Is somebody after you, Jack? Maybe those guys you mentioned before? The ones you thought had the Reuben sandwich?"

"Shhh," he whispered, trying to calm her. "Don't worry. Everything's going to be fine. In fact, if I can pull this off, everything's going to be great. But right now, I'd settle if just tonight went great. So, will you help me?"

Alice considered. "Fine. What do you need me to do?"

Jack stood. "I need to go change. Again. Can you find something I can pass off as dinner?"

"Like what?" Alice asked.

"How about something Italian?" he suggested.

Alice gestured to the pantry. "I think there's some pasta."

"That's great! If you can handle that, I'm going to go ahead and get changed. Into what, I have no idea." He started down the hall but turned after a few feet. "Oh, hey, and Alice?"

"Yeah?"

"About the speakers. I'm sorry I yelled at you."

"Thanks, Jack." She offered a soft smile as he turned and headed down the hall once again. Then she spun on her heel and strode toward the pantry. She opened the door and stood there with her hands on her hips. Alice put a thoughtful index finger to her lips.

"Something Italian."

CHAPTER 25

Harding Estate
Jack

"Spaghetti rings and mini meatballs?" Trinity arched a perfectly shaped eyebrow over her bowl. She pushed one of the tiny meatballs with her spoon.

"Come on," Jack joked. "A conveniently shaped pasta in a robust tomato and cheese sauce. What's not to love?"

Trinity's laugh was genuine. "It's fine, really. Brings back memories of my college days. I think I lived on Chef Boyardee and ramen noodles for most of my undergrad."

Her lighthearted attitude dissolved some of Jack's stress. Granted, this wasn't exactly what he had in mind when he'd suggested Italian to Alice.

But beggars can't be choosers.

A thought which brought him around to part of the reason for asking Trinity here tonight. It wasn't exactly begging, but his back was up against the wall. He chased a lone meatball around his bowl with his spoon.

"So, um, Trinity," he began. "I wanted to tell you how much I appreciated the belief you expressed in my ROAR program."

Trinity wiped a tomato sauce smile from her mouth with a

napkin before she spoke. "It's a solid concept. One I don't feel got a fair shake at the demonstration."

"Believe me," Jack agreed. "You're preaching to the choir."

He considered his next words. "What if I were to tell you that my software engineer and I have tweaked it a little since that fiasco and discovered that the program has much more far-reaching implications than we originally intended?"

Trinity crossed her long legs and leaned forward, her reporter's interest visibly piqued. "Like how far-reaching?"

"Let's just say that what we believe we've discovered might boldly take us where we've never gone before."

Puzzlement clouded Trinity's face. Suddenly, realization flooded her features and her eyes grew wide. She gripped both sides of the dining room table. "You've cracked the Mars puzzle?"

"Yes," Jack replied, a twinkle in his eye. He leaned back in his chair and sighed. The twinkle dissipated. "At least, I think we have. Problem is we need to run more testing. Testing which requires collider access. Something I regrettably no longer have."

"Jesus, that would be a hell of a story." Her eyes gleamed. "It's practically got Pulitzer written all over it."

"And I would love nothing more than to see your name on that byline," Jack agreed excitedly. "But it's going to cost money."

"So, what are you going to do?" Trinity asked.

"I have no idea." A long moment of silence hung between them. "There's another problem too."

"What's that?" Trinity asked.

"Someone else knows what I've discovered."

"Who?"

Jack unconsciously touched his shoulder. "Someone with less than altruistic intentions. What's worse, they've stolen some of our research."

"So, why don't you report it to the police?" Trinity urged.

Jack shook his head vigorously. "These aren't the kind of people you cross. Not unless you've got a hell of an ace up your sleeve. No. The only solution I see to getting out from under all this mess is to beat them to the punch."

"You're going to try and get to Mars."

Jack nodded. "I was hoping, maybe with your connections, you might know someone who can help me get back into the P1AL labs."

Trinity shook her head slowly. "Jack, I'm just a science correspondent. I don't have any clout with anyone important. And definitely not anyone with a padded bank account."

"There's no one? Not even Travis Locke? You did say he liked you."

"Travis Locke?" Trinity's eyes narrowed. Her tone took on a sudden sharp edge. "What I said was he accosted me in a coat closet."

She pushed away from the table and stood. "Is that why you asked me here? To try and use me as leverage to get to Locke's money?"

Jack tried to push back from the table too, but the legs of the chair caught in the area rug. He braced his hands against the table, gave a hearty shove, and tumbled ass over elbows. He scrambled to put himself to rights. "No, no, no. Christ, this is going so wrong!"

"You bet your ass it is," Trinity snapped. "You know, back at the bar, when I suggested you get into the Mars race, it was so you could beat Locke. Not jump into bed with him."

Hurt pulled her mouth into a frown. "You may be willing to prostitute yourself in the name of science, Jack, but you do not get to use me like that."

The doorbell sounded through the house.

Jack threw a sudden nervous glance toward the front door. Trinity followed his gaze.

"Are you expecting someone?" she asked.

Jack shook his head slowly. "No."

Jack took several measured steps toward Trinity and pulled her slowly behind him.

Trinity tugged herself loose from his grip. "Hey! What are you doing? Let go of me!"

"Shh!" Jack ordered, his tone tight and rigid.

"Don't you shush me!" Trinity grumbled. "What's going on?"

Jack turned to look at her, his gaze cold and hard. "Remember those not-so-nice people I mentioned before?"

Trinity tensed. "Wait. You think that's them?"

Jack nodded.

"What do we do?" she whispered, her long fingers gripping his shoulder.

"Go grab the kids. They're all down the hall there. Bring them all into Charlie's room—that's the one at the end of the hall—and lock the door. No matter what you hear, don't come out, okay?"

"You need to call the police, Jack," she whispered tersely.

"No!" Jack interjected. "No police. That will just make things worse. I'll take care of this. Just go."

Trinity stared at him, doubt flooding her face, but she eventually nodded and slipped off down the hall. Jack took a deep, steadying breath. It had to be Valeni at the door. The gangster probably couldn't get past Bart's computer security and, now, he was here to take his frustrations out on Jack. Jack set his jaw.

Fine, then. If this is the way you want to play it, so be it.

Jack grabbed an umbrella from the hall stand and lofted it above his head for ready use. He reached out for the door handle, slowly turned the knob, and threw open the door.

"All right, bring it!" he bellowed.

Sarah Copeland stood shapely in a clingy red dress, holding a bottle of Dom Perignon. She blinked in mild surprise at the sight of Jack brandishing a ladybug umbrella.

"Well," she replied nonchalantly. "I brought Dom. Does that work?"

*****

Jack quickly dropped the would-be weapon. "Wow, um, I'm so sorry, Ms.—"

Sarah reached out a manicured hand. "Copeland. Sarah Copeland. I am lead counsel for Locke Industries. Mr. Locke has sent me to request a meeting."

"He couldn't have called?"

Sarah let out a coy chuckle. "He felt this would be more… personal." Her long lashes fluttered. "May I come in?"

Jack stood transfixed for a moment, then finally looked awkwardly over his shoulder toward the kids' rooms. "Yeah, now's not a really good time."

Sarah pulled up short. The look on her face told Jack she was not accustomed to hearing the word no.

"Really?"

"Yes. You see, I actually have company," Jack began. He was a physicist, not a chemist. But he definitely knew that the combination of these two women would be combustible.

"No matter." Sarah placed the champagne in Jack's hands. "At least this won't go to waste."

She looked over Jack's shoulder to see Trinity peeking from the half-open door to Charlie's room. In fact, Trinity wasn't the only one peeking. It looked like a mismatched totem pole as Lucas and Oscar peered out from the bottom, topped by Alice and Julia just below Trinity.

"Well," Sarah murmured seductively as she leaned in and whispered in Jack's ear. "When you're done playing house and are ready to discuss business, Mr. Locke will be waiting for you. Tomorrow morning. 9 a.m. sharp. His office."

She slipped a business card with the address of Locke's offices on it and planted a siren-red kiss on Jack's cheek before turning on a five-inch stiletto and walking back to her jet-black BMW X6 M G-Power Typhoon Wide Body. Jack remained mesmerized as he watched her hips sashay in rhythm before she slipped into her vehicle, pulling her long legs in after her. It wasn't until she was well down the winding driveway that he noticed Trinity had slipped up behind him. She looked at the bright red lip marks on his face.

"Wow. She really beat you up, huh?" The sarcasm dripped. "It's a wonder you survived."

Jack turned to Trinity. "She wasn't who I was expecting."

"I'll just bet," Trinity said.

"What was that about, Jack?" Alice asked as all the kids, save Charlie, trickled into the living room.

"Yes, Jack," Trinity agreed. "What was that about?"

"A–job offer, I think," Jack said.

"That's great, Jack!" Alice congratulated.

Trinity's gaze furrowed. "What kind of job offer comes with champagne and suicide heels?"

Jack rubbed the back of his neck. "She was an attorney. The attorney for, uh, Travis Locke."

Trinity leaped forward. "Locke! Oh, tell me you're not considering it, Jack."

"What else can I do?'

"Gee, I don't know. Say no?"

"I don't know that I have that luxury. I should at least hear what the man has to say," Jack offered.

"The 'man' is a slime. If you're even thinking of going into business with him, then you're not the man I thought you were," Trinity responded.

"A man with five kids and a massive mountain of debt and no way to get out from under?"

"You were a scientist. You saw a problem, and you asked all the right questions until you came up with a solution that made something incredible." Trinity grabbed her bag then turned on her heel to look at Jack one last time. "That was the man I liked. Let me know when he decides to show up."

With that, Trinity stormed from the house. Jack sighed.

"Jack?" Oscar's small voice called from the dining room table.

"What, Oscar?" Jack sighed.

"Does this mean the mad lady's not gonna eat her S'ghettiOs?"

CHAPTER 26

Harding Estate
Jack

"Where in the hell is my dress shirt!" Jack bellowed as he dug through the hamper, tossing laundry every which way. He let out an exasperated groan and stalked toward the kitchen, where he slapped peanut butter and jelly on slices of bread and mushed them together in frustration.

He could not be late for this meeting!

Things wouldn't have been so bad if the meeting took place at Locke Industries' main offices right here in Palo Alto, but Locke wanted to meet at his San Francisco office. That meant an extra forty minutes on the 101–and that was on a good day.

Jack wasn't certain if it was the frustration of trying to get five children ready for school that had him so on edge or the wagging finger of his own conscience. He would have to have been an idiot to have missed the hurt in Trinity's eyes when he had suggested she use her influence to get him a meeting with Locke.

Influence? Right. He'd practically been willing to pimp her out.

Just call me Huggy Bear.

The concept left him feeling a bit queasy. Even when Sarah Copeland had shown up on his doorstep, absolving Trinity of any involvement whatsoever, Jack knew in his gut he should have said no.

But he didn't.

And he didn't have time to berate himself for it right now either. "Dammit! Has anyone seen my last decent dress shirt?"

"I put it in the wash, Jack," Charlie sniffled as he steered his wheelchair into the room. "You're so busy; I thought I would help. The dryer cycle just finished, I think."

"Thank you, Charlie. Finally, something's gone right!"

"Jack," Alice tapped Jack's arm. "I need to talk to you about something."

Jack waved her off. "Um, not now, Alice, okay? I'm already late. Can we do this another time?"

Alice shook her head. "But this is important. It's about my parents."

Jack made a beeline for the laundry room, Alice scrambling along behind him. "What about them, Alice?"

"About the day they died."

Jack stopped and turned to face her. He took her small hands in his. "Look, kiddo. I know you miss them. I miss them too. But I really cannot miss this appointment this morning. This could be my one shot at getting back into the **P1AL** labs and replicating the same phenomenon that occurred with Thom-Thom."

"But that's kind of what I want to talk to you about, Jack. I read an article. About the plane crash. Do you know why my father was going to Paris that day?"

"I dunno, kid. I think it was a vacation, wasn't it?" Jack was hard-pressed to keep the exasperation from seeping into his voice.

Alice shook her head. "No way. Not when they were getting

ready to run an important test at CERN. My father wouldn't have missed that. Not unless it was for something really important. I think maybe it had something to do with Thom-Thom. I was thinking. I remember he used to keep journals. He was always scribbling in them. Maybe he wrote something down about it. When they sent you all his stuff, did you see anything like that?"

"I don't know. Yes, I think maybe there were a few boxes with journals in them, but I don't have time to look for them now. I'll try to go dig down in the basement tonight, okay? But right now I really need to get to that appointment."

Jack popped the dryer door open and rummaged through the freshly laundered clothes—superhero underwear, a red sock, assorted pajamas…wait. A red sock?

Oh crap!

Jack hurriedly dug through the rest of the clothing in the dryer, searching for his white dress shirt. What he found was his *pink* dress shirt. The red dye of the sock had insidiously leached into the warp and woof of his white shirt, turning it a pleasantly brilliant shade of bubblegum pink.

"Son of a bitch!" The boom of Jack's voice echoed throughout the manor, stopping each of the Johansson children in their tracks. Charlie's eyes widened at the sight of his error.

"I'm so sorry, Jack. I'm so, so sorry. I only wanted to help."

"You only wanted to help? Well, that's just great. And I only wanted to make a damn difference in this world, but ever since being saddled with the five of you, the only difference I've made is to the balance in my checkbook—and it's all negative! Just—just get in the van."

The five children stared at him slack-jawed. Julia nodded to Charlie. "It's okay, Charlie. Don't worry about it. Let's just get to school, huh?"

She guided her younger brother outside. The twins shuffled

186

off quietly behind them.

Alice stared balefully at Jack. "Yeah. If you were going to try and be better, Jack, that wasn't it."

She hefted her satchel over her shoulder and walked outside.

Jack stared after them, then looked down at his pink shirt that hung like a limp piece of chewed gum.

CHAPTER 27

Locke Industries, San Francisco
Locke

The Locke Industries' executive tower jutted above the San Francisco skyline like a shard of dangerous glass. Its jutting edges stood harshly stark against the gingerbread feel of the Ghirardelli factory and the art deco design of nearby Coit Tower in Telegraph Hill. Locke's interest wasn't trained on either of these two iconic San Francisco landmarks, however, though the view from the fiftieth floor afforded him a panoramic view of the entire city.

No. His focus settled on another historical landmark, albeit one with a much darker past.

Alcatraz.

Over the years, a host of notorious men had passed through the iron cells of the federal penitentiary—men like Al Capone, Robert Stroud, also known as the Birdman of Alcatraz and perhaps one of the most violent inmates on the island, and Alvin Karpis, public enemy number one and member of the infamous Barker Gang.

A wry smile tugged at Locke's mouth as he thought about the Barkers. Ma Barker was rumored to have been the criminal mastermind behind the wave of crimes committed by the gang—including bloody bank robberies, kidnapping for ransom, and hijacked mail deliveries.

Truth of the matter was, Locke thought, as admitted by a contemporary gang member, Ma Barker "couldn't plan breakfast." Conspiracy theory held that the great J. Edgar Hoover himself circulated the rumor to justify the FBI's hand in the sixty-two-year-old woman's death.

Locke chuckled. Apparently, evil wasn't just reserved for the rank and file of gangsters and lowlifes.

He was in good company.

Locke pressed a long, manicured finger on the intercom. "Has Mr. Harding arrived yet, Connie?"

The receptionist's voice came over the speaker crisply and efficiently. "Not as of yet, Mr. Locke."

"Hm," Locke tilted his wrist to check the time. A scowl twisted his face into a disgruntled grimace. Locke did not like to be kept waiting. "Ms. Copeland has likely just arrived. Please give her the latest reports from Dr. Binderkampf to bring me. I'll also take a double espresso."

"Right away, Mr. Locke."

Within moments, Sarah strode briskly into the room, balancing a fine china cup on a saucer in one hand and leveraging a copious stack of computer readouts and lab results in the other arm. She carefully laid both on the desk before Locke. The tall, leggy lawyer momentarily distracted Locke from his building anger.

"You're slipping, Ms. Copeland."

Sarah wheeled on her heel, her blonde tresses whipping across her face with the force. "Pardon me?"

Locke began casually thumbing through the paperwork. "It's just, normally I would have expected any man to have rushed to attend a meeting at your invitation."

Locke cast a pointed glance at his expensive watch.

"Doesn't appear that Mr. Harding is in all that much of a rush to be here, now, does it? Perhaps he found something more—" Locke's eyes traveled the length of Sarah's lithe body, "interesting."

Sarah planted both palms flat on Locke's desk. Her cold blue eyes bored into Locke's own black. "Don't worry. He'll be here."

Locke stared back coolly. "You'd better hope so."

*****

What the hell else could possibly go wrong!

Jack should have known better than to ask that question.

Of course he would get stuck behind a puttering, rusted-out pickup coughing noxious black exhaust fumes. And, of course, the electric motor on the driver's side window would choose that precise moment to cease working. And, of course, the morning could not have been complete without the pickup hitting a pothole and bouncing the truck bed so hard a box of roofing nails launched out onto the highway, several lodging themselves in the tread and sidewall of Jack's radials and grinding his harried morning commute to a decided halt.

Not friggin' now! Not today!

"Son of a bitch!" Jack exploded for the fifty-seventh time. Mid-century poly-resin spoked tires couldn't go flat, but they certainly could shred. He slammed a well-placed kick into the ruined tire of the van. A galaxy of stars exploded before his eyes as the pain radiated through his foot and up into the pain receptors of his brain. Angry car bleeps screamed past him as he instinctively grabbed for his foot and hopped on the shoulder of the 101 like a mad imp.

"Come on, man," he finally admonished himself. "You've got a 142 IQ. You can figure out how to get yourself to a simple business meeting!"

Once the pain had subsided from his ill-advised assault on the disabled vehicle, Jack tugged at his suit and smoothed the pink wrinkles of his shirt. He tapped his wrist-comm and spoke in a few commands. Then he closed his eyes and leaned against the van. He took a deep breath and waited.

His eyes fluttered open about fifteen minutes later when tires crunched on the loose gravel.

"Somebody call for an Uber?" He heard a familiar voice call. His eyes opened wide.

"Bradley?" Jack exclaimed with surprise as he leaned down to look into the window of the Honda Civic that had pulled up behind the disabled van.

"Jack? Is that you? Oh my goodness. I thought the van looked familiar."

"You're working as an Uber driver now?" Jack asked, incredulity sliding into his voice.

"Ahem," Bradley cleared his throat. "I did say I was making the jump to the corporate sector. Uber *is* a Fortune 500 company, you know. What did you do to my ElectroVan?"

"I didn't do anything to the van!" Jack moaned. "But it's left me stranded, and I need a ride to a meeting that I'm already late for. How fast can you get me to San Francisco?"

Bradley's voice took a serious tone. "Get in."

Jack clambered into the car and merged into traffic. Bradley adjusted the rear-view mirror and met Jack's gaze. "Not that I'm judging, Jack, but what's with the pink shirt?"

Jack looked ruefully down at his stained button-down. "Yeah, uh, Charlie tried to help out with the laundry."

"Oh, how are the kids? I already miss them so much. And

how is Charlie? I hope you've been keeping an eye on him. You know how dangerous even a low-grade fever can have on his condition."

"The kids are great," Jack mumbled, stealing glances as his watch. "Charlie too."

Bradley frowned. "Tell me you have not forgotten his doctor's appointment on Wednesday."

"No," Jack muttered. "I haven't forgotten, but if I don't get to this meeting soon, I won't have the cash to get the van fixed to get him there, so can you put some lead in it?"

"Yes, sir," Bradley replied.

As they pulled up to Locke Industries, Jack practically vaulted from the car. He skidded to a sudden stop and turned back to Bradley. "I know this is a big ask, but can you wait here for me?"

Bradley shook his head. "Jack, Jack, Jack. How are you ever going to survive without me?"

Jack grinned wryly. "I probably won't."

"Fine. For old times' sake. I'll wait over there."

Jack smiled gratefully and tapped the roof of the car before he turned toward the sleek office building and headed for the glass doors.

Once inside, something gnawed at his gut, a general feeling of unease which Jack attributed to being completely unprepared for this meeting.

With a final ding, the sleek silver doors opened onto a virginal white expanse of carpet. Jack took one step out and was greeted by the svelte Sarah Copeland.

"Well, well, well, Mr. Harding. I was starting to worry. You were beginning to make me look bad."

"I am so, so sorry," Jack gushed. "My van got a flat. The kids were an absolute handful. I would never do anything intentionally to make you look bad."

Sarah slithered to Jack's side. She drew a manicured finger down his cheek and pursed her lips. "Don't worry. Like Mae West said, when I'm good, I'm very good, but when I'm bad, I'm even better."

She leaned in to plant a kiss on Jack's cheek, but a voice interrupted her motion.

"Sarah, Sarah, Sarah." Locke's bass rumbled behind the lawyer. "There will be plenty of time for small talk later. Right now, Dr. Harding is here to discuss business. Isn't that right, Jack?"

Jack smiled broadly and stepped forward. He held an outstretched hand toward Locke and allowed it to fall awkwardly limp when Locke refused to take it. Locke surveyed Jack from head to toe, taking in the cheap suit and his shirt's alarming shade of pink. Jack followed Locke's gaze and looked up sheepishly.

"Yes. About that. Little bit of a mixup with the laundry this morning," Jack offered by way of an explanation. Locke waved a hand nonchalantly. "Silly me. I took quantum physics. Probably should have stuck to organic chemistry."

"Well, fortunately, I'm not interested in whether you separate your whites from your darks. What I am interested in is," Locke lowered a dark glare toward Jack, "how can this…thing get me to Mars?"

He turned, holding Thom-Thom aloft.

Alarmed at Locke's possession of his stolen ferret, Jack leaped forward. "Where did you get that!"

Two black-suited security guards seemed to materialize out of nowhere and gripped Jack by the arms. He might have struggled a bit more, but he noticed a very serious Sig Sauer peeking from the gap under one man's jacket lapel.

"Now, now, now, Mr. Harding. You seem to be confused. I am the one asking the questions here."

Locke passed the ferret to Sarah. He slipped a slim gold cigarette case from his pocket and pulled a Sobrani from inside. Locke noticed the odd, off-kilter glance Jack gave him. He smiled.

"One of the advantages of having as much money as God," he brought his lighter to the end of the cigarette and coaxed an orange glow from its tip. He clicked the lighter closed and pulled a long drag on the cigarette. "No one tells God where he can and cannot smoke."

He exhaled a large cloud of blue-gray smoke into Jack's face. Jack exploded in an uncontrollable coughing fit. Still, Locke's guards held him fast.

"I thought this was a legitimate business meeting, but you're in bed with Valeni," Jack growled, gritting his teeth.

Locke let out a genuine belly laugh. "In bed with Valeni? My dear Dr. Harding, my dealings with Mr. Valeni are simply a means to an end. And when he ceases to prove useful, believe me, I mean to end it. The true question is, will you prove to be useful in my endeavors to launch a successful manned Mars mission?"

Locke looked at Thom-Thom and back at Jack. "Like what can you tell me about this little fellow, hm?"

"It doesn't belong to you," Jack spat.

"Oh, let's not quibble about the finer points of ownership, shall we? Possession is nine-tenths and all that. Anyway, as I understand it, you weren't at all concerned with rights of ownership when you broke into your old laboratory the other night. I have to ask myself, what could be so critically important that a man, a family man as I'm to understand it, would risk being jailed by trespassing in a facility he no longer owns?"

Jack opened his mouth to speak but thought better of it and tightly pinched his lips.

"I'd venture to say it had something to with this…creature."

Locke took the ferret back and strode toward the panoramic

window. He looked out toward Alcatraz. "It's amazing what you can see when you're this high up."

He motioned to his guards, who brought Jack closer to the window. Jack looked away, crushing his eyes shut.

Locke nodded. "It can be a little dizzying, I know, but I suppose when you can fly, you've nothing to fear."

He let Thom-Thom go. The ferret floated obligingly to the ceiling.

Locke's eyes narrowed. "But then, I don't suppose you fly, now do you?"

The security guard on Jack's left rammed Jack's face into the wall of glass.

Locke leaned in remarkably close to Jack's face, so close Jack could taste the businessman's expensive cigarette. "But you can see clearly up here. Can't you, Mr. Harding?"

Locke slid around to whisper in Jack's other ear. "You can clearly see the wisdom in joining my team."

Jack struggled against the guard's tight grip, but the man held him fast.

"The only thing I can clearly see is you're a lunatic," Jack offered.

Locke's upper lip stiffened, but only for a millisecond. He made a nearly imperceptible gesture. The security let Jack go. Jack quickly backed away several feet.

Locke smiled serenely. "Mr. Harding, I apologize. We seem to have gotten off on the wrong foot here."

"You can say that again," Jack agreed.

Locke leaned against his desk, long legs crossed in front of him. "Please forgive me. It's just that I'm, well, rather passionate about this particular project."

Jack rubbed his arm where the guard had grabbed him. "Yeah? And what project is that, Mr. Locke?"

"Mars, Jack. Yes, I am passionate about being the first to reach Mars, and sometimes that passion goads me into being a bit forceful. But it's going to take force to propel a manned ship all the way to the red planet. I have a ship. But I don't yet have an adequate propulsion system."

Locke stood and took a step toward Jack. "That, Mr. Harding, is where I believe you and your furry little friend come in."

Jack cast one wary eye toward Thom-Thom, bobbing on the ceiling. "I don't have any idea what you're talking about."

Locke clucked his tongue. "Please, Jack. I don't appreciate playing hard to get. Not in my women and definitely not with potential business partners."

Jack's wrist-comm vibrated, but he kept his attention riveted on Locke. "You manhandle all your potential partners?"

Jack slid a sideways glance toward Sarah, who cast her eyes downward.

"As I said, sometimes my passions get the better of me," Locke continued. "But the stakes are astronomical. Who could blame me?"

"Gee, I don't know. Trinity Watson, maybe?"

"Who?"

Jack scoffed. "Jesus. You can't even remember the name of the woman you accosted?"

Jack's wrist-comm continued a second cycle of vibrations.

"Clearly there must have been some misunderstanding," Locke offered smoothly.

"Yeah. You clearly misunderstand if you think for one hot second, I would be willing to work with you."

Locke's jaw tightened. His knuckles whitened. He momentarily closed his eyes and took a deep breath. When he opened them, he stared at Jack.

"I don't quite think you comprehend the gravity of the

situation, Mr. Harding. It's more than just the voyage to Mars that is important. It's the egrets."

"Birds?" Jack shook his head. "You're worried about birds?"

Locke shook his head. "I'm speaking of the life-forms on Mars."

Jack tilted his head. "Life-forms?"

Locke strolled around his desk toward an antique globe of the earth. He casually spun it on its axis. "You're a scientist, Mr. Harding. Surely you can understand the reality we are not the only life in the known universe."

"Of course," Jack replied warily.

"Granted, the Mars egrets don't measure up to our stature or definition of civilization. They're tiny little things, really. Hardly worth noticing, in fact, except for one thing."

Jack took the bait. "And what's that?"

Locke stepped in close to Jack. Jack held his ground.

"Immortality, Mr. Harding," Locke hissed. He stepped back. "These infinitesimal beings hold the secret to regeneration. The power to resuscitate dead cellular matter and prolong life indefinitely. Whoever gets to them first will retain control and, of course, the power."

Holy crap!

"Mr. Harding, I believe you and that thing," Locke pointed toward Thom-Thom, "hold the key to my Mars project. I am prepared to offer you a sizable sum if you join my team. How do six figures sound?"

Jack's heart skipped a beat. He hadn't been expecting that sort of windfall offer. He thought of the creditors, Charlie's medical expenses, and now the damaged van.

Six figures? A light at the end of the tunnel!

Jack frowned.

With your luck, Jack, old pal, it would probably be a train.

He groaned inwardly. Not to mention it would mean selling his soul in the process.

Locke must have seen the doubt wavering in Jack's face. He stepped forward. "And as you seemed quite eager to get back into your facilities at P1AL labs, I will acquire the mortgage from the bank as part of the deal. You would be free to use the facilities at your leisure. Insofar as the work relates to this mission, of course."

The lab!

To get back into the lab would mean unrestricted access to the collider. Regardless of Bart's miraculous feat with rebuilding the ROAR system, they still needed the collider to replicate Thom-Thom's phenomenon.

The wrist-comm buzzed yet again. Jack jammed a hand into his pocket and depressed the ignore button. He had to think, and the damned comm device was just distracting him!

He paced in a tight little circle. He thought about the hurt in Trinity's eyes the night before. Slowly, he shook his head. "I'm sorry, Mr. Locke. Your offer's generous, but I'm afraid I can't…"

He was interrupted by a sudden flurry of activity behind him at the elevator. As the elevator doors slid open, Bradley appeared, tussling with another security guard in a generic black suit.

"I understand protocols, you gorilla! I practically run my life by them! But this is a medical emergency, so you can take your protocols and give yourself a security enema! Oh, Jack! Jack! Thank God I've found you. Why aren't you answering your phone, man?"

Locke appeared ruffled by the sudden intrusion of Bradley and his high-waisted jeans and penny loafers.

Jack just looked confused. "Bradley? What in the hell are you talking about?"

Bradley jerked free of the guard's grip and rushed to Jack's side. Deep concern etched a line in the former nanny's forehead.

"The school's been trying to get hold of you, Jack. They finally contacted me. Apparently, I'm still listed as an emergency contact."

Jack's eyes widened at the word "emergency." He grabbed Bradley by both arms. "Emergency? What's wrong? Did one of the twins get hurt?"

Bradley shook his head. "Jack, it's Charlie. The school had to call 911. He's been rushed to the hospital."

"This is a limited time offer, Mr. Harding," Locke interjected. He produced a sleek business card and handed it to Jack. "I need your answer."

Jack locked gazes with Locke. "And my kids need me. Come on, Bradley."

He shoved the card into his pocket, and the two men ran toward the bank of elevators. Jack couldn't help but notice the seething fury in Locke's face as the shiny elevator doors slid closed.

CHAPTER 28

Lucille Packard Children's Hospital Stanford
Jack

The bitter bite of antiseptic assaulted Jack's nostrils as he burst through the emergency room doors, Bradley fast on his heels. The nanny had driven with an aggression Jack had not realized he was even capable of, pressured, he assumed, by lingering concern for Charlie's well-being. They had managed to avoid any entanglements with the California Highway Patrol. Jack wouldn't have wanted to be the accusing officer if they hadn't. Bradley was a man possessed.

In between his violent verbal outbursts to lollygagging cars on the interstate, Bradley had thoroughly berated Jack for his apparent failure in tending to the needs of the Johansson children. He had thrown a hand up in the air as the other had jerked the wheel to slip the Honda behind a speeding eighteen-wheeler.

"I mean, Jesus, Jack! I haven't even been gone a day, and look what you've allowed to happen!"

Jack hadn't offered up a response. He couldn't argue with his former employee. He sucked at the entire parenting thing... lock, stock, and two smoking barrels. If failed parenting were an

Olympic event, Jack thought, no doubt, he would have brought home the gold.

Acid churned in his gut. Sucking was one thing. But what kind of incompetent jerk would allow something to happen that could threaten the children's lives?

A schmuck. That's who.

That was the word written across the faces of the Johansson children as they huddled around the worried-looking Bart and Mrs. Pulldraw. The twins sat on Mrs. Pulldraw's lap, one on each knee, their tear-streaked faces buried in her ample bosom. Julia stood near the older woman's shoulder, furiously chewing at the nails on her right hand as she stared at the imposing double doors that led to the emergency department treatment rooms. She didn't so much as glance at Jack as he barreled into the lobby.

Alice, on the other hand, ran unexpectedly toward Jack. He reached out his arms to catch her in a comforting embrace, but she ran immediately past him and into the comforting embrace of Bradley behind him.

"Oh, Bradley! I'm so glad you're here! It's awful."

"Oh, my sweetie," Bradley clucked, pulling her in close. "I'm sure it's all going to be fine."

Even Jack could hear the wavering conviction in the nanny's voice. Jack stepped toward Bart, who had headed in his direction.

"So, *is* it going to be fine?" Jack murmured under his breath as he and the software engineer stepped off toward the side, out of earshot.

Bart shook his head. "Honestly, man, I don't know. Technically, we're not family, so the docs wouldn't tell us much. HIPAA and all. The only reason we were even able to bring the kids is because you have Mom and me on the authorized pickup list. Alice called us in hysterics from the school. We couldn't just leave them there. Not after Charlie collapsed like that. Alice said he had some kind of seizure or something."

"No, no. You're right. Thanks for that, brother." Jack's eyes scanned the room, looking for some official medical personnel–a doctor, a nurse–somebody. "But I need to go find someone who can tell me exactly what's going on."

Bart grabbed his arm. "What happened at Locke's?"

"I'll tell you later, okay?"

Bart nodded, his double chins wagging. "Yeah, yeah. Sure. Of course."

Jack walked past Bart's mother, laying a hand briefly on each of the twins' shoulders. Mrs. Pulldraw smiled sadly.

"Julia?" Jack ventured as he looked at the teen.

Julia glowered at him. "This is all your fault, you know."

"What do you mean?" Jack countered.

Julia stood up straight. "Charlie told you last night he didn't feel well, and you just blew him off. You were more worried about your date and your stupid little lab."

"Hold on, JuJu Bee," Jack began.

"No!" Julia burst. "You do not get to call me that! Only Charlie can call me that, and because of you, I may never get to hear him call me that again. I hate you, Jack. I hate you!"

She stormed down the linoleum hallway, cheeks flushed, fists clenched. All heads in the ER swiveled in Jack's general direction. After a moment of silence punctuated only by a hospital intercom announcement, Bart walked up and patted Jack on the back.

"I'll go get her, man," he offered.

"No. Let her go. She's angry. And, on some level, she's right. I don't know what I was thinking, letting Oliver and Elsa name me guardian. I can't even take care of myself."

Jack stormed off toward the nurses' station, leaving Bart to exchange glances with his mother and Bradley and just shrug.

*****

"Excuse me?" Jack tried to gain the attention of the nurse behind the counter. She held up a halting finger as her other hand held the comms device to her ear.

"Yes, Doctor. We have four more nurses coming on at shift change, so we'll be covered."

Jack tapped the counter impatiently. "Ma'am, I'm sorry to interrupt, but I need to speak to someone right away."

She gave an exasperated, end-of-shift look to Jack and disconnected from her device. "Are you having chest pains, are you bleeding, or have you sustained any type of head injury, sir?"

"What?" Jack looked down at the collection of cuts and abrasions along his body. "Yes. I mean no. I mean, what does that have to do with anything?"

The nurse started ticking off boxes on a form. "Hm. I see. Confusion is often a symptom of a concussion, sir."

"I do not have a concussion!" Jack bellowed. "What I have is a child in your ER and no doctor around to tell me what's going on!"

"I see," the nurse said calmly. "When was the child brought in? What's his name?"

"He was only just brought in a little while ago. His name's Charlie...Charles Johansson."

The nurse's fingers flew across her keyboard. "Yes, sir. And how old is the child?"

"Seven. He's wheelchair-bound."

"And your name, sir?"

"Harding. Jack Harding."

As Jack uttered the mismatched name, the nurse peered over her glasses. "And your relation to the child?"

"Will you stop calling him 'the child'? His name is Charlie. I am his legal guardian, and I demand to know what is going on!"

"It's okay, Nurse Jones. I'll take it from here." A calm, quiet voice spoke behind Jack. Jack whirled to see a man in a white lab coat standing there. A stethoscope draped around his neck. A laminated identification badge indicated his name was Dr. Logan Pershing. "Mr. Harding?"

"Yes," Jack replied. Dr. Pershing extended a hand and shook Jack's firmly.

"I'm Logan Pershing. I'm the attending on-call this evening. You're obviously aware that your ward," the doctor quickly checked the chart in his hand, "Charles Johansson, suffers from vanishing white matter disease?"

Jack nodded. "Yeah, um, leukodystrophy. It presented when he was five. But he's been stable for quite some time. He, uh, even had an appointment scheduled two days from now to discuss a bone marrow transplant."

The doctor nodded somberly. "Yes. We noted that in his file. I'm afraid, however, that a transplant will not be an option now. Are you aware of how the disease works?"

"Just that it's a bit like MS in that the protective sheath around the nerves deteriorates. Patients begin to lose motor function as the central nervous system is affected…"

"And eventually results in death as cerebellar ataxia and chronic neurological deterioration worsen. When Charlie was brought in, he presented with a high fever. Did no one ever mention that febrile episodes can accelerate the course of the disease? Has he been sick?"

Jack's heart fell. He thought of the kids trapped out in the rain when he had gotten so caught up in the ROAR project with Bart he'd forgotten them. He remembered Charlie's sneezing–just a common cold symptom to any other kid, but what should have been a klaxon warning in Charlie's case.

"So, what are our options, Doc? You can help him, right?"

Dr. Pershing inhaled deeply. "We're transferring him to the ICU. The best we can do at this point is make him comfortable, but the outlook isn't promising. The fever has caused an aggressive breakdown of the remaining myelin in Charlie's brain. Unless someone comes up with something that can regenerate the lost white matter and quickly, the prognosis is, I'm afraid, quite grim."

"What are you saying? He's going to die?"

"What I'm saying is, if you're a believer, you might want to get out there and wish on the brightest star you can find."

Jack watched the doctor tuck Charlie's file under his arm and walk slowly back into the recesses of the ER. Jack slid his hands into his pockets, mostly to keep himself from throwing them into the air and screaming. He turned and looked at the eager faces of his family, who searched for some sign of hope in Jack's features.

Jack's fingers fumbled across Locke's business card in his pocket. He drew out the linen card with its cold black lettering and gilt accents. Jack looked out at the darkening evening sky.

I don't know about a star, Doc, but there's a planet that just might help.

CHAPTER 29

Harding Estate
Jack

Jack stood in the dim light of the early morning, alone on the front porch with his coffee. The kids were asleep, passed out from the emotionally exhausting events of the night before. The sun had not yet risen over the horizon, but he could just make out the wisps of steam drifting up from his mug and dissipating into the atmosphere. The image left him feeling alarmingly unsettled.

Sure as hell hope that's not a visual metaphor for my immediate future.

Last night, he hadn't even waited till they left the hospital to put the call into Locke. He'd stepped out of the emergency room lobby, leaving the kids with Bart and Mrs. Pulldraw, and dialed the number on the linen business card. Locke's crisp tone answered on the first ring.

"Travis Locke," Locke's curt voice announced.

Startled, Jack fumbled for composure.

"Mr. Locke?" he squeaked.

"I thought I had already established that. Who you are and what you want, however, remains to come to light," Locke replied coolly.

"Yes." Jack cleared his throat, his voice still thick with angst over Charlie.

Come on, you jackass. That's why you're making this call. Don't screw it up.

"Mr. Locke, this is Jack Harding. Dr. Jack Harding? If the offer's still valid," Jack paused, his conscience giving one last gasp for morality, "I'd like to accept the offer to work for you."

And that had been that.

Jack knew he had struck a devil's bargain. Crap, he was probably going to hell already–what with how he'd let Oliver and Elsa down–but it was the only way he could think of to help Charlie. Somehow, he had to get his ass to Mars, snag the Mars egrets, and get them back to Earth. He'd worry about the proprietary rights issues later. Right now, he just needed Locke and his resources to get to the red planet.

Jack stared at the golden semicircle of sun just starting to peek over the horizon and sighed. Devil's bargain or not, he'd only made one stipulation to Locke.

Keep his name out of it.

He didn't want the kids to find out about the Mars plans just yet. At least not until he figured out how to break the news to them. He wasn't sure they would understand him building, then boarding a ship that would take him a hundred and forty million miles away. Especially not when he considered Charlie's condition. The preliminary studies with the Mars egrets were just that–preliminary. The only work that had been done so far was with mice. No human testing had been attempted. There were no guarantees. Would they understand he had to take the chance?

Then there was Trinity.

Jack ran a hand through his tousled hair. He didn't suppose the gorgeous reporter would approve of his alliance with Locke even one iota. Just the concept of it had driven her to storm out the night of their abysmal date.

Correction. Our second abysmal date.

He remembered the night at the Rust Bucket.

Jesus.

He was really batting a thousand where Trinity was concerned. Problem was, he truly liked her. Growing up in the system, connections had never been easy for Jack. In fact, until he'd met Oliver and Elsa, he hadn't made a single one. By the time he'd settled in one foster home, he was uprooted and plunked down in yet another strange place where he had to learn more new names and faces and routines. Eventually, he stopped trying to learn them. He was just a body, drifting through space like a comet, cold and lonely.

He had felt something with Trinity though. Something that had started to melt the iciness inside. Maybe it was her enthusiastic belief in his work.

Who the hell knows?

All he did know was he had no intention of striking out completely with her by admitting his cooperation with Locke Industries.

He took a cautious sip of his steaming coffee and leaned down to pick up the morning paper. He'd read the paper, finish his coffee, and get dressed. He'd have just enough time to drop the kids at school, then stop at the hospital and check on Charlie's condition before he headed back to the labs to start running the ROAR testing with the accelerator and try to replicate the phenomenon that had occurred with Thom-Thom.

If he could master gravity, he could master Mars.

He had hardly settled into the kitchen chair with his coffee and paper when a furious pounding sounded at the door. Jack jumped to his feet and ran to answer it before the kids woke up. He threw open the door to find Bart standing on the threshold, cherubic face flushed.

One hand held a disposable tablet of the morning *Mercury* aloft while the other hand tapped the digital headline with rapid agitation.

"You're going to freaking Mars?" Bart's voice squeaked as he pointed to the news article. "With Locke?!"

"What?" Jack balked, snatching the tablet from Bart's hand. His eyes rapidly scanned the lead story.

"Travis Locke, CEO of Locke Enterprises, announces a surprise move in the Mars race late last night. Locke Industries has signed particle physicist Dr. Jack Harding to the company's Mars team."

Jack purpled and smacked the tablet back into Bart's chest. "Son of a bitch promised to keep my name out of it!"

He wheeled on his heel and stormed back into the house.

Bart followed Jack and continued reading where Jack had left off. "Despite Harding's recent debacle with the failed ROAR program, Locke remains confident that Harding's research will prove critical to the success of Locke Industries' efforts to send a manned mission to Mars."

Bart dropped the tablet to his side. "Were you planning on sharing this little nugget of information with me?"

Jack angrily started stacking packed boxes by the front door to load into the van. "Of course I was. Things have been a little hectic in the last twenty-four hours, in case you haven't noticed."

Jack made a sweeping gesture that encompassed the whole of the room.

"Not so hectic you couldn't make travel plans…to freakin' Mars! I mean, I've heard of midlife crises, man, but couldn't you opt for something a little more terrestrial? I don't know, like Disneyland?"

Jack teetered a fourth box of **P1AL** materials on top of the stack before he turned to his friend. "This isn't a midlife crisis, Bart. I don't have a choice. Oliver's kid is lying in that hospital, fighting for his life, and the odds aren't exactly stacked in his favor. His only hope is if I can get to those egrets first and bring them back to Earth. I owe Oliver that, at least. God knows I've jacked everything else up three ways from Sunday. No pun intended."

"And you really think the Mars egrets are the answer?"

"Think about it, Bart. The DNA protein structures on the ends of our chromosomes," Jack began.

Bart nodded. "Telomeres. Yeah? What about them?"

"They protect our cells from degrading and even allow cells to repair."

"Right. Kinda like that jellyfish. You know. Damn. What's its name?" Bart snapped his fingers. "What's the crazy lady with the snake hair?"

"Medusa?"

"Yeah! That's it! The Medusa jellyfish. They call it the immortal jellyfish because if it becomes injured or damaged in some way, it basically regenerates itself."

"Yeah, well, that's kind of what I'm hoping for with the egrets. Even in a normal, healthy person, the telomeres shorten every time the cell divides. Eventually, when the telomere gets too short, the cell starts to die off or flat out just dies off altogether. In Charlie's case, his telomeres are deteriorating at an insane pace. His DNA is basically telling the myelin on his nerves to go to hell in a handbasket. But, with the egrets, Charlie's got a shot."

Bart scoffed. "Even if they could modify the RNA to carry instructions from the genes of the egrets' DNA to the protein-making areas of dying cells, all the scientific journals have reported is a theory that it can restructure the nucleotide chain and rebuild the telomeres and stem cells."

Jack responded eagerly. "But what if it could? Charlie's cells would quit dying off. What's more, they could rebuild themselves. Think about it. Theoretically, he could walk again."

"So, let me get this straight. You're going all the way to Mars...for a theory?"

"Wait. We're going to Mars?" Alice's voice suddenly interjected.

Both men whirled to see the preteen standing slack-jawed in a robe and slippers behind them.

Jack looked at Bart for an assist. Bart simply shrugged. Jack took a tentative step toward Alice. He held his hands out cautiously in front of him as if he were approaching a dangerous, wild animal.

"Now, Alice, when you say 'we' are going to Mars..."

Any remnants of sleep dropped from Alice as her eyes gleamed with anticipation.

"You mean we're going to get the egrets!" She bounced on her toes eagerly. Her words tumbled out faster than her lips could form them. "Oh, Jack, I've read all about them. They're these amazing creatures. Scientists think they can use them to help fix terrible things like dementia and Alzheimer's."

She froze. Her next words came out slow and considered. She stared at Jack as she spoke them.

"They could help Charlie," she murmured under her breath.

Inwardly, Jack breathed a sigh of relief. It seemed at least one of the Johansson children grasped why he needed to travel halfway across the solar system.

She straightened. "I'll go pack. When are we leaving?"

The momentary relief deflated like an expiring balloon. Jack smiled gently. He took Alice by the arms. "You're not going, Alice."

"That's funny, Jack. Of course I'm going."

Jack shook his head slowly. "Alice, this isn't like Space Mountain at Disneyland. Mars is over a hundred and forty-two million miles away from Earth. No human has ever made the trip. I still don't even know if it's possible. No one's ever been able to build a ship that could manage it. Gravity is just too powerful."

Alice's eyes widened. "But we have Thom-Thom."

Jack's head began a slow shake.

"But you said, Jack. You said you were so close to figuring out what made Thom-Thom float, and you could make whatever it was happen to something else. You could make a spaceship, Jack. You could make a spaceship and make it float. Then you could get to Mars."

"I don't have Thom-Thom anymore."

Shock blanched Alice's face. "You…lost him?"

"I didn't lose him," Jack offered. "I know exactly where he is. I'm going to work for the man who has him."

Bart shot Jack a puzzled look. Jack gave a curt shake of his head and held up a silencing finger.

"You gave my dad's ferret to him?" Alice accused.

"Not exactly. The terms of the exchange were a little one-sided."

"Wait," Alice started. "This man *stole* Thom-Thom."

"Stole is a strong word," Jack suggested.

Alice started pacing the kitchen floor. Her hands flailed in the air. "Why didn't you call the police? Thom-Thom belongs to us! It was the last thing my dad ever gave anybody. He gave him to you! You should have taken better care of it!"

A pang of regret stung Jack like a slap across the face. He tried to shake it off. Jack waved his hands in a shushing motion. "Quiet down, Alice. You'll wake the twins. And I can't call the police on Mr. Locke. He's allowing me to get back into the lab with the collider and finish my testing with Thom-Thom."

Bart grabbed Jack's arm and pulled him out of Alice's earshot. He lifted the black bowler from his head, today's chapeau of choice, and scratched his scalp. The big man whispered.

"I don't know, Jack. I mean, I'm beginning to think this Locke's a seriously dangerous guy. You remember what Trinity said at the bar. How he practically attacked her? And from what you've told me, he didn't exactly roll out the red carpet for you either. And that was just supposed to be a job interview!"

Jack plucked Bart's hand from his arm.

"I know what I'm doing," he said.

"No offense, Jack, but that's what you said before the ROAR demonstration went tits up."

Jack tossed a nervous glance toward Alice, who eyed them suspiciously from across the room.

"Locke's just used to getting what he wants," Jack mumbled sotto voce to Bart, keeping one eye on the girl.

"And when he doesn't? What do you think's going to happen then?"

"I'll jump on that grenade if it shows up."

"Okay, Steve Rogers," Bart began. "And what if things blow up before you ever get to the grenade?"

"What's that supposed to mean?" Jack's brow creased. He stopped watching Alice and leveled a concerned look at Bart.

"Locke. Ever since you mentioned Locke's little proposal, my gut's been bothering me."

"That's more likely your diet," Jack considered.

Bart shook his head in response. "Something just doesn't feel right about this. I'm telling you. I started thinking about what Trinity mentioned that night at the bar. About the rocket misfire at one of Locke's facilities working on the Mars project? At least, that's what they're calling it. I did some more digging on your new apparent bestie. Did you know Locke was supposedly there when it happened?"

Jack shrugged. "Sounds like a mechanical engineering error. Wouldn't be the first time something's happened with new tech. Hell, different field, but it happened to us."

Bart shook his head. "My errors don't turn a physicist into a charcoal briquette."

Jack paused. "Wait. Someone...died?"

Bart nodded. "Yeah. And here's the thing. The rocket testing area is specifically designed so the rocket engine cannot fire when a human is inside the test compartment. There's always someone inside the control booth, plus they have a butt load of monitoring equipment."

"So, what exactly happened?"

"The firing button was somehow engaged while the guy was inside."

Jack ran through the calculations in his head. His eyes widened at the sum.

"Locke?" he whispered.

Bart shrugged. "Can't know for sure. The camera feed was malfunctioning. At least that's what all the papers are saying."

"So, we don't know for sure that Locke had anything to do with the guy's death, do we?"

"You want to take that bet when you're floating a hundred million miles from Earth?"

Jack paled a little at that last.

A deep look of concern puckered Bart's own expression. He poked Jack squarely in the chest with a fat finger.

"That's not all. I even heard rumors he was in bed with the mob."

Jack looked Bart square in the face. "He is."

Bart froze, then blinked twice. He suddenly exploded into action, expelling a cloud of air, stalking away, and throwing his hands in the air. "Oh, that's just great! As if we weren't in deep enough with the cement boot crew with Valeni! Now, you're getting mixed up with Locke's goons."

"Keep it down, will ya!" Jack hissed, looking nervously back at Alice, but the girl was nowhere to be found. He looked back to Bart. "If it makes you feel any better, it's the same goons."

Bart gave a hearty Bronx cheer. "Oh yeah. That makes me feel so much better! So, now you're telling me that Valeni and Locke are working together?"

"Well, think about it. How else is Locke going to have Thom-Thom unless he's in league with Valeni?"

Bart bounced on his toes. "Crap! Did you see my computer there?"

Jack shook his head. "If he has it, he was keeping it out of sight."

"Dammit," Bart cursed.

"What? You said you uploaded all the information we need to the cloud," Jack responded.

"Yeah, yeah, yeah. But ROAR is installed on that computer. If he cracks my security, then he'll have it too. That's proprietary information, Jack."

"Which we hold the patent on. Stop worrying. Locke needs us."

Bart frowned. "Until he doesn't."

A moment of weighty silence hung between the two of them. "Shit."

"You said it, brother."

"I need to get to the lab." He gave Bart a pleading look. "I can't do this without you. Are you with me?"

Bart sighed. "I must be *meshuggener*, but if there's an outside chance it'll help Charlie, I'm in."

Jack grabbed one of the file boxes marked **P1AL** from the

stack near the door. "Help me get some of this stuff in the van."

"Roger that," Bart answered. He grabbed a box and started after Jack.

Once outside, Jack started loading the boxes in the back of the van. He and Bart shuffled back and forth, piling more boxes in like a game of Tetris. Jack tried to ignore the twinge in his gut as he tried to stack the boxes around Charlie's wheelchair lift.

"I'm not going to let you down this time, Oliver. I promise," he mouthed under his breath as he thought about the misplaced trust his old friend had placed in him.

His reverie only lasted a moment as hurried, heavy footsteps sounded behind him. Julia skidded to a stop on the driveway gravel as Jack turned.

"Julia," Jack began.

Julia interrupted. "What are you doing? Where are you going? Why is Alice babbling on about Mars?"

Bart walked past, carrying a box. "We are, apparently, headed to Mars, JuJu Bee."

Behind him, Jack wildly waved his hands and shook his head vehemently. Bart's face clouded with confusion.

Julia's gaze volleyed between the two men.

"What!" she exclaimed. "Are you kidding me? Like actually in space? Alice was serious?"

Jack stepped forward and tried to grab Julia's arms. The teen jumped back. "Don't touch me!"

"Let me explain."

"You can't explain this."

"I'm trying to, if you'd let me."

"Why?" She looked at the P1AL scrawled on the sides of the boxes in the van. "It looks like you're getting ready to go to the lab and play Einstein while Charlie is lying in a coma at the hospital. Yeah, Alice told me about that too. Nice move, Jack."

She practically spat out his name.

"Now, hold on just one second, young lady." Jack's tone shifted from defensive to scolding. "Did she also tell you I'm doing this *for* Charlie? For all of you?"

Jack gestured to the remaining Johansson children, who huddled near the front door watching the exchange.

Julia scoffed. "I'm thirteen. Not stupid. Don't think I can't see this for what it is. You're just doing this for yourself."

The muscle in Jack's jaw twitched as he gritted his teeth.

"Guess you'll screw that up too."

With a stern gaze, he raised a finger toward the house. "Get back inside the house, Julia. We'll discuss this later."

"You're not my father."

"No," Jack replied. "No, I'm not. I probably can never hope to be the kind of amazing father your dad was. But I *am* responsible for you, and I say get back in the house."

They stared each other down for a few silent seconds.

"Fine," Julia finally replied. "I just have one question for you, Jack. Even if we forget about jet-setting off to Mars for a hot second, if you and Bart are going to the lab today, who exactly do you plan on watching us? The school is still closed for pest control."

The sudden reality of Julia's statement hit Jack like a ton of bricks.

Bart leaned forward and whispered in Jack's ear, "Houston, we have a problem."

CHAPTER 30

This could prove to be a problem. Four problems, to be precise.
The troubling thought drifted through Locke's mind as his gaze fell on the miscellaneous children gathered behind Harding. His stomach soured.

What was the word for a group of children?

An ingratitude.

How ironically apropos.

It would have been easy enough to arrange for some sort of accident to befall Harding once he had unlocked the floating ferret's secret and ushered Locke's space program to the forefront of the Mars race. An accident, perhaps, like the one that had befallen poor Dr. Engleton.

A deep line blemished Locke's otherwise unlined forehead.

It was another thing entirely to dispatch an entire family. It wasn't that he had qualms about the possibility. Over the years, the age of his victims had run the gamut. He just wasn't particularly keen on leaving such a large trail of bodies that could potentially lead back to him.

Which brought him back to his quandary.

Jack Harding needed to die.

Not immediately, of course. Jack Harding and his tech had a very crucial purpose to serve. Binderkampf and Vashtin had clearly outlined the necessity for technology that could ascertain the quantum aspects of gravity and determine the effects of subatomic alterations. In this case, specifically the effects on the ratty-looking little beast Valeni had brought to his offices. There was absolutely no doubt in his mind unlocking the animal's secrets would solve the issue of manned deep space travel.

But if the ferret was the lock, Jack Harding's technology was the key, and apparently, it was encrypted on the Strontium Power Core computer Peter Valeni had "appropriated" using Advanced Encrypted Standard 256 (AES-256)–impossible to access. At least, that's what every single one of the idiots in Locke's tech department had blathered on about when he called for a status report on the stolen computer.

AES-256, they explained, was the gold standard of encryption. The brainchild of Belgian cryptologists Joan Daemen and Vincent Rijmen, AES-256 was the result of a contest sponsored by the US government to replace the powerful but lagging triple DES–Data Encryption Standard–developed by IBM. It wasn't just a randomly generated password–an arbitrary string of numbers, capital letters, and symbols to keep your teenager from logging into your Amazon account and ordering the latest fashion craze.

No.

AES-256 provided 1.1 x 1077 variable combinations to crack by brute-force attack if you wanted the data it protected.

And, goddamn it, he wanted that fucking data!

Last night's conversation with Sarah Copeland drifted to the forefront of Locke's mind.

"But even if you can get to it, you can't use it. Not legally, anyway," Sarah Copeland had whispered in his ear before she nibbled on his lobe when she came to his house last night. Her efforts to arouse him went unnoticed. He sat on the edge of the silk sheets, staring through the glass walls of his Monterey home out at the midnight sky.

The only body that held any interest for him was a heavenly one—Mars.

Sarah hadn't let the obvious snub faze her. She stood, the ivory skin of her perfect body glowing in the light of the full moon shining through the windows, and padded barefoot to the wet bar across the room. One thing you could always find at Locke's was a decent scotch, even if sex was off the menu.

The sound of the ice cubes clattering in Sarah's glass drew Locke's attention. He tilted his head toward her, chin balancing atop tented fingers.

"What do you mean, not legally?" he asked as she poured a generous dram of the amber liquid over the cubes of ice. "There's a reason I pay you twice the price of what's in your glass, you know."

She raised the Baccarat whiskey tumbler, swirling the alcohol around in the crystal, then watched as it formed little eddies around the ice. "What? This ancient swill?"

Locke sneered. The 1937 Glenfiddich was anything but swill. At $120,000 a bottle, the pre-World War II whiskey was yet another of the finer things he chose to surround himself with. He was beginning to wonder just how much longer Ms. Copeland would remain in that category.

Sarah lifted the heavy glass to her full scarlet lips. She took a sip then leveled a steely gray stare at Locke. "I'm worth a case of this, you know."

Locke stood, his long legs taking him to Sarah's side in two easy strides. He towered over her, dark eyes flashing as he grabbed her roughly by the wrists.

"Then tell me exactly what you mean when you say not legally," he hissed.

"Harding holds a patent on the analysis program," she replied, wincing at the pain from his vise-like grip but disguising it well. "But because his program is so targeted and its process so narrow—the testing of quantum particle measurements..."

Locke scowled. "The typical technological disclosure—the trade secrets of the program that competitors usually have access to when the first patent application is filed..."

He stormed off toward the window.

"Aren't available, giving you no legal recourse to compete," Sarah finished. She also finished her scotch in one steadying swallow. "If you managed to gain access to Harding's tech, and that's even assuming that Binderkampf and Vashtin could figure out how to operate it, and you used that tech to advance your Mars program, as your lawyer I would have to warn you, you would be opening yourself up to a devastating lawsuit if Harding decided to pursue. And I'm pretty damned sure he would pursue. So, whether you like it or not, you *need* Jack Harding."

But what if Harding was removed from the equation?

"I take it he wasn't too keen on your proposition of employment?" Sarah continued.

"The outcome of our little tête-à-tête was less than desirable," Locke grumbled. "Truth be known, he walked out before I received his definitive answer."

Sarah slid behind him and trailed a polished fingertip down along his spine. She kissed his shoulder. "So, it's entirely possible you could still get what you want."

He turned abruptly, wrenched her to him, and kissed her hard. As he pulled back and released her, even in the abbreviated light of the moon, he could see the dark red marks of his fingers tattooed against her porcelain skin.

"I always get what I want," he replied. "One way or another."

That was when he'd received the call, Harding agreeing to his terms. The physicist had stipulated a few rules of his own—like keeping his name out of the news—but Locke had never been one to play by the rules.

Rules were made to be broken.

Locke stared at the motley crew standing before him now in the P1AL facility.

And so was anything that got in his way.

"Mr. Locke? Ahem, Mr. Locke? If I may?" Binderkampf's grating nasal tones interrupted Locke's reverie.

"Yes, Dr. Binderkampf?" Locke brought himself back to the moment.

"Ah yes. Very good. As I was saying, you know Dr. Jack Harding, of course. Dr. Harding, this is Dr. Emry Vashtin, my colleague. And may I just say, Dr. Harding, I am very excited to be working on this project with you. This is truly groundbreaking stuff here. If your program can do what you suggest, well, we'll be able to accomplish the impossible!"

"I don't suppose you can start by ending the incessant babbling and move on?" Locke suggested. He cast a glare at the older man, who withered under Locke's intense gaze.

"Yes, um, of course, Mr. Locke. After all, time is money."

"Imagine that, Doctor. We finally agree on something," Locke sneered. "Now, if you'll please continue. He gestured to the remaining members of the party.

"Here we have Mr. Bart Pulldraw, Dr. Harding's associate who I'm to understand was instrumental in the development of the ROAR program."

"Ah, Mr. Pulldraw. I believe we have something of yours," Locke stated. He gestured to his attaché, who produced the Strontium Core laptop. "Let's just say it was turned into our company's lost and found."

Pulldraw grabbed the computer and snorted. "Yeah, right."

An immediate look of regret passed over his round face as Locke's attaché grunted.

Locke surveyed the round software engineer, his scrutiny stopping at the deerstalker atop Bart's head.

"Fan of Sir Arthur Conan Doyle, are we?" Locke's eyebrow arched.

Bart looked askance at Locke for half a second before he remembered his hat. He touched the iconic headgear and offered a nervous grin. "What, this? No. I just like hats."

"And I like results. I trust we can expect to see some and rather quickly, Dr. Harding?" Locke queried.

"Of course, Mr. Locke," Harding answered. "I just wanted to thank you again for this opportunity and for your faith in our program."

"Oh, make no mistake, Dr. Harding. My faith lies strictly with the almighty dollar. What I hold for you is expectation. Don't make me demonstrate what happens when I am disappointed."

Locke's coal-black eyes met Harding's, the implied threat only thinly veiled. He broke the stare only when a furtive movement at Harding's side distracted him. A small boy, five years of age at most, gripped Harding's pant leg. The boy's lower lip trembled. An older girl, her hair an odd mix of cotton-candy colors, stepped forward and drew the boy back behind the physicist.

"And who do we have here?" Locke asked, feigning interest.

Harding looked behind him and drew the children forward. "Oh yes! I'm sorry. I don't normally bring children into the office. I'm afraid it was unavoidable today as their school is closed, and I could not locate a sitter. I promise they won't be in the way, and it won't happen again. These are my wards. Their parents...well, their parents are no longer with us."

"How very tragic," Locke lied.

"Yes, they were victims in the Styrfjäder Air crash several years ago."

Locke's interest keened. "In Geneva? Near the CERN collider?"

"Yes," Harding replied. "Were you there?"

Locke took several seconds to answer. "No, no. I believe I was in Paris at the time. It was big news though."

"Yes, well, the children's parents were extremely close friends of mine. I am now their legal guardian."

Harding gestured to each child in turn. "These are Julia, Lucas, and Oscar."

The children looked at Locke warily, stepping back behind Harding as soon as they had been introduced. The boys, twins Locke surmised, clung to the girl.

"How do you do?" Locke asked stiffly.

"There is another boy, Charlie." Harding appeared to hesitate like he was searching for the right words. "He isn't here."

Locke had a vague sense of unease. There was more to that story, but he let the matter drop for now.

Harding placed a hand on the slight shoulder of a second girl, this one slightly younger than the other. Her blonde hair was pulled back in a messy ponytail, and Locke wasn't entirely certain, but he thought he saw one of her toes peeking out of a hole in her worn tennis shoe. He shuddered inwardly.

"This is Alice," Harding offered. "I guess you could say Alice is the scientist of my little army."

"Oh, isn't that wonderful!" Binderkampf began. "My son has a keen interest…"

Locke's head whipped toward the scientist and cut him off mid-sentence. Binderkampf immediately started picking at a piece of imaginary lint on his lab coat.

"She tends to be pretty inquisitive," Harding expounded.

"Really?" Locke asked with a modicum of curiosity.

The girl didn't seem as timid as the others. She cocked her head, studying Locke. He studied her right back.

"Where's my ferret?" she abruptly demanded, her blue eyes cold and hard. For a moment, Locke felt a fleeting appreciation for her boldness.

"Alice!" Harding reprimanded the child.

"And demanding too," Locke smiled, baring his brilliantly white teeth.

"I'm sorry about that, Mr. Locke. I'm still new to the whole parenting thing. We're working on the manners. It just takes a lot of time and patience."

"Two things I have precious little of," Locke stated. "So, if the introductions are out of the way?"

"Her manners may need fine-tuning, Mr. Locke, but I'm afraid Alice is right. In order to begin, we will need the ferret."

"Of course." Locke bobbed his head. A muscled guard stepped forward and pulled Thom-Thom from a steel-sided case. Alice leaped forward, snatching the animal before Harding could grab her.

"This belongs to us!" she snarled.

Locke's face broke into a wide, intimidating grin. He stepped forward and leaned down to look Alice in the eye. "No, you see, that's where you're wrong, young lady. Things belong to those with the will to take them. It has nothing to do with aspiration, diligence, or even legality. The sheer will to take is the dominant factor. And make no mistake. If there is something I want, like Mars…I…will…take…it."

With that, he wrenched the ferret from her small hands. A sharp gasp escaped her lips. Both Harding and Pulldraw instinctively leaped forward, giving Locke more insight into

Harding's dynamic. Locke shoved the stuffed animal into Harding's chest.

"Keep your animal under control," he spat and stormed from the facility.

CHAPTER 31

P1AL *Laboratories*
Jack

A cloud of nervous energy hung over everyone as Locke left, leaving the room cocked like a loaded gun. Jack drew in a long, slow breath.

Guess I'll pull the trigger.

He clapped his hands together. The sound cracked like a shot through the empty offices.

"Okay, gentlemen. We don't have time to waste. I know we've already done most of the heavy lifting, but we've still got work to do! Let's finish unpacking these boxes and get cracking," he ordered, pointing to the stacks of cardboard file boxes. "Those over there have some of the data we need to get this shit up and running again, so open those first and get them down to the collider staging area."

"Jack!" Bart whispered, giving a surreptitious nod to the Johansson children standing behind Jack.

Jack whirled. He rolled his eyes and groaned.

"Stuff. Get this *stuff* up and running. Pretend I didn't say that, okay, guys?"

Julia hefted Lucas up on her hip. "Why not? We've been

pretending like you've been taking care of us. Pretending we didn't hear one little curse word oughta be a cinch."

Jack scowled at her. "Look, just stay out of the way, all right? I've got some serious work to do."

"What are we s'posed to do, Jack?" Oscar chimed as he looked around the bare offices. "I don't see no toys here."

"Any toys," Jack corrected. He shrugged. "I don't know. Play hide-and-go-seek or something."

"We're going to leave early enough that we can go check in on Charlie, though, right? Visiting hours end at 8:00 p.m.," Julia reminded. "You promised."

"Dr. Harding," Binderkampf tapped Jack on the shoulder. "We really need to get started."

Jack nodded impatiently. "I know, I know. I'll be there in a second."

"Jack?" Julia emphasized his name, her question emphatic.

"Dude," Bart interrupted. "Once I get the computer set up, do you want me to start running the reverse algorithm to establish the parameters of the original experiment? Experiment? I mean, is that what we're even calling it? The thing that happened with the ferret?"

Jack waved his hands in exasperation before pushing through his hair. "Yes!" he exclaimed.

Bart looked confused. "Is that a yes for me or for her?"

"Yes," Jack repeated. "Yes, I want you to start running the algorithm. And yes," he turned to Julia. "I'll make sure we get to go see Charlie before visiting hours end."

"All righty then." Bart gave a quick nod and walked away. Alice watched as Jack dropped his face in his hands and rubbed vigorously.

"Jack, I want to help," Alice tugged on Jack's sleeve.

"I don't think so, Alice. Building a levitron is one thing.

Colliding subatomic particles is something else entirely."

"But I'm the one that found Thom-Thom. If it wasn't for me, you wouldn't even be here."

"I know. But Mr. Locke is expecting me to figure out how to make this work." Alice leaned in to whisper in Jack's ear. "I don't like him, Jack."

"I don't like him either, kid, but I need him to get to Mars. And," he spun her in another direction, "I *need* you guys to back off and let me work."

He pushed off in the direction of her siblings.

"But," she protested.

Jack scowled and waved his hands like he was dismissing an annoying fly. "Go! Shoo!"

He turned and ran a frustrated hand through his hair. The clock was ticking. He needed to create a viable means to get to Mars. He was right on the cusp. He could feel it in his gut.

Then again, it's probably an ulcer.

His shoulders deflated as he expelled a heavy sigh. He surveyed the frenetic activity of Bart and the scientists as they began to bring the P1AL labs back to life. His eyes drifted to the snarling countenance of the white ferret sitting on a nearby desk, teeth bared, beady eyes glinting. A fleeting thought of Shelley's Frankenstein passed through his mind—the mad scientist and his monster. Victor Frankenstein had only sought to prolong life and instead wound up creating his own downfall.

Would Jack's own creation turn out to be his downfall?

The question reeled in his head as he cast a worried glance back at the twins, who were gleefully amusing themselves by dumping files from the remaining boxes and building a cardboard fort.

Forget Thom-Thom and ROAR, he groaned inwardly.

Who was going to control these monsters?

*****

"I won't do it for less than twice my old salary," Bradley stated. Jack's former nanny-turned-Uber-driver stood in the parking lot of the P1AL labs, arms crossed nearly as tightly across his chest as the belt cinched around his high-waisted pants.

"Twice your old salary!" Jack's face purpled in apoplectic fury. "That's highway robbery!"

"No," Bradley stated. "Highway robbery is what the ride-share companies are doing to their drivers. Besides, don't act like you can't afford it now that you're working for one of the richest men in California. Travis Locke's got his finger in a lot of pies, mister. His name's on at least half the buildings in Silicon Valley. If that's the name on the bottom of your paychecks, now, I might be persuaded to come back."

"And if," Bradley dotted the air with a manicured finger, "you ask nicely."

Jack raspberried. He threw his hands up and let them fall defeatedly to his side. "Fine. You can come back at twice your salary. Just take the kids to the house and get them out of my hair."

Bradley shook his head and waggled a finger. "Ah, ah, ah. I also want Sundays off. I've realized the critical importance of self-care and want it clearly understood that I need to be able to take some time just for me. No Jack. No house. No children. Just me, myself, and I...and maybe a Nicholas Sparks novel."

"You want Sundays off too? What am I supposed to do on Sundays then?"

"You're a smart man, Jack. A terrible dresser," Bradley gave Jack's wardrobe a dubious glance, "but a smart man. You'll figure it out. Now, do we have a deal?"

Bradley held out an expectant hand. The wheels in Jack's head spun wildly, but he arrived at the inevitable conclusion. Bradley had Jack's back against a wall, and he knew it. He reached out and shook the man's hand.

"Deal."

"Excellent!" Bradley exclaimed.

"Just get them out from underfoot," Jack continued. "Locke may have money, but he's running low on patience. The official gun sounds on the start of the land grab in less than a month. If we're going to be the first to get to Mars, I still have a lot of work to do."

Jack fished in his pocket and plonked his keys in Bradley's hand.

"Here are the keys to the van. Take the kids back to the house. They'll need dinner. Make sure the twins get a bath before bed. Oh, and Julia mentioned something about stopping in to see Charlie at the hospital. Could you maybe see about making that happen?" Jack rattled off the list of orders. He paused when he observed Bradley's tapping foot and stern gaze.

Jack grinned sheepishly. "Please?"

"Thank you." Bradley's foot stopped tapping. Jack breathed a sigh of relief.

A smile broke out across the nanny's face as he clapped his hands together and rubbed them eagerly. He headed toward the building. "So, where are my little darlings?"

With the kid situation handled, all Jack needed now was to get the collider up and running, implement the ROAR analysis, and hope to hell it pointed him toward the means of getting a ship to Mars. No pressure, right?

Nah. No pressure at all.

CHAPTER 32

P1AL *Laboratories*
Alice

It was like feeding time at the Aquarium of the Bay shark tank.
Bradley's presence had whipped all the children into a mad frenzy. All of them except Alice. She dragged along behind the rest of them, her worn tennis shoes shuffling along the asphalt of the parking lot.

"Can we have mac 'n' cheese?" Lucas pleaded.

Oscar put his two cents in, as well. "With all the hot dogs cut up in it?"

Alice watched, a strange pain twinging in her gut. It was probably just a hunger pang, she knew—she hadn't eaten breakfast—but it wasn't Bradley's famous macaroni and cheese with all-beef hot dogs she was craving. Alice craved knowledge.

Besides, there will be plenty of time to eat mac 'n' cheese after I make sure Jack gets this to work.

She cast a glance at the lab entrance then back at her chattering siblings trailing behind Bradley. She had a sudden, sobering reminder of Jack's less-than-stellar track record. She sighed.

Or I might just starve to death.

"I'm so glad you're back, Bradley," Alice overheard Julia talking to the nanny as they walked toward the van. "You'll take us to the hospital to visit Charlie, won't you? I know he might not even realize we're there, but..." Her voice trailed off. Alice longed to visit her brother, too, but she also knew how much he was relying on the success of the Mars mission. She had to slip from under Bradley's watchful eye and sneak back into the lab. She remained alert, waiting for an opportunity.

"Of course I will, Julia," Bradley answered. "And he may not be awake, but I think he'll know you're there." Bradley's tone was heartfelt and sincere.

The teen smiled appreciatively, then placed her earbuds into her ears, oblivious to the rest of the world.

"Now, let me count heads," Bradley announced with his familiar tone of organized authority. "Would you two *please* hold still! You're going to make me miscount."

The twins bounced madly at Bradley's feet, each clamoring for attention from the harried man. Alice waited patiently for Bradley to tap her on the head.

"And four," he finally stated after a few vain attempts at enumerating the Johansson children.

"All present and accounted for. Gracious! I know it's only been a few days, but I forgot how much it's like herding cats!" Bradley tried to extricate himself from the twins' clutches. "That's it! Everybody in the van!"

Alice waited until the twins were buckled into their car seats and were arguing over possession of the forgotten Twizzler Oscar had found in his seat and Julia was tucked into her corner in the far back row of the van, eyes closed, listening to her tunes.

As soon as Bradley rounded the corner of the van, heading for the driver's seat, Alice slid the door closed and made a mad dash for the lab's entrance. She ducked behind the thick shrubbery near the door, blue eyes peeking out toward the van. She watched as Bradley put the vehicle in gear and drove the van out of the lab parking lot. Her gaze followed its red taillights as they disappeared into the distance.

Now, to go help Jack before Charlie's chances disappear in the distance too.

*****

Inside, the lobby was deserted. Jack had said something about the urgent need to run testing with the collider. Alice tiptoed, eyes darting, toward the collider staging area. That's where everyone would be, she supposed.

For as desolate as the lobby had been, the interior lab was a beehive of activity. The large, curved beam pipe of the collider ring was just barely visible to her as she boosted up on her tippy-toes to peer through the glass wall separating the monitoring equipment from the collider itself. It was so much smaller than the Large Hadron Collider at CERN, but to Alice, it was still monstrous.

Alice darted behind a stack of brown cardboard boxes as an unfamiliar scientist in a white lab coat strode briskly past. When she dared peek out and survey the room, she marveled at all the people scurrying back and forth—connecting cables, powering up systems. She found it a little hard to believe the place had been so desolate just days ago when she'd been packing things up with Jack and Bart.

Some faces she recognized. Others, like the red-haired man with the enormous glasses, were wholly unfamiliar to her. Binderkampf, she thought she remembered someone saying.

He looks nervous.

Alice watched as he timidly gave instructions and seemed to

be fighting the urge to push his falling glasses back up his nose.
I wonder if those horrible bruises have anything to do with it.

The bruises Alice observed had started to turn a sickly yellow-green. Alice found herself starting to turn a sickly yellow-green, too, as her own nerves started to jangle. She began to second-guess her brilliant plan.

Her heart leaped into her throat as an alarm klaxoned throughout the facility. She dove back behind the boxes.

"Attention! Attention! Collider going online. Prepare for beam event! Powering systems up," a slightly accented voice announced over the PA speaker just over Alice's head. She clapped her hands over her ears. She poked her head out once more to see if the coast was clear. Spying an opening as everyone's attention was currently glued to their computer consoles, Alice hotfooted it across the linoleum toward a dark, unpopulated hallway. It looked like a safe place where she could observe the test.

"Engaging power to magnets," the announcement system blared.

She stumbled backward, falling through the door behind her. She winced as she landed square on her rump. Alice got up and dusted herself off, rubbing the sore spot. She quickly forgot about the pain in her backside, however, as she surveyed the dizzying array of information spanning out before her.

As many times as she had been to the **P1AL** lab, Alice had never seen this room before. It was expansive. A large, polished conference table stretched nearly the length of the room, encircled by executive chairs. Interactive smartboards hung every few feet along the white walls.

"What is all this?" she whispered under her breath.

She reached a hesitant finger out, gently touching it to the nearest board. It glowed to life, complex physics equations dancing across the screen, holding her in awe.

It's like being inside Jack's brain.

She could almost imagine him speaking the variables out loud as he had scribbled them on the boards.

"Alice?" Jack's voice called.

Uh-oh. That's not my imagination.

Alice whirled to find Jack standing in the doorway, arms crossed, tapping his foot.

"Jack!" she exclaimed, then found herself at a loss for words.

"What are you doing here?" Jack asked, though it sounded more like an accusation to Alice's adolescent ears. "You're supposed to be with Bradley. Why *aren't* you with Bradley?" Concern creased his brow. "Christ! I'd better call him. He's going to flip when he realizes you're missing."

Jack tilted his wrist and spoke into the microphone. "Call Brad…"

Alice lurched forward and grabbed Jack's wrist. "No! Please, Jack. Please don't call him. I want to stay. I want to be here."

Pleading filled her eyes. He sighed. "Fine. I suppose. But can you promise to stay out of the way? We're already light-years behind. I can't spend time watching you. In fact, I really need to be getting back." He'd, of course, call Bradley later and update him on the situation.

He jabbed a thumb down the hall. Alice walked the perimeter of the conference room, brushing a hand across each smartboard as she passed it. Each one illuminated, some showing more equations, some outlining timetables, others noting dates and times.

"I promise, Jack. But what is all this stuff anyway?" Her eager eyes drank it all in.

"This? This is our Mars project." Jack stepped further into the room, following along behind her. "A project that all started with your dad's floating ferret."

"Thom-Thom helped you come up with all...this?" She made a broad, sweeping gesture that encompassed the whole of the room.

Jack nodded. "He's the key. We had to outline our primary objectives, of course. That's what you see on the board behind you."

Alice turned to see the bullet points of the program.

Jack pointed. "First, we have to isolate the sequence of events that made Thom-Thom float in the first place. Then, we have to try and replicate the event with other matter. See what the application could be for space travel."

"A ship that can defy gravity?"

"A ship that can defy gravity," Jack repeated. "Mr. Locke's company is providing the ship. I just have to make the damned thing hover...and sooner rather than later."

He gestured to the timelines, illuminated in bright red alphanumeric characters on another board. "Because we are showing up more than a little late to the party."

He picked up the smartpen and underscored a date with several harsh lines.

"April 1. That's when every ship lined up at the starting line just outside Mars' gravitational pull will haul tin can and buckets to Mars' surface and stake a claim to whatever Martian land each ship can get its hands on."

"April Fool's Day?" Alice looked dubiously at Jack, one eyebrow arched high over a blue eye.

Jack held up his hands in defense. "I swear it's not a joke. The best time to launch for Mars is between mid-July and mid-August. The ship can use the Hohmann transfer orbit. It saves on fuel because the ship will use Mars' own gravity to move into Mars' orbit once it gets there. Most teams are slated for takeoff as soon as the window opens on July 15."

"Jack, that's less than three months away!" Alice voiced weighty concern.

"Don't you think I know that? What's worse, if we don't take off by August 15, we'll miss the window entirely. That's why it's so important I get back to work."

He returned the pen to the tray. "It takes approximately two hundred sixty days to get to Mars. About eight months, give or take. Not everybody is going there for the same reason, but it doesn't matter what our reasons are if we can't be there when the race starts."

Jack sighed.

"And if we're going to have any hope of helping Charlie," he tapped the bottom of an astrogeological photograph of the red planet on another of the screens, "we have to get to Mars' south pole before anyone else."

"The south pole? Why there specifically?" Alice asked.

"Because that's where the greatest concentration of egrets has been found. Whoever stakes a claim on a parcel of land will also own any resources, like the egrets, for example, that are found on that land."

He gestured to all the boards. "I'm just hoping that somewhere in all of this, we can figure out a way to get there faster."

CHAPTER 33

P1AL Laboratories, One Month Later
Jack

"What do you mean, the accelerator's not working?" Jack bellowed into the hands-free receiver as his car zipped along the interstate toward the exit for the lab. Jack's body lurched back and forth as the electric car's self-drive mode whipped in and out of the heavy traffic that always seemed to congest California's motorways. It didn't help that it was Friday night. Everyone was on the road, searching for the next best place to let off steam from a grueling workweek.

The only steam Jack was letting off came from his ears as Bart imparted the bad news.

"I don't know." Anxiety ratcheted up the timbre of Bart's voice. "One second I was down in my mom's basement, running simulations on ROAR.2 with the data coming in from the lab, you know? Since we've pretty much been running the accelerator round the clock now."

The last month had seen Jack and Bart's research move light-years ahead. Using ROAR, they had successfully reverse-engineered the exact circumstances which had led to the bizarre occurrence of Thom-Thom's mass excess. They had even managed to recreate the effects with other organic matter. The challenge still remained of how to apply those effects to an entire inorganic spacecraft though.

Almost a week ago, on the previous Sunday, Jack had experienced a moment of divine inspiration in the park with the kids. It just sort of hit him...

*****

Bradley had been off, per his newly renegotiated employment. He'd suggested Jack take the children for a picnic in the park. The theory was the fresh air and exercise would tire them out, making them more docile for the inexperienced Jack—especially the rambunctious twins—until Bradley returned on Monday. Jack had taken the nanny's advice and piled the boys along with Alice and Julia into the family van, and headed for Bol Park on Laguna.

Named after Cornelius Bol, a Holland-born Stanford physicist and research associate, the 13.5-acre Bol Park was bordered by Matadero Creek on one side and a serpentine walking path on the other. Stately redwoods and scattered oaks provided welcome shade. The sloping meadow in between used to be a donkey pasture. In fact, one of the highlights of the park was the two donkeys who visited the park on Sundays. The twins had been eagerly anticipating petting the animals.

"Just be sure to slather them both in hand sanitizer when they're finished," Bradley had warned.

It was just as Jack was dutifully squirting generous dollops of sanitizer in the boys' hands that inspiration hit. Well, more like a Frisbee.

"Oof!" Jack exclaimed as the flying saucer smacked him in the forehead—hard. He collapsed in a heap on the grass.

"Oh God!" he heard a feminine voice exclaim. Soft hands

grabbed his own. "Oh God! Oh God! Oh God!"

Woozy, Jack grinned. "All the ladies say that when they're with me."

He was vaguely aware his hand was abruptly dropped.

"He's fine," he heard the woman's voice quip.

"Jack?" Alice's voice filtered through his consciousness. "Can you sit up?"

Jack struggled to a sitting position. His vision swam in and out of focus. He raised a hand to his forehead. He winced as his fingers brushed a sensitive lump forming there.

"What happened?" he asked.

"You played Frisbee," Lucas offered.

"You lost," Oscar expounded.

"Frisbee?" Jack questioned, still a bit muddled from the hard hit. "With whom?"

His blurred gaze wandered to the Frisbee dangling next to a pair of long, shapely legs. He crushed his eyes closed, trying to bring things back into focus. He opened them and followed the legs up the curved figure of Trinity Watson.

"Trinity?"

And then he promptly blacked out.

*****

"UFO!" Jack blurted when he awoke once again, probably concussed but functional, in his own bed at the house.

"Are you hallucinating?" Trinity's voice sounded from the corner of the darkened room. Jack squinted toward the shadows before reaching for the bedside lamp.

"Because hallucinations can be a sign of a concussion. Although, truth be told, I really don't think I hit you *that* hard."

The shapely reporter stood and walked into the wedge of

light. She was as drop-dead gorgeous as he'd remembered her. She sat on the edge of Jack's bed.

"Wanted to after that abysmal last date. If you can even call it that."

Jack hung his head. "Yeah. I was a Class-A jerk. I never should have put you in that position. I'm so sorry."

The hint of a smile played about Trinity's lips. "Apology accepted."

"Did you drive me home?" Jack looked around the room, a sudden look of panic in his eyes. "Oh man! Where are the kids?"

He started to leap from the bed. Trinity firmly placed two hands on his shoulders and forced him down. "Calm down. The kids are fine. They've eaten dinner, had their baths, and we even checked homework for school tomorrow."

Jack exhaled in relief. "You are a godsend. I can't even begin to thank you enough. God knows I don't deserve it after the way I treated you."

"Sounds like maybe that Frisbee knocked some sense into you."

Jack managed a chuckle. He reached up and gingerly touched the egg on his forehead. He winced. "Yeah, maybe it did."

Her voice took on a more somber tone. "Alice told me what happened with Charlie. Is he going to be okay?"

"The doctor's prognosis was less than stellar. He's a tough little guy though. Strong spirit." Jack wasn't certain if he was trying to convince her or himself.

"I'm so sorry," Trinity offered.

"It's funny, you know? How it takes something that devastating to make you realize things."

"Realize things? Like what?"

"How fleeting things are. How we only get a moment, then the moment's gone."

Trinity leaned a little closer to Jack. The warmth of her body seeped through the sheets. Jack could feel it against his skin. The scent of citrus and daisies wafted through the air. He inhaled deeply—as much to drink it in as to steel himself for what he was about to ask.

"That's why I'm going to ask something I probably have no right to," Jack continued.

Trinity sat up straight, her jaw set. Jack stumbled through the words before she could think the worst.

"Give me another chance?" he begged.

A beat passed. Jack held his breath. Before he could prepare for it, Trinity leaned in and pressed her full lips against his own. Electricity surged through him. He brought his arms around her supple waist and pulled her in even closer.

When they finally came up for air, a broad smile spread across Trinity's face.

"Now, that's how our first two dates should have ended," she suggested.

"I wholeheartedly agree, Ms. Watson," Jack grinned.

"And to think, all I had to do was clobber you over the head with the old Pluto Platter."

Jack shook his head. "I'm sorry. The what?"

"You know. The Pluto Platter. It's one of the original names of the Frisbee. Guess they figured it sounded better than the Flying Saucer."

"Flying Saucer?" Jack froze. He suddenly grabbed Trinity by the shoulders, pulled her in for another deep kiss, then released her, looking her squarely in the eye.

"Trinity Watson, you are a genius! An absolute genius! I need to make a comms call."

*****

That same night, Jack had called Bart with the idea for the saucer.

I just wish I had one now to get me to the lab faster than this stupid car!

As the electric car moved at its steady pace, he thought back to the scientific experiment Trinity's Frisbee had reminded him of.

Thomas Townsend-Brown had experimented with flying disks in his own antigravity experiments back in the 1950s. The inventor had charged metal disks with over twenty thousand volts of electricity in an effort to demonstrate an antigravity effect. Experts determined it was merely ionic drift that caused Townsend-Brown's disks to float, but after getting smacked with Trinity's Frisbee, Jack decided that coupled with their Thom-Thom technology, Townsend-Brown's concept had merit.

If they could alter the subatomic structure of a saucer-shaped device and mount it to the surface of the main craft, they could manipulate the thrust of its existing gravity hills and wells by adjusting the electrical charge applied to it. With enough voltage, a full-sized ship could rapidly be propelled through space toward Mars.

They had set up to run inorganic testing this upcoming Monday.

We just have to have a working accelerator to run the damn tests!

"Nothing was wrong, though, was it?" Jack needled. "The accelerator was working fine, right?"

"No. Everything was good. I just wanted to make sure we don't run into another fiasco like what happened with the CERN test," Bart continued. "The next thing I know, my wrist-comm starts going nuts, buzzing like a nest of angry hornets."

"I know. I got an alert too," Jack replied. "But what the hell happened?"

"I checked my messages. Turns out, the utility company shut down power to the grid. Rolling brownouts to adjust for increased demand. I don't get it. We're getting ready to colonize freaking Mars. You'd think we'd have come up with a viable energy solution by now. I talked to Gordon already. He says the lights are running on the backup generators, but no way in hell can they crank enough juice to run the accelerator."

Gordon Tooley had rejoined the P1AL crew along with Rosa Hernandez. With the date of the land grab bearing down on them like a freight train, Jack had been able to convince Locke he needed more help. Locke agreed to allow him to bring the former P1AL employees onto the project. It wasn't just that he needed the help to ensure they met the deadline. Jack didn't quite trust Locke's scientists. He felt far more comfortable having some of his own people on board.

Bart's news didn't make him feel comfortable at all.

"Shit!" Jack smacked the dashboard so hard the car gave a slight bobble. "Locke is scheduled for an on-site visit on Monday! Fat lot of good that's going to do if we don't have a working accelerator. You can't just flip the switch. Accelerators are inclined to get a little bit pissy if they don't get turned off nicely."

"That's the understatement of the decade," Bart muttered. "The whole damn thing's going to need to be re-tuned."

"All right, well, it's all hands on deck then. Call Rosa. Tell her we need her ASAP. Then get Binderkampf and Vashtin on the horn. Nobody sleeps until we get this under control. Understood?"

"Got it."

"I'm at the exit now. I'll be there in a few minutes. Meet you there. Hopefully we can avoid the sucking black hole of failure… again."

Jack disconnected the call. A wry grimace contorted his

features as he considered his particular choice of metaphors.

A black hole.

Regardless of its mass or size, the gravitational force at the event horizon of a black hole, that theoretical boundary skirting around its edges, beyond which nothing could escape, equated to 1.2 x 1044 Newtons.

That was the real gravity he had to break.

*****

Gravity threatened to pull his eyes closed. As the clock pressed on toward 7 a.m. on Saturday, it was a universal force operating on each of the scientists who had worked through the night. Once power had been restored, everyone had manned a station.

"Check the console display," Jack barked. "Make sure the beam's not too loose. If it is, it's going to shed too many particles. You'll have to tweak the quadrupole magnets. Focus the beam to keep the particles together."

"I'm on it," Gordon's gravelly voice rasped, sandpapered by years of cigar smoking.

"Beam path is out of calibration," Rosa added. "Realigning dipole magnets to compensate."

Jack gave a quick head bob. "Good." He called to Bart, "How are things looking on the control hub?"

Bart didn't respond.

"Bart?" Jack called again, this time glancing over to Bart's station. The software engineer was vertical. Barely. His double chin rested in the cup of his hand as his elbow rested on the desktop. A thin line of drool stretched from his generous lower lip. It yo-yoed with each inhale and exhale, his low-pitched snore rattling in counterpoint to the vibration of the accelerator.

Jack walk over and knocked Bart's arm out from under him. Bart nearly face-planted in his cup of now-cold coffee. Startled, his arms flailed in all directions. Coupled with the straw porkpie atop his round head, he looked like an Oz scarecrow.

"I'm up! I'm up!" he squawked like the crows his counterpart was meant to discourage.

"Yeah?" Jack challenged. "Well, up is exactly what we're trying to accomplish here, so, by all means, we'd appreciate your insight. Again, how are things looking on the control hub?"

Bart dragged a sleeve across his mouth. "Levels are stabilized. Looks like we've got everything back on track."

"Well, isn't that excellent news." All heads swiveled to the entrance where Locke stood, looking crisply expensive and alert despite the early hour.

CHAPTER 34

Locke's intense gaze bore down on the quivering Dr. Binderkampf. The nervous scientist took a cautious step behind Emry Vashtin, as though the thin man's frame could even remotely protect him from Locke's wrath.

Locke owed this little field trip to the good doctor. Binderkampf had been the one to rouse Locke with tales of disaster at the P1AL labs after he himself received the alert from Pulldraw to report immediately to the collider facility.

"The collider's down!" Binderkampf's strident voice had warbled through the wrist-comm. Without so much as a word, Locke had slid from his bed, called his driver to prepare the car, jumped in the shower, and readied himself to determine if this incident was going to kill his Mars project.

And determine who I'm going to kill because of it.

Now, as that idiot with the ridiculous bowler hat atop his round head—what was his name again?—announced the collider was stable again, it became readily apparent to Locke that Binderkampf had prematurely called foul.

Well, you cried wolf, Doctor.

Locke's lip curled as his gaze locked with Binderkampf's. *Here I am.*

As the portly scientist cowered, Locke's sneer morphed into a sardonic smirk. The wolf metaphor amused him. He looked at the assemblage of white coats before him, his own little herd of compliant sheep doing his bidding and, right now, his bidding was to make the goddamned ship float. The soles of Locke's shoes clicked on the tile as he strode toward Harding.

"Now that we're 'back on track,' Dr. Harding, as your colleague in the Magritte chapeau so conveniently informed us," Locke began, pulling the cuffs of his silk shirt taut, "perhaps you can update me on when I can expect to see some tangible results on your team's efforts."

"Well, as you are aware, we have a demonstration scheduled for…"

"Now," Locke stated.

Harding blinked at Locke's sudden mandate. He exchanged an uneasy glance with Pulldraw. The sentiment rippled through the rest of the team, low nervous murmurs undulating through the group. The software engineer offered a limp shrug to his partner. Harding's gaze swiveled back to Locke.

"Now? But," he verbally stumbled. "My people haven't slept, and we weren't scheduled to initiate that testing until Monday."

Locke interrupted. "And I wasn't scheduled to be this far behind in the land grab initiative."

The black gravity of Locke's eyes sucked everything in and obliterated it, burgeoning complaint and opposition included. *Everything except fear.*

"We all have our own little trials, then, don't we?" Locke surveyed a manicured hand, tilting it this way and that.

"The only difference? In this trial I am the sole judge, jury…" He allowed his voice to drift so everyone in the room would feel his gravitas. "And executioner."

It pleased him to see the collective bobbing Adam's apples as everyone in the room swallowed the bitter taste of fear.

Maybe now I'll start to see some results.

Harding cleared his throat. "Very well, Mr. Locke. It's your circus. Let's get started, shall we?"

Harding moved toward the bank of consoles, barking orders. The crew members quickly fell in line, each manning a different aspect of the equipment. Some took up positions at the monitoring screens. Pulldraw's fingers sped over the keyboard of the control hub. Locke heard the warning alarm blare through the facility, heralding the initiation sequence of the collider. He watched it all with keen interest.

"Injection sequence complete. Protons loaded," Vashtin announced.

"Ramping sequence initiated. Collider powering up," another of the scientists called, a woman, her coarse black hair pulled back in a tight bun. Dark purple shadowed the ochre skin beneath her eyes, exhaustion showing its toll.

"We hope," Locke heard Pulldraw mutter.

"Proton beams accelerating to collision energy. 6.5TeV per beam." Binderkampf's nasal tone voiced.

"If you'd be so kind as to illuminate the process for my 'friend' here." Locke gestured to the grim-faced gentleman behind him. The molded earwig earpiece in his ear and muscles straining against the seams of his tailored black suit belied the true nature of his acquaintance with Locke.

Harding jotted down some relevant notes on his clipboard before answering him.

"We're attempting to replicate the event in which the ferret's mass excess was altered."

Harding moved toward the observation window. "When the

ferret interrupted the collision path inside the collider," Harding pointed, "like the one we have here, his molecular makeup—the number of protons, neutrons, and specifically electrons—his mass, was altered."

Locke nodded. "And that's what gives him the ability to hover in midair?"

"Exactly. The ability we're working toward applying toward your spacecraft."

"Not quickly enough. The Paramus Aerospace Group, as I'm sure you're aware, has already launched their vessel."

Harding pulled at his collar. "Yes, well, the problem was determining the exact details of the inciting incident, like the ferret's original mass and the strength of the beam. Critical factors if we wanted to replicate the effect of the event. That's where the ROAR program comes in. Mr. Pulldraw created an algorithm which allowed us to reverse engineer the event and run subsequent simulations using inputted data for other organic matter."

"Simulations?"

Harding nodded. "It's what we designed ROAR for in the first place. And we would never have been able to figure out why the ferret floats without it. Its quantum computing capabilities worked through an infinite number of experimental observations and calculations using the data from the original event and processed them through every potential outcome."

"CliffsNotes version, if you don't mind, Doctor," Locke said.

"Right. Right. Basically, ROAR predicts experimental outcomes."

"So, we can tell if something's going to work virtually before we affect a real-world application?"

"Essentially, yes. Since Thom-Thom—"

"Thom-Thom?" Locke interjected.

"The ferret," Harding replied.

"The rodent has a name?"

"Well, technically, ferrets aren't rodents. They're a member of the weasel family." Locke silenced him with a look. Harding continued. "Anyway, since Thom-Thom is carbon-based, organic material, we began our experimentation with other organic material—*Lumbricus terrestris*, mostly."

"Lumbricus terrestris?"

"Earthworms."

"Earthworms? Why the hell aren't we using lab mice?"

"The particle accelerator isn't always…friendly…to living matter. Just ask Anatoli Bugorski."

"Who in the hell is Anatoli Bugorski?" Locke challenged.

"Kentucky-fried Russian," Pulldraw interjected from his post. "Back in '78, the Russkies were having trouble with their collider, so he stuck his melon inside the proton channel and his brain came out crunchier than the colonel's extra crispy."

"Not exactly," Harding embellished. "But the proton beam did burn a hole through his brain. It destroyed nerves and tissue and permanently paralyzed one side of his face. If word got out that we were subjecting live mice to that potential risk, it might have brought some very unwelcome attention from groups like PETA."

"If it gets us to Mars, I don't care if we fry Mickey Fucking Mouse," Locke hissed through clenched teeth. "Is that understood?"

Harding took a cautious step backward. "Yes, but the point is moot. After repeated successful simulations, we've been running the collider nonstop."

"And?"

"And we've successfully floated the worms, but it's the inorganic matter test that will have the greatest effect on the

Mars project. If the data we've collected through the ROAR simulations is correct, we could theoretically use the collider to rearrange the subatomic mass of an external apparatus, making it, in effect, an asymmetric capacitor. We affix it to the ship, and by reducing or ramping up the voltage pumping through it, we can control the thrust or pull of the gravity wells and hills."

"And how does that give me an advantage?"

"You won't be restricted by the same physics. The other teams are likely counting on a gravity assist from Venus. Basically, their spacecraft will slingshot past Venus, harnessing the planet's gravity to alter course toward Mars. A gravity assist reduces the expenditure of energy for the Mars trip, cutting the weight and increasing the speed of the trip. You won't need to rely on Venus' gravity, or the gravity of any other heavenly body for that matter. With this tech, you," Harding pointed at Locke, "will be able to create or subvert gravity. At will."

A slow smile spread across Locke's face.

At will.

It made perfect sense. It was how he did everything else in his life. He took the women he wanted…at will. He shredded business competitors…at will. He killed.

At will.

Why shouldn't he conquer the heavens the same way?

"Let's see if your theory holds water, Dr. Harding." Locke gestured toward the collider, which hummed in anticipation.

"Rosa!" Harding called. "Squeeze the beam. This whole thing goes pear-shaped if we don't zap the disk."

"Disk?" Locke asked.

"The apparatus I mentioned. We're using a design based on Thomas Townsend-Brown's work with electrogravitics. Think of it as a giant Frisbee. It's already loaded into the collider."

"Preparing for beam event," another man called.

Locke read his identification badge. Tooley. One of Harding's people. Tooley reached a lanky arm toward a cluster of buttons on the console and depressed several of them. "Here comes the flat-top! Beam energy leveling out."

"That means the beam is reaching its targeted position."

"Beams stabilizing and...we have collision event!" Pulldraw let out a hearty whoop. Cheers went up from the others in the room.

"We're not done here, people!" Harding warned. "Initiate beam dump."

"On it!" Pulldraw flopped back into his seat. He rapidly typed a sequence at the control hub.

"Beam dump?" Locke queried.

"We've got bunches of protons traveling at nearly two hundred miles per hour in there. You can't just flip the switch. It would be like asking a crossing guard to stop an Amtrak. That's why there was some concern when the power grid went down. What should happen is we divert the protons to a new track into a beam dump. Basically, it's a solid graphite cylinder over twenty-six feet and a little over three feet around. The whole thing's filled with nitrogen gas, and it's sheathed in stainless steel covered by iron and concrete."

"Beam dump complete," Pulldraw announced.

Harding clapped his hands together. "All right, then. Let's see if there's really such a thing as a flying saucer, shall we? Gordon?"

Tooley nodded and donned some nearby safety gear before proceeding to the maintenance tunnels. Tension hung thick in the room.

Locke felt a surge of adrenaline building in his gut, much like the feeling he'd had just before he sent Donny Newton to his maker all those years ago.

There was an inexplicable thrill in firsts.

Now, he hovered on the cusp of a discovery that would catapult him to first in the Mars land-grab.

And if Harding failed, there was always the old thrill to fall back on.

All eyes remained focused on the exit to the tunnels. No one spoke. Tooley's immensely tall, lanky frame appeared in the doorway. In his hands, he held a large, convex disk, nearly stretching his ample arm span to its six-foot-six-inch limit. He paused as he stepped into the center of the room.

"Well?" Harding asked, nearly bouncing on his toes.

In response, Tooley released the huge disk. Everyone, including Locke, stood slack-jawed as they watched the saucer-like object bob upward to defy gravity and linger just over their heads.

Harding beamed. "Mr. Locke, it looks like my tech's going to send you to Mars."

"No," Locke intoned. He snapped his fingers and signaled to his men to collect the hard drives and data readouts from each of the computer stations. "My tech is sending me to Mars. Oh, and we'll be needing *that*."

He pointed to the saucer.

The joyful jubilation that had filled the room just moments before sank like a lead balloon. Locke paid it no mind. He turned to leave, then turned back to face Harding.

"I want everyone at Locke Industries' assembly facility in the morning. You may have taken one giant leap for mankind today, but there are still a hundred and fifty-three miles to go."

CHAPTER 35

Harding Estate
Jack

"He took *everything?*" Alice asked as she sat, legs tucked beneath her on the sofa in Jack's living room.

Jack paced furiously in his sock feet, fuming. "The hard drives, the saucer...everything! He called it 'his tech,' like Bart and I had absolutely nothing to do with it."

He whirled to face her. "We had *everything* to do with it!"

He stomped his foot for emphasis. Unfortunately, he stomped right on top of one of Lucas' Legos. The insidious piece of molded plastic sent electric jolts of pain through his foot and up into his leg as the sharp corners bit through the thin weave of his socks.

He started hopping like a frog on a hot plate, clutching his injured appendage. He knocked into the coffee table, lost his balance, and fell in a useless, moaning heap. Alice brought her hands to her mouth and gasped. She leaped to his aid.

"Oh my gosh! Jack! Are you okay?"

Jack struggled to right himself. "Yeah, I'm fine. Apparently, two hours sleep over a forty-eight-hour period is not conducive to good balance."

Alice clucked her tongue. "Probably not."

Jack rubbed his foot vigorously, trying to rub out the pain. He picked up the offending Lego. "You know, the military's got it all wrong. They really want to injure the enemy? Toss a couple of these suckers on the battlefield."

Alice's eyes glittered. "But you actually got it to work?"

Jack's pain instantly melted away. He grabbed Alice's hands in his. "We actually got it to work. It was amazing, Alice! It just hovered there, like it was floating on an invisible cushion of air. I mean, we've really got a shot at getting to Mars now."

He got to his feet and limped toward the kitchen. Alice clambered over the back of the sofa and followed him.

"I guess the next step is going to be to affix the saucer unit to a rocket and test the antigravity propulsion theory with an actual ship," Jack suggested. "Of course, I have to run an electrical conduit from the interior of the ship to the saucer to regulate power output and thrust, but that will be a cakewalk compared to what we've already accomplished."

A small frown darkened Alice's petite features. "But how are you going to do all that if Mr. Locke took everything?"

"Oh no. It's not like that. He took it all to his rocket assembly facility. Can't make a rocket fly if you don't have a rocket. Uncle Bart and I are going to go work there and finish the rest of the project there. We start tomorrow." Jack tilted his wrist and glanced at his watch. "Which will be here sooner rather than later. You need to get to bed, and I need to get some sleep, or I might screw everything up and wind up on Pluto instead of Mars. Talk about the wrong planet!"

He ushered her down the hallway toward the bedrooms.

"Yeah," she agreed. "Especially since Pluto's technically not even a planet anymore. It's a dwarf."

"A dwarf, huh? Well, I'm a dwarf too. Wanna guess which

one?"

"Grumpy, for sure."

"You got that right. Now, you go be Sleepy, and in the morning, we'll both be Happy."

"Okay, Jack," Alice giggled and scampered off to her room, humming. As she disappeared through her doorway, Jack was almost certain he heard the words "off to work we go."

He would be off to work soon himself, he thought as he heard the grandfather clock in the living room toll the hour. Once in his bedroom, he collapsed across the queen bed, ready to fall into an easy sleep.

But tired as he was, falling asleep proved to be anything but easy. The feeling gnawing at his gut had him staring blankly at the ceiling.

Why had Locke taken all the data, the saucer, and the hard drives from the **P1AL** *labs?*

More importantly, why had he let him? Any tech developed with the use of **ROAR** technology was proprietary. Jack sighed heavily.

Charlie.

As his thoughts turned toward the boy, he knew Charlie was the real reason he kept jumping through all of Locke's hoops— why he'd just allowed Locke to walk out the doors of the lab with everything and why he was going to dutifully report to the assembly facility in the morning. He still needed Locke.

And Charlie needed him.

Tired as he was, there was somewhere he had to be.

"House?" he called out loud to the smarthome's concierge. "Call Trinity."

*****

The sound of the ventilator hissed and wheezed quietly in the background. The steady blip of the pulse monitor was illuminated in jagged green hills on the screen, tracking Charlie's heartbeat.

Jack sat in the faux leather chair in Charlie's hospital room, the kind that reclined into a single bed for long, watchful nights at a patient's bedside. He ruminated that despite all of society's advances—self-driving cars, smart dust, volumetric readouts, and holographic displays—hospitals had remained largely unchanged. The astringent bite of antiseptic still permeated the air. The page of cryptic medical codes still squawked over the public address system. Nurses never let you sleep at night—always poking and prodding. And seeing someone you cared for hooked up to a battery of machines made the person seem so small and frail, and you felt hopelessly inadequate to help.

Jack reached out to hold Charlie's small hand in his own. It wasn't much. Just a small gesture, really. He wasn't even certain if Charlie was aware of his presence, but until he got to Mars and secured those egrets, it was all he could really do. After his fever, Charlie had slipped into a coma. Jack shook his head in disbelief.

He thought of all of Locke's veiled threats. Of Bart's suggestion that the man had something to do with the horrible death of the scientist in Houston. Locke was dangerous. Of that, Jack had little doubt.

But this disease, vanishing white matter syndrome, was downright insidious. Hiding in the DNA, in mutated genes, it could lurk undetected, as it had in Charlie, striking without notice. Then, it robbed you.

It stole your legs. It stole your vision. It stole your mind.

Jack gazed down at Charlie's face.

It had stolen Charlie's smile.

The doctors were uncertain whether Charlie would even

wake. Even if he did, mental degeneration was a very real possibility. There was no way to know—at least not till he awoke.

"Hang in there, champ," Jack whispered. "I'm doing everything I can."

He leaned forward and rested his head on the edge of the bed. A sound over his shoulder made him lift his head.

"Oh, I'm sorry. I didn't realize anyone was here with him. I was just making rounds."

Jack sat up and rubbed his eyes. The doctor had entered the room.

"I hadn't planned on being here tonight," Jack responded. "I guess I just felt like I needed to be here though. So, I called a friend to sit in with the other kids and headed over. Any change?"

The doctor looked at the chart, flipped a few pages, then shook his head somberly. "No. No change since the initial onset of the coma. Sometimes after an episode, we witness signs of partial improvement, but in this case?"

The doctor placed a comforting hand on Jack's shoulder. "I think you need to prepare yourself for the very real possibility that he may never wake."

Jack leaped to his feet. "No! I won't do that!"

The doctor made a shushing motion. "Please, Mr. Harding. I must ask you to keep your voice down. This is a hospital."

"Yes. It is a hospital. A place where people come to get help to get better."

The doctor sighed. "Yes, but sometimes the science hasn't caught up to every disease or illness we see."

"Then you know what? Maybe science needs a boost."

Like a big fat rocket shoved up the backside.

He grabbed his jacket and stormed through the door.

CHAPTER 36

Locke Industries Assembly Facility
Jack

The titan towered.

Jack and Bart stood in the vertical assembly building of Locke Industries and craned their necks upward to follow the two-hundred-and-twenty-foot barrel as it climbed toward the ceiling of the high bay.

"We're going to Mars in *that?*" Bart murmured, awe tempering his normally boisterous tone.

Jack shook his head. "No. That's the propulsion system. Locke's backup plan. You know, in case we go the way of Newton's apple."

"You mean fall flat on our faces," Bart translated.

Jack shrugged. "And did you have to wear *that?*" He pointed to the wide-brimmed, wooly gray conical hat rising from the younger man's head. "I mean, today of all days."

Bart scoffed. He jabbed a thumb at the monstrous rocket. "Do you really think anyone is going to notice *me* when *that* is in the room?"

"That, gentlemen," a voice behind them addressed, "is the *Horus* rocket."

The men turned to see a slight brunette woman in a white lab coat peering at them from behind round glasses. She looked almost Lilliputian next to the behemoth rocket. From her smooth unlined skin, Jack assumed she was rather young. In fact, there was an almost impish air of childlike glee about her as she blew at a stray lock of hair that had worked loose from her messy bun and fallen over her eyes.

Jack read her identification badge. Locke Industries–Midge Evers, PhD.

Another of Locke's people.

Yet, unlike the others he'd met, like Binderkampf and Vashtin, Midge Evers wore a jovial expression, and her tone was friendly. Still, Jack remained cautious.

There's too much riding on this.

"Yep!" Midge continued. "Primed, this baby carries nearly seven million pounds of binary rocket fuel composed of liquidated oxygen methane cooled to near freezing. But don't you worry. Things'll get hot enough when those thirty Peregrine engines fire up and produce seventy-five meganewtons of maximum thrust. That's three more meganewtons than Musk's old hunk of junk, Super Heavy, I'll have you know. But the rumor mill has it we might not even be needing this bad boy now that you're here. In fact, you fellas might just put me out of a job."

"I'm sorry?" Confusion filled Jack's face.

The woman grinned from ear to ear. "Dr. Midge Evers, aerospace engineering here at Locke Industries. Smartest gal to ever come out of Bellville, Texas, and youngest ever to graduate from Cal Tech, thank you very much."

Texas. As Jack surveyed her petite frame, he chuckled inwardly.

Guess not everything's bigger in Texas.

"Cal Tech? I went to Cal Tech!" Bart grinned. "I'm Bart. Bart

Pulldraw."

"And that would make you Dr. Jack Harding, both from P1AL labs if I'm not mistaken," Midge ventured.

She reached out to shake both men's hands. Her hand was small, but her grip was firm.

"Pleased to meet you," Jack said.

Midge put her hands on her hips.

"Well, I think I'm supposed to give you guys the ten-cent tour. Wouldn't want you to get lost on your first day." She swung her arms out in a wide, sweeping gesture meant to encompass the entire facility.

"As you can see, the assembly facility takes up a pretty big footprint at nine hundred acres. More than the Mouse here in California, less than the Mouse in Florida, but either way, we've got better rides."

She jabbed a thumb.

"*Horus*," Bart restated, staring awestruck at the big rocket.

Midge nodded. "Egyptian falcon god of the air. Loosely translated, the name means 'that which is above' or 'the distant one.' Both of which describe Mr. Locke to a 'T' if you ask me."

She snorted, then checked herself.

"Ahem, but I do believe Mr. Locke chose the name in light of the nature of this project. You know—up there—among the stars." She waggled her fingers in the air.

"And the name of the engines? Peregrine is a falcon too. Correct me if I'm wrong, but I'm sensing a theme here," Jack suggested.

"I think it's Mr. Locke's way of thumbing his nose at Mr. Musk. You know he's named a lot of his engines after birds too. The Kestrel, the Raptor, the Merlin," she began.

"I think you mean 'marlin.' Merlin was a wizard," Bart interrupted. "That's fifteen years of Supanova Comic Con talking here."

"I love Supanova Comic Con!" Midge blurted. "I have this Plasma Girl outfit I use for cosplay…" Midge began. Bart froze, his eyes glazing over just a little. Jack nudged him until he blinked.

"But that's ridiculous," Midge continued. "You don't want to hear about my silly old hobbies. And, besides, if you can pull off the kind of magic everyone's been talking about, I might have to start calling *you* 'Merlin.'"

She snorted again and playfully shoved Bart's shoulder. "By the way, love your hat."

He blushed right to the tips of his ears.

"And, no, I don't mean 'marlin.' Merlin is the proper name for the bird colloquially known as the 'pigeon hawk,'" Midge explained. "But it's the peregrine, you see, that's the fastest bird. Can reach speeds up to two hundred miles per hour. Guess when he went about picking a moniker, Mr. Locke wanted to suggest he was going to be the fastest to Mars."

She blinked at both of them from behind her round frames and rocked forward on her toes. "What do you say we get this tour going, eh? Please keep your hands and arms inside the vehicle at all times, and away we go!"

She spun on the ball of her ballet flat and headed off into the heart of the facility, motioning for the men to follow her.

"I think I'm in love," Bart mumbled.

"Easy. Cool your jets, Casanova. Remember where we are. We can't be certain who we can trust…" Jack stared after the diminutive rocket scientist, who was practically skipping.

"No matter how adorable they are."

*****

"The Locke Industries Assembly Facility features just under

1.5 million square feet of manufacturing space and plenty of room for expansion," Midge stated as the trio walked through the facility. "The vertical assembly center alone is fifty thousand square feet."

She gestured above her head as they passed through another wide-open area. "As you can see, we have several high bay spaces, most of which are extensively equipped with an industrial overhead crane network. We also employ robotic tools to aid in rocket assembly and to stack oversized vertical structures."

She snorted again. "Compared to me, I suppose everything is oversized!"

Another snort. "But seriously, it's super helpful when it comes to putting these monsters together. And, of course, we do a lot more here. Pretty much anything you can think of to further rocket science. We have friction stir-welding capabilities—"

"Friction stir-welding?" Jack interrupted. "What's that?"

"Basically, it's a method of joining two workpieces without destroying any of the material the way you would with traditional welding methods. Saves a bunch of money since you waste less material. We just use a specialized tool to generate friction, which then provides the heat needed to conjoin the desired pieces."

Bart leaned forward to whisper in Jack's ear. Jack suspected a racy double entendre and held up a warning hand.

"Don't even," he said.

Midge blathered on, oblivious. "We also fabricate the composite materials necessary to build out the rocket pieces and have the facilities for testing right here in-house. We have industrial 3D printers and gantry machining centers for milling, drilling, threading, and cutting needs."

She turned to face them. "Well, there you have it. We pretty much have everything—a one-stop-shop for all your space travel needs. Well, almost. You haven't seen the icing on the cake yet.

Wait till you get a load of this!"

She ushered them into yet another bay. Once inside, Jack's jaw dropped. Standing upright at almost a hundred and sixty feet tall was a sleek bullet of a spacecraft. The wind left Jack's chest as Bart smacked a hard hand into it.

"It's Ming the Merciless' rocket!" Bart gasped. He bit his fist.

Jack's forehead furrowed in consternation, but as he looked at the starship, he couldn't deny the resemblance to the villain's ship in the 1930s cult classic comic, *Flash Gordon*. The ship's body tapered from the nose cone downward, wider at its crest and slimming toward the bottom, where four triangular fins flared. Jack searched his brain for the correct archaic term.

Delta wings.

Delta, huh? Don't suppose they'll give me frequent flyer miles for this trip.

Peeking from beneath the fins, Jack was certain he spied several more Peregrine engines–power, he supposed, for after the ship broke free from the rocket booster.

If all goes according to the ROAR simulations, hopefully we won't need those.

A large viewing window curved near the top of the ship.

"A window?" Bart asked. "I'm all for stargazing, ahem, with the right person," he tossed an eager smile toward Midge, "but isn't that a little on the dangerous side for a spaceship? I mean, structurally speaking. Not to mention, you're asking for a helluva sunburn with the solar radiation up there. The stewardess handing out SPF 3000 instead of peanuts?"

Midge returned his smile, which made Bart blush again. "We've taken all of that into consideration, of course. The window is actually a three-pane system. The outer pane is composed of fused silica. It stands up well to high temperatures that may present at atmospheric entry. We've infused it with cerium oxide to be able to absorb ultraviolet light–that radiation you're worried about. The pressure pane, the inner pane, is composed of tempered aluminosilicate. That strength is needed to stand up to the interior cabin pressure. The middle pane is the best-of-both-worlds pane. It can withstand high temps from the outside and stand up to the cabin pressure from the inside. So, you see? No worries. It's a room with a view. Not a doom with a view."

"Helluva room," Jack muttered.

Bart looked at Dr. Evers. He gave her an enthusiastic thumbs-up. "You're absolutely brilliant. You know, in case no one's ever mentioned it."

Now, it was Midge's turn to blush. She toed the ground.

"Gee, thanks."

Jack continued surveying the ship. Its silver surface gleamed. Jack held up a shielding hand to protect against the glare.

"What is that? Stainless steel?"

Midge shook her head. "No, although stainless *is* pretty cheap. Comes in at about three bucks for just under two and a half pounds. Has a high melting point too. Probably some of the reasons why Musk decided to use it. But we went another route. Used a newly developed aluminum alloy. Aluminum is so incredibly light, it only makes sense to use it in the construction of spacecraft. You want to reinforce it, of course, with an alloy to make it stronger. Problem is the residues of most aluminum alloys break down with exposure to the radiation in space."

"That could be a problem," Bart muttered cynically.

"Yes, I suppose it would dampen your day if you were cruising past Saturn and your ride home started disintegrating." She paused, lost in momentary contemplation. "But our specific alloy is radiation-resistant. So, no harm, no foul. Dr. Engleton, one of the scientists at our Houston facility, suggested it before…" Midge's voice faltered, and an uncharacteristic gloom clouded her features. She started fiddling with her identification badge.

"Before what?" Jack asked. Midge opened her mouth to speak.

"Before we built this incredible piece of machinery!" Locke's authoritative tone echoed in the wide expanse of the hangar bay. Jack and Bart whirled at the sound of his voice. Midge angled herself slightly behind Bart, who noticed the discreet shift and straightened his shoulders, standing a little bit taller.

"But that is neither here nor there," Locke continued. "Our ship is now built and brilliant and eagerly awaits the addition of your breakthrough technology, Dr. Harding. So, if Dr. Evers has completed your orientation?"

Locke looked down the length of his aquiline nose at the rocket scientist, eyes narrowed. She stepped fully from behind Bart and nodded.

"Yes, sir, Mr. Locke. As far as I know, there is nothing else standing in the way."

A slow, satisfied smile spread across Locke's face. "About damned time."

*****

Locke paced through the assembly facility, the flock of scientists scurrying subserviently in his wake. As he walked, he ticked off tasks on his long fingers. Several of the scientists scribbled furiously with their styluses, noting his instructions on their tablets. Jack just listened, wondering with every step exactly what he'd managed to get himself into.

"Firstly, get the engineers to secure the upper stage to the rocket assembly. Then I expect to have the gravitator assembly secured to *Horus* by end of week. No excuses."

Jack was secretly pleased Locke had gotten on board with calling the saucer a "gravitator," although Jack suspected it had less to do with honoring the late Thomas Townsend-Brown whose work had influenced Jack's own invention and more to do with just not being bothered with trivial detail.

A trivial detail had stirred Jack's curiosity though. Most of the scientists hung on Locke's every word, trailing the billionaire by less than six inches. Midge Evers lagged behind. She seemed reluctant to get too close to Locke. Jack fell in step with the petite rocket scientist.

"Everything okay?" he asked.

The concerned expression on her face lingered for just a moment more, then evaporated, her familiar smile returning once more. "What's that? Why yes, of course, Dr. Harding. We are on the cusp of something truly amazing here! Why wouldn't things be okay?"

"I couldn't help but notice, you seem a little...flustered," Jack said.

"Flustered? No, really. I'm fine. Although," she began, "I tend to get a bit unsettled at the mention of Dr. Engleton. I used to work with him, you know. At the Houston facility? Such a kind man, and brilliant too. After I finished my doctorate, he was the one who interviewed me at the TitusBane facility. I wanted to be close to home, you see. And Houston's only an hour from Bellville. After what happened, though, I couldn't bring myself to stay."

"After what happened?" Jack's mind raced to catch up.

Midge stopped walking. She stared into Jack's eyes. "I'm the one who found his body."

"Engleton!" Bart hissed in Jack's ear. "That's the guy Trinity mentioned. The one I was telling you about!"

Jack waved him away.

"Dr. Engleton was the scientist who got, er, incinerated by the rocket engine?" Jack asked Midge.

She nodded. "It was awful. No one knows exactly how it happened. There are protocols in place to prevent things like that."

A sniff hitched her breathing. She dabbed at her nose with a tissue she pulled from her pocket. She returned it as she took a deep, cleansing breath. "Anyway, the memory was so tragic, I couldn't stand going to work every day. I just kept seeing his... charred corpse. I still wanted to work on the Mars program, so I requested a transfer to work here. I thought a change of scenery would help. Now, I'm not so sure it was the right decision."

She looked up. Locke cast a wary glance over his shoulder toward the young woman. She stopped talking and worried at an imaginary stain on her lab coat.

Jack remembered how Bart had hinted at Locke's involvement in the affair. Jack leaned in, whispering. "Do you think Mr. Locke had anything to do with the incident at TitusBane?"

Midge's gaze darted toward Locke, who was engrossed in barking orders. She ducked behind a barrel assembly platform and dragged Jack with her. He grabbed Bart at the last second, just before they all disappeared from Locke's line of sight.

Midge whispered, her voice taut with tension. "All I know is there was a test firing scheduled for that day—the CRX2221. We were all there to witness it. But for some reason, Mr. Locke ushered us all out at the last minute. Said something about needing privacy with Dr. Engleton."

"Did he say why?" Jack asked, his curiosity piqued.

Midge shook her head. "I mean, the team was a bit behind schedule. As lead scientist on the project, I was worried Dr. Engleton might be getting fired. That didn't sit well with me at all. This was groundbreaking tech. Mr. Locke had to expect some stumbling blocks."

"What happened then?" Bart queried.

Midge shrugged. "Most everyone returned to their workstations. I hung back though. I wanted to express to Mr. Locke how unfair I thought he was being. How I thought he should give Dr. Engleton another chance. So, I waited just down the hall for the two of them to come out."

"And?"

"And only Mr. Locke came out," she murmured. "I followed him to the parking lot to tell him what I thought."

"What did he say?"

"I don't know. I never actually spoke to him. His car was pulling away just as I got outside. Not too long after that, I found Dr. Engleton's body."

"Did you mention any of this to the police?" Jack pushed.

Midge shook her head. "You don't make accusations against a man like Travis Locke unless you're damned sure and have the proof to back it up. There was no security video from inside the firing bay that showed Locke engaging the rocket, and there was more than enough time for someone else to slip into the bay while I was chasing after Mr. Locke."

She sighed. "Look, maybe I should have said something, but ever since I was a little girl, I've dreamed of being a part of something big. This Mars project is big! I didn't want to jeopardize my job."

"So, why mention it to us now?" Bart asked.

"Whether Mr. Locke wants to admit it or not, Dr. Engleton made a huge contribution to this team's Mars effort. Our ship is lighter than any other ship heading for Mars. Between his efforts and your contributions, we're going to outstrip any team making the voyage, but Dr. Engleton didn't live long enough to see that happen. I don't want to see the same thing happen to you. Watch your backs."

With that, Dr. Evers peered from behind the barrel assembly platform and slipped back into the gaggle of scientists walking behind Locke. As she cast a worried look back toward the spot where Jack and Bart stood, she didn't see the sidelong glance Locke cast in her direction.

Jack saw it though. He also saw the studied look Locke gave him as he and Bart rushed to catch up to the moving group.

CHAPTER 37

Locke Industries Assembly Facility
Jack

"Gravitator assembly anchored!" the engineer called down from the lift.

A collective whoop soared up from the gathered crowd at the foot of the *Horus* StarCraft.

Jack exhaled. He felt like he had been holding his breath all week. Things had been moving forward at Locke Industries at a dizzying pace. Mars was getting closer by the second. He could feel it. The upper stage had been secured to the rocket assembly earlier in the week, and he and Bart had been poring over the ROAR data, verifying and cross-checking. Everything pointed toward a green light for today's test.

So, why did he feel like a supernova on the verge of collapse?

The answer was simple. The conversation with Dr. Evers had unnerved him. She was right. She had no actual proof Travis Locke had been involved in the incident at TitusBane. At best, Jack could only consider her evidence hearsay and conjecture. Still, it left him feeling skittish about working so closely with the man.

But it's not like I have a choice.

His gaze drifted up to the observation deck high above the *Horus* hangar bay. The man in question stood stoically, one arm folded across his trim waistline, the other propped beneath his sharp chin, watching. He hadn't participated in the shared cheer. He seemed to be waiting for greater accomplishments.

He was waiting for the miracle.

"You and me both, Mr. Locke," Jack murmured to himself.

"What did you say?" Bart asked, fingers typing at his optical virtual keyboard at Jack's elbow.

"I said, it's time to get this show on the road." Jack didn't wait for any prompt from Locke. Instead, he shifted into high gear and started cranking out orders for the gravitator test.

"Make sure the feed wires are connected. The lift should increase exponentially with the amount of voltage we run through the gravitator, but it won't mean crap if the juice has no way of getting to it. Remember, we've got to positively charge the outboard wire on the leading edge. And the body of the gravitator itself should be negatively charged," he barked. A sinuous, twisted bundle of insulated wires had been fed to the gravitator from the interior of the *Horus* StarCraft, where it was connected to the fuel cell power plants. It looked like a python twisting its way down through the hull of the craft.

The power plants themselves, twelve in all, were proton-exchange-membrane fuel cells (PEMFCs). Simpler, lighter, and safer than traditional fuel cell assemblies, the PEMFCs had the added benefit of providing a source of potable water for the spacecraft's crew. Each cell could provide up to twelve thousand volts of power. The cells were connected to a discreet accessory section where the crew could control and monitor performance. Today, however, the accessory section controls were being monitored remotely by Bart—in case anything should go awry.

Like, say, the rocket explodes.

A shiver of dread rippled down Jack's spine.

"This is going to work," he said to Bart.

"You trying to convince me, or you?" Bart replied, a crooked grin on his face. He clapped Jack on the shoulder. "Don't worry. We've got this."

Despite his shared misgivings with Jack about Locke, Bart had been particularly jovial as of late. Jack suspected it had something to do with the software engineer's lunches with the lovely Dr. Evers. Turned out, the duo had much more in common than an affinity for buxom, Lycra-clad, feminine superheroes.

"By the way, how are things going with the doc?" Jack asked.

"Great!" Bart answered eagerly. He folded his arms smugly. "We actually have a date this Friday. Roller derby."

Jack grinned.

You might just get those grandkids yet, Myrna.

Bart's face clouded. He looked around. "Although, I kind of expected she'd be here for this. I mean, it's kind of a big deal."

Jack frowned. "That is a little weird. Where do you suppose she is?"

An alarm, similar to the one they had at the P1AL labs, klaxoned through the facility, interrupting him. "Attention all personnel. Attention. Gravitator test will initiate in five minutes. Clear the area. Repeat. Clear the area."

Everyone vacated the hangar bay and repaired to the lower observation deck behind the safety glass. The announcement repeated a second time.

"Dr. Harding, are we good to go?" Locke's cool voice came over the intercom.

Jack depressed a button and answered. "Yes, sir."

"Then let's make some history, shall we?" Locke's tone made it clear he didn't require a verbal response. Only action.

"Power the fuel cells," Jack ordered. Bart typed rapidly on the holographic keyboard.

"Fuel cells active," Bart replied.

"Get ready to disengage holding clamps as soon as we have liftoff."

"Holding clamps standing by."

"Retract roof."

"Check."

Here goes everything.

"Engage power to gravitator," he said. "Set maximum voltage to fifty thousand."

"Maximum voltage set at fifty thousand," Bart confirmed.

"Jesus, I hope I don't kill anybody," Jack said under his breath.

Bart chuckled. "Don't worry. It's not the volts that kill you. It's the amps."

Jack smiled weakly at Bart's attempt to cheer him, but they both knew fifty thousand volts mixed with the right current would turn anybody into a charcoal briquette.

A charcoal briquette like Dr. Engleton.

Jack looked around at the gathered engineers and scientists. Where was Dr. Evers? He was so focused on locating her face in the crowd, he didn't notice the perplexed looks on their faces.

Bart nudged him. "Jack, nothing's happening."

Ice slurried in Jack's veins. "Wait. What? What do you mean nothing's happening?"

Jack's gaze flew to the huge ship. "*Something* should be happening!"

He could hear the hum of the power plant cranking voltage, but the *Horus* StarCraft sat, impotent, without so much as a wiggle.

"No, no, no!" Jack groaned. He rapidly scanned the monitors.

"Is the voltage at fifty thousand?"

"Yes," Bart responded.

Jack whirled to the engineer who had connected the gravitator to the fuel cell. "Did you make sure all the connections were viable?"

The engineer nodded. "Yes, sir. Checked them all twice."

"Dammit!" Jack pounded a fist into the wall.

"Dr. Harding?" Jack cringed as he heard Locke's voice. "Can we expect to see some sort of action here today?"

"Yes, yes, sir, Mr. Locke. We are just, um, building the anticipation, sir."

Jack whipped toward Bart. "Push it to maximum voltage."

Bart's eyes widened. "That's sixty thousand volts, Jack. We never ran the simulation for that amount of voltage. We don't know how the gravitator's mass excess will react to that kind of power."

Jack shrugged. "You only live once, right?"

"You're the boss. Pushing voltage to maximum threshold."

The hum grew louder, rattling the coffee mug on Bart's desk. Jack wasn't certain, but he thought he spied a tremor of movement on the rocket platform. He leaped forward.

"Disengage holding clamps, now!" he bellowed.

Bart struggled to disengage the clamps. All eyes snapped to the monstrous rocket with its attached StarCraft and gasped as slowly, then steadily, it began to rise from the ground.

"Adjust the gravitator orientation!" Jack demanded. Bart's fingers flew.

Without so much as a peep from the powerful Peregrine engines, the rocket gave a sudden lurch and lifted. Stunned silence hung over the facility as all three hundred and eighty feet and four thousand tons of the *Horus* StarCraft hovered ten feet off the ground.

When Bart finally broke the silence, it came out as nothing more than a reverent whisper.

"We have liftoff."

*****

"I thought she'd be here by now." Bart's mouth was set in a tense, thin line as his eyes darted around the celebrating crowd. He nearly hit the deck as someone popped the cork on another bottle of champagne. Jack patted his friend on the shoulder, though the crinkle between his own eyebrows hinted at his own misgivings.

"Don't worry, buddy. I'm sure she's around here somewhere. After all, 1.5 million square feet is a lot of real estate for someone to get lost in," Jack suggested.

Bart caught Locke's intense gaze from across the crowded room and frowned. His voice dropped to a whisper. "It's also a lot of real estate to hide a body."

Jack's followed Bart's worried look to where Locke stood, arms folded serenely across his chest, ignoring the excited babbling of Dr. Binderkampf at his elbow. The billionaire seemed avidly interested in what the muscular bodyguard whispering in his opposite ear had to say.

Jack caught a snippet of Locke's *sotto voce* reply. "Make sure it gets aboard the StarCraft. Put it in the heat-melt compactor. When they run the first disposal protocol, it will just go out with the rest of the trash."

"You don't really think..." Jack began. He looked over just in time to snag Bart as he began to storm toward Locke. "Hey! What do you think you're doing?"

Bart's breath came quick and heavy as he fumed. "I'm going over there to ask Richie Rich what he's done with Dr. Evers, that's what! And if he lies about it, well then, I'll just call the cops."

"Like hell you are!" Jack whispered tersely. "You might as well kick in a hornet's nest! We need him. Charlie needs him. Without Locke Industries, we don't get to Mars, and he is Locke Industries!"

"So, we just let him get away with murder?" Bart's rising blood pressure had flushed his perspiring skin to a near ruby-red. A few of the surrounding celebrants were starting to take notice of their awkward conversation. Jack grabbed Bart by the elbow and steered him into a nearby alcove.

"Come here, genius. We don't have a lick of evidence proving that Travis Locke murdered anybody. If we went to the police, they'd laugh in our faces."

Bart threw his hands up in exasperation. "But you heard him. Plain as day. He told that bodybuilder in a monkey suit to put her body in the heat-melt compactor. He's planning on burning the evidence. Burning her!"

Jack shook his head vehemently. "We heard him say put something in the compactor. We don't know that it's Dr. Evers' body."

"What else would it be? And, I mean, don't you think it's just a little weird that right after she tells us her suspicions about Locke's involvement in the TitusBane incident, she goes missing?"

Jack shrugged. "It could be a coincidence."

"Yeah, well, you know what Ian Fleming said about coincidence," Bart offered.

"What's that?"

"Once is happenstance," Bart quoted as he stuck out his index finger.

"Twice is a coincidence." He stuck out his thumb.

"Three times?" He pointed the finger gun directly at Jack's

head. "Three times is enemy action."

Jack lowered Bart's hand. "All right, Double-Oh-Dimwit. But without Locke, exactly how do you propose we get to Mars? Jet pack?"

"I don't know, man." Bart's eyes brimmed with tears. "All I know is I do not want to be stuck in a tin can in the vacuum of space with somebody who might be a cold-blooded killer."

"Ladies and gentlemen," Locke's voice boomed. Jack pulled Bart, and they melted back into the gathered crowd. Locke stood elevated on the platform of the articulated boom lift. He held a champagne glass aloft in one hand.

"When Neil Armstrong became the first man to walk on the moon, he uttered those famous words, 'One small step for man, one giant leap for mankind.' And, indeed, that historical moment certainly was. And many made a similar giant leap with the great moon land grab just a decade ago. One might say we have truly conquered space travel to our closest neighbor."

Locke raised his glass in a toast. A swelling cheer rose from the crowd. As Locke lowered his glass, the cheer subsided.

It's almost as if he's conducting them.

Jack surveyed the faces. It seemed everyone hung on Locke's every word, but whether it was attention driven by interest or fear, Jack couldn't tell.

Locke continued. "But space is vast. There are eight official planets in our own solar system, just waiting to be conquered, such as Mars. But the question has always been, how can we get there quickly and efficiently? Our current methods are bulky and cumbersome and have stymied us in reaching our true potential."

Locke handed his glass off to an attendant. He turned back to his audience. "There is another quote from the storied Mr. Armstrong, however, one not so widely known. 'If it's there, I believe technology will step up.' And, as you have all been witness to today, technology has indeed stepped up. Today, Locke Industries has conquered Mars travel."

He raised both arms into the air, exultant. The gathered scientists and engineers cheered on cue.

Bart snorted. "Locke Industries, my ass. Our tech made that monster float. As if it's not bad enough, he's potentially offing humans here on Earth. Now, he's probably going to use it to start knocking off aliens."

He tugged the brim of his USCSS Nostromo crew cap down over his eyes. Childlike, he blinked away more tears.

"Yeah, well, he'll have an easier time of it than Ripley since the only life-forms that have been found are the egrets, and they're microscopic," Jack quipped, attempting to make light of a bad situation. "But small as they are, they're the only thing that can save Charlie. We've got to get to the southern pole of Mars before Locke and stake the claim. If he beats us, he'll own the rights. There's no doubt in my mind he'll be mercenary. That's if he relinquishes control at all. Charlie would just be another of his casualties."

"So," Locke continued, "it is with great aplomb that I make the following announcement. With today's successful test, Locke Industries will be launching for Mars in just two short months. You have all made great strides, but the celebration is over. We still have work to do. So, go home, and be back bright and early to continue our forward progress."

He stepped down from the articulated crane, apparently unfazed by the deflating jubilation in the room. Jack watched as Locke moved sleekly through the crowd, weaving through the undulating crowd like a shark. The analogy sent a ripple of unease coursing through Jack. Sharks *were* nature's perfect killers.

He recalled an intense shark documentary Charlie had insisted on watching. The twins had had nightmares for a week. They had even refused to get into the bath! Jack remembered a few facts.

As apex predators, everything was on the menu for sharks—smaller fish and even large mammals—who did not hesitate for a second to swallow their prey whole or rip into it with mighty jaws to tear off huge chunks.

What did Dr. Evers say? That fits Locke to a T.

Certain species, like tiger sharks, ate garbage—cans, tires, bottles, even the occasional unexploded bomb—cast-off junk that society had long since forgotten. Jack watched Locke, followed by his bodyguard, move across the floor, his dead black eyes disappearing into the darkness of a nearby passageway.

Something niggled at the back of Jack's brain.

Junk.

He tapped Bart with the back of his hand. "I don't know about a jet pack, but I might have an idea of how we can get to Mars without Locke and, if we play our cards right, we might just be able to beat him at his own game. But if he's really planning on launching in two months, then we don't have a second to waste. We need to get back to the **P1AL** lab."

"What in the hell are you talking about, Jack?"

"I think it's high time for our apex predator to meet another apex predator."

CHAPTER 38

St. Michael's Alley
Jack

He couldn't let anything go wrong. Not this time.
Jack felt his heart hammering in his chest. He started to feel lightheaded when he realized he was holding his breath and let the air out. Slowly. Carefully. What he was attempting required skill and finesse. Any number of things could go desperately wrong.

CRASH!

Jack cringed as a waiter dropped a tray of wineglasses. Shards of broken glass splintered everywhere.

Jesus, I hope that's not a sign of how this evening's going to go.

He'd chosen St. Michael's for his dinner date with Trinity for several reasons. First, it was a public place, and there was less likelihood, at least in his mind, that she would cause a scene when he confessed his mad plan to secure his own ship and beat Locke to Mars.

The second reason was St. Michael's was a romantic venue. The stage was set right as you approached the entrance with its hand-carved sign, rustic lanterns, and blossoming red-orange ixora. The interior was warm and inviting, with whitewashed wainscoting along the walls. A gleaming table made of a single piece of sequoia was set for group service.

Jack sat at an intimate table for two in the far corner, waiting for Trinity to return from the ladies' room. The third reason he had chosen St. Michael's wasn't because of any particular faith–Jack's faith in anything was a little on the shaky side given his track record–but if there was the remotest chance of the restaurant's namesake throwing a little protection his way, he was all for it. Jack fiddled with the steak knife next to his empty plate. The overhead light glinted off the razor-sharp blade as he tilted it to and fro.

"I'll just cut to the chase," he murmured to himself.

"You talk to yourself often?" Trinity asked as she returned to the table.

Jack forced a smile. "Cheaper than a shrink."

He took a healthy sip from his own glass–a little Dutch courage–then tilted the bottle into Trinity's, filling it to the brim. She held up a hand.

"Oh no, thank you. I've had enough."

"I don't think you have," Jack offered.

Especially considering what I'm about to suggest.

"Why, Dr. Harding," Trinity said coyly. "Are you trying to get me tipsy?"

"Heh, not exactly," Jack replied.

Trinity hadn't been too keen on the idea of Jack working for Locke Industries. She'd tried to warn him off once before, a caution Jack not only had ignored but had thrown back in her face when he had asked her to parlay Locke's attention into a round-trip Mars ticket. Even after the Frisbee incident, it had taken some explaining–okay, a *lot* of explaining–about Charlie's condition and the dire need to get to Mars and the egrets before anyone else before she came around.

He wholeheartedly expected Trinity to get up and storm out of his life once again with the plan he was about to share. Jack wiped his mouth with his napkin and set it gingerly on the table.

"Um, Trinity?" he began.

Trinity set down her fork. "Uh-oh. My daddy always used to say when I started a sentence with 'um,' it either meant I was about to admit to something or ask for something. So, which is it?"

Jack grinned weakly. "Actually, both. I'm admitting to something that, well, might be a little crazy, and I'm asking for your opinion on it."

"I thought we already established that you were a little Bellevue when you agreed to work for Locke," she smirked before her face turned solemn. "But you had your reasons, and they're valid ones. I don't fault you for that anymore. You're a good person. Locke is simply a means to an end."

She paused, worry flitting across her beautiful face. "Just be careful. Bad things seem to happen to good people around Travis Locke."

Jack tugged at his collar. "Yeah, about that. Another scientist has gone missing."

Trinity's eyes flew wide. "Wait...what? Who? When? Where?"

"You forgot 'how' and 'why.'"

"Don't try to be funny, mister. Who's missing?"

"Dr. Midge Evers. She works at Locke Industries as an aerospace engineer. She used to work at the TitusBane facility in Houston."

"Where Bill Engleton was killed," Trinity said.

Jack nodded in agreement. "Dr. Evers was the one who found his body. She was pretty shaken up. Turns out Engleton was something of a mentor to her."

He hesitated. He wasn't certain he wanted to share the next

bit of information. "She was even more shaken up when she realized Locke likely had something to do with it."

"Dammit!" Trinity pounded a fist into the table. Restaurant patrons turned to stare. Jack smiled at them weakly.

Okay. Maybe she will cause a scene.

As he motioned for her to settle down, Trinity pushed her chair back hard and stood. Jack frantically tried to get her to return to her seat.

"Dammit, Jack! I told you this guy was dangerous!" Her face pinched as the reporter in her competed against her indignation. She fumed for a few moments and slowly sat down again. "Did this Dr. Evers have proof?"

Jack exhaled, nervously glancing at the maître d', who gave them a baleful stare. Jack thought back to the P1AL eviction.

Wouldn't be the first time I've had my ass kicked out of someplace.

Jack shook his head. "Circumstantial at best, but enough to make her nervous when Locke was around. She looked especially worried when Locke saw her talking to Bart and me."

"And now she's missing?" Trinity accused. "Did it ever occur to you that the two of you might be next?"

"I have entertained the thought." Jack sucked in a deep breath. "Particularly when I overheard Locke talking to one of his goons about secretly disposing of something in the heat-melt compactor aboard the *Horus* once it got into space."

"Like a body?"

"Maybe."

"Is that even plausible?" she asked.

Jack stood and walked toward her. "Well, when you crunch the numbers, each crew member on a long trip like the one to Mars will generate about a kilo of trash a day. You can't follow the protocols they use on lunar excursions or the Space Station, where the astronauts basically take their trash to the proverbial curb by dumping it in an empty spacecraft returning to Earth. The spacecraft then ejects the waste at a given point, letting it burn up on reentry. A Mars mission is just too far away for another ship to meet it."

Trinity scoffed. "I can't even get my garbage guy to put my can back on the curb."

"That's where the heat-melt compactor comes in. It's a compactor and incinerator all in one. It can compact the waste so it takes up less than one-eighth of the original volume. Then they incinerate the trash, boiling off water and venting off noxious gases. The system is even set up so that the noxious gases can be reprocessed into usable gases within the ship's life support system. Any boiled-off water can also be recovered for the crew's needs."

"Talk about upcycling," Trinity muttered.

"Yeah, well, the system can also be used to burn and dispose of a body," Jack added somberly. "Any ashes remaining after incineration are then ejected during a waste protocol. They are loaded into a small launch vehicle, and when the ship is close to a celestial body with orbital capabilities, the vehicle is ejected into orbit."

"Oh, that's just great! Bad enough we've trashed our own planet. Now we're trashing space!" Trinity exclaimed.

Jack shook his head. "No, no, no! The payloads are small enough so when the vehicle goes into orbital decay, it all burns up on reentry. It's similar to what companies who offer space memorials do. Gene Rodenberry's ashes went up in 1997."

"The creator of *Star Trek*? And I suppose you're going to tell me it was aboard the Enterprise," Trinity joked.

Jack delivered his most sincere look.

"Seriously?" Trinity voiced her disbelief. "So, let me get this straight. Theoretically, Locke's henchman could sneak into the ship while it's docked here on Earth, incinerate Dr. Evers' body, and when the crew initiates the first waste protocol, any traces of her will be vented into space?"

"And Locke would get away with murder."

"You can't go to Mars. Not with Locke. It's too dangerous."

"I couldn't agree with you more," Jack responded. Trinity tilted her head, a puzzled look on her face.

"What?" Jack said.

"I...I don't know. I guess I just expected a little resistance to the idea, is all. So, you're just giving up then? Giving up on Charlie? You're going to let Locke win?"

"Like hell I am." Jack's communicator began to buzz on his wrist. Jack was so incensed by Trinity's comment, he didn't feel or even hear it.

"Oh yeah?" Trinity put one hand on a cocked hip. The wrist-comm continued to buzz. "So, what's your brilliant plan?"

"I know where I can get a ship of my own. I am going to beat Locke to Mars." The words tumbled from his mouth. Afterward, he immediately crushed his eyes shut and balled his fists, bracing for the expected mushroom cloud.

It never came.

Trinity blinked. A beat passed. She calmly folded her napkin and placed it in her lap. She looked pointedly at Jack. "Then I guess I'd better start packing."

Jack gave his head a quick shake, still ignoring the buzzing communicator. "Wait. What?"

"I'm coming to Mars, of course," she stated matter-of-factly.

"Like hell you are," Jack bristled. "Are you out of your mind?"

"Sure as hell sounds like you are, but even if I'm certifiably nuts, I know one thing for sure."

"Oh yeah? What's that?"

"This is going to make for one *hell* of a story. Are you going to answer that?" Trinity pointed to his wrist.

With a frustrated look, Jack tilted his wrist and looked down. When he saw the name on the display, a look of concern settled into his features. He tapped a button.

"Bradley? Is everything all right? What is it?"

The nanny's pinched, nasal tone came through the speaker.

"It's the hospital, Jack...it's Charlie."

CHAPTER 39

Jack burst through the door of Charlie's room and immediately pulled up short. Sitting up in bed, looking wan but smiling, was Charlie. Dr. Pershing stood next to him, checking Charlie's vitals.

"Hi, Jack," Charlie waved weakly.

A wave of emotion nearly brought Jack to his knees. Recovering on less than steady legs, he stepped to Charlie's bedside. "Hey, bud. How are you feeling?"

Charlie shrugged. "Doc Pershing says I took a really long nap. He says it was just my brain's way of trying to heal itself. I must be A-OK now, though, 'cause I woke up. Right, Doc?"

Charlie looked up at the doctor, who exchanged a knowing look with Jack. The doctor looked down at the frail boy. "You're better, but we've still got a long way to go. If your vitals stay strong, I'm going to let you go home tomorrow, but I think it would be a pretty good idea for you to increase the visits to your neurologist."

An orderly came into the room with a gelatin cup and spoon.

"Ah!" Dr. Pershing commented. "Looks like your snack is

here. And it's your lucky day. It's red!"

Charlie's face puckered. "I hate the green kind. Bradley buys those from the grocery. I think they're disgusting."

"Me too," the doctor agreed. "Why don't you tuck into that while I go talk to your guardian out in the hall, okay?"

"Sure thing, Doc," Charlie agreed as the orderly helped him open the snack. Out in the hall, the doctor's demeanor changed almost immediately.

"Is he really better, Dr. Pershing?" Jack asked, wringing his hands unconsciously.

The doctor drew in a long, measured breath. "In conjunction with an electromyogram, we conducted a nerve conduction velocity test to measure how quickly electrical impulses move along a nerve. In the case of a healthy nerve, the signals are conducted with higher speeds and strength. The speed is influenced by the myelin sheath, which in Charlie's case, as you know, was slowly deteriorating due to his disease."

"*Was* deteriorating? Do you mean the deterioration's stopped?" Jack felt a surge of hope at the doctor's words.

The doctor's shoulders slumped. He shook his head. "The deterioration hasn't stopped. It's speeded up. I hate to say it—he's such a sweet kid—but Charlie's living on borrowed time."

Jack's chin dropped to his chest. A heavy silence punctuated the air with a dire exclamation point. Moisture brimmed along the rims of his eyes when he finally raised his head to look at the doctor.

"How long?"

"Twelve to eighteen months at the outset. And that's if he doesn't have another attack. It's one of the reasons I'm letting him go home. He's going to lose more motor and possibly cognitive function by the day. It will be incredibly scary for him. At least being home in a familiar setting, surrounded by people who care for him will hopefully alleviate the stress until…"

Jack didn't need the doctor to finish the sentence. "Until he dies."

"He'll need round-the-clock care. Do you have someone who can stay with him?"

"We, uh, have a nanny," Jack mumbled. "He's extremely capable. He's been taking care of Charlie and his siblings for a while now."

"Good to hear," Dr. Pershing replied. He reached into his pocket and pulled out a business card. He handed it to Jack. "This is the number of a good family therapist. Charlie's not going to be the only one affected by his illness. His brothers and sisters are likely going to experience some coping issues. I would highly suggest giving her a call."

Jack half-heartedly took the card from the doctor's hand. He rubbed his chin absentmindedly. "Yeah, thanks, Doc."

The doctor caught Jack's lost gaze. "She works with adults too."

Jack snapped out of it. He slid the card into his own pocket and vigorously rubbed his hands on the legs of his pants. He dragged an angry arm across his eyes to wipe away the threatening tears.

"Thank you, Doctor. I appreciate all you've done for us. For Charlie, I mean. I'm just going to, uh, go in and see him now. Let him know what time I'm going to come get him tomorrow to take him home."

Pity filled the doctor's eyes. "I'm sorry we couldn't have done more, Mr. Harding, but the odds were stacked against you from the outset. Leukodystrophy is a brutal opponent. It's like Vegas. The house always wins."

Jack's jaw tensed. His lips set in a hard, thin line.

"Oh yeah? Watch much World Series of Poker, Doc? Nick

Dandolos said it best. 'The house doesn't beat the player. It just gives him the opportunity to beat himself.'"

But I've got an ace up my sleeve.

CHAPTER 40

En Route to BrutForce Labs
Jack

On the way to meet his ace, Jack picked up a joker. Literally. Bart tumbled into the car wearing a brilliantly colored cockscomb. Jack shook his head from side to side.

At least it doesn't have bells.

"Would it kill you, for once, to dress like a professional?" Jack quipped. "Maybe then somebody might actually take you seriously."

Bart adjusted the cap and spoke softly, "Dr. Evers took me seriously. She liked me exactly the way I am." The oversized, childlike man closed his eyes.

"I know, buddy. But she also chose to work for Locke. Even after she suspected him of murder. And now she's missing. I'd say her judgment was a little off."

"We work for Locke, too, though," Bart pointed out the elephant in the room.

Jack programmed the car's destination. BrutForce Labs. "Not for long, we don't."

*****

Jack drummed his fingers on the steering wheel the entire ride to BrutForce Labs.

I only hope I'm not too late.

The last time he had seen Major Earl Cotton was in the subterranean section of the major's facilities—facilities which, if Jack had any luck on his side, held the key to Jack's plan to beat Locke: an abandoned ship.

If he was going to beat Locke to the punch, Jack didn't have the time or the wherewithal to build a ship from scratch. Then he had recalled the ships, in various stages of disassembly, just sitting in the major's underground cavern. He needed to convince the major to let him have one—likely even convince him to help him to outfit it for a Mars mission. He just prayed the major hadn't finished closing up shop.

The car slowed as it pulled into the abandoned parking lot of the major's business. A single box truck sat near the entrance, its cargo door open, Jack assumed, to receive the remaining materials to make the move to Mars.

"Good!" Jack exclaimed as the car rolled to stop. He disengaged his safety belt. "Maybe he's still here."

"Who's still here?" Bart questioned as he fumbled with his own belt and hurried to catch up to Jack. "I thought we were going to the P1AL Labs."

"Not *to* the labs—*under* the labs. You know the tunnels that run under our facility?"

Bart nodded.

"Well, we're not the only ones who took advantage of the space. Major Earl Cotton—he runs BrutForce Labs—has a huge hangar area down there which connects to our own tunnel network. Haven't I ever mentioned him before?"

Bart shook his head.

Jack shrugged. "Yeah, well, I've bumped into him a couple of times in the tunnels when I've had to service the collider. The last time was when we were closing P1AL down. I went down into the tunnels to shut off the main breaker, and that's when I first discovered the hangar...and the ships."

Bart pulled up short. "Ships?"

Jack nodded. "That's the major's business. Disassembly and refurbishment of lunar vehicles. The major's got three or four of 'em down there. Granted, none of them looked very space-worthy when I last saw them, but I'm hoping I can convince the major to not only let us have one but maybe help us get it in shape and retrofit it with gravitator tech."

"Jack?" the major's voice bellowed. Jack and Bart looked up.

"Speak of the devil," Jack grinned.

The major strode toward the duo. His mirrored aviators hid the expression on his face, but the wide smile projected warm friendliness. He held out a beefy hand.

"Jack Harding! Good to see you again, son. You've come to make me an offer on the labs, haven't you? Knew you'd be back. It's a solid investment, without a doubt. Didn't think you'd be able to pass it up."

The major stationed his hands on his hips and cast a glance back at the building. The sun reflected off the mirrored windows, catching Jack in the eyes. He held up a protective hand.

"Tell you the truth," the major continued, "I'm glad to see the old place going to somebody deserving. Made a lot of money here. Maybe some of the luck it brought me will rub off on you, eh?"

He gave Jack a hearty slap on the back and chortled deeply.

Jack and Bart exchanged glances. Jack spoke. "As much as I would like to buy this place from you, sir, I've got a little something else in mind. A counteroffer you might be interested in. You have some time?"

The major eyed them both. "Not much, truthfully. I'm just here to finish closing up shop. If I'm not around to supervise, things tend to turn into a regular soup sandwich, if you know what I mean. Then I've got to muster my crew, pack up the transporter, and haul my ass to Mars. Won't open up shop there until we're a little bit closer to the land grab, mind you, but gotta get things ready. Fail to prepare, and you'd better be prepared to fail."

"Ben Franklin," Jack said.

"Bravo Zulu, Jack! You know your founding fathers," the major congratulated, though the praise couldn't overcome Jack's disappointment.

He needed the major's help!

Jack's shoulders sagged as his chin dropped toward his chest.

The major's head tilted, and he reached up to pull his glasses from his face. He squinted against the sunshine, crow's-feet playing at the corners of his intense blue eyes, as he studied Jack's face.

"Going to admit, though, you do have me a little intrigued about this counteroffer of yours. What did you have in mind?"

Relief flooded Jack's face. He stood tall, straightening his shoulders, and cleared his throat.

"Ahem. It's just I was wondering, Major, if I could convince you to keep the shop open for maybe another month or two."

"Whoa!" the major exclaimed, waving his hands before him. "That's a tall order, son. If I were going to even consider that, you'd certainly have to make it worth my while."

Bart nudged Jack in the ribs with an elbow. "Tell him."

Jack nodded. He turned back toward the major. "Well, sir, remember all those rare earth elements the Chinese found on the moon?"

The major nodded. "Suckers made a pretty penny off 'em, too. Mark my words, it will be the same thing with those egrets on Mars. Whoever gets to those puppies first will be able to write their own check!"

Jack beamed.

"Well, then, you know what else Franklin said?" Jack said.

"What's that?" the major replied.

"An investment in knowledge pays the best interest."

The major's brows rose in ardent curiosity. "And you're saying you have some knowledge?"

Jack nodded and grinned from ear to ear.

"Interested?"

CHAPTER 41

Locke's Estate, Monterey, CA
Locke

As he listened to the thunderous crash of waves against the cliffs below, Travis Locke marveled at nature's raw, unbridled power. While the cliffs appeared strong, towering over the frothing water, the punishing waves had the power to brutalize the rock into nothing more than sand—helpless particles subject to the whim of wind and water.

Part of him was envious in a way. Nature didn't answer to conscience. It had no social and moral code that judged against a violent act. In the wild, if something decimated something else, it was just...nature.

A hurricane devastated the Gulf region, killing nearly two thousand people. The Loma Prieta earthquake brought the San Francisco Bay area to its knees with sixty-three people dead and over thirty-seven hundred injured.

And yet, no one went on trial. No one went to jail. It was simply nature enforcing its will, social mores be damned.

So, why then was acting in accordance with his own nature supposedly so wrong?

If society knew how often he had done just that, the needle

would have been in his arm faster than you could say Lizzie Borden. Of course, he had never used such a rudimentary tool as an ax. No, he had always been a bit more…creative. Like with good old wheezy Donny Newton.

But there had been other instances.

His mind flashed back to a party. Not a children's party with balloons and cake, but a catered soiree his parents held at their Sonoma estate—one of many. His father, Trenton Locke, had been a formidable businessman.

More like corporate raider.

He threw the events to entertain clients. Travis, however, was anything but entertained. He had always found the events incredibly boring and often sought alternative means of keeping himself occupied—methods his parents apparently found quite distasteful.

He remembered his mother's shocked face when a distressed yowling drowned out the jazz quartet they had hired. She and his father came rushing onto the patio to see the thirteen-year-old swinging the family cat in circles by its tail, accelerating with every rotation. He remembered his mother's horrified scream.

He also remembered letting the cat go right in front of her— without so much as a twitch of remorse—just to hear its skull crunch against the brick wall of the house. That's what prompted the first psychiatric evaluation. He didn't understand its necessity then, and to this day, he still didn't. He had identified a problem. He had solved it. All the psychobabble about impaired capacity for empathy or remorse, depressed neuroticism, and low impulse control was just noise—an overreaction from his hapless parents.

Locke stared at the dark expanse of the California night stretched across the heavens. He rather enjoyed the darkness when he thought about it. He felt at home in it. It reminded him of that dark space on the PET scans all those years ago, a hollow hole in his orbital cortex the psychiatrist had told his parents was the culprit for Travis' aberrant behaviors. And in just two short months, he was about to rocket deeply into that star-pricked darkness, secure those egrets, and become the richest man on Earth.

Fuck that. The universe.

And anyone who stood in his way and became a problem? *He'd solve it.*

CHAPTER 42

CLUNK! CLUNK!

The double-tap slap of the major's hand on the metal hull of the small spacecraft reverberated throughout the vast expanse of the cavern.

"Here she is. The sardine can you'll be calling home for the next six to eight months," the major announced. He stationed his hands on his hips. "She's nothing fancy. An old Russian Yalik-18 that's been lying around here for ages. Dropped her off and never came back for it. Seems the Russians have a habit of leaving their space junk to rot and rust."

Bart groaned. "Oh, that makes me feel incredibly comfortable."

"No joke," the major continued. "They've *still* got two shuttles and a rocket rusting out at the Baikonur Cosmodrome in a couple of disused hangars in the Kazakh steppe. Leftovers from the Cold War, if you can believe it. Part of the Buran program. Buran—means blizzard in Russkie."

"So, what does 'yalik' mean?" Bart asked.

"Dinghy," Trinity answered. After she'd learned that the

302

major had agreed to outfit Jack with a ship and crew for a share in the profits of the egret recovery, she'd tagged along on this little orientation as a self-proclaimed crew member. She hadn't given Jack much of a choice.

Bart frowned. "Is the name-calling necessary? I'm simply asking a question."

The major let out a hearty belly laugh. "No, no. The little lady's right. 'Yalik' is Russian for 'dinghy' or 'skiff.' Originally, this craft was fitted as a tender for the International Space Station. Hauled people, gear, and provisions back and forth to the moon during all the brouhaha with the moon land grab."

He patted the hull.

"Saw a lot of action, this girl. When we first got her, looked like she had taken some hits from some micrometeoroids. Couldn't have been too big, or they would have pierced the hull and depressurized the craft, and that wouldn't have been too healthy for anybody. She did all right though. My crew didn't find any dead bodies aboard," the major chuckled.

Jack squirmed.

Probably can't say the same thing about Locke's Horus StarCraft.

"Anyhow, if you come across anything like that, it's probably better just to execute debris avoidance maneuvers than take a chance of getting starstruck, so to speak. So, keep your eyes on the road out there, right?"

Jack gave a little snort. The major made it sound like he was talking about driving his mother's Volvo instead of an interstellar space vehicle. Although...

Jack cocked his head and surveyed the Yalik-18. It did sort of look like a Volvo. Not the sleek electric models you could find zipping along the maglev highways of Southern California these days. Rather, it resembled the boxy versions the Swedish car company had churned out in the latter part of the twentieth century. Sixty feet of sharp angles headed by a small crew cabin that housed the flight deck, Jack supposed. The forward fuselage of the craft was separated from the aft by a recessed midsection. The aft fuselage bowed out on both sides to accommodate the orbital maneuvering system and reaction control system modules. Normally, the OMS—a system of rocket engines fired by hypergolic liquid propellant—wouldn't be near adequate to propel a craft all the way to Mars.

But that's where the gravitator assembly comes in.

Even though Locke's ship also had Jack's tech onboard, Jack was banking on the weight differential between the two crafts to help him gain ground over Locke's monstrosity.

Well, that and I'm hoping to launch before the psychotic son of a bitch.

Dr. Evers had never reported back to work. At Bart's behest, Jack had dropped what he hoped was a discreet inquiry to human resources. If you believed the abrupt woman with a chignon so tight it made Jack's head hurt, Dr. Evers had tendered her resignation the same day of the Horus test. Convenient.

Convenient. Suspicious. It was a fine line.

"When will she be space-worthy?" Jack asked.

"Ah, hell. Had my boys knock out all the dents and dings. And, per your specs, the engineers connected the gravitator assembly to the orbital maneuvering system. After I show you all the bells and whistles inside, I'd say you'll be Oscar Mike by the end of next week."

Three days before Locke's scheduled to lift off.

The major's face grew stony. "Now, what I need you to understand is this is not a joyride. I will be providing you with a pilot and two crewmen, sure. But on a trip like this, everybody better damn well know everybody else's job. Two is one and one is none, you read me?"

"What in the hell does that mean?" Bart asked quietly.

"Always have a backup plan," Jack muttered.

The major continued his tirade. "Do not think for a hot second that you're going to be sitting on your keisters, taking selfies with the man in the moon and posting to your SynchMind account. Everybody on the ship works, and I mean *everybody*. Affirmative, Boot?"

He eyeballed Bart, whose hat today read "Not from Around Here." Bart looked over his shoulder innocently. "It's Bart, sir."

"I said 'affirmative!'" the major barked in Bart's face.

This time, Bart, Jack, and Trinity instinctively responded in unison. "Yes, sir!"

Bart saluted.

The major's jovial attitude returned. He clapped his hands and rubbed them together vigorously.

"So, who wants to take a peek under the hood?"

*****

They entered the small craft from the crew ingress hatch, which brought them onto the mid-deck. The headroom wasn't very generous, and Jack knocked his noggin pretty hard on the overhead.

"Yeah," the major warned belatedly. "Pardon the pun, but space is at a premium in this baby. Mind your melon."

Jack rubbed at the sore spot. "Thanks for the warning."

The major grinned and pointed. "This is the avionics bay. Basically, it's the brains of the spacecraft. The system either controls or supports crew control, just about every system aboard this tub."

"It's HAL," Bart whispered in Jack's ear.

"Shut it, or I'm deep-sixing your ass over the moon's SPA basin," Jack warned.

305

"He's not wrong. The system automatically detects status and operational readiness. It can control the OMS, guidance, navigation, and control, and it makes sure the right amount of juice gets to where it needs to go. Like your gravitator assembly."

"Sounds like it can practically fly itself," Trinity suggested.

"Damn near close. The only part of the trip it's not programmed for is docking. Flight crew handles that manually."

Jack looked at the intricate spaghetti assembly of tethered wiring feeding into black boxes. A feeling of dread crept through him, moving slowly like an icy glacier.

"What happens if the system fails?" he asked, almost fearing the answer.

The major scoffed and waved a hand in the air nonchalantly. "Those black boxes are hooked up through party lines to three different computers. Having that many black boxes gives you dual or sometimes even triple redundancy for every single beep, bell, and blip on this damn thing. It's a fail-safe operational arrangement. But enough about that. Let's see where the real magic happens."

The major spun and hefted his muscular frame up the flight deck access ladder, motioning for them all to follow. Trinity nimbly climbed up after the major. Bart struggled a bit, his bulky frame getting wedged, but finally managed to squeeze through the slender opening between decks. Jack watched Bart's high-tops disappear and grabbed the rung above his head and climbed, pulling himself up and through.

As his shoulders breached the deck of the upper section, his gut tightened at the blatant shock plastered across both Trinity and Bart's faces. Even the normally effusive Bart stood silent, his mouth hanging slack. Jack's head swiveled nervously between them. He shot a glance at the major, who stood off to the side, chuckling, behind one of the five flight seats squeezed in the cramped crew cabin.

"What's wrong?" Jack asked, anxiety infusing his voice with deep gravity.

"It's like Christmas," Bart whispered.

Jack turned his head to see what the software specialist was staring at. Just beyond the pilot and commander's seats was a brilliantly lit assembly of panels and displays configured in a U-shape. Red bulbs blinked, demanding attention next to the solid glow of passive green buttons. It was a bit reminiscent of the Christmas tree the kids had insisted Jack erect in the living room the previous December.

Except it was my blood pressure rocketing into the stratosphere, trying to get the damned thing to sit straight in the stand.

He felt a sudden surge of overwhelming panic.

This hunk of junk is rocketing my ass to Mars.

Jack broke through the immobilizing fear and pulled the rest of his body through the hatch, dusting himself off. "What is all this?"

"Welcome to mission and payload operations," the major declared with a sweeping gesture. He pointed to different sections of the cockpit in succession. "Over here, we've got closed-circuit monitors. The feed will let you keep an eye on things going on around the ship—both inside and outside. Helpful in watching out if you've got any bogeys on your six."

Like Locke.

Jack prayed to God they would have enough of a jump on the billionaire to avoid any entanglements. Jack already feared Locke suspected something. He and Bart still had been clocking in regularly at Locke Industries. They had been going through the motions, playing the part of good employees, fine-tuning the *Horus'* gravitator assembly functions in preparation for launch day. They had been slipping out, however, reporting to BrutForce during their lunch hour. More than once, Jack thought he spied a familiar black SUV in his rear-view. Had Locke put a tail on him? He remembered the menacing Sig Sauer in the jacket holster of Locke's goon.

The thought chilled him cold.

Jack tried to focus on the major, who continued explaining. "Over here, you've got your payload handling controls. Below that are the access panels for flight deck stowage. Gotta make use of every square inch, you know. Now, like I said, the ship's onboard AI will handle most of the actual flying, but the crew is responsible for docking and landing protocols. For that, you need to know where these bad boys are."

He pointed to several molded black handgrips—one at the southern corner of the port aft-viewing window and one set dead center on the operations panel. "This here's the docking rotational hand control, and this one's the docking translation hand controller. These controls will allow you to adjust roll, pitch, and yaw. In other words, keep your ass upright."

"Good to know," Jack noted. He pointed to a third handle. "What's that one for?"

"That is the rotational hand control for the remote manipulator. Basically, it's a massive robotic arm designed to either retrieve or deploy space hardware and cargo from the payload bay."

"Handy," Bart commented.

"Sure as hell will be when you have to unload the tank from the rover to the shuttle," the major agreed.

Trinity stepped forward. "About that. Tell me again how all this is going to work again. Please."

Jack turned to her to explain. "The shuttle has a thirty-gallon empty tank onboard. Once we get to Mars, we'll load it onto the rover along with a pumping assembly and open personnel basket.

When the gun goes off, we haul ass for the south pole."

"Where the underground aquifer is," Tiffany said.

"Right. And the egrets. Plan is to lower ourselves to the aquifer in the basket with hoses, sample the water for egret population, and, if we get the results we're hoping for, pump thirty gallons back up to the tank." He looked to the major. "Where exactly is the tank?"

The major jabbed a thumb. "In the aft fuselage. Past the galley in the modular stowage."

"Is that also where the sleep stations are?" Jack queried.

The major nodded. "Three horizontal sleep pallets and one vertical sleep station."

Bart counted on his fingers. "But counting the three crew members and the three of us, that's not enough. Where are the rest of us supposed to sleep?"

"Son, in a hostile territory like space, you're always gonna want a warm body on overwatch."

Jack swallowed hard, the mysterious SUV in the back of his mind and the implications.

"Couldn't agree more, Major."

Problem is, who's doing the watching?

CHAPTER 43

Locke Industries Assembly Facility
Locke

"Hand me that o-scope, will ya?" Harding's voice crackled over the monitor. Locke watched, like a falcon tracking its prey, from his perch high above the assembly floor. He watched as that useless lump Pulldraw bumbled down the scaffolding and grabbed a slender box from the tool chest on the platform. He scrambled back up, holding it aloft.

"Here you go, boss man!" his annoyingly cherubic tone filtered through the speaker.

Harding scowled. "Not the digital multimeter! The oscilloscope!"

Pulldraw looked down at the instrument in his hand. "What's the difference?"

Harding sighed. "I need to see the waveforms to check the signal strength, not check the current. Don't think Uber picks up as far as Makemake, and if I don't make sure the signal to the gravitator's strong enough, thumbing it's about the only other option."

Locke watched curiously as Harding's glance lifted to the observation booth. He couldn't be certain, but it was as if

Harding was intent on ensuring Locke heard his conversation. Harding would know he would be listening. It was common knowledge that Locke kept tabs on all the activity and dialogue surrounding the *Horus* StarCraft.

Locke's eyes narrowed.

Was Harding putting on a piece of theater for his benefit?

Despite Harding's regular attendance and apparent diligence at his duty station, Locke had recently begun to harbor unsettling suspicions regarding the man's loyalty. His brows pinched, and he subconsciously shook his head.

No. Loyalty wasn't the right word.

Fear.

Locke was no longer sensing the level of delicious fear that had radiated off Harding when he first joined the Mars project. Locke stroked his chin thoughtfully. What was the quote often attributed to Hermann Göering, Hitler's right hand?

"The only thing you need to make people into slaves is fear. And if you can find something to make them afraid, you can make them do anything they want," Locke muttered.

He just wasn't certain he still inspired the requisite fear in the good doctor.

"What's that, sir?" Sarah Copeland strode into the observation booth. The silk shantung dress she wore clung to her every curve, inviting the eye to travel from the slip of her shoulder, down the indent of her waist, and over the curvature of her hip until it slid the length of her legs all the way to her Jimmy Choos.

Locke grunted. Sarah Copeland was a tantalizing distraction, one that usually satisfied some of his other base urges, but the dangling reward of securing the Mars egrets was a much greater incentive than rough sex with the attractive attorney—one that the overactive reward system in his psychopathic brain craved maddeningly.

Locke waved a hand. "Nothing. Tell me about Harding. Have you been following him as I instructed?"

Sarah nodded crisply, carelessly tossing her leather attaché to the side as she sat. "Yes, although I can think of better uses for my $500 an hour billing."

"Your money is always on the side table, isn't it?" Locke leered.

Sarah glowered at him. Locke took no heed of her displeasure at the analogy.

"So? Where has he been going?" Locke demanded.

"The P1AL labs," Sarah spat.

"The P1AL Labs?" Locke scowled, puzzled. "But we've completed all the testing required. He should have no need to keep going back there. Are you absolutely certain?"

"He leaves every day on his lunch break with that short, round guy, hops on the 101, and drives to the labs. They park in front of the building and disappear inside for forty-five minutes to an hour, then come out again and hotfoot it back here."

"What about after work?" Locke pressed.

"Same deal, except then he usually stays a bit longer. He's always home by seven though. Guy's got a whole herd of knee-biters. I've seen them a couple of times."

Locke looked up sharply. "But have they seen *you*?"

Sarah stood and sashayed around Locke's desk to stand directly in front of him. She bent forward, ample cleavage heaving at her plunging neckline, and placed her hands on his knees. She slowly slid them toward his crotch.

She shrugged off the question. "Although I know *exactly* how to make a man look at me when I want him to…"

Locke began to lean toward her, meeting her halfway, when she shoved him forcefully back into the leather of his chair and walked away.

"I kept my distance."

Locke smiled. He stood and walked toward the window to watch Harding again.

"Good," he replied, partially in response to Sarah's aggressive actions and partially in approval of her success in carrying out his orders.

"Good," he repeated. "Harding's already suspicious enough. He and that buffoon Pulldraw were chummy with Dr. Evers." He huffed. "I can only imagine what information she may have shared."

"Are you worried about the authorities?" she asked.

"Hardly. My endeavors are generally discreet. If not," he pulled her into a hard, painful kiss. "I have you."

Sarah stumbled back as he released her, drawing her hand to her lip. She pulled back blood. Locke continued on as though nothing had happened.

"Still, no sense in leaving loose ends. Make sure he stays around long enough for the *Horus* launch."

"Why the launch?"

A malevolent grin widened across Locke's face.

"Because it has become readily apparent to me that Dr. Harding and Mr. Pulldraw need to be a part of the crew. I mean, it is their tech that is making this flight even possible. What if something should go wrong?" His voice took on a mockingly innocent tone.

"After all," he continued as he sat in the Italian leather executive chair behind his desk. He tented his fingers. "Space can be *such* a hazardous place."

CHAPTER 44

Harding Estate
Jack

It was time.

Anxiety sat like a two-ton lead weight in the middle of Jack's gut. Or maybe that was the third helping of Myrna's brisket. He probably should have abstained, but he had figured if he was stuffing his mouth, he wouldn't have to talk—and right now, talking was the absolute last thing he wanted to do.

But they were all gathered—right here in front of him—waiting to hear what he had to say.

Myrna had finished clearing the dishes with Bradley's help and now sat firmly ensconced in his grandmother's overstuffed armchair, the twins pulled up in her ample lap.

Light snoring drifted from the corner of the room. Bart sat slouched in the wingback, the all-too-willing victim of a food coma. He'd had four servings of his mother's cooking.

I wonder how he's going to handle freeze-dried mac 'n' cheese.

Jack's own tongue might as well have been freeze-dried for as parched as it felt. He reached for his glass of water. At the last second, he caught Alice's baleful stare from across the room.

He reached for Trinity's wineglass instead.

Trinity placed a gentle hand atop his and whispered. "Hey. Don't worry. It's going to be okay. They'll understand."

"You think so, huh? The girls already know about the trip."

"And?" Trinity asked.

"Well, one is pissed at me because she thinks I'm abandoning them, and the other one is pissed at me because I won't take her along."

"They'll get over it. This is for Charlie. He's their brother."

Jack nodded and looked over at the seven-year-old. Charlie had been home from the hospital for a while now, weakened by his episode but still as cheerful as ever. Due to his weakening muscle control, he now wore a helmet and was strapped into his wheelchair to protect against any inadvertent falls. Not that such a thing would happen with eagle-eyed Bradley on duty. The nanny kept a keen watch on his charge, tending to any of the boy's needs.

Jack couldn't help but feel grateful to the man. Bradley had already heard the speech he was about to give. Jack had pulled him aside earlier in the day and laid it all out for him. Jack knew this family was going to need someone capable to really step in and keep the ship afloat. Altruistically, Bradley had agreed to be the ad hoc captain.

Okay. Mostly altruistically and for a small percentage of the profits.

Jack looked up as the twins' laughter bubbled through the air. Despite his condition, Charlie was still making his little brothers giggle uncontrollably as he weakly nodded his head and bobbled the deely boppers Bart had affixed to his new headgear.

Julia's nose was buried in her tablet as usual.

I could probably just leave for Mars without saying a word, and she probably wouldn't even notice.

That left the brooding Alice. The eleven-year-old sat next to Julia, her thin arms folded tightly across her chest. Jack stood from the table and walked toward her.

"Alice," he began. She got up and stormed from the room. Jack tossed an "I-told-you-so" glance toward Trinity.

Yeah. She'll totally understand.

A door slammed in the hallway, startling Bart awake and riveting everyone's gaze on Jack.

"Well, um, I guess now that I've got your attention, we can call this little family meeting to order. As some of you already know, I have to go on a small business trip."

Julia snorted. "Little?"

"Okay, fine. I'm going to Mars."

The twins' faces lit up.

"You're gonna be an astronut?" Lucas gaped.

"Astro-*naut*, and yes, Lucas, I guess you could say that's exactly what I'm going to be." Jack pointed. "And Uncle Bart and Ms. Watson are coming with me."

"That's cool!" Lucas exclaimed, bouncing on Myrna's lap. Oscar didn't seem to share his brother's keen enthusiasm. He cocked his head and studied Jack's face.

"You going in a rocket?" Oscar asked.

"Sort of," Jack explained. "It's more like…a space car."

"Does it have lasers?" Oscar continued.

"No, but it does have a really neat robotic arm that can grab things."

Oscar considered. "Okay!"

Two down, three to go.

"Are you going for something important, Jack?" Charlie asked. His feeble voice ripped Jack's heart from his chest. Jack kneeled in front of the wheelchair. He grabbed Charlie's hands.

Jack didn't want to tell Charlie about the egrets–about the promise they held for people with conditions like his. He also hadn't told Charlie about the doctor's prognosis. Why ruin what little time the child had left? Wasn't it better he continue to live out his days bright and upbeat in the sunshine of his optimistic personality than to tell him and cloud his days with gloom?

Besides, if this mission failed, if he told Charlie and he didn't bring back the egrets successfully, all he would have managed was to give the boy false hope.

So, what could he tell him then?

"Yes, Charlie. I'm going for a very important reason," Jack finally managed.

Charlie considered Jack's words, beamed from ear to ear, and gave a weak nod. "Then you have to go."

A derisive sniff sounded over Jack's shoulder. He turned to see Julia sneering. "Oh yeah? Ask him how long he's going to be gone."

"Jack?" Charlie asked.

He turned back to the boy. "Twelve months. Maybe more."

"A whole year?" Charlie said.

Jack nodded. "It takes a long time to get to Mars, and then I have to fly all the way back too."

Please, God, just let it be enough time to get the egrets back to help Charlie.

"You'll still get to talk to me. We'll have video communications aboard the ship. The signal's delayed, but it's better than nothing, right?"

Jack watched Charlie for a response. He sat in protracted silence.

Bradley stood, wiping his hands on his jeans. "Okay, I think this was a lot to take in. Maybe I should just get Speed Racer here off to bed now."

"Who's going to stay with us?" Charlie asked.

"Oh, well, that's easy!" Bradley explained. "That will be me! Except on Sundays, of course, but Mrs. Pulldraw has kindly offered to hold down the fort on those days."

The twins squealed with delight. Jack knew it was because that meant rugelach. Regardless of the reason, Myrna delighted in the sloppy kisses and hugs the twins lavished on her.

"Ooooh, come here, my little *ziskayts*!" She scooped them both up in a crushing bear hug. "It's been a long day. Let's get you two to bed."

She stood up and waddled off down the hall with the boys. When things had settled, Jack looked to Charlie for a final response. Finally, he grinned. "Take a lot of pictures. Okay, Jack?"

"You bet I will, kid," Jack replied.

Bradley wheeled Charlie off to bed. Jack turned to Julia. "Well?"

"You didn't tell him about the egrets." She lowered her tablet and looked up at him.

"I didn't want to build up his hopes."

"In case you screw this up too?" She stood. "Well, at least you didn't make another promise you couldn't keep. Have a safe trip, Jack."

She disappeared down the hall. Jack started after her, but Trinity held him back. She shook her head.

"She's angry. Not only is she a teenager, which itself comes with its own universe of drama, but the kid's also lost her parents, and now, she's watching her little brother waste away, and she's powerless to help. To top it off, the person to whom her parents entrusted her care is getting ready to travel millions of miles away. Can you blame her?"

Jack opened his mouth to say something, then thought better of it.

"Her world is crumbling down around her. Be the father she needs you to be. Make this mission succeed. She'll come around."

Sure. Easy peasy.

Jack sighed. "Actually, it's probably the most civil conversation we've ever had. Guess I'd better go talk to Alice now."

"Good luck," Trinity said and kissed him on the cheek.

"Thanks," Jack replied and squared his shoulders before setting off toward Alice's room.

Right now, I need all the luck I can get.

*****

Jack tapped on Alice's bedroom door. "Alice? Alice, it's Jack. Can I talk to you?"

"Go away!" Alice's voice, thick with tears, was muffled through the door.

Jack leaned his head against it and sighed. "Easeplay etlay emay inway."

Two years ago, when Alice first came to stay with Jack, she didn't speak much. Truthfully, Jack reminisced, she didn't speak at all. For the first several weeks after arriving at Jack's house, she just stayed in her room, only coming out for the bare necessities. But still, no speech. The trauma of losing her parents so unexpectedly had been too much for the then-nine-year-old. Jack had been at his wit's end. He had no idea how to be a parent, let alone communicate with a troubled child.

That's all Jack wanted to do with her now.

Communicate.

He had been watching Bart write the code for the ROAR program when the idea had struck him.

Code.

That night, Jack had drafted a quick anagram for the word "hello" and had slipped it under Alice's bedroom door. After a few moments, the paper came back under the door, unscrambled. That's how his communication with her had begun. For a while, all communication with her had to be in some kind of code. Morse code, ciphers—at one point, he'd even made a scytale. Her quick mind loved deciphering the patterns. Soon, the codes gave way to speech. The codes still played a part. Her absolute favorite way to communicate was Pig Latin.

"Ellohay?" Jack tried again.

Silence met him from the other side of the door.

Ohway ellway.

He turned to leave when, suddenly, the door handle turned. Alice stood on the other side, face streaked with tears. "Ellohay."

"Hey, kiddo."

"Hi."

"I'm so sorry I've upset you. It's not what I wanted. Believe me."

She sniffed and dragged a sleeve across a runny nose. "I know. It's just that I should be going too. If it weren't for me, you would never have figured out how to make the gravitator work!"

"You're right, and if I could take you along, I would. But I really need you to keep those smarts here on Earth. Be my mission control."

Alice looked pensive for a minute, then slowly nodded. "Okayway."

Jack smiled and grabbed her in a huge hug. "That's my girl!"

And, for the first time since she'd arrived at his house, that was how he thought of her.

Suddenly, Bart came barreling down the hall, arms waving like an inflatable tube man. "Jack! Jack! Jack!"

Jack put Alice down and shushed Bart. "Keep it down, will ya? Your mom just got the twins to sleep."

"Okay, yeah, sorry. It's just, we've got a problem."

"A problem? What kind of problem? Is something wrong with the ship?"

Bart nodded. "Something's wrong with the ship, all right. We've got two first-class tickets...on the wrong one!"

CHAPTER 45

BrutForce Labs
Jack

"We don't have a choice," Jack explained. "Locke's pushed up his launch date. He expects us to be there!"

He strode past Bart for the fifteenth time, hurriedly hefted another box of supplies, and carried them into the shuttle. His determined footsteps on the steel ramp echoed off the rough-hewn stone walls of the hangar bay.

Bart didn't follow. Rather, he stood on the loading dock, wringing his hands. He tugged on the brim of his baseball hat, which sported a sexy green alien posing like a trucker's mudflap icon.

"But, Jack, this is crazy. We weren't supposed to leave till next week. We don't have all our supplies stowed yet, and I haven't finished brushing up on the ship specs. What if I accidentally grab the wrong handle and flush myself out of the airlock instead of flushing the toilet?"

Trinity laughed as she passed him, carrying a box of her own. "Didn't go through Space Potty Training 101, huh? Don't worry," she assured. "It's not the flushing that'll get you. It's missing the four-inch hole you've gotta aim for. Miss that, and you'll clog up the air vents that provide the suction."

Jack returned, nodding his head in agreement. "Then you'll have a real shit show. Kind of like the one we've got on our hands now."

He stopped and looked Bart straight in the eye. "Locke's gotten what he needs out of us. He's got the hover tech. Not to mention, he knows we talked to Dr. Evers, and things didn't work out so well for her, now, did they?"

Bart shook his head.

Jack jabbed a determined finger into Bart's chest. "Forget the airlock. If we so much as set a foot back at Locke Industries, let alone on the *Horus*, we'll be the next ones to wind up in the heat-melt compactor. Now, quit whining and help us load the ship!"

Bart grabbed an available box and scurried to the ingress hatch.

He'd never admit it, but Jack shared his friend's misgivings. They hadn't been scheduled to leave for another week, but Locke was forcing their hand by pushing up his launch date. If they were going to succeed in getting the jump on him, staying alive in the process, they had to leave soon.

Like today.

Jack stood on the loading dock, staring at the vehicle that was supposed to take him into space. The ship, though a little worn around the edges, was solid. The gravitator tech assembly was in place.

All he needed now was a crew.

The major had promised him a top-flight three-man crew, all of whom, the major guaranteed, had knocked a generous amount of space dust from their boots during various lunar excursions and stints on the International Space Station—all of them military veterans.

And none of them here yet.

A knot of worry gripped his insides.

"Jack!" He heard the major's voice call across the cavern. "Jack! Come here! Got someone you're going to want to meet."

The major approached with a strapping African American gentleman who clocked in at just a hair under six-foot-three.

"This here's Captain Rondell Stennis," the major began. Jack exhaled a mental sigh of relief.

"Rondell here is your shuttle commander. Served under me, so I know he's rock solid. Would have shoved a boot up his ass if he wasn't. Listen to him," the major ordered sternly.

"Yes, sir," Jack answered, resisting the urge to salute.

The major shook his head. "I am dead serious. The commander's job is to enforce order and discipline on the mission—from the moment the shuttle door closes until it lands back on Earth. He says 'jump,' you say how high. No questions asked. The crew's primary directive is to perform whatever actions the commander deems necessary for the success of the mission and the safety of the ship and its crew."

Stennis reached out a hand. Jack thought his rich mahogany face hinted at a readiness to split into a brilliant white smile, but it looked like the man put considerable effort into maintaining a stoic expression demanded by the magnitude of his position. It was apparent he took his job seriously. "I think the mission's a noble one, Dr. Harding. Proud to serve. I'll do whatever I can to make sure your boy gets what he needs."

My boy.

The words gut-checked Jack like a heavyweight prizefighter. It was time to admit it to himself. He had started to think of all the Johansson children as his own—his own little crew. Even the recalcitrant Julia. Yet, here he was about to abandon them to fly halfway across the solar system. But like the major said, that was the commander's job, wasn't it? To do whatever was necessary for the safety of the mission?

And his mission was to make sure this family survived—all of them.

"I need to start the preflight checklist. See you aboard, Dr. Harding." The captain had moved on, heading for the spacecraft.

"Chas Brown," a hearty baritone captured Jack's attention. His head swiveled to see the extended hand of a short, stocky man sporting a head buzzed down to stubble. "First lieutenant, United States Air Force. I'm gonna be the one flying this here bus. I'll try to give you a smooth ride. Avoid any potholes, ya know? Just don't go sticking any gum under the seats, and we'll get along just fine."

The man chortled, pleased at his own joke. He slapped Jack on the back. "Pleased to meet ya, hoss!"

The major shook his head. "Meet your pilot, Charles Brown, though most days I think he's just a frustrated comedian. But don't worry. What his humor lacks, he makes up for with his piloting ability. He can fly just about anything. Hell. Wouldn't surprise me if he could fly a carpet better than Aladdin. And here comes our last crew member. We good to go, Odd Job?"

"Odd Job?" Jack queried.

A small man, no more than five-foot-three, walked by. A tool belt was slung on his slim hips, carrying a variety of tools Jack considered probably weighed more than the man himself. "You bet, Major. Got my wrench. Got my boots. And I got my union card."

Jack looked to the major, puzzled.

The major explained. "Second Lieutenant Francis Xavier Moretti, or as we like to call him, Odd Job. He's the mission specialist, which basically means he's a plumber, a spacewalker, and a construction worker all rolled into one. The commander may be in charge, and the pilot might fly this thing, but Odd Job here pretty much handles everything else. He'll be the one helping you retrieve the egrets once you get to Mars."

"Good to know," Jack had replied.

"Good men to the last," the major confirmed. "Now, seeing as how we're about to hit the go button on this thing, I'm going to make sure everything's copacetic. Oh, look. Here's your family."

The major pointed to the hangar entrance where Bradley waited with Myrna Pulldraw and the children, all of them wide-eyed and slack-jawed. Even Charlie was here.

"Best say your goodbyes," the major said softly.

Jack swallowed. Hard.

*****

"You goin' on a trip…today?" Lucas blubbered. The five-year-old's lower lip trembled. Tears welled at the rims of his blue eyes. Oscar's expression mimicked his brother's.

The boys had been all excited at the idea of Jack being an "astro-nut." Now that the time for the actual departure had arrived, they seemed a lot less keen on the idea.

"We don't want you to go," Oscar moaned and threw his chunky little arms around Jack's neck. Tears began to form in Jack's own eyes. He patted the crying child on the back.

"Hey, hey. It's okay, little man. Jack will be back. Maybe I'll even bring you your very own Martian rock. You can take it to school for show-and-tell."

Oscar picked up his head. "A space rock?"

Jack nodded vigorously. Anything to stop the tears. He couldn't take it. Hell, if he could, he'd bring the kid freaking E.T. himself. He looked toward Charlie, sitting in his wheelchair.

Wasn't that kind of the plan?

Jack turned Oscar over to Bradley and knelt in front of the

seven-year-old. "Don't worry. I'll be back soon."

"I know you will, Jack," Charlie replied. A small smile tugged at the corner of Jack's mouth. How this kid, who had been dealt the worst possible hand life could give, could remain so positive…it was a mystery more complex than subquantum mechanics.

He looked at all the kids. Julia hung near Myrna's side, looking nervously at Jack while clutching something tightly in her fist.

At least it isn't that damned tablet.

The twins had gravitated toward Bradley. Jack smiled. The nanny would take good care of them, making sure they were fed, driving them to school.

Hopefully they don't drive him crazy first.

Alice stood on the periphery of the group. Her pixie face seemed pinched—from pain or difficult thought, Jack couldn't determine. She rocked back and forth on her worn high-tops, a petite bundle of kinetic energy. Jack moved to speak to her next, but surprisingly, Julia intercepted him.

"So, uh, Jack, I didn't know if your eardrums clog up in a spacecraft. You know, like they do on an airplane?" Julia said, casting her eyes to the ground. "And, it might be kinda dumb, 'cause I know space is like…a vacuum, so there's not supposed to be any sound anyway."

The teen toed the stone floor, searching for the words. "But, well, when you're in the ship, I figured it might be kind of important to be able to hear what's going on. Gum always helps my ears pop, so, well…here."

She shoved a pack of bubblegum into Jack's hand then darted behind Bradley, hiding her head in embarrassment.

Trinity leaned forward. She whispered in Jack's ear. "Told you she'd come around."

"But who's gonna make up bedtime stories for us while

you're gone?" Lucas asked with concern.

Jack squatted next to him. "You know who's really excellent at making up stories? Alice. I'm sure Alice would be happy to…"

His voice trailed off as a buzzer sounded loudly. A red lamp rotated as an accented feminine voice announced over the address system.

"Oxygen purge completed. Prepare to initiate launch status check."

Jack looked nervously back at the shuttle. Odd Job was gesturing madly, urging them to get to the ship pronto. Jack looked back at his family.

His…family.

Bart tugged his shirtsleeve. "Come on, man. We've got to go."

Jack looked around frantically. "But where's Alice? I have to say goodbye."

"Don't worry," Bradley assured. "She probably ran off because she was upset. We'll tell her. Now, go!"

"Bartholomew Pulldraw! You come here this instant!" Myrna threatened. She pulled him close and planted a lipstick kiss on his cheek.

Bart groaned. "What, Ma? I gotta go. Voyage of discovery and all that."

She frowned, licked her thumb, and rubbed at the red smudge. "Voyage of discovery. You want to discover something? Discover how mole-kas I'm going to be if you don't come home to me safe and sound. Do you understand me?

"Yeah, Ma. Love you too," he replied a little less harshly and followed Trinity toward the shuttle.

Jack looked at Bradley and Myrna. "I can't begin to express how much I appreciate this. Thank you. Both of you."

"Dr. Harding!" Odd Job called.

"Go!" Bradley urged.

Jack gave a weak wave and ran to the ship.

*****

"Buckle up, Buttercup," Odd Job suggested as Bart slid into his seat. "Pull those overalls over your pumpkin suit."

Bart slid the straps of the thick harness over the bright orange of his OCCS suit. Clearly, used, no two of them seemed to be the same.

"Why's it so orange?" he grumbled.

"So they can find your ass if you accidentally flush yourself out over the Atlantic," Odd Job laughed.

Bart sneered and shot a nasty look toward Jack. Jack shrugged inside his own harness.

Maybe he shouldn't have shared Bart's fears about mixing up the shuttle levers.

Jack marveled at his own suit. The next-generation Advanced Crew Escape Suit (ACES) and the specially designed seat were engineered to meet the punishing conditions that space travelers might find themselves subject to high-landing loads, g-forces, extremes in temperatures, unexpected bailouts—even unexpected bladder issues.

Bart squirmed in his suit. The maximum absorbency garment urine containment trunks were a lot like incontinence underwear.

"It chafes," Bart complained. "I feel like I'm wearing Pampers."

The suits, lined with pressure bladders, also came equipped with an integrated ventilation system for use with the shaded, full-pressure helmet. Textured gloves attached to the suit to allow crew members full manipulation of switches, buttons, and levers necessary during ascent and reentry. Each suit even came with a life raft tucked into a survival kit.

Only thing missing is the kitchen sink.

"Look. You're famous," Odd Job quipped. He hooked his thumb toward the closed-circuit screens.

The feed displayed a crystal-clear image of their little ship clamped down in its docking bay. Red lights flashed against the metal hull in rhythm, warning the ground staff the area was hot.

"Attention all personnel. Attention all personnel. Clear platform area for launch," the female voice announced.

"What do you say we get this show on the road, gentlemen?" Stennis' bass rolled as he flicked several overhead switches.

"Roger that, Captain," Brown responded.

Jack felt his stomach quiver.

Nerves or excitement?

He couldn't be sure.

"Initiate launch status check," the shuttle commander said.

"Initiating launch status check," Brown responded.

Normally, there would be a host of team leaders—conductors, directors, engineers— participating in a standard launch. Now, three men conducted the work of twenty different departments. Jack chuckled inwardly.

This launch is anything but standard.

"OMS function?" Brown called.

"Go," Odd Job responded. Each system would be met with a go/no-go response.

"Flight and ground systems?"

"Go."

"Payload systems?"

"Go."

"Launch processing system?"

"Go."

"Gravitator assembly?"

Jack held his breath.

"Go."

He exhaled a sigh of relief.

"Weather?"

"Open skies and clear sailing."

"All systems go. Proceed to launch," Stennis announced.

"T-minus one minute," the female voice announced.

"This is it," Bart murmured. "The countdown."

Jack frowned. "I'm doing the right thing, right?"

"Of course you are!" Bart assured.

"Then why do I feel like I'm going to puke?" Jack replied.

Odd Job laughed. "Think you're going to puke now? Wait till you hit zero gravity for the first time."

"Do not turn my ship into the Vomit Comet, son," Stennis warned.

"Vomit Comet?" Jack questioned.

"It's the shock to the body's vestibular system," Brown explained. "Helps you maintain balance on the ground. Can't do shit when you take gravity out of the equation."

"Nobody can hear you scream, but everybody can see you blow chunks," Odd Job added.

Jack dry swallowed.

I am so not ready for this.

"Five, four, three, two, one."

A chorus of noises assaulted Jack's ears all at once.

WAANNK! WAANNK!

The jarring launch alarm blared through the cavern. He heard the thudding ca-chunk as the securing clamps released.

Brown looked back at Jack. "Okay. Time to see if your magic Frisbee's gonna fly."

A sudden rising hum of power flooded the cabin as Brown rocked the gravitator's power lever upward. The crew grabbed for purchase as the small craft made a sudden lurch and bobbled uncertainly over the launchpad.

Brown grabbed for the control and pulled back. He looked around the cabin. "Got a little kick, don't she?"

Stennis barked at the pilot. "Give me a pitch adjustment, now, or this girl's gonna need a nose job before she even thinks about prom."

"Transverse axial adjustment. Check." Brown rapidly attended the rotational hand controller and stabilized the vessel.

As the ship slowly lifted toward an opening at the peak of the ancient aquifer, Brown engaged the small thrusters, which would serve to propel the ship up through the earth's atmosphere.

Odd Job glanced at the trio of wide-eyed passengers. "Don't worry. The ride smooths out after the first three hundred and ninety-one thousand miles."

Jack groaned.

The ship moved toward the top of the exosphere, and light gave way to velvet night. Jack, Trinity, and Bart stared in reverent wonder through the viewing windows. It was a sudden sea of stars, Jack thought. In all his life, he'd never seen anything so beautiful.

Trinity gasped. Jack turned to watch the expression on her face.

Then again, maybe he had.

His thought was interrupted by the shuttle commander. Stennis turned to face them. "Gentlemen," he began. "It suddenly occurred to me that this vessel doesn't have a proper name—only a manufacturing designation. Since it's largely your tech that's driving this mission, I think naming rights fall to you. Any suggestions?"

Jack floundered, his mind blank. He looked to Bart for an assist. Bart only shrugged.

"Can I make a suggestion?" Trinity offered. Jack nodded gratefully.

"I like *Hover*," she said. "It's rather poetic, all things considered."

Stennis nodded. "Not bad, ma'am. Not bad at all."

Jack beamed.

Hover.

He silently turned the word over on his tongue, mouthing it silently.

"It's perfect."

CHAPTER 46

Hover Shuttle Craft
Jack

"Good morning," Trinity began, then looked out the viewing window at the blackness of space. "Hm, then again, I guess it's always 'good night' up here."

Jack grumbled. They were only three days into the six- to seven-month journey, and he was already sick of sipping freeze-dried coffee through a straw. "I miss Starbucks."

It had been a rough night. He hadn't slept well at all. His dreams were filled with vague images of ferret-faced aliens, Martian dust storms, and the feeling of dread that he'd forgotten something critically important. He'd stayed awake for hours running mental calculations for the gravitator's power, desperately trying to remember if he'd forgotten to drop a nine or carry a one. The gravitator created the gravity hills and wells on its own, creating thrust without any outside interference, but it needed the extraneous power boost from the added voltage if they were going to get all the way to Mars.

He rotated his neck, trying to work out the kinks. His body still hadn't adjusted to the microgravity environment present aboard the *Hover*. It had been compounded by the vertical sleep station he had been assigned.

Man was not meant to sleep standing up.

He yawned deeply.

Or to drink diluted mud.

Trinity laughed. "Oh, come on. The coffee's not so bad."

Jack gave her a baleful stare. "I'd rather drink battery acid."

Before Trinity could counter, Odd Job rushed in and demanded their attention.

"Battery acid might sit better on your stomach than my news, Doc. You're needed on the flight deck, pronto."

Jack and Trinity exchanged worried glances.

"Is something wrong with the gravitator?" Jack asked, the concern of his nightmares flooding his brain.

"It's not the gravitator, Doc." Odd Job paused. "It's Locke."

*****

Jack and Trinity hurried after Odd Job as quickly as one could in the bizarre gravitational environment and headed for the forward fuselage. At that moment, Bart emerged from the personal hygiene station, the sucking whoosh of the air toilet sounding behind him. His brow rose as he observed the sudden, panicked flurry of activity. Jack rushed past him.

"What?" Bart asked. "Don't tell me I missed breakfast?"

Jack barely looked back as he responded. "Locke's here."

"Oh crap," Bart mumbled. He started after Jack when a rustle from the second vertical sleep station caught his attention. His head swiveled toward it.

"Are you coming or not?" Jack called.

Bart looked nervously between Jack and the slightly bulging sleeping bag mounted to the bulkhead. "Yeah, um, coming."

"Well, get your ass in gear. Something tells me this isn't going to be a happy reunion."

Jack's head disappeared toward the avionics bay and the interdeck access point to the flight deck.

*****

"He's close," the mission operations specialist informed the gathered crew. He pressed his hand against the earpiece of his headset. He frowned and turned to look at them. "And he's pissed."

The shuttle commander stood over him, bracing his huge frame with a flat palm against the overhead. "How close is close?"

"We can't see him yet, but he's got to have engaged his rocket boosters at the periapsis and cleared the far side of the moon, or we wouldn't be able to hear him."

"What's he saying?" Jack asked.

Odd Job handed him the headset. "Listen for yourself."

Jack exchanged glances with the crew and reluctantly took the headset from Odd Job and placed it on his own head. He immediately cringed at the sound of Locke's shrieking tirade. Jack motioned for Odd Job to transfer the call to the ship's overhead coms. The billionaire's blistering voice suddenly echoed through the ship.

"–ding? Harding, you fucking son of a bitch!" Locke's voice quavered with fury. "How dare you try to beat me with my own tech!"

Jack started. He yelled into the mic. "Your tech? You mean my tech, you psycho!"

"A matter of perspective, and from my perspective, your little tugboat doesn't stand a chance against my ship."

Stennis spun to face Jack. "What's he talking about? Does his ship have weapons capabilities?"

"I-I-I don't know," Jack sputtered. "I mean, I don't think so."

"Now, hold on just a goddamned minute!" Odd Job interjected. "This was just supposed to be a market run. You know, like go to the corner store, pick up some eggs and milk, and head home. Granted, the 'corner's' a hundred and forty-one million miles off, but I sure as hell didn't sign up for any interstellar combat! I did my tours."

Stennis got in Jack's face. "The safety of my crew and this mission are on the line, Dr. Harding. Were there or weren't there weapons on Locke's ship?"

"How am I supposed to know?" Jack exploded. "I didn't see anything that looked like a weapon when Bart and I were still working at the assembly center. But I wouldn't even begin to know what I was looking for. I'm just a scientist!"

"Holy shit," Brown gasped. All eyes swiveled toward the closed-circuit screen to see what had drawn the expletive from the pilot's lips.

At first, it was difficult to determine what exactly they were seeing. The entire screen was bright white.

"What? What is it?" Trinity asked nervously.

Stennis leaned forward, craning his neck toward the screen. "What are we looking at, Brown? I can't make anything out."

Brown didn't answer. His hands moved deftly over the controls, adjusting the pitch and yaw until he had turned the vehicle around and they could see the object that had filled the aft camera lens.

"Mother…" Stennis mumbled. He motioned to Odd Job to mute two-way communication. He held up a hand to shield against the sudden glare as the sun reflected off the shining hull of the mammoth spacecraft bearing down on them.

"What the hell is that thing?" Brown muttered.

"That, gentlemen," Jack responded, "is the *Horus* StarCraft."

A look of intense concern pinched Trinity's face. "How much trouble are we in?"

"I don't know about us," Bart's voice suddenly interrupted the conversation. "But somebody is."

Everyone turned to see him at the edge of the interdeck access…and he wasn't alone.

Alice, garbed in an oversized OCCS suit, wiggled her fingers and grinned sheepishly.

"Hi, Jack."

Jack's jaw dropped.

CHAPTER 47

Horus StarCraft
Locke

"What happened?!" Locke bellowed to his communications specialist. "Where are they? Get Harding back on the line! Now!"

He stood on the bridge, frustration causing his body to tremble. You couldn't pace in space, and it was driving him to distraction.

The fury he felt was nothing compared to the volcanic eruption that had occurred when Sarah Copeland had informed him of Harding's P1AL launch.

Under my fucking nose the whole goddamned time!

Sarah's nose had paid the price. He thought of the bright crimson blood that had gushed when he lashed out and punched her for failing to alert him sooner.

A brief smile fleeted across his face.

He was going to have to acquire new counsel when this was over.

The plan had been to dispatch Harding and Pulldraw aboard the *Horus*. Discreetly—disposing of their remains where they would never be found. He smiled again when he thought back to his exploits with the family feline all those years ago.

More than one way to skin a cat.

He turned to the captain, a stern-faced man with a bristling mustache.

"Tell Dr. Binderkampf to engage the Marx generator," Locke ordered.

"Already done, sir," the captain nodded crisply. "The high-voltage pulses generated from its parallel-charged capacitors are being fed to the gravitator. Its thrust, coupled with the gravity-assist from sling-shotting around the moon, will allow us to outstrip Dr. Harding's craft and arrive at Mars well before him."

Locke's eyes narrowed.

"I don't want to 'outstrip' him," he spat. "I want to *obliterate* him."

The captain fell silent, frozen by the murderous intent readily apparent in Locke's expression.

"But, seeing as how I have no missiles aboard, I was hoping the good doctor could redirect the generator's pulse toward Dr. Harding's ship."

The captain frowned. "But the electromagnetic pulse would shut down all power to their ship. It would fry the capacitors to the computer systems, disabling flight controls...and life-support systems."

Locke let the gravity of his intent settle with the captain for a few moments before he spoke. "Is that a problem?"

"No," the captain shook his head. "No problem at all, sir."

CHAPTER 48

Hover Shuttle Craft
Jack

"You bet your ass it's a goddamned problem!" Jack bellowed.

Jack, Trinity, Bart, and the admonished Alice were gathered in the crew quarters. Jack's face, already puffy due to the effects of near zero-gs, flushed red with his increasing blood pressure.

"I just wanted to help, Jack," Alice whimpered.

"Helping would have been to stay with Bradley and Mrs. Pulldraw!" Jack's hands rose slowly to his head. "Shit! Bradley! He's probably mobilized the entire California Highway Patrol by now!"

Bart, awkwardly standing there with a *totally* busted look on his face, said, "I told Bradley...I knew she was onboard. And to be honest, I'm more than a little surprised no one else saw her. It was almost comical. We're just lucky there's redundancy...extra sleeping bags, two extra environment suits. Food will be tight, but I'm eating half rations..."

Jack shot Bart a death glare. Then, looking at Alice, he offered up a half smile.

"Not that this isn't important," Trinity interrupted, "but shouldn't we be addressing the elephant in the room?"

Jack turned to her. "What are you talking about?"

"Locke?" Trinity gestured out the viewing window.

Shit.

In the sudden upset, he'd nearly forgotten.

"And unless your plan is to chuck Alice out of the airlock, she's here to stay." Trinity pointed. "If *that* thing has any kind of a weapon, I don't think I can say the same about us."

Jack pulled at his hair. He looked at Bart. "I don't know. Do you remember seeing anything that looked like a weapon on board the *Horus* when we were working on it?"

Bart shrugged. "I mean, I didn't see a rail gun or missile port or anything that could cause external damage to the ship."

Trinity breathed a sigh of relief. "That's good."

Bart frowned.

Jack's own face puckered. "No. No frowns. Frowns are bad."

"That's not the only thing," Bart muttered.

"Explain," Jack demanded.

Bart shifted in his spacesuit. "Well, every sci-fi movie I've ever seen, there is one incontrovertible tenet."

Jack nodded.

Get there faster, bro.

"And that is?" Jack finally verbalized.

"Power is life. It controls the guidance systems, the life-support systems, even the stupid airflow on that ridiculous aim-for-the-bullseye toilet! If you can figure out a way to take out a ship's power, anybody onboard…" Bart hesitated as he looked at Alice.

"Anybody onboard what, Bart?" Jack snapped.

"Anybody onboard would be as good as dead."

Suddenly, the *Hover* lurched. The overhead lighting flickered as rapid-fire popping sounded from the avionics bay. Jack dove through the air, propelling himself toward the sound. He found

Odd Job helplessly scrambling to disengage wires from their ports, sparks flying.

"What can I do?" Jack offered.

"Not a goddamned thing!" Odd Job blurted. "It's a fucking cascade failure. The son of a bitch hit us with an EMP!"

"An electromagnetic pulse?" Jack asked.

Odd Job nodded as the ship plunged into sudden darkness. Alice let out a little scream. Stennis' voice, filtering down from the flight deck, barked orders to Brown.

What bothered Jack was the sound he *didn't* hear—the deep, droning hum of the engine and the internal power plant that ran it.

What do we do now?

Jack heard the crack of one of the glow sticks that came standard with every OCCS. He jumped as Odd Job's face glowed in the ambient green light of the mixed hydrogen peroxide and dyed tert-butyl alcohol.

"He's left us dead in the water."

*****

"How bad is it?" Stennis asked. His brown face took on a dull, moss-green cast from the emergency glow stick around his neck. Still, Jack could see the thinly veiled concern on the shuttle commander's face as he stood over Odd Job.

The mission specialist picked up the burnt ends of countless wires waving loosely from the avionics bay. He turned to his commander. "I don't know, sir. I've got no guidance, no navigation—forget flight control or communications. It's all gone. The whole system is fried."

Stennis sighed heavily. Jack saw the man weighing his next words.

And the load looked unbearable.

"Life support?"

Odd Job looked up. "If saturation levels were at maximum when the pulse hit?"

The commander nodded.

"Twenty-four hours."

Alice buried her head in Trinity's chest, hugging her tightly.

Jack looked around at the despondent faces of the crew. Because of what he had done, Locke had crippled their ship and left them to die drifting in space. That meant Charlie would die too.

He felt a sudden surge of nausea.

Way to go, Jack. You have now succeeded in failing on a galactic scale.

It was Bart who finally broke the silence. "What about the International Space Station? It's close. Relatively speaking. If we could get to it, we'd be okay."

"And how do you propose we get to it?" Odd Job quipped. "In case it escaped your attention, we've got no juice. Our engines? They're dead!"

Bart wasn't dissuaded. Jack heard the undercurrent of excitement in the software engineer's voice. "The gravitator. We use the gravitator. The gravity field it generates is intrinsic to its subatomic makeup. The pulse shouldn't have affected it."

Brown scoffed. "But it did affect the drivers that control it."

Jack shook his head.

"Even if the gravitator was an option in this situation, the time it would take to reach the station and make the repairs? It would be too late to reach the Mars race." He paused. "And too late for Charlie."

"And Charlie's your son?" Odd Job asked.

Jack nodded.

"Son," he heard Alice repeat.

"Yes, Alice," Jack floated to her side. "I called Charlie my son because that's how I think of him now. That's how I think of all of you now. *My* kids."

Alice pushed him away. "No. Not 'son.' I said 'sun'!"

"Alice," Jack began, looking after her as she pulled herself toward the cargo bay. "What are you saying?"

He maneuvered after her. Bart, Trinity, and the rest of the crew followed suit. Alice stopped next to the personnel rover lashed down in payload. She held her arms out to encompass the thin solar panels affixed to the rear of the vehicle, a panel which, when fully deployed, would power the unit across the deserts of Mars to look for the egrets' aquifer.

"S-U-N!" she announced with a wide, beaming smile. "I noticed the panels when I first snuck aboard."

Jack's eyes narrowed. "Which, under different circumstances, was a move that would get you grounded...for life."

Alice sighed. "You'll get your chance to punish me later. I really think this idea will work. We can use the panels from the rover to provide power to the shuttle!"

Jack felt a surge of hope. Then his brow creased. He turned to Odd Job. "But didn't you say the system was totally fried?"

Odd Job nodded. "Every piece of electronic equipment on this ship is toast."

Bart floated forward. "Not every piece."

Everyone's gaze riveted on the pudgy young man. Bart squirmed under the attention.

"Explain yourself," Stennis ordered. "And sooner rather than later."

"Well, the rover has a lot more than just solar panels," he began, pointing to the vehicle. "You have to understand, the human body is composed of 60 percent water. That means even we can conduct electricity." He looked at Brown. "How many times have you scuffed your feet across a carpet then zapped yourself when you grabbed a doorknob?"

Brown shrugged. "More than a few."

"Exactly!" Bart burst.

"Electrostatic discharge," Odd Job added, slowly nodding.

"That voltage alone can reach twenty thousand volts! So, imagine you're tooling across the Mars desert in your rover, and a dust storm flares up. Talk about a nightmare for the rover's onboard computers! The low atmospheric pressure and windy, dry-as-hell climate is the perfect environment for the triboelectric charging of dust. A discharge of that magnitude could shut the rover down, and you'd be stranded...about a hundred and forty-two million miles from AAA."

"That's great, Bart," Jack admonished, his concern building as he knew the available air was dwindling. "I'm impressed you're such an expert on the rover."

Bart shook his head. "I'm not a rover expert, but I *am* a computer expert. I read an article on how commercial rover designers incorporated Faraday cages to protect the delicate onboard computer systems from the charged Mars dust."

"Holy shit," Odd Job murmured.

Jack shook his head. "Wait. A Faraday cage? Wouldn't that protect against the effects of an electromagnetic pulse?"

"Exactly," Bart confirmed.

"So," Jack continued. "That means there's a viable computer system aboard the rover we could use to get the shuttle back up and running?"

"No." Bart shook his head. "There are two. If we can install the solar panel as Alice suggested, we can reprogram the computers to get the shuttle up and running again."

Stennis looked at Odd Job. "Are they right?"

Odd Job shrugged. "If enough of the wiring survived to

connect the rover units to the avionics system, I suppose it's possible. It's going to require a helluva programmer, though, to make the two different systems talk to each other."

Bart interlaced his fingers and stretched them to crack his knuckles. "Leave that to me."

"Can you get the panels installed?" Stennis asked the mission specialist.

Odd Job's face looked grim. "Bad news? Conditions aren't optimum. Normally, for a spacewalk, you'd want your walkers to spend a whole day in the suits breathing 100 percent oxygen and gradually decompressing to avoid getting the bends once you open the door."

"Well, we don't have twenty-four hours," Stennis pointed out.

Odd Job nodded. "And with no power, we also don't have the means to decompress the airlock."

"So, what's the good news?" Bart asked.

"Good news? The whole ship started decompressing the minute the power went out. Technically, the whole vessel's a decompression chamber right now. We could seal off the flight deck for most of the crew, but then someone could still suit up and wait as long as possible before opening the exterior door manually. Can't wait the full twenty-four, for obvious reasons, but," he shrugged, "maybe it will be enough."

"Okay. So, do it," Jack urged.

"That's going to cut the clock on the available breathable air for whoever is on the flight deck."

Jack suddenly realized the implications of what the man said. "By how much?"

"Fifty percent. That means we have to complete the whole operation outside the ship in less than four hours."

"Good thing we're wearing pressure suits, huh, Jack?" Bart mused.

Jack attempted a smile.

This kind of pressure...he didn't need.

CHAPTER 49

Hover Shuttle Craft
Jack

"You ever done a spacewalk before?" Odd Job asked Jack as they stood near the airlock. Almost twenty hours ago, they had exchanged their OCCS suits for two extravehicular activity suits that had been in the cargo stowage of the rover. He had drawn the proverbial short straw. Now, he and Lieutenant Moretti were breathing pure oxygen and watching the clock.

"Does dancing to Michael Jackson's 'Billie Jean' count?"

Odd Job whistled. "That is some old school right there. But no, don't think the 'moonwalk' qualifies."

He looked at Jack's deepening worry lines.

"Don't worry. Your EVA will keep you safe. It's designed to basically be a mini-spaceship. Can handle radiation, debris, and extremes of heat and cold. And," he thumped the pack on Jack's back, "it'll keep you breathing out there."

Jack laughed nervously. "Something I'm very interested in doing."

"I'm just glad these suckers are standard in the rover's emergency survival kit. Otherwise, this whole crazy plan of yours would have been impossible. The PLSS system is electrical."

"PLSS?" Jack asked.

"Portable life-support system. Interfaces with the HUT."

"Jabba?" Jack attempted some humor to try and warm the icy dread that threatened to consume him.

Odd Job laughed. "Hard Upper Torso. I know this is a lot. Consider it a crash course Space camp for grown-ups. You'll be fine."

Yeah. You know what FINE stands for?

"Okay. We can't wait any longer. Let's do this thing!" Odd Job thunked his bulbous helmet. "You might want to hold onto something. When I pull this handle, it's really going to suck."

Believe me, pal, it already does.

"In a perfect world, the pressure would be equalized before we stepped outside. Otherwise? Explosive decompression. Not pretty. Only option? Without juice, the cabin decompresses on its own. Hope it's enough. Either way, I'm expecting there to be a bit of a breeze, so hang on."

Jack bobbed his head inside the big bubble of a helmet and threaded his foot through the airlock foot restraint. His gloved hand grabbed a metal grip installed on the bulkhead. The solar panels they needed for the ambitious plan were safely secured nearby so they wouldn't be sucked out when the open airlock created a monster vacuum.

"Now, when we get out there, be careful. It's no walk in the park. First thing you do is attach your tether. Then, you keep your eyes on me. Do what I say, when I say. Got it?"

Jack braced as Odd Job strained against the metal lever. He could see the man's face reddening with the effort. Odd Job let go and leaned back, puffing.

"I can't do it. It's not budging."

Jack started. "You can't give up. Alice, Bart, Trinity...the rest of the crew...they're sealed on the flight deck. They've only got four hours of air left. We've got to make this happen!"

Odd Job look at the plaintive expression through Jack's visor. He nodded and resumed his efforts with the airlock's manual lever. It still refused to budge. Jack had just started to believe that the whole plan was for naught when he saw the lever begin to give just a fraction.

"It's moving! Come on!" he urged. Odd Job gave one last, concerted effort, and the lever released. The airlock door opened, causing a massive suction of air. The men braced until the atmosphere stabilized.

"Yes!" Odd Job shouted in exultation. "Michael Jackson's about to have nothing on you, Doc. Let's go."

They released the solar panels, each man grabbing one of the long rectangular units, and moved toward the black rectangle of space.

Jack reached the edge of the airlock and pulled himself out into the universe.

*****

Jack surmised he had taken approximately one million three hundred and fifty-one thousand six hundred and forty steps in his lifetime. As he took the one million three hundred and fifty-one thousand six hundred and forty-first into the vastness of space, he knew this one–this single one–would be the most memorable.

As a foster kid, he'd spent countless nights lying under the night sky–flat on his back in a bare postage stamp of a backyard or on the gravel-strewn roof of some anonymous apartment building–watching the stars and wondering if somewhere out there, there was someone who truly wanted him. Now, he was "out there," walking among the very stars he had longed for so long ago. The brilliant blue orb of Earth hung like a giant, beautiful marble beneath his feet. Slowly, he turned to see the massive specter of the man in the moon staring down him. The intense beauty of it all took his breath away.

"No time for sightseeing, Doc. We're on the clock." Odd Job's voice crackled over his headset. Jack mentally shook himself alert. He connected his tether to the eyelet on the exterior of the shuttle.

Odd Job motioned. "This way."

The man's tool bag bobbed along behind him. They reached the gravitator near the bow of the craft. It had been decided that was the only location where they would be able to connect the panels in order to feed the energy they collected into the ship's fuel cells.

"How are you doing?" Odd Job asked. "Any symptoms?"

"What's that?" Jack shook his head, a slight ringing in his ears.

"I said do you feel okay? Any dizziness? Confusion? Those are symptoms of decompression sickness."

"No. Looks like twenty hours did the trick."

"Yeah, well, we got lucky," Odd Job commented. "Hold this panel while I set things up. Angle them so they can charge while I'm working."

Jack took the panel from the mission specialist. The six-junction solar cells that comprised the panels were specially designed for optimum photovoltaic efficiency, capturing energy across the spectrum of the solar rays to maximize the output even with Mars' notorious dust storms. Yet, each cell measured no thicker than the width of a human hair. Jack had run the calculations. Each one of the panels would produce 7.5 kilowatts. Roughly translated, that meant they could expect somewhere in the neighborhood of fifteen thousand volts of power from the joined panels. Only a fraction, Jack knew, of the power Locke was pumping into the Horus and its gravitator. At best, the Hover could only hope to limp along—but they would get there.

Please, God, just let it be on time.

If they didn't make it before the starting gun fired, the whole trip would have been fruitless.

As Odd Job worked, Jack watched the clock. The laborious process stretched on nearly three and three-quarter hours.

"There!" Odd Job finally stated triumphantly. "Got it!"

Jack observed the man's handiwork. His vision blurred. He squinted his eyes to bring things back into focus.

The two panels, connected at the hull and wired into the gravitator and the ship's fuel cells, jutted up from the craft at forty-five-degree angles like the antennae of some giant space bug.

"Looks like a giant cockroach," Jack mused, his words slightly slurring.

"Yeah?" Odd Job responded. "Let's hope God or whoever else is up here doesn't decide to step on us. We'd better get back. If your friend's done his job, they should be able to get systems back online as soon as we're back on board. Let's head back."

Jack nodded. The two men made their way back to the ingress. Odd Job disconnected his tether and pulled himself in through the door. Jack took one last look at the blue globe below him, the streaks of white frothing across the oceans. As Jack reached for his own tether, it sounded like the surf of the entire ocean pounded in his ears. The light began to dim as he unhooked the latch.

"Dr. Harding?" he heard Odd Job's voice faintly in the distance.

That's funny, he thought. *In space, usually everything seems so much closer. Like the moon is right now. Bet if I just reached out, I could touch it.*

"Dr. Harding?" Odd Job repeated. "Jack!"

Free of his tether, Jack floated. The last thing he remembered was reaching out to shake hands with the man in the moon.

CHAPTER 50

Hover Shuttle Craft
Jack

"Is he going to be okay?" Jack heard Alice's worried voice filter through the blackness. He focused his energy and blinked, opening his eyes to see the eleven-year-old standing on her tiptoes at the edge of the horizontal sleep pallet. Trinity hovered beside her.

"Well hello there, Sleeping Beauty," Trinity smiled.

Jack shook his head weakly from side to side. "Nope. Just Jack."

"Huh?" Trinity replied.

"If I was Sleeping Beauty, you'd have woken me with a kiss," he explained.

"We almost kissed you," Odd Job's voice sounded from behind the girls. He came around with a tablet, punching in some pertinent data. He looked up. "Kissed you goodbye, I mean."

"What happened?" Jack mumbled.

"Decompression sickness. You got the bends, my man. You passed out after you disengaged your tether and started floating out into the void."

"Damn," Jack whispered.

"If Odd Job hadn't jumped out after you, we might have lost you forever," Trinity agreed.

"Still could have," Odd Job continued. "But your science whiz here," he tapped Alice on the head, "ingeniously suggested rigging the airlock as a hyperbaric chamber to recompress you. Took some creative engineering, but looks like it did the trick. Sorry to say it won't help us get to Mars on time though."

"Wait! What?" Jack tried to sit up, whacking his already aching head on the overhead of the pallet. He rubbed the sore spot. "What about the solar panels? They should be providing enough power to boost the gravitator and our speed."

Odd Job shook his head. "Not enough. Even if we push the gravitator to the max, Locke's little stunt with the EMP slowed us down just enough to keep us from arriving in time to meet the gun. Captain Stennis has ordered us to set a course for Earth."

"Earth!?" Jack slid from the pallet. "No, no, no. I have not come this far only to fall flat on my face!"

He pulled himself through the craft and up through the interdeck access to the flight deck.

"Captain Stennis!" he began. "Captain Stennis!"

"Ah, Dr. Harding. Good to see you up and about. Thought we lost you there for a minute."

"Part of me wishes you had. If we don't succeed in getting to Mars in time for the land grab, I may as well be dead. Why are you taking us back to Earth?"

A serious look settled on Stennis' features. "It's my job to make the best decision for the mission and the crew. After looking at all the data, I've decided the wisest course of action is to abort and return home."

"Home? You know what's at home, Captain Stennis? A little boy. A *sick* little boy whose only hope is on Mars. Not Earth. Mars. And now you're telling me Locke is going to get there, and we aren't?" He turned to Brown. "Major Cotton said you were the best pilot he's ever seen. Can't you fly this hunk of junk any faster?"

Brown snorted. "Not on two small solar sails, I can't."

Jack bellowed in frustration.

There has to be a way!

Stennis put a hand on his shoulder. "It's not your fault, son. You went up against Goliath. You're lucky you got this far."

Jack stared out the viewing window. Venus, the evening star, winked in the distance like the universe was in on some great cosmic joke. Suddenly, a thought occurred to him. Stennis had mentioned Goliath, the biblical behemoth that a shepherd boy brought down with nothing but a slingshot. Maybe that's all they needed.

A slingshot.

"Can you steer us toward Venus?" he asked Brown excitedly.

"Now, hold on, son," Stennis growled.

Jack turned to the shuttle commander. "Wait. Please listen."

"Make it good," Stennis ordered.

"Okay, look. It's just like going around the moon. If we can get just close enough to Venus until the planet's gravity pulls us in and increase our speed just until our own gravity pulls at Venus, a momentum exchange will occur as we arc around. Venus won't feel it one lick, but our ship? That will be a different story. What momentum it takes from Venus will bump up the momentum we already have and, if we engage the gravitator at exactly the right time, the combined power will launch us, like David's slingshot, straight toward Mars at an exponential rate!"

"And we'll beat Goliath," Stennis murmured.

"What do you say, sir?" Jack asked. "For the good of the mission?"

Stennis nodded. "For the good of the mission...but mostly

because I just want to kick Locke's ass all the way to Pluto."

*****

Jack's wrist device vibrated, letting him know the prearranged time for the next call home was quickly approaching. The P1AL's comms equipment was situated at the back section of the cockpit. Captain Stennis had helped to get them set up. Configuring communications telemetry between two separate objects in space, one which was Earth, one which was the P1AL, traveling at many thousands of kilometers per hour, was not for the feeble minded. But that was how Jack felt right now, looking at the array of blinking lights on the multiple rows of rack-mounted equipment.

Charlie's excited voice crackled from the speaker. "Jack? Are you there, Jack?" Only then did his face appear on the display. Of course, any synchronization was off between video and audio, but it didn't really matter. It was just good to see the little tyke again, looking so happy.

Before Jack could reply, Alice leaned forward and said, "Hi, Charlie...can you see me?"

It took a few moments before Charlie responded, "No...all I see is an alien. Or maybe it's a swamp creature."

"Ha ha," she said with a laugh.

They talked to all of the kids, one at a time. Two minutes each was all that we were allotted. Captain Stennis reminded Jack the open window of time for this session was quickly coming to an end. Bradley was the last to speak. Although looking a tad frazzled, he seemed surprisingly upbeat. He did scold Alice again for stowing away without telling anyone except Bart, who had informed Bradley via a short text message just moments before liftoff. She apologized, and so did Jack for not foreseeing that this could have been predicted very easily.

The comms channel began to fragment and distort while the audio skipped and then broke off completely. Jack and Alice stared at a still shot of Charlie making a face at the camera.

CHAPTER 51

Mars Orbit, Six Months Later
Jack

Brown let out a long, low whistle.

"Damn," he finally breathed. Outside the viewing window, they could see ships–hundreds of ships–entering Mars' orbit. A fleet of space-going vessels in all shapes and sizes, all filled with New Boomers. The term had historical roots in the 1889 Oklahoma Land Grab back on Earth. Like the original Boomers, many of the New Boomers were explorers, prospectors, and would-be landowners–poised to take their chance on the new frontier–interested in specific geological locations suspected to contain rare earth minerals–locations far-removed from their target location of the south pole.

"I thought they were called 'Sooners'?" Alice asked as she marveled at a long, cigar-shaped vessel nearby. Lights blinked along the length of its hull. Smaller utility vessels zipped close.

Bart shook his head. "Sooners were cheaters. They're the ones who snuck onto the land before everyone else and 'claimed' it ahead of time."

Jack grumbled. "Sounds like something Locke would pull. He's probably already down on the surface, on his way to the south pole."

They still had to beat him to the south pole though.

Jack's science had been dead to rights. Coupling the gravitator capabilities with a slingshot around Venus had gotten them to Mars on time. The ground they'd lost due to Locke's sabotage had more than been made up. A good thing, too. The solar sails hadn't held up too well during the long journey. The cosmic radiation and space debris had taken quite a toll. The ship had limped the last few leagues to the red planet. The likelihood of it making the return journey was zero to nil. Jack pushed the thought from his mind.

I'll cross that bridge when I get to it.

"About Locke," Bart grinned stupidly. "I don't think you need to worry about him."

Jack turned. "What are you talking about, Bart?"

"I *may* have uploaded a virus into the *Horus'* navigational systems when we were at the assembly facility, and it may have sent him a *little* off course."

It took a minute for Bart's revelation to marinate. Suddenly, Jack grabbed him and planted a fat, wet kiss on the man's cheek.

"You big, geeky, beautiful nerd!" Jack exclaimed. "You so deserve a raise!"

"Oh sure." Bart wiped the offensive gesture away. "I've been trying to tell you that for years."

Jack scooped Alice into his arms. "We're gonna do it! We're gonna save Charlie!"

"BrutForce Base Camp to *Hover* shuttle. Come in," a familiar voice crackled through the earpiece of the shuttle commander's headset. Stennis gestured to Jack.

Jack picked up his headset and placed it on his head. "Hover shuttle to BrutForce Base Camp."

"Well, it's about damned time!" Major Cotton's voice replied.

"Where have you been, Harding? Cutting it a little close, don't you think?"

Jack grinned. "Ran into a little trouble, Major. Brown hit a pothole."

Brown stuck out a tongue.

"A pothole? What in the hell are you talking about? Never mind. You can explain later how I took off *after* you and beat you here. Right now, you'd better get your asses down here. The race hasn't begun yet, but there's an encampment set up near the starting line. You'll need to check in and be at the starting line in the morning. I'll try to get there in time to see you off, but I've got my hands full here setting up the salvage-refabrication operation."

"Yes, sir! Any word on Locke?" Jack asked.

"Oh, there's word, all right…a few of them. And not a one I can say in polite society. Some of my guys picked up chatter from Locke's ship. He landed some three hundred miles away. Apparently, there was some trouble with his navigational systems."

Bart snorted. Jack waved him silent.

"He didn't sound too happy about it. Anyhow, he's hotfooting it to the start via his private personnel transport. Even at top speeds and without any trouble, it's going to take him five or six hours. If he makes it, it'll be by the skin of his porcelain veneers."

"Dammit," Jack cursed.

"Listen, don't worry about him. Get to the encampment. Get some sleep. Mars is a more brutal opponent than Locke could ever be," the major suggested.

Unless he's armed with an EMP.

"It's going to take everything you've got to overcome the hazards. You want to talk potholes? Try driving across the Martian terrain. Then there's the crappy air and dust storms that'll sand a man clear down to his bones if he's not wearing the right gear. Run through your checklists tonight. Make sure you're ready. How's the rover?"

"Um, good," Jack hesitated. "Major, if we, uh, run through our checklist and discover we need anything–extra hoses, work lamps…solar panels–could we get those at the encampment?"

"Well, there's no store, per se," the major replied. Jack exhaled in relief. The major hadn't heard him slide solar panels on the list. "But you can likely haggle with some of the other New Boomers and get whatever you may need. Good luck, son."

"Thank you, Major. For everything."

"BrutForce Base Camp. Over and out."

Over.

Jack sighed. The long six-month journey to Mars was over, but the adventure?

It was far from over.

CHAPTER 52

Mars Surface – Utopia Planitia
Jack

The sight of the *Hover* coming in for a landing had caused quite a stir on the planet's surface. Jack admitted to himself, he had felt a surge of pride as a crowd gathered near the perimeter of the landing area, pointing and exchanging words. He couldn't hear what they were saying from the confines of the ship, but he imagined he knew what they were all talking about.

His hover tech.

The touchdown area for incoming craft largely resembled NASA's launch facilities back on Earth. Forward teams comprised of international crews had made the long, slow journey to the red planet in cargo ships carrying payloads of construction materials. In preparation for the anticipated land grab and in the interest of safety for the arriving New Boomers, the teams had erected several lightning towers, obelisk-shaped staves connected by wires, to transmit electrical energy and protect landing craft from lightning. The "lightning" on Mars didn't hold the same devastating voltages as lightning on Earth, but the swirling dust on the red planet certainly created enough electrical discharge events to be of some concern. A feeling of remembered dread gave Jack a chill as they flew past the towers.

I'm all for a little protection against electricity.

A flame trench, stretched the length of almost two football fields, had been dug as well to contend with the propulsive landings of incoming craft. Emergency crews stood by with extinguishing equipment. In the distance, Jack noticed a smoking pile of charred metal and cringed.

Guess landing on Mars really is rocket science.

Thruster rockets were standard equipment on most craft, firing explosive tongues of flame and power—power critical to slowing the ships from their seventeen-thousand-mile-per-hour orbiting speed to a velocity that wouldn't shatter human bones to dust when the ship made contact with Mars' rough, unforgiving terrain.

Not a single flame danced from the *Hover.*

Jack smiled appreciatively. The major hadn't inflated Brown's skills as a pilot. He deftly manipulated the gravitator so the ship rode the crest of a gravity hill as if it were surfing off the coast of Waimea, then reoriented it so they slid down the face of the wave and coasted to the trough of the gravity well before repeating the process. The landing legs extended, and the *Hover* bumped to a gentle stop on the pad.

A feeling of pride and satisfaction flooded Jack as the crew gathered their supplies and prepared to disembark the ship. They loaded the rover with all the supplies they would need—heavy-duty habitats, rations, water—adding them to the materials already on board like the hoses and tank they would need to retrieve the egrets. Everyone donned EVAs, a necessity given that Mars' atmosphere was over 95 percent carbon dioxide and exposed visitors to radiation levels of thirty μSv per hour. Stennis had them all set their communicators to the universal short-range channel established by the encampment. This would allow them to hear and speak to personnel in close proximity. When they finally stepped from the ship, Jack fully expected to field a barrage of questions about the *Hover's* technology.

The reality…didn't quite coalesce.

"Looks like a goddamned half-cooked rabbit," he heard one gruff voice chide as they passed through the crowd. Jack tried to resist, but he couldn't help turning to assess the description himself.

With the blackened charring where the EMP had fried electronics near the hull's surface and the damaged solar panels angling lop-eared from the top of the ship, Jack had to admit, the Hover did sort of resemble an overdone *hassenpfeffer* stew.

A beefy, redheaded man, heavy face scruff behind his visor from a six-month journey, checked Jack in the shoulder. "Sure as hell hope you don't plan on getting back to Earth in that tin can."

The man guffawed. Jack groaned inwardly. They *were* going to need to find other transport home.

"W-o-o-o-w-w-w-w."

Alice's protracted interjection snagged Jack's attention. He turned his head to see a sea of red-dusted igloo-like structures. Utopia Planitia, the largest impact basin on Mars' surface, had been chosen as the start point for the race largely due to the expanse of its size. Government officials couldn't determine just how many New Boomers would show up for the land grab or how many ships they would bring with them. They needed to select a location conducive to landing, but that could also accommodate temporary encampment facilities to house an unknown number of people and their equipment. Utopia Planitia fit the bill. The northern plains stretched a little over two thousand miles across the Martian surface.

It was also hell and gone from where they needed to be.

"Where the hell are we?" Bart's voice crackled through Jack's headset.

"Nowhere Land," came Jack's quick retort.

Bart cast a dubious look beyond the encampment at the desolate hills and crags in the distance. "You ain't kidding."

Jack turned to look at Bart, whose pudgy frame inside the EVA really pushed the Michelin Man visual. "No. That's its name. Utopia Planitia means 'Nowhere Land Plain.'"

"Where's that on the map?" Bart unfolded a topographical readout he'd pulled from NASA's Mars Trek online tool before they'd left Earth.

Jack didn't even bother to look. "Pick a point furthest from the south pole, and you're close."

Bart dropped the map to his side. "Do you mean to tell me we've come all this way for nothing?"

"No. We've still got a shot." Jack gestured through the ruddy haze at the motley assortment of gathered crews. "Most of these guys are here to secure mineral rights."

"Like the Chinese on the moon."

Jack nodded. "There's not been any research to indicate anything like that's been found in the direction we're headed. We'll be all alone out there."

"Except for maybe Locke."

"Except for maybe Locke," Jack agreed. "But if we're lucky, he won't get here in time to start the race. Although there's a part of me that wishes the son of a bitch makes it."

Bart's eyes widened in surprise. "Why would you want that?"

"So I can knock his ass into a Martian crevasse and leave him to die. A little tit for tat."

"Make murder plans later," Stennis suggested as he walked past. "Right now, we've got to set up the habitat." He pointed to the setting sun. "Night's coming fast. Temperatures will likely hit a hundred. The insulation of the habitat will protect us."

"A hundred degrees?" Bart exclaimed. "That's hotter than Laguna Beach in August!"

Alice laughed. "A hundred degrees *below* zero."

The eleven-year-old followed after Stennis, leaving Bart stunned in frozen silence.

*****

The habitat Stennis had referred to was a remarkable invention in and of itself. Its replicable modular structure made for a relatively quick and painless setup and disassembly. The three-layer panels locked together to form a geodesic dome-like structure.

"It looks like we cut a soccer ball in half," Alice remarked as Brown secured the portable airlock at the egress hatch of the first unit.

"Yeah," Jack remarked. "Well, this 'soccer ball' will protect you and Trinity from the elements while I go get the egrets."

"What?" Alice cried. Her slight shoulders began to quake.

Trinity reached out to try and console Alice. Jack didn't like leaving her here.

His gaze drifted to Trinity.

Either of them.

Jack's head tilted slightly. He'd never noticed the smattering of freckles across Trinity's nose before. It wasn't that he hadn't looked at her face before. He'd stared at her often enough on the six-month voyage, wishing like hell the ship hadn't been so damned small.

No fucking privacy.

A smile twitched at the unintentional double entendre. Like microgravity would have even made such a thing possible.

Okay, maybe possible, but damned difficult.

But it was more than just the physical. Right now, the moment just seemed more poignant. He was about to set out on an incredibly dangerous trek—one from which he might not return. If he made it through this, he planned on taking their relationship to the next level.

He stepped toward her. "Will you guys be okay here?"

Trinity nodded, her pupils wide and large in the green of her eyes. She shrugged. "We'll be fine. I'll probably take her around and interview some of the folks here. It's going to be a hell of a story."

She poked him in the chest. "Forget the land-grab angle. The *bigger* story? Reluctant father figure travels two hundred and forty-two million miles to save son from a life-threatening illness. It's got Pulitzer written all over it."

Trinity stepped in close and almost whispered. "But I'm not interested in writing that one. I'm living it. And I can't wait to see how it ends. You're the hero of that tale, Jack. You've got to succeed."

The curve of her visor touched his.

Wish to Christ I didn't have this stupid helmet on!

"I'm not staying here!" Alice blurted, redirecting Jack's focus. She attempted to stamp her boot, but with Mars' diminished gravity, Jack doubted it was as forceful as she'd hoped.

He tried to convince the preteen. "Alice, we have to go through the Hellas Planitia on our way to retrieve the egrets. It's twelve hundred miles of hell on an already rough planet. Winds are stronger; dust storms last a hell of a lot longer; temperatures are off the charts. Not to mention we have to get across some of the worst terrain on the Martian surface. The crater's deeper than the Grand Canyon and filled with deep pockets of sand that can suck you in."

"Jesus, Mary, and Joseph," Odd Job remarked. It had been

decided he would be the member of Cotton's crew to accompany Jack and Bart to retrieve the egrets. "Forget how far away it is. How in the hell are we supposed to cross it once we get to it?"

"Ah, you see, I've already thought of that," Jack said, his voice dropping to a whisper. "We use the gravitator. Can you refit it to the rover?"

"What? Make it like a hovercraft?"

"Exactly. Plus, if we can find some replacement solar cells, it will give us the extra boost to cover the distance we need."

Odd Job scratched the top of his helmet. "It will take me all night. I'll have to get some supplies from the shuttle–but, yeah. I could do it."

"Good," Jack said. "We'll finish getting the girls set up here– Captain Stennis and Brown are setting up the second habitat– then Bart and I will explore the encampment. See if we can rustle up some solar panels."

Time to be a hero.

CHAPTER 53

Mars Surface – New Boomer Encampment
Jack

The system was overloaded.

The incoming data barraged his senses. The energy of the Utopia encampment buzzed. Bodies bumped from every side as Jack and Bart maneuvered their way through the throng of space-suited New Boomers. The speaker in his headset thrummed with the warp and woof of international languages, a colorful weave of accents and sounds.

Flags snapped above his head. He glanced up and saw many of the land-grab participants had planted the flags of their home nations outside their habitats—the iconic red dot symbolizing the rising sun for Japan, the bold red crisscross of Britain's Union Jack, Canada's familiar maple leaf, and, of course, the good old red, white, and blue. The pennants whipped in the Martian wind, cracking through the air like gunfire, but the only gunfire that mattered was the shot that would sound tomorrow morning, Jack thought.

And if we don't find some solar panels for the rover, the race'll be over before we even get started.

So, he and Bart had set out to find some. It only took

a few inquiries before it became apparent the cantina was where everybody who was anybody conducted business in the encampment. Jack pushed through, following the directions of an old Swede a few tents back. The information had cost a questionable rations trade. Bart trailed a few steps behind, holding a container of round brown pellets.

"I probably shouldn't have given up my protein bar for these, but I've been craving chocolate ever since we left Earth. I tell you one thing. If I had chocolates, I sure as hell wouldn't be trading them for a tasteless, chalky energy ration. It's like manna from heaven."

"Did he mention if there were rats on his ship?" Jack replied without dropping his pace.

"Why? You think the rats got into the chocolate, and that's why he traded?"

Jack sighed and shouldered his way to the right.

Bart pointed to the left, looking over his shoulder instead of where he was going. "I think it's this way."

He stumbled over two burly Russians arm-wrestling over a metal supply drum. A swelling, cheering throng surrounded them. Bets in all currencies exchanged hands. The crowd swallowed him.

The PLSS of Bart's suit knocked into the barrel, tipping it over and disrupting the game. A roar of discontent erupted. Bart backpedaled away as the Russians advanced. Bart waved gloved hands in front of him.

"I am so, so, sorry," he apologized profusely. The Russian didn't look at all appeased. "I am such a klutz. In fact, I'm pretty sure my mother considered naming me that at my bris."

One of the men lifted Bart by the shoulders of his suit.

"*Mudak*," he spat and threw Bart to the ground. Mars' low gravity prevented the assault from causing any measurable injury, but the large foot the man was driving toward Bart's midsection was likely going to make up for it.

"Whoa there, Gorbachev!" Jack suddenly inserted himself between the bear of a man and his friend. "How about a little *glasnost* here, huh? We're just trying to get to the cantina to make a deal for some solar panels."

The Russian studied Jack curiously.

"*Krepkiy napitok,*" the Russian growled.

Jack had no idea what that meant. He looked to Bart, behind him. Bart shrugged, shaking his head. Jack looked back to the strapping man. It wasn't like he could right-cross the guy. The visors made throwing a punch a non sequitur. His eyes lit upon a length of metal pipe. It was just within arm's length. If he was fast enough, he could drive it into the man's stomach. With any amount of luck, it would knock the wind from him.

"*Krepkiy napitok,*" the Russian repeated, this time more forcefully.

Fuck it.

He wasn't about to let Bart be mushed into beluga. He dove for the pipe when the Russian spoke again, this time in broken, stilted English.

"Buy me drink."

Jack paused but still held the pipe defensively. "Excuse me?"

The Russian shrugged. "Buy me drink. We talk shop."

A current of laughter rippled through the crowd. They dispersed as the big man threw an arm around Jack's shoulders and steered him toward the cantina.

"You have solar panels?" Jack asked.

"Drink first. Business later," the man said.

"Yeah, um, okay," Jack said. "What's your poison?"

The man laughed as he gave a thick slap to his broad chest—a deep, throaty chuckle that reverberated in Jack's headset. "I am

Russian! Vodka, of course! Much vodka! Then we get you your solar panels."

Solar panels for nothing but the cost of a bottle of vodka? *Nostrovia!*

*****

By 3:00 a.m., Jack firmly believed the world's problems could all be solved with a shot of Stolichnaya.

Okay. Maybe eight.

As he and Bart stumbled back toward the habitat, two solar panels in tow, he decided all the world leaders just needed to get together and play beer pong or something. Several rounds at the encampment cantina had certainly done wonders for international relations as far as he was concerned. Not only had his new Russian friend gotten him the solar panels they needed for the rover, but Jack had also learned how to say "I love you" in Russian.

"*Ya lyublyu tebya,*" he slurred as they made their way through the almost deserted encampment. Most of the New Boomers had already turned in, wanting to be bright-eyed and bushy-tailed for the race. That, and the ambient air was more than a little chilly. Fortunately, their suits protected them.

"That's drunk talk," Bart responded, his own words a little mushy around the edges. "You're not making any sense."

Jack shook his head. "No, no, no. It's a Russian term of… term of…ah hell. It's what you say to a girl when you really like her, and I'm going to say it to Trinity."

He looked around, trying to ascertain the direction of their camp. He decided and trundled on. Bart followed loyally.

"When?" Bart asked.

"When what?"

"When are you going to tell her? Now?"

Jack stopped again. He turned to Bart.

"You know what? You're right. No time like the present. What time is it?" He looked down at a nonexistent watch. "Damn. I got robbed."

"You're in a spacesuit. You weren't wearing one."

"It's one in the morning!" Jack exclaimed. "That's okay. It's all good. The early bird gets the worm, right? Oh, look! We're here."

They had, in fact, reached the girls' habitat. Jack handed Bart his panel.

"I'm just gonna go in here for a second. Be right back." He entered the airlock to the girls' quarters.

"Trinity?" he whispered. He stumbled through the dark, looking for the battery-powered lantern. "Trinity? Ah, here."

His hands found the lantern and switched it on. Fear immediately gut-checked him sober.

The girls were gone!

Trinity's cot was empty, pillow abandoned, and blankets rumpled. Alice's cot lay on its side, her bedclothes tangled and strewn across the floor to indicate a struggle. Jack broke loose from his frozen fear and leaped forward. He dove to the ground, looking under Trinity's cot and searching through Alice's blankets.

"No, no, no!" Jack cried. That's when he saw the scrap of white on a supply crate–a scrap of paper held down by a Martian rock. He ripped the paper from beneath the rock. A note had been hastily scrawled across its face. Jack read it out loud.

"I have something you want. You're going to make sure I get what I want. Stay away from the egrets, or there will be a different reason to call this the red planet. Locke."

Locke's words sank in, curdling Jack's own blood. He screamed primally, picking up the rock and hurling it at the wall of the geodesic dome. Only gravity kept it from doing irreparable damage.

Bart stumbled in. "What the hell is going on?"

Jack whirled.

"Locke. He's here. And he's got the girls," Jack snapped.

CHAPTER 54

Mars Surface – Starting Line
Jack

The starting line pulsed.

It was a living, breathing thing stretched as far as the eye could see. Wind blew hot and dry across the plain, eddies of crimson swirling in sandy dervishes. The encampment had come alive early, just as the Martian sunrise crested the red hills in the distance. Around 8 a.m., officials called for racers to form up. Electric energy crackled as buggies were loaded and teams started jockeying for a prime starting position. Per the land-grab regulations, the starting cannon would sound at noon. Once it sounded, teams would race to collect beacons attached to designated parcels. Be the first to bring one back, and that land and all its resources would be registered as yours.

Teams surged to the front of the pack, held back only by the armed, watchful guard of race officiants a scant hundred yards away. The clock ticked down the minutes to the cannon boom.

Jack's team was nowhere to be found.

Back in the encampment, Jack packed final provisions into the rover, his pace frenetic and harried. Bart paced behind him, wringing his gloved hands.

"You're going through with it?" he questioned, worry forming lines in his own face as he watched the murderous scowl on Jack's.

Jack heaved a coil of hose onto the back of the rover. "You bet your ass I am. This is my family we're talking about here, and Locke is not calling the shots."

"Except that he kind of is," Bart pointed out. "He has one of your kids, not to mention your girlfriend. He's going to kill them if he finds out you're going after the egrets."

Jack turned to face him. "Then he'd better not find out. Look, that's why we're not queued up with the rest of the pack. If I know Locke, he'll be frothing at the bit right at the front of the line. He'll want to, but he won't take the straightest route to the egrets—too treacherous. He'll take the most logical path to the egrets, through the Meridiani Planum. The ground's rocky, but a hell of a lot smoother than the Hellas highlands."

"And that's the hotbox with the sixty-grit sandstorms, the quicksand, and the Grand Canyon, right?" Odd Job interrupted.

Jack nodded. "Hellas Planitia. It's the quickest way to the egrets. If we survive getting there, we'll be in and out before Locke even realizes we're in the race."

"I am lovin' this gig more every minute," Odd Job quipped.

"Once we have the egrets stored safely in the tank," Jack patted the thirty-gallon container, "we'll rescue the girls, haul ass back to the *Hover*, and get the flock outta here."

"About that," Bart raised a gloved finger. "While I'm all for getting outta Dodge, I'm a little fuzzy on just how we're going to do it on the *Hover*. In case you forgot, the ship is toast, man."

Jack shrugged. "Okay. So, the ship needs repairs. Fortunately, we have a vested partner in our little venture here on Mars, who happens to be pretty damned good at that sort of thing."

Bart rolled his eyes in a classic "duh" moment. "Major

Cotton."

"Major Cotton," Jack repeated. "Captain Stennis and Lieutenant Brown started for the BrutForce camp as soon as we discovered the girls were missing. They'll make sure the ship is space-worthy while we beat feet to the egrets and get the girls. Undoubtedly, Locke will have the girls with him. A man like that will want to retain complete control over his bargaining chips. After we secure the egrets, we'll take cover and wait till he arrives. When the moment's right, we'll grab the girls and rendezvous with the *Hover*, then get the hell home."

"I still say this is a bad idea," Bart said.

"I agree," Odd Job said.

"Well," Jack began. "You know what they say."

"What's that?" Odd Job asked.

Jack grinned. "Anything worth doing always starts as a bad idea."

CHAPTER 55

Mars Surface – Locke's ARV
Locke

"Any sign of Harding?" Locke demanded as Binderkampf entered through the ARV's airlock. He struggled in the abbreviated space before it gave way to the more spacious and luxurious interior of the vehicle. Vashtin was already inside, seated in one of the leather captain's chairs, poring over topographical maps of the Martian terrain. He looked up as Binderkampf entered.

Once fully inside, Binderkampf stomped his boots, sending plumes of Martian dust into the air. "And stop pawing the ground, will you? That goddamned red dirt is getting everywhere!"

"Sorry, Mr. Locke. Won't happen again," the scientist babbled, anxiety warbling his tone.

"See that it doesn't."

Binderkampf began to strip out of the EVA. Locke's expression soured.

Like squeezing a sausage from its casing.

He shook the image from his mind. "Well? Harding?"

Binderkampf shook his head. "Nowhere to be seen. Guess

he's heeding your warning."

"And what of my warning, Mr. Locke?" Vashtin piped.

Locke turned. "What of it?"

Vashtin stumbled over his words, hesitant to suggest anything. His Adam's apple bobbled as he took a hard swallow. "Do you agree the best route is over the Meridiani Planum?"

"It's the safest route to take if we want to increase our chances…your chances for success," Binderkampf concurred.

I am so ridiculously tired of people telling me what I can and cannot do!

Locke dragged his hands through his thick hair and pulled. He let out a guttural growl. *Fuck rational thought. Fuck scientific principles. I just want those goddamned egrets!*

Locke waved an annoyed hand. "Yes, yes. Fine. Go tell Rico where to point us. And take this imbecile with you."

He pointed to Binderkampf, who appeared only too happy to vacate Locke's presence. As for Vashtin, he nodded profusely, gathered up his maps, and disappeared with Binderkampf toward the pilot's cabin.

Locke dragged his finger across the dusty red surface of the marble countertop. The exterior of the armored carrier might have been utilitarian, loaded for bear against the harsh Martian elements, but true to form, Locke had spared no expense for luxury inside the vehicle. He padded across the silk Isfahan rug to the two hooded figures huddled in the corner and squatted beside them.

"I do hope you ladies are comfortable. I'm sorry I can't offer you some refreshment—it must be quite stifling under those hoods—but, well, we are on Mars, and water is such a precious commodity. Wouldn't want to waste it."

The larger of the two figures struggled violently against her bonds.

"So, that's it, then? You're going to kill us no matter what

Jack does," Trinity's voice came heatedly from beneath the black fabric. Alice whimpered beside her.

"Oh, without a doubt," Locke confirmed. "I was more than a little pissed off to discover Dr. Harding had ripped off the tech he had promised to me and launched his own Mars mission."

"That tech was Jack's from the start," Trinity insisted.

Locke laughed softly. "My dear woman, you are laboring under the delusion that there are rules to ensure fair play when, truly, there is only one hard and fast rule."

He leaned in so Trinity could feel the heat of his breath. "Rules are made to be broken."

Trinity lunged her head forward, cracking the solid bone of her forehead against Locke's face, connecting with his nose and mouth.

He heard the crunch before he felt it. Crimson spurted, dripping fat, wet drops all over the Isfahan as he scrabbled backward, hands to his face, trying to stanch the gushing blood.

"You bitch!" he howled. He drew back a foot, propelling all the weight of his body forward to kick Trinity in the head, which snapped to the side as his foot made contact. She slumped lifelessly against Alice, who screamed.

Locke dragged an angry forearm across his face, smearing a bright red trail along his cheek.

"You know what else is made to be broken, Ms. Watson? People!" He spat a glob of bloody phlegm at her bound feet. "Body and mind. And after I break every bone in both your bodies, I'm going to throw your sorry carcasses at Harding's feet...and break his very soul."

Suddenly, the deep boom of the cannon reverberated through the ARV. Locke braced himself as the unit lurched to life. As Trinity lay motionless against Alice's shaking, sobbing body, Locke calmly reached for a cloth and dabbed gingerly at his wounds.

"But first, it's time for me to make history."

CHAPTER 56

Mars Surface – Hellas Planitia
Jack

"Now I know why they call it Hellas!" Bart screamed over the moaning roar of the wind. "This is hell, all right!"

He gripped the rollbar of the rover tightly as they zipped over the red blur of Martian terrain. They had waited until the first surge of Boomers had taken off from the starting line, slipping in with the last stragglers. They had dropped back, gradually widening the gap between them and the rest of the pack before they broke south and engaged the gravitator.

With the gravitator, they had covered an incredible amount of ground, flying over treacherous terrain that would have crippled a normal transport. And now, they were only a few short leagues from the lobate debris aprons, the area where the Mars explorers had found the first egrets in underground glaciers.

The winds, however, they could do nothing about.

"Yeah," Jack hollered back. "It's getting pretty dicey. Think we're dealing with one of those nasty dust storms Hellas Planitia is so famous for!"

He nudged Odd Job, hollering over the wind. "We should be coming up on Hellas Montes. Look for a cave or outcropping of rock we can use for cover! Otherwise, the dust is liable to gunk up the rover's gears, and we'll *really* be stuck in no-man's-land."

"Roger that!" Odd Job yelled back. A few hundred feet further, Jack tapped Odd Job's shoulder and pointed to a shadow in a ridge face. Odd Job directed their rover toward it. As they got closer, it did, in fact, prove to be a cave. Well, less of a cave and more like a deep alcove. Regardless, it was large enough to shield them from the blistering storm, which continued to gather force and howled like a monster.

As he watched the swirling vortex of red dust clouds beyond the outcropping of rock, Jack's thoughts turned to Trinity and Alice and the monster they were with.

Hang in there. I'm going to save you.

The wind screamed.

Even if it kills me.

CHAPTER 57

Mars Surface – Meridiani Planum
Alice

"What the hell do you mean there's no place to secure the ARV?" Alice heard Locke scream from the front of the vehicle. They had stopped moving a while ago. Now, the ARV just lurched from side to side. She heard the wind howling, the outside elements scratching at the exterior like ravenous creatures trying to claw their way in.

Get it together, Johansson. The real monster's in here with you.

"We're in the middle of the Meridiani Planum. As in flat. No mountains, ridges, or outcroppings that we might use," she heard another voice explain with a tinge of sarcasm. Accented. That would be the man they called Vashtin.

CRAACK!

Alice cringed when she heard the sudden crunch of bone followed by the thud of a collapsing body. She still had the hood over her head. She could feel Trinity's limp body still leaning against her.

"Trinity?" she whispered. "Trinity? Are you awake?"

Trinity moaned weakly but didn't arouse.

Guess it's up to me.

Alice couldn't see it, but she felt the wall her shoulder was braced upon. She tilted her head and leaned her cheek against the surface, feeling the cool against her cheek. She rubbed her cheek downward, inching the fabric of the hood up just a fraction.

Dammit.

She felt a twinge of guilt for the curse word, but given the circumstances, she figured Jack would forgive her.

She took a deep breath and tried again. This time the fabric gave a little more. Light seeped in from the bottom of the hood. She cast her gaze downward and could just see her pinkie toe wriggling through the hole in her high-top.

I can do this.

She repeated the motion once more, sliding her whole body downward in one fluid motion until the hood worked completely off her head.

"Trinity! Trinity! I got the hood off my head," she whispered tersely. "I'm going to look for a way out."

Alice's blue eyes darted around the cabin of the transport. She saw the crumpled form of Dr. Vashtin at the cabin's fore.

Is he dead?

She breathed a sigh of quiet relief when she saw his foot begin to move.

Her relief was short-lived, however, as Locke stormed toward the aft of the transport, Binderkampf and a wobbly Vashtin in tow.

"Rico," he called over his shoulder. "Get us out of here. Find us somewhere–anywhere–to hunker down and ride this shitstorm out. I need a drink."

"Can't, boss." Alice heard a new voice–Rico, she supposed–reply. "The sand's clogged the engine's ventilation system. It's sucking in buckets of this red dust. Unless somebody wants to get out there and clear the vents, we ain't goin' nowhere."

Locke turned to Binderkampf. "Well, you heard the man. Get out there and clear the vents."

Binderkampf looked shocked. "You can't possibly be serious. Martian dust storms are dangerous things. Forget what it can do to an ARV engine. The winds in these storms can reach up to sixty two miles an hour, and that's just the ones we've been able to clock! Then there's the accompanying radiation that's swirling around! Martian dust storms are dangerous things."

"No, Dr. Binderkampf," Locke began as he slid open a drawer and removed something Alice couldn't quite see. Locke turned, a serious black gun in his hand. Alice's eyes flew wide. "I'm a dangerous thing."

BLAM!

The sharp retort of the pistol drowned out Alice's gasp. A splatter of red and bits of gray matter dotted the silk rug under Binderkampf's body before it collapsed to the floor. His head lolled to the side, empty eyes, staring at Alice–but Alice wasn't looking. All she could focus on was the ugly black hole, rimmed with charred flesh, and the trickle of blood that dripped from it.

She opened her mouth, but no sound came out. Inside, she screamed.

Jack! Help us!

CHAPTER 58

Mars Surface – Centauri Montes
Jack

"Watch your step there," Bart warned Jack just before he lost his own footing and tumbled down the narrow, road-like outcropping of sand-covered rock descending into the gully. Odd Job followed along behind them in the rover. They had located the Hellas beacon and secured it in the rover. That was the easy part. The hard part was going to be actually locating the egrets.

Bart's disjointed directions hadn't made the effort any easier. After more than a few wrong turns and dashed hopes, however, the party had made their way to a gulch cut into an oblong crater in the Centauri Montes.

Jack watched as Bart came to an abrupt stop when he came to the gently sloping ridge of a lobate flow, a rippling feature indicative of glacial movement in the red planet's past.

With any amount of luck, the not-too-distant past.

Jack knew the first Mars exploration crews had found small pockets of water and, subsequently, egrets in the region—further evidence that Mars had once been covered in ancient rivers and lakes. What he was banking on was finding one of those bodies of water alive and well, hidden somewhere beneath

Mars' mysterious surface. The plan was to locate one of these underground reservoirs and, after verifying the presence of egrets, siphon some of the water into the thirty-gallon tank.

The Centauri Montes, so close to the south pole, seemed as likely a place as any for that to be possible.

The Mars Orbiter camera had picked up data showing new deposit activity–much like you could see around the delta of a river like the Mississippi. A bright spot had popped on the Orbiter's lens, lighter than the area around it, with sinuous branches breaking around low obstacles as it exhibited characteristics consistent with the movement of fluid behaving like water.

This has to be the spot!

"I'm okay! I'm okay!" Bart assured, though Jack wasn't certain who he was trying to convince. Bart struggled to his feet and dusted himself off.

"You'd better watch it, Bartholomew Cubbins! One misstep out here, and you'll find your hat-wearing ass at the bottom of a Martian cliff," Odd Job called.

Bart grimaced. "It's Pulldraw, not Cubbins. I'm not a Dr. Seuss character."

"Tell that to your five hundred hats," Jack quipped. He stood on the precipice of a ridge, squinted through the red haze, and looked around, frustrated they hadn't located the reservoir yet. He threw his hands in the air and growled. "Christ! I wish the damned Cat in the Hat was here. At least maybe he'd be a better navigator than YOUUU–"

Jack's voice faltered as his foot slipped off the edge, and he disappeared from sight. In a near-reflexive action, one gloved hand gripped the climbing pick on his tool belt and drove it into the face of the rock wall in front of him. Even with the low gravity, he still winced as the momentum of his falling weight tugged at the muscles in his shoulder.

"Jesus Christ!" he burst out.

As he dangled, he dared a slow look down. He was suspended over what appeared to be the mouth of an open cavern—a dark hole yawning wide to swallow the uncertain Martian light. Jack's heart swelled.

I found it!

"Jack! Jack, buddy! Oh God! Please don't be dead!" he heard Bart's plaintive voice calling out.

They must not have seen where I fell.

"Bart! Bart, I'm okay! I'm over the cliff edge! I've found it! I've found the entrance to the reservoir!"

A crack popped, echoing against the walls of the cavern. Jack looked up at a growing fissure where his pick met the rock. His eyes widened. He called up to his friend. "But, um, I could use a little help down here."

The bulbous dome of Bart's helmet suddenly popped over the cliff edge. Bart looked down at him. "What are you doing down there?"

"Oh, you know. Just hanging around." Jack's voice took on an immediate and urgent tone. "Will you quit asking fucking questions and pull my ass up!"

The sound of splitting rock sounded again. The crack near the pick tip widened.

"Like, now!" Jack bellowed.

Bart suddenly realized the severity of the situation. Jack felt a wave of relief when the winch cable threaded down close enough for him to grab with his free hand. The motor whined as, slowly, it retracted and pulled him back to terra firma.

His heartbeat gradually slowed as Bart dusted him off. Jack smacked his hand. "Stop that! Now, come on! The egrets have got to be down there. We need to get in and get out. We don't know exactly how long it will take Locke to show up, and I'd prefer to be in another zip code when he does."

A puzzled look flitted across Bart's face. "What about the girls?"

Jack didn't want to think about the girls. If he did, he just might lose it.

"We'll cross that bridge when we get to it. Right now, Charlie's counting on me to get those egrets. This is our only shot. So, let's get moving!"

Odd Job hopped from the driver's seat and helped them unload the open-gauge basket from the rover. Jack and Bart would use it to lower themselves into the crevasse with the hose.

"Has it been secured to the tank?" he asked Odd Job.

Odd Job nodded. "Yep. And the pump is set to run at max."

"Good," Jack replied. "We don't know how deep this thing runs. Mars' atmospheric pressures are lower than Earth's. We're going to need the extra juice to manipulate the pressure-potential energy to ensure the reservoir water can make the trip up the hose."

"Roger that," Odd Job gave a jaunty little salute.

Bart wiggled the cable line attached to the basket. "You sure we have enough slack?"

Jack turned, his face serious as death.

"We have to."

*****

The winds had started picking up again. Not enough to warrant shelter, but enough to sway the basket as it lowered into the deep cavern.

"I think I'm gonna be sick," Bart moaned.

"Suck it up," Jack ordered, looking down into the black abyss.

The wind moaned around them, though, leaving even Jack with a sense of unease.

He swallowed his fear. This was Charlie's only hope.

He had no choice.

Suddenly, the basket lurched. It slammed against the red cavern wall, the clang of metal echoing off the unforgiving rock. Jack and Bart both scrabbled for purchase as the basket plummeted thirty feet before it jerked them to an abrupt stop. Their descent halted. Jack looked back up toward the lip of the cavern.

"Odd Job! Odd Job! Come in! What the fuck is happening up there?"

Odd Job's voice, tense and harried, crackled through the communicator. "Yeah, shit, man! Sorry! The goddamned sand shifted, taking the rover with it. Maybe you should tell Round Boy to lay off the Twinkies, huh?"

Jack looked at Bart.

"Oh, really? This is my fault?"

Jack looked back up toward the disembodied voice. "We good now?"

"Looks like for now. Although you may want to do some calisthenics before you head back up. The rover's only a few feet from the edge of the cavern. There's no guarantee the ground won't shift again under the weight of pulling you guys up."

Jack grimaced. "Hopefully, the weight of the water in the tank will help keep it stabilized. What do you say we finish this thing, huh?"

"Roger," Odd Job replied, and slowly began to lower the basket into pitch oblivion.

As light gave way to impenetrable darkness, Jack and Bart turned on the headlamps affixed to their EVAs. The space into which they descended was so massive, the darkness swallowed the beams of their lamps well before it revealed any wall or bottom.

"I wonder how far down it goes," Bart pondered aloud as he looked down into the dark.

Jack's foot kicked a small rock on the basket floor, launching it out over the abyss. Jack followed its fall until it disappeared but heard a sudden splash within seconds.

"We're almost there," Jack uttered.

"That's good," Odd Job's voice called. "Because we're just about out of hose and cable."

The basket bumped to a halt. Jack played his light about the space.

"I can't see crap. Bart, grab that work light, will ya? The one with the forty-five hundred lumens."

Bart hurried to hand Jack the battery-operated spot. Jack switched it on and gasped.

"Holy shit," he uttered in sheer awe.

The bright beam of the work light illuminated massive stalactites jutting from the ceiling within the cavern—most of them thicker around than Bart's ample midsection. They descended to meet rising stalagmites, sharp and dangerous-looking—like the teeth of some massive Martian beast ready to devour whoever dared violated the sanctity of the space. Moisture dripped from the tip of the descending mineral formations. As Jack heard the ping of water hitting water, he trailed his beam down to reveal an expanse of crystal-clear, unadulterated water. Concentric rings rippled across its surface as drops from the stalactites hit the water's surface. The water stretched as far as the light would penetrate.

Bart let out a long, low whistle. "This thing's gotta be at least nine hundred feet long by two hundred and fifty feet wide."

"And that's just what we can see," Jack agreed. He stepped forward, trying to see more. "If the water tests positive, can you imagine the number of egrets an environment this size would hold?"

"Enough to cure the world," Bart mumbled.

Jack's voice dropped to a whisper. "I don't need to cure the world. Just one little boy."

Jack took a moment to drink it all in, then exploded into action.

"Let's do this." He climbed from the basket and took the testing kit to the water's edge. He extracted a test tube and dipped it into the water. Once the tube was nearly filled, he lifted it up and dropped the reactive agent into the tube. It swirled in an almost instant cloud of aqua blue.

Jack looked up at Bart. "A reaction this fast? It's swimming with egrets. Get the hose."

Bart unlatched the hose nozzle from its housing on the basket and dragged it over to the water. "So, we've found the egrets. What's to stop Locke from finding them?"

Jack considered Bart's point. "A cave-in."

"A cave-in?" Bart asked dubiously.

Jack nodded. "You heard Odd Job. The substrate around here is unstable. After we get out of here, it won't take much to cave in the entrance."

"Okay. I'll buy that. That takes care of the egrets here, but how are we going to stop Locke from following us and zapping us with another EMP? Not to mention we need to rescue the girls."

"Already thought of it," Jack replied. "While Locke's busy digging in the dirt for egrets, we get to the *Horus* and steal the hover tech. He'll never get back to Earth without it. We call for an exchange. The tech for the girls. We make him come to us. That way, we're in control of the situation—not him."

"You really going to give him back the tech?"

"Hell, no!" Jack exclaimed. "We'll drop it off in some remote location and, if he's lucky, we tell him where to pick it up."

"That's insane."

"Yeah, well, people do crazy things for the ones they love."

And Bellevue's got a bed with my name on it for damn sure.

"Odd Job, turn on the pump. We're sending them up," Jack called into his headset.

"Check. Pump on."

As Jack watched the hose swell, pumping life-saving egrets up toward the waiting tank in the rover, Jack allowed himself to breathe a sigh of welcome relief.

"Hang in there, Charlie. I'm coming home."

CHAPTER 59

Mars Surface — Centauri Montes
Locke

"Where in the fuck are my egrets!" Locke's voice bellowed across the sand and rock. Vashtin stood nearby, the topographical map in his hands quaking. The temperature had dropped, but the scientist's hands more likely shook because of the splattered drops of crimson across his spacesuit.

Binderkampf's blood.

Locke's eyes narrowed at Vashtin, the blood splatter only reminding him that unless Dr. Vashtin could find the damned egrets, Locke's mission would quickly suffer a similar fate as Binderkampf.

Death.

Once the dust storm had passed, Locke had unceremoniously dumped Binderkampf's limp body on the Martian plain. Four people had witnessed the murder–an egregious oversight he would have to address once he secured the egrets.

If he secured the damned egrets.

"Well," he verbally prodded the scientist. "Where are they?"

Vashtin consulted the map. "I don't understand. The coordinates indicate they should be right here." He looked around. "But the landscape doesn't match the map at all."

Locke advanced on Vashtin. The scientist cringed. "So, are you telling me we're in the wrong place?"

Vashtin shook his head. "No, sir, Mr. Locke, sir. I would never tell you that."

Locke paused. Maybe the scientist wasn't a complete idiot after all.

But he still hasn't been able to tell me where to find what I'm looking for!

He grabbed Vashtin by the front of his suit, lifting him off the ground. "What would you tell me?"

"That the surface of Mars is always undergoing change. We're in the right place, but it's entirely possible, what with the dust storms and thermal inertia changes, that the topography has altered, obscuring the egrets' location."

Locke began to undergo a thermal inertia change of his own. His blood began to boil as the object of his desire remained just out of reach.

"So, where's the beacon then?" Locke hissed. "At least I can retrieve it so no one else can claim the rights to the egrets. After the claim is filed, we can return with the right equipment and excavate for the damned things."

Vashtin stammered. "I-I-I don't exactly know, sir. It should be here."

"My point exactly," Locke agreed. "It *should* be here. But it quite clearly isn't. Am I supposed to believe that a breeze picked it up and carried it off to parts unknown?"

"That would be highly unlikely, sir."

"THEN WHERE THE FUCK IS MY BEACON!!!"

His lips curled back over his teeth, and he let out a bloodcurdling howl toward the red-streaked sky.

It had to be Harding.

"I have spent billions on getting to Mars with the sole intent and purpose of securing those egrets. Nothing, and I mean nothing, is going to stand in my way!"

Rico walked toward Locke from the direction of the ARV. "Mr. Locke, sir. I'm picking up some chatter."

Locke waved his hand. "Not now!"

He was sick of interruptions–sick of obstacles. Some shrink had once tried to sell him on the concept that obstacles were a character-building exercise, meant to be overcome.

"Mr. Locke, I really think you should take this," Rico insisted. "It's Harding. He says he's got the Horus' hover tech. He wants to make a trade."

Harding.

Locke seethed.

"Fuck that shrink," he hissed.

Obstacles were meant to be obliterated.

CHAPTER 60

Mars Surface — Utopia Planitia, Outer Perimeter
Alice

"Go on. Move!" Alice felt Rico's broad hand shove her in the back, causing her to stumble down the angled ramp leading from the ARV.

"Hey!" Trinity contested. "Leave her alone. She's just a kid!"

The protest earned the reporter a shove of her own. She ran into Alice, nearly toppling her. The industrial zip-tie securing her small hands in front of her allowed little give for maneuvering. If she fell, there would be no way to break her fall. Alice righted herself, taking a final step onto the dusty surface Jack had chosen for their rescue.

Well, at least I can see.

They both were wearing EVA suits and helmets. Probably no point in veiling locations or identities any longer—now that they were being rescued.

Or it could be because Locke plans on killing us anyway.

The sobering thought chilled Alice to the bone.

We might not have time to wait for Jack!

Her nimble mind started calculating an escape.

"Where are we?" Trinity asked.

"Isidis Planitia," Alice murmured, making sure they were far enough away that Locke's communicator wouldn't pick them up. "When I found out Jack was going to Mars, I studied every Martian map I could get my hands on. I thought I could help, you know. Be Jack's navigator on the trip or something. I even told him how I'd learned the name of every single plain, rock, and crater on the surface. There's even a rock called Snoopy. But he pretty much ignored me. Told me I wasn't coming. That I'd wasted my time."

Tears started to well in her eyes. She blinked hard to dispel them. "Anyway, I think we're just south of where we landed. Yes. Look!"

She gestured with her bound hands as they crested the top of a sandy dune. "There's the encampment. Off there, in the distance. Maybe we can get out of these and make a run for it."

Trinity held up her hands. "We won't get far trussed up like this."

Alice looked down at the restraints. "There was this physics lesson in school. It was all about leverage. A lever can amplify an input force, resulting in an increased output force. Leverage. If we splay out our elbows, kind of like chicken wings, and yank our hands down toward our hips, the restraints should snap."

Her eyes caught the watchful stare of Locke's bodyguard in the distance. She smiled weakly.

"But we should probably wait till we're not being watched," she suggested. As the guard walked toward them, she prayed he hadn't overheard her plan.

Jack had given Locke instructions to bring the girls to Isidis, a section of plains on the outskirts of Utopia Planitia, largely open but with mounding hills of sand. The arrangement was Jack would meet them there in the repaired *Hover*, exchanging the girls for the tech. Alice looked at the foreboding pistol located at

Locke's belt.

I definitely don't think he's going with the plan. It's now or never.

"Trinity?" Alice began and nudged the reporter.

"Quit talking!" Locke barked from in front of them. "All these ridiculously stupid names. Planiti-*ah*. Terr-*ah*. Hesperi-*ah*. Why can't scientists name anything in fucking English!"

"Says the guy who named his rocket after an Egyptian god," Trinity muttered under her breath.

Locke stopped, his head swiveling to the right and left. "Where in the hell is Harding? Get him on the radio! Patch it through to the headsets."

Alice turned her own head, scanning the horizon for any sign of Jack. He had to come. He wouldn't leave her.

All the same, a faint niggle of worry began eating at her soul.

Vati said he'd never leave me either.

Trinity leaned toward her. "Don't worry. He'll be here."

"For your sake," Locke threatened as he turned and stalked toward the girls, "he'd better be. If Harding even *thinks* of trying to pull a fast one, I will put a bullet in both your heads without so much as blinking."

"Isn't that what you're going to do anyway?" Trinity challenged.

Locke drew back an arm and instinctively backhanded her, forgetting about the polycarbonate visor of her helmet. His glove merely bounced off the rounded plastic, but the sheer momentum caused her to stumble backward.

Locke leaned in. "Perhaps you would rather I do it sooner than later?"

Trinity's lips set in a hard, thin line. She looked away. Locke smiled coolly.

"Didn't think so." He stalked away.

Trinity kept her gaze pointed down. Alice felt a tiny nudge at her elbow and turned. She looked at the reporter, who twitched her head toward something on the ground. Alice followed her gaze to four distinct depressions in the ground. Perfectly rectangular, spread equidistant apart. These weren't natural features of the Martian landscape, Alice thought.

These are marks from the landing struts of the Hover!

Alice nearly gasped and checked herself as Jack's voice popped in her earpiece.

"Horus, Horus, Horus. This is the Hover on channel sixteen. Over."

Alice's heart leaped into her throat.

"Told you he'd be here," Trinity said.

"Harding! Harding, where the fuck are you?" Locke screamed. He immediately looked to the sky, searching for Jack. He motioned to his bodyguard to leave the girls and search the perimeter.

"Now *that* is not proper radio etiquette, Mr. Locke," Jack quipped.

"Screw etiquette," Locke spat into the receiver. "I know what you've done, Harding. You took the beacon. *You* took my egrets."

"Don't forget...took your hover tech too. Sure hope you like the neighborhood, 'cause without it, you're going to be stuck here for a pretty long time."

"Dammit, Harding! GIVE ME WHAT'S MINE!" Locke frothed.

"Not until I have proof of life. I want to know that the girls are okay. Put Alice on the line."

"Jack? Jack, I'm here. We're okay." She looked at the murderous rage in Locke's gaze. "For now."

"Don't worry, Alice. I'm coming to get you soon. Once you're safe, and all this is over, we can go to the Utstray Arksmay with Trinity and look for the Asketbay under the Martian sands."

Alice's eyes grew wide.

"More asinine Martian names!" Locke growled. He shoved the women to the ground. "Enough! You can plan your little family trip after I get what's mine."

"Oh, don't worry, Mr. Locke. You'll get what's yours. Meet me over the crest of the next hill. *Hover* out."

"Finally!" Locke grumbled. He pointed to Dr. Vashtin. "You! Watch them. Don't let them out of your sight. Rico!"

Locke looked around for his bodyguard, but the man hadn't yet returned.

"Goddammit. I guess if you want something done right, you have to dig it yourself." He stormed off toward the dune, periodically glancing back to ensure Vashtin was doing his duty.

As soon as Locke disappeared over the crest, Vashtin turned quickly to the girls. "I wish I could help you, but I'm just a scientist."

The frightened man seized his opportunity to run frantically in the direction of the encampment.

Alice scrambled to her feet. "Quick, Trinity. Come on!"

She yanked her arms toward her, and the restraint around her gloved hands split open. Trinity did the same and started running toward the encampment after Dr. Vashtin.

"NOOOOOOO!!!" Locke's bloodcurdling scream carried across the barren landscape. Alice looked over her shoulder to see Locke hurtling back toward them. Trinity waved her on.

"Come on, Alice! The encampment's this way! We've got to hurry! He's coming!' Trinity screamed, pointing.

Alice shook her head and started in the opposite direction. "No, Trinity! We'll never make it. He'll run us down in the ARV! We have to go this way!"

Alice pointed toward empty sand. Trinity frowned.

"Are you nuts! There's nothing in that direction! At least this way, we have a snowball's chance."

"Utstray Arksmay!" Alice shouted, looking nervously at Locke, who was gaining ground.

Trinity pulled up short. "You want to go sightseeing now?!"

Alice shook her head and fell to her knees in the sand.

"Yeah," Trinity agreed. "Praying might be a good idea right now."

"I'm not praying," Alice responded. "I'm digging! There is no Utstray Arksmay on Mars. I know. I've studied the maps, remember?"

"So, what is it?"

"It's Pig Latin for 'strut marks!' And 'asketbay' means Jack buried the open-gauge basket under them! Jack's going to pull us up and out of here! Now, dig!"

"Jack?" Trinity asked. Alice pointed up.

There, a few hundred feet above their heads, the repaired Hover bobbed silently in the air. It grew closer along with Locke, who ran toward them, sliding in the loose sand and screaming.

"DIG!"

The two of them worked frantically, digging at the red sands, throwing up plumes of red dust. Several inches below the sand, they found the basket and climbed in. A winch cable lowered from the cargo door of the *Hover*. Jack leaned out and hollered.

"Hook it on!"

Trinity reached up and grabbed the hook. She had just secured it when Jack yelled.

"Look out!"

Trinity whirled just in time to see Locke raise the pistol. She opened her mouth to scream just as the basket lifted into the air and knocked the weapon from Locke's outstretched hand. It fell to the ground and was immediately covered by an avalanche of shifting sand. Locke leaped for the cage, his fingers latching around the bottom. His weight made it lurch. Alice was nearly thrown. Trinity grabbed for her, saving her from falling.

Up above, the *Hover* was having difficulty staying steady with the shifting weight below. Alice watched as it tipped, dumping Jack out the side.

"Dad!" Alice screamed before she even realized what she said.

They watched in horror as Jack clung by his fingertips to the deck of the ship.

"We've got to stabilize!" Trinity yelled, but Locke was wreaking havoc as he started to climb up the side of the basket and caused everything to sway to and fro.

A determined look came across Alice's face as she stumbled toward Locke. "You can do anything," she began, "if you just use your head!"

With that, she drew back and rammed her helmet visor into Locke's. The sudden impact caused Locke to rock backward, his own weight pulling him off the basket. His scream crackled in their headsets as he fell fifteen feet to the ground and groaned.

Alice immediately looked up to check on Jack. With the ship now steady, Bart was pulling him to safety. Alice threw her arms around Trinity and breathed a sigh of relief.

"I don't know about you guys," Jack's breathless voice came over their comms. "But I'm sure as hell ready to go home."

"Me, too," Alice replied. A beat passed. "Dad."

CHAPTER 61

Earth – One Year Later
Jack

"Are we there yet?" Lucas groaned for the umpteenth time.

"That's *my* necklace you're wearing, isn't it?" Julia sniped at Alice in the van's back row.

"Is not," Alice retorted, fingering the amulet fashioned from a Martian rock Jack had picked up before the long journey back to Earth.

"Is so! Dad gave it to me, and you just took it without even *asking* me!" Julia shoved her sister's shoulder.

"Will you two please start acting like human beings!" Bradley's nasal voice corrected from the driver's seat. "Don't make me turn this van around."

"Lucas," Trinity's voice warned. "Get that action figure out of your nose."

Jack's head repeatedly bounced on the headrest as Oscar kicked the back of the passenger seat. Jack inhaled deeply and sighed.

Ah…home sweet home.

Well, not quite home. There was something decidedly missing before his life felt complete.

Not that he was complaining, mind you. All things considered, circumstances had worked out pretty well.

Dr. Vashtin had managed to make it all the way back to the encampment at Utopia Planitia and alerted the authorities about the cold-blooded murder of Dr. Binderkampf. Upon investigating, they had also found trace remains of Peter Valeni in the compactor aboard the *Horus*.

Turned out, Dr. Evers was alive and well after all, to Bart's exuberant delight. He had been ridiculously excited to show her the latest addition to his hat collection—the helmet to his EVA suit. Her unexplained disappearance was a result of temporary protective custody after providing authorities with information about the Houston incident. Now a full-scale investigation was underway to determine Locke's involvement in Dr. Engleton's death as well. In any case, Locke was looking at some serious jail time once he made it back to Earth.

Things with Trinity had blossomed. She and Jack had shared some long talks on the six-month ride home. They'd also shared a few other things. He grinned lecherously.

Turned out you could do certain things in zero gravity.

Now, they were an officially exclusive item. Trinity had even moved into the house. He had been so proud of her when she won a Pulitzer for her story on the Mars land grab. She had been equally as happy for Jack when he won the Nobel for his antigravity work.

He had turned in his beacon for the Hellas region on Mars and registered full ownership rights to the Mars egrets. The general public had not yet seen the benefits of what the egrets could provide, but groundbreaking research was already underway to help people afflicted with devastating illnesses—cancer, Parkinson's, multiple sclerosis, and more. Major medical research facilities had signed contracts with Jack to gain access to the egrets, lucrative contracts which had made Jack a very rich man. He now owned **P1AL** Labs outright and had a new full partner–Bart.

But as much as it was all coming together, there was still one missing piece to the puzzle.

Charlie.

As they pulled up to the Lucille Packard Children's Hospital in Stanford, Jack almost found himself holding his breath.

Even though none of the procedures using egrets was officially vetted by the FDA, Trinity had called on some of her connections and got the approval pushed through for egret use in the treatment of vanishing white matter.

Charlie had undergone his procedure a week ago. All signs pointed toward the success of the operation, but doctors had wanted to keep him under observation. No one had ever gone through a procedure using alien technology before. No one could be 100 percent certain it would work.

It had to work.

The van glided to a stop in front of the hospital. Everyone tumbled out and headed into the sweeping lobby. Jack stopped short and turned to the group.

"Do...do you guys mind if I go up alone first? I don't want to overwhelm him right away. They'll be plenty of time for that once we get him home."

The kids started to balk, but Trinity reached out and touched his shoulder. "You go on ahead. We'll be here when you're ready."

"Thanks," he said.

Trinity turned to the kids. "All right! Who wants to get ice cream in the cafeteria?"

A cheer of excitement went up from the children. Bradley groaned.

"They'll spoil their dinner." But he followed them off toward the cafeteria anyway. "I'll have chocolate."

Jack turned toward the bank of elevators and headed up to Charlie's floor.

*****

When he arrived at the pediatric floor, Jack's stomach was in knots. He had traveled over two hundred and forty-two million miles, nearly died floating in space, and he had escaped the clutches of a madman to try and save Charlie's life.

And there were still no guarantees.

He reached Charlie's door, and his heart fell. The bed was empty. The wheelchair was abandoned in the corner.

Jack whirled. He rushed toward the nurses' station and tapped rapidly on the counter. "My son. Where's my son? Charles Joh– Harding. Charlie Harding. He's not in his room!"

The nurse behind the counter put her hand over the receiver. "Now, sir, if you'll just calm down a minute, I'm sure we can straighten this out."

"No. I will not calm down, and I will not wait one second, let alone one minute. I want to know what happened to my son right now!"

"Dad!" Charlie's voice made Jack spin.

There, standing in the hallway, holding himself up with arm-brace crutches, was Charlie.

"You're–you're standing!" Jack exclaimed. "I'd hoped the procedure would save you, but…oh my God, you're standing!"

He rushed toward Charlie and gave him a great big hug, crushing the wind from the eight-year-old.

Dr. Pershing, who was standing nearby, put a hand on Jack's shoulder. "And he'll likely be running soon. That is, if you don't stop his breathing before then."

Jack abruptly let go and stood back a pace or two. "Oh! Wow, I'm sorry. I'm just so…God, this is unbelievable."

"It truly is," Dr. Pershing admitted. "And it wouldn't have been possible without you, Dr. Harding."

"I just went to the store, Doctor. You did the cooking."

Dr. Pershing laughed. "Now, test results have indicated that Charlie's disease is in remission. Not only will there be no further degeneration of white matter, but any deterioration he had experienced prior to the procedure has reversed itself. Indeed, even the muscular atrophy that had set in over the last two years is gone. Like it didn't even exist, which is the only reason he is able to walk right now. In a standard case, it would take months of physical therapy to get to this point. Of course, this case is anything but standard. As he gets even stronger, he'll eventually be able to do away with the crutches."

"Amazing."

"Can we go home, now, Dad?" Charlie asked.

"You bet we can, champ. Come on."

They slowly walked to the elevators and rode the car down to the first floor. Everyone waited in the lobby. After the initial shock wore off, there were hugs and tears and feelings of joy and elation.

There was something else too.

Completion. Jack finally felt complete. Like he really belonged to something. He looked at Trinity. Like he really belonged to someone. The twins tugged at his pant legs.

Okay, fine. To six someones.

He had a family.

Trinity whispered in his ear. "You ready?"

"Without a doubt."

EPILOGUE

Jack helped load all the kids into the van as Bart pulled up behind him in his electric Mini Cooper. Bart and Midge Evers both jumped out from the small car. Midge carried balloons and an oversized teddy bear.

"Am I late? Am I late? Did I miss anything?" Bart's words tumbled from his mouth.

Jack looked at the Mini Cooper. "What happened to Leia, Bart?"

Bart tossed a glance over his shoulder.

"Thought it was time for an upgrade." He cast a devious look at Midge. "Needed more space."

Jack shook his head.

"Hi, Bart!" Charlie beamed as he stepped from behind Jack.

"Holy midi-chlorians, Yoda! You're walking!" Bart exclaimed.

"That's right! Don't need the old speed buggy anymore!"

Jack slapped his forehead. "The wheelchair! We left it upstairs. You probably don't need it anymore, but I should go get it. Bart, come with me."

"Sure thing!"

As they walked back toward the hospital, two men in black suits and mirrored aviators stepped toward them.

"Dr. Harding?" one of the men asked.

"Yes?"

"Dr. Jack Harding?"

"Yeah, I've already said that's me. Can I help you, gentlemen?"

"Department of Homeland Security." Both men flashed badges.

"What does DHS want with me?" Jack queried cautiously.

"Not you, Dr. Harding. Your tech. Both your antigravity work and the egrets. For reasons of national security, I'm afraid we're going to have to ask you to relinquish any and all materials pertaining to the findings of your antigravity studies and immediately cease all activities which may involve the application of said findings."

"You've got to be joking," Jack said. He laughed and looked at Bart. "Did you put them up to this?"

"I have nothing to do with this," Bart said.

"As such, Dr. Harding, we will be assuming control of the P1AL labs and the collider located therein. We currently have agents at the facility as we speak, securing all pertinent data and equipment. Additionally, the rights to the Hellas Planitia region of Mars will revert to the government of the United States."

"This is bullshit!" Jack spat.

"No, sir. This is over." He handed Jack a business card. "Should you have any questions, please don't hesitate to call this number."

The men turned in tandem and slipped into a black SUV that hummed away.

"Can they do that? I mean, can the government just swoop in and take away everything we fought so hard to create?" Bart started. "I mean, dude...we went to Mars!"

"Yeah. I guess they can," Jack remained oddly calm. He wondered if Locke had had something to do with it. But with mounting legal problems, including murder charges still being levied against him, that was unlikely. The billionaire was still on his way back from the red planet. Apparently, his ride had suffered engine problems en-route. But soon enough, the psychopath would be facing the music.

"Forget curing cancer or Alzheimer's," Bart continued. "They're probably going to use the egrets to create some kind of super-soldier or something."

He followed Jack back to the van, where everyone stood watching.

"What was that all about?" Trinity asked.

"Homeland Security. They took everything!" Bart moaned.

"Not everything," Jack grinned.

"What are you talking about?" Bart asked. "They just said they're securing all the hover-tech data at the labs."

"Julia, can I see the necklace I gave you?" Jack asked.

"Why?" Alice interjected, "It's hers. You gave it to her."

Julian worked the clasp at the back of her neck and then handed the Martian rock necklace to Jack.

"I want that back," Julia said.

"Bart, do you still have that jerry-rigged ROAR system set up in your mom's basement?"

"Yeah. Why?"

Jack fiddled with the necklace, eventually pulling the rock loose from the bail of the pendant and revealing a hidden data storage device. He held up the opened pendant, "'Cause we have all we need to rock and roll right here."

The End

Thank you for reading HOVER. If you enjoyed this book, PLEASE leave me a review on Amazon.com–it really helps! To be notified the moment any future books are released–please join my mailing list. I hate spam and will never, ever share your information. Jump to this link to sign up:
http://eepurl.com/bs7M9r

Acknowledgments

First and foremost, I am grateful to the fans of my writing and their ongoing support for all my books. I'd like to thank my wife, Kim—she's my rock and is a crucial, loving component of my publishing business. I'd like to thank my mother, Lura Genz, for her tireless work as my first-phase creative editor and a staunch cheerleader of my writing.

This book was most definitely a team effort. I'd like to thank Margarita Martinez for her fine work copy and line editing the manuscript. Melinda Falgoust you were a total rockstar—with your help we brought the ball over the finish line. For this project there were multiple advanced readers who supplied creative and technical reviews that made this book so much batter. I'd like to thank Eric Sundius, Stuart Church, Sue and Charles Duell, Jack Herris, John Harrell, Nancy Wichmann, Jim Sturtz, Richard Moseley, Ed Hilterman, Hank Scheibe, Peggy Casarella, and James Hall. I'd also like to thank Lura and James Fischer for their unwavering moral support of this project.

Check out my other available titles on the following page.